THE ISLAND REMEMBERS.
DO YOU?

LIGHT
OF THE
SECOND
STAR

VANESSA
RACCIO

THE ISLAND REMEMBERS.
DO YOU?

LIGHT
OF THE
SECOND
STAR

VANESSA
RACCIO

Cover design by Cover Dungeon Rabbit

ISBN: 978-1-7778630-3-6 (eBook)

ISBN: 978-1-7778630-4-3 (Paperback)

ISBN: 978-1-7778630-5-0 (Hardcover)

Printed in the United States of America

For my baby girl—I checked under your bed, your closet, under the dresser, and outside your window. There are no monsters. I promise.

And for my son—thanks for reminding me it's okay to be a crocodile when being a mermaid doesn't cut it.

AUTHOR'S NOTE

"Check the window, mama. Check. Check again."
- Baby girl, Age 3

My daughter was three years old when she started asking about the **MONSTERS** in her bedroom. She would lie under her covers at night and stare wide-eyed at the shadows in the far corners until I reassured her she was safe. Objectively, I knew there was nothing there, that an acute fear of the dark wasn't uncommon for children. So, when my daughter asked me, night after night, to check her room for the scary beasts, I shouldn't have been surprised.

The problem, though, was that my kiddo watched no television, and we didn't read her scary stories. She didn't go to nursery school or have an older sibling to scare her. I was confused as to where she may have learned the term **MONSTER**, let alone how she could have developed such a profound fear of them. The mom in me wanted nothing more than to make that fear go away; the writer in me thought it would be *awesome* if kids really could see things we grown-ups couldn't.

Her fear eventually did resolve. But while *she* might have

forgotten all about the creatures that went bump in the night, the seed of an idea had already been planted in my mind. And, like any good idea for a story, it didn't go away.

My son was only a baby at that time, so he wasn't yet able to talk about any **MONSTERS** he might have seen. However, a big part of me liked the thought of this book becoming a gift to both of my children. As my boy shared a name with one of the iconic characters in the story of *Peter Pan*, I endeavoured to connect the popular fairytale with my daughter's fear of imaginary creatures. My initial idea became a fully fleshed-out world with characters I was excited to write.

But becoming a mom of two did more than give me the fun concept for *Light of the Second Star*. I began to notice the way adults wished my children would grow up faster and how I felt pressured by those adults to do the same. I learned pretty quickly just how fragile childhood really was; every choice I made as a mother held the power to permanently alter my children's lives. Finally, I learned that postpartum anxiety didn't care whether I was confident or shy, outspoken or timid, or if I had a support system to help me cope or not—it simply came into my home and took up unwanted space in my mind. It unearthed my demons and forced me to face my own childhood trauma. Motherhood gave me a new perspective on how *Peter Pan*'s lost children might have come to be, and you're now holding their story in your hands. It's a story I hadn't set out to write. Sometimes, mistakes are good like that.

Gambles don't always turn out so positively. But the alternative is forgetting that some gambles are worth taking and choosing to stay still instead. That, to me, is much worse than failing.

Speaking of forgetting...

I've written and rewritten this note to you more times than I care to admit. The goal was to reach out and tell you a bit about what influenced the story. I wanted to bring you a piece of childhood that might have been forgotten when you grew up.

We sometimes forget what it felt like to be a child. We forget to play as much as we work, to give the benefit before the doubt, to believe in magic. To leave our window open at night. We forget to check for **MONSTERS** under our beds because we believe they're nothing more than childish fears.

We growns forget a lot.

I hope Lou and Jay pull you into these pages.

I hope the lost children you're about to meet find a small home in your heart.

I hope that living on the island, even if only for a little while, helps you remember. It sure helped me.

This was the story I needed to tell at the time I needed to tell it. And while every author would like every reader to love their work, there may be some triggering situations for you.[1] Please be kind to yourself.

Light of the Second Star is my heart turned inside out. It's grief and love and trauma and healing. Most of all, it's *human*. And it helped me slay my own **MONSTER**. At least, for now.

See, baby girl? I have them, too.

Happy reading, my fellow grown. And enjoy your time on the island.

Just be sure not to get lost.

Much love,

Vanessa

---

1. Content warning: Amputation (not explicit), anxiety, attempted rape, blood, death, depression, homophobia, infertility, mention of child abuse (not explicit), mention of incest, pregnancy, sexism, sexually suggestive content, suicide (not explicit), violence.

I'M CANADIAN, O-K'EH?
A QUICK WORD ABOUT LANGUAGE

Please note that, as the author of this book is Canadian, she has adhered to Canadian spelling standards. Therefore, you will find many more *U*'s than you might be used to. For example, color is spelled colour, favor is spelled favour, behavior is spelled behaviour . . . you get the idea. These words are not, in fact, typos. While this author realizes this might annoy some of her readers, the memory of Mrs. Sanchini's red pen is more powerful and more terrifying than her very Canadian aversion to upsetting anyone.

That's saying something.

Serio*U*sly.

PART I

Children almost always hang onto things tighter than their
parents think they will.
——E. B. White, *Charlotte's Web*

The moment you doubt whether you can fly, you cease forever to
be able to do it.
——J. M. Barrie, *Peter Pan*

PROLOGUE

Lou

My first memory in this life was the day I learned I would die.

At the age of four, existence is a never-ending cycle of day and night, the love of mothers with warm arms and fathers smelling of cloves and ripe oranges. Mother and Father were born full-grown with me tucked safely under their arms. And forever we would stay. At the age of four, time is infinite, never to be considered. Or feared.

Until it jumps out at you in the night.

As a child, I would watch Mother slice fruit. I tracked the journey of the knife moving through ripe melon with greedy eyes, the nectar spilling over the sharp edge like blood from a wound. Destroying the fruit was the only way to create the perfect crescent moon, all sweetness and colour. And I would stand by her hip, relishing in that destruction with a watering mouth.

Mother was my favourite person in my world, as most mothers are to their own children, I suppose. And for a short time, I was her favourite too.

Come here and help with the dishes, Louisa, she would say.

My heart would explode with pride at having been chosen. It was always nice to be wanted.

Let me show you how to fold your tights, darling.

Yes, please, Mother. Show me. Never forget to show me.

Our hands would work in silence, folding, soaking, washing, cooking. That was our conversation, and it was good because it was *ours*. We were together, and in those moments, I couldn't imagine any better life. But every so often, she would ask a question I did not have the answer to. And on those occasions, I would fail her. Disappointment would flash, quick as a sword swipe, across her fine features, and I would flush from the shame of it. And at that moment, I would hate myself before I even knew the meaning of the word.

When I was four, however, Mother was still patient. The questions would continue to come, and I would search my mind for what she wanted to hear like a stray dog leaping on a shaft of meat-bare bone.

Do you like yellow or pink better for your Sunday dress, Louisa?

Purple, actually. Always purple. Her eyes would turn away from me, then. I'd chosen an option I hadn't been given. I'd chosen wrong.

Would you like your hair in curls or a braid today, Louisa?

Can we cut my hair shorter, Mother? It's too hot. Suffocating.

A braid, Mother. Please. Thank you.

I learned to say the right things. I changed until the questions came quicker along with her rare smile. That was when I knew I had to lie to keep her love. Small questions, tiny droplets of dew on dry grass that, together, made my world glitter.

Until one day, everything changed.

The summer before my fourth birthday was especially warm, and the fruit at the market had been exceptional.

Would you like to come with me to the market, Louisa?

Yes, I would, please.

Hand in hand, we'd browsed the baskets of peaches and strawberries, succulent figs and fresh basil leaves in pots of black earth. But the melons were my favourite, a sweet secret hidden within an ugly bumpy shell. Mother's youngest sister had come to visit from the city during a violent heat wave that July, her sticky one-year-old in tow. We served them melon slices at night. The sky would shift from blue to red to green, and we would turn our reddened faces to the breeze weaving through the woods behind our home so our skin could cool. My cousin's thick fingers dug into the fruit, pulverizing the flesh until it slithered in a sticky mess down her chin. I wanted to take the melon away; that wasn't how to cherish something so beautiful, how to handle something Mother and I had taken great care to prepare together.

And then another question came: *How long do you think it will take your cousin to finish her fruit, Louisa?*

One hundred years, Mother.

An intelligent answer, one that had given me pride. One hundred was a large number, one Father had taught me when we were alone, because numbers were wasted on little girls. But Mother had only laughed and said, *Silly girl. We will not be alive in one hundred years.*

She'd gone to break open another melon, the nectar spilling through her fingers. I'd sat in my chair, watching the wedges melt away to nothing under the knife. *We will not be alive in one hundred years.* The words beat at my skull, forcing me to consider them. There would come a time when Mother would be gone. She would no longer exist. The same would happen to me.

Death was a monster in the closet.

Death was a shadow under our feet.

Death would get Mother. It would find me too. Someday.

The night slouched on as though Mother had not just announced the world was not the safe place I thought it was. My stomach sank into my knees, the room swam and lurched, and the colours of the world flickered like they, too, were not real. Like the colours wouldn't last forever.

I wasn't the same after that night.

Slurp, slurp. Away went another melon slice, orange pulp spilling over fat fingers. So greedy. So temporary.

Later, I'd wrapped my arms around Mother's leg, burrowed my face into her skirts, and cried. She hadn't understood why I was so upset, and at the tender age of four, I could not find the words to explain my torment. All I knew was if I squeezed her tight enough and learned to answer all her questions, perhaps I could slow time. Perhaps I could learn to breathe again.

But, of course, life never gave us what we wanted; just as it was fleeting, our existence was also cruel and unforgiving.

From that day forward, I never longed for another of Mother's questions for fear of getting one wrong. That would mean the end.

And I never touched a melon again.

CHAPTER 1

Too old for climbing.

Too old for the woods and reading frivolous stories.

Louisa Webber had heard those words her entire life. Interestingly, they'd come more frequently since her twentieth birthday the month before. What a nuisance birthdays were becoming.

Too old for games, nightmares, independent thought.

Louisa Webber was now a woman of twenty.

Louisa Webber was therefore *too old* for all the things she'd come to love.

"Slow down, Rosie!" she called. "I didn't wear my boots today!"

"Come on, Lou! You're taking too *long*."

The solid oak banister slipped under her palm as she raced down the steps from the second floor to the parlour. She pushed her legs to move quicker, but she was always too slow to catch up with her sister, Rose. A whisper of lavender lace and a burst of giggles bubbled out the door into the summer wind, calling Lou outside. Fragments of Rose flickered in and out of view, always out of reach. Lou could only chase and chase and hope to catch up. She never did.

The gold light of midsummer was blinding as Lou burst through the door. Their home sat atop Silverton Lane, a road that began at the top of a hill and spilled down from Lou's feet in a streak of grey stone and packed earth. Identical row houses coated in ruddy red brick lined the drive, each one boasting an identical square lawn peppered with neat tulip patches. Fences wore fresh coats of white paint. Gardens were carefully plucked free of weeds. It was a place of straight lines and straighter backs, and it was of no particular interest to Rose that day. Her black head flashed blue under the swollen sun, around the corner of their home, and off to where the opposite side of the hill waited. The wilder side.

"Slow *down*!" Lou's chest burned, but she picked up her pace anyway.

"Hurry *up*!"

More laughter, fresh and featherlight, pulled Lou far away from the road and all its painful perfection, past the rose bushes lining the bay window on the west side of their home and around the old swing creaking against the slatted porch. The familiar earth path through the back garden melted under Lou's slippers, and the weight in her chest melted with it. She knew where Rose was going, and she quietly relished it as much as her sister did.

A black iron gate wrapped their land in strong arms, but it was no match for Rose. The ten-year-old girl pushed through it, the soles of her riding boots kicking up dirt. While Silverton Lane ran down one side of the hill, the Briarwood sprawled down the other. The forest encroached on the earth with gnarled fingers. Moss and pastel flowers bled poisonous colour onto the soft ground. Leaves and vines trimmed in thorns crept through the trees unchecked. It was a wild place, an ancient place. A maze of shadows and irregularity.

There, in the Briarwood, nothing was ever *too old*.

Not even Lou.

"Rosie!" Lou broke through the woods and scanned the darkness for her sister. A set of narrow footprints was pressed into the mud, disappearing across a thick carpet of pine needles. "You know there are wild animals here and a lake you'll fall into if you're not careful! You must wait for me!"

Silence greeted her like a terrible foe. Her heart kicked behind her ribs. Rose was her charge, her responsibility when their mother couldn't carry the burden.

Father had once said fairies lived among the elderberry bushes lining the main path through the Briarwood and that if she were ever to become lost, those fairies would lead her home. Lou had spent an entire summer hiding in the shadows, turning over leaves in hope of catching one. Lou smiled at the memory as she moved down that very same path, past the old boulder carved with her and Rosie's initials and the hollowed-out tree trunk housing a family of racoons. Every touch of bark and call of birdsong was a piece of home. But even that wasn't enough to ease the anxiety clawing up her throat at Rose's continued absence.

"Louisa!" Rose chanted, her voice coming from everywhere. "Do you want to race to the maple tree by the cave? I bet I win."

"I cannot race you if I do not know where you are."

"You're no fun!"

"Your words are cruel," Lou called, "but I can bear them. Now, would you please stop running so we can visit the lake together?"

No answer.

Lou hiked up her skirt and marched deeper into the woods. The dome of leaves overhead bathed the world in jade, the maze of branches pointing her down false paths and into pockets of darkness. A fly buzzed past her ear, so loud, *so loud*. The ground pitched under her feet, and the flicker of a headache scratched behind her eyes. What if Rose was already on her way to the lake?

She'd been reminded many times never to approach the cold black water alone, but the girl was a creature of her own making, beholden to no one. Not yet, at least.

"Rosie?"

The Briarwood was a place of magic and colour, but both were quickly fading. In their place, darkness blanketed the woods in ash.

"*Rose!*"

The trees swayed, spiking the pain behind her eyes. The Briarwood waited for an answer, and so did she. "As you wish, sister," Lou said. "Let us make a bargain: you come out of whatever tree you're hiding in, and I will let you borrow that toy boat you seem to love so much."

"Deal!" A veil of raven hair swung out ahead of Lou from a low-hanging branch, and a pair of leather riding boots thudded to the ground. Chocolate-brown eyes flecked with gold beamed with satisfaction from a round tan face. Where Lou had inherited all their mother's pallor but none of her grace, Rose carried their father's mischievous spirit and warmth. Both were so different, yet forever bound by love and blood.

"You had me properly worried!" Lou said.

Rose shrugged. "I promise to take perfect care of your boat. Mother bought me a new paint set; I can freshen up the varnish on it, if you like."

"I like the boat faded."

"Have it your way. But please, do *not* call me Rose again. You sound like Mother."

"You may borrow the boat, but the chipped paint adds character . . . *Rosie.*"

She smiled her impossibly sweet smile. "That's better. You never told me where you got that boat anyway. Does it have a story? It doesn't seem like something Mother would approve of for a lady."

"I don't remember. It must have been a gift from Father."

Rose linked her arm with Lou's, pulling her down the elderberry path. There wasn't a fairy in sight, but in Rose's presence, magic was alive anyhow. Warmth soaked into Lou's blood, birdsong filled the fragrant air, and the world righted itself once more. Together they would visit the lake and skip rocks across the glassy surface. Together they would remove their shoes—always too tight, always too scuffed—and cool their toes in the shallows.

Together. The way they were meant to be.

"Can you tell what bird that is just by its call?" Rose asked, squinting up at the leaves.

Lou nodded. "It is a goldfinch. They're quite common, actually."

"Have I ever seen one? Are they pretty? They sound very pretty."

Lou grinned, planting a kiss on the crown of Rose's head. "They are. I used to wait by my window all winter to hear their song in the spring. Father used to say they chased away the cold and made room for the new sun."

"I didn't know Father liked studying the birds too."

"I liked them, so he liked them."

Rosie nodded at that. "That sounds like him, I suppose. Do you know the names of all the birds, then?"

Something sharp twisted in Lou's chest. "Some. I would never say I knew all of them."

"Why not?"

Branches unfolded before them, all brown and green sinew. She thought of Father's rough hands scratching the parchment paper of a new present he'd brought her from the city. His delight when she pulled a new book free of its wrappings and took it straight to her room to read was a greater gift than the book itself. Her thirst for novelty and knowledge was his pride. She missed his rough skin and his glowing smile.

"I prefer to imagine an infinite number of birds left to discover than to think I've learned them all," Lou said. "That would be unbearable."

Rose wrinkled her nose. "I do not understand."

"That is because I am much older and wiser than you." Lou winked and gave Rose's arm a squeeze. "You see, something that has not yet been discovered cannot be caged, let alone named. It can simply . . . *exist*. Just how it is. Forever. Not knowing something means there is the possibility of everything."

"Even magic?"

"Perhaps even that."

Rose perked at that. "There is a place like that, Lou. I've told you so a thousand times."

"Yes, I've heard all your stories of the island and its creatures. Tell me, how do children learn to fly if they haven't got any wings?"

Brown eyes so deep they swallowed the darkness turned up to meet hers. "Not *all* children. Only those who become fairies. You know that. Or you *did*. Once."

The island. The fairies. The crocodiles with the large teeth, and the women with fins as bright as polished gems. Lou had heard it all before and would gladly hear it all again. Because the scent of wild grass was heavy in the air, and the earth squelched underfoot. The Briarwood was a magical place, perfect for the whispered secrets of fantastical creatures. Such talk wasn't permitted on Silverton Lane, but the trees never seemed to mind. Perhaps they, too, believed in magic.

"You'll tell me all about the island again when we reach the lake, Rosie. I seem to have forgotten much."

"Not even Louisa Webber can be perfect, then."

Rose laughed, but Lou pulled her sister closer, the knot in her stomach tightening, squeezing, choking. She'd chased perfection her entire life, but it was as tangible as a shadow. She had never managed to erase the disappointment from her mother's eyes. Perfection was elusive, a myth as impossible as Rose's fairies and the island on which they lived. Still, she wanted it badly. She would chase that impossibility for as long as Mother was disappointed in her. Perhaps longer.

But she wouldn't tell Rose any of that. Perfection was a burden for the eldest sibling, and she would bear that alone. In the meantime, she would protect Rose's innocence until adulthood fell upon her, too.

"We're almost there!" Rose said, hopping on her toes. "Do you think the ducks will be there today?"

"They might be."

"I'll race you!"

Rose broke away for the lake before Lou could agree, taking her warmth with her. Lou's whole world had once been bathed in heat and sun and colour. Now it existed only in the Briarwood with Rose by her side.

Once, Lou had wanted to make a home in these woods, be a bird among the boughs.

But childhood dreams had no place in the heart of a woman. The forest would never be her home. After all, colours faded, and nothing was guaranteed.

Not even perfection.

THE WEBBER HOUSEHOLD placed great importance on routine, and bedtime was no exception. Lou's father had taken pride in escorting her to her room after dinner, his big hand wrapped around hers. He would brush her hair before tucking the sheets under so the nightmares couldn't get in. Once the noise of the day had settled and the blue moonlight washed over the world, he would read from one of her books. Mother was busy with other things, but Lou preferred it that way. Bedtime was for her and Father.

Now Lou kept him alive by brushing Rose's hair, tucking her sheets nice and tight under her slight body, and hoping the nightmares chose her instead of her sister. They usually did.

Rose's bedroom sat opposite Lou's on the second floor, the plush runner connecting them well-worn. Teacups and dolls littered her floor, books with missing pages and shoes with missing partners scattered among them. There had been a time when Mother had tried to bring order to the carefully arranged chaos, but those efforts were wasted; Rosie was happiest in the mess. And Rose's happiness was the only thing Lou and her mother could agree upon.

"I wish my hair were as dark as yours." Lou dragged the boar bristles through Rosie's hair, marvelling at the way the strands poured through her fingers like blue ink shining under the moon. Beside her on the bed, plush bears, horses, and rabbits watched in reverent silence, their eyes shining, their fur soft. "Mine looks like it is made of straw."

Rose leaned into Lou's legs from her place on the floor. "And I look like a crow. Anyhow, I thought tomorrow we could try the narrower path through the woods instead of the large one we always use. I already know you are going to say no, but I've found all the good hiding places, and I'm bored."

"Perhaps if there is time. Tomorrow may not be possible."

Rose frowned over her shoulder. "We go to the woods every day."

"We do, but tomorrow is different."

One floor below, Mother's voice hummed a familiar tune to the tinkle of dishes clinking into place in the cupboards. A lifetime ago, a deeper voice had joined hers, always a touch off-key, always managing to coax a breathy giggle from her. Now there were only wooden notes delivered on chapped lips.

"What is it?" Rose asked. When Lou didn't answer, Rose plucked the brush from her hands and climbed onto the bed, toppling Henry Horse and the raccoon twins onto their sides. "Well? Out with it."

The light in the room wavered, turned from blue to grey, and another headache rolled behind her eyes, scratching a fresh wound in her skull where the last had only just left its scars. Above the quiet whisper of the breeze through the gossamer curtains, a low gurgle of water bubbled behind the walls. After the absence of colour, the sound of the sea was a terrible presence in the house. Try as she might, Lou couldn't shake it.

"Mother invited the Rileys for tea tomorrow," Lou said, her cheeks heating. "She thought I would like to join them."

Rosie pulled the brush through Lou's tangles with careless strokes. "Since when are you invited for tea? Mother hates it when you're late to social visits, and you're *always* late."

"Rosie!"

"You know it's true. And Mrs. Riley is awful. She smells like cats and old food."

"The way Mrs. Riley *smells* is hardly a reason to avoid going to tea," Lou said around a smile.

"It is reason enough for me. What is the occasion, then?"

Lou toyed with the ends of her hair: muted blond laced with dull copper, neither the shiny locks of her sister nor the spiralling curls of her mother. "Samuel is visiting from the city. Mother thought it would be sensible for someone his age to be there when his parents came to call."

"Samuel? Isn't that their son that moved to the city a few years ago?"

"Yes."

"And Mother wants you to have tea with him?"

"*Yes.*"

"Oh." The brush slowed. Rose fell silent.

"They think we'd make a good match."

To Lou's surprise, Rosie laughed. "Samuel speaks of nothing but their family cat, and he probably wears a smoking jacket to bed. You could do better than him."

"What do you know about the things boys wear to bed?"

"Not much." Rose tossed the brush onto the floor and reached over to her nightstand for a ribbon. "I, unlike *Samuel*, have an imagination and brains. You're not really going to sit through an afternoon with them, are you?"

She wanted to say no, but Lou knew her place; her options were limited by the rules of her mother and the desires of men. Even men like Samuel.

He really does have an unhealthy attachment to that cat, she thought. "He's respectable," Lou said instead. "We have not seen him in years. The city might have done his character some good. Matured him a little."

"He never smiles," Rose countered. With deft fingers, she worked Lou's hair into a braid before fastening the end with a black velvet ribbon. "You need someone who smiles. Someone who likes to laugh and tell stories and watch the birds."

Lou's heart swelled at her sister's concern. "It is only tea."

"It is *never* only tea," Rose muttered. "Mother thinks I do not understand why she invites boys over to see you. She does not think it is my concern. But it is, you know. They'll have him court you and visit us too often with presents you won't like. Then you will marry and have children and a few awful cats, and I will never see you again. That has *everything* to do with me."

"That isn't true."

"It is. I hear it from the Milligan boys all the time. Their older sisters have suitors who come to court them and wed them and take them away. It's all so nauseating."

Lou's smile was tight. *That will be* my *fate, not hers. She will never need to suffer this way. She can live.* "Everyone must grow up,

Rosie. It is my turn to do what needs to be done to keep our family in good standing. A solid match and a proper marriage to Samuel might bring Mother some peace of mind. You know how all the ladies whisper about her being unwed. The last thing she needs is an unwed daughter."

"You speak like Mother never married at all. Father did not leave us or do something else to bring us shame. He *died*. There is a difference."

Lou flinched at how easily the words tumbled from Rose's lips. "Not to the other ladies. And if I marry well, you might not need to."

Tears shimmered in the corners of Rose's eyes, tiny pearls nestled in pink flesh. "I don't want you to do this because of me."

"I am doing this because I am a woman grown, and this is what grown women do." *And what needs to be done to make Mother happy.*

"Timber says the growns forget what it is to play and laugh and climb trees and make messes in the puddles," Rose said. "You've already forgotten so much. I couldn't stand you losing any more."

"Ah. So, this is Timber's doing, then."

Timber had been Rose's first word, followed closely by *no*. It was only later that Lou understood it to be a name instead of a term of affection for the woods they both loved so much. But then the stories followed, and they were strange—even for a child.

Timber lives on an island with the fairies.

Timber told me I can meet a mermaid if I want. They have teeth to eat little girls.

Something is wrong on Timber's island. Boys are disappearing, and the stars are too far away.

Sometimes there were nightmares; on those nights, Lou wanted nothing more than to scoop the imaginary boy from her sister's memory. And sometimes the breeze through Rose's window smelled of salt and copper, and she could almost taste the sea.

But it wasn't real. None of it was ever real.

"Tell me he is wrong," Rose said, breaking through Lou's thoughts. "Tell me you will not do any of those things."

Lou took Rose's hands in hers. "You knew as well as I that this day was coming. Girls grow into women, then into wives. It is the normal course of things, even if we do not wish it to be so. But I would never forget you, not even for a moment, so please tell Timber to stop scaring you."

That seemed to calm Rose. Her face was thoughtful, her pause leaden. "I won't ever get married or have children."

"Why do you say that?"

"I like my life the way it is. Everything I see makes me believe that growing up is the end of all good things. Timber says that being a child forever is pure magic."

Beyond Rose's open window, crickets chirped farewell to the day. Father would have known what to say to quiet Rose's worries. But he was underground and far away, and Lou could never find the words to hold the same weight.

Still, as she tucked Rose into bed, she had to try.

"Perhaps Timber should tell you stories of mermaids in pink lagoons instead of filling your head with such worries."

Rose placed a warm hand on Lou's cheek. "They are not *stories*. Timber would never lie to me. I will see everything he has spoken of for myself one day."

Lou laughed. "You are so afraid of being left behind. If I understand you correctly, you are the one planning on leaving *me*. Perhaps you will take me with you when you visit Timber's island."

But Rose wasn't amused. Her dark eyes grew solemn, and her delicate fingers pressed urgently into Lou's cheek, as though trying to trap her in her fist. "He told me you're not allowed there. Not unless Peter says you are."

"I wish I had your imagination," Lou said, stifling a yawn.

"You did once. You had a friend just like Timber who loved you like a sister. Jay still waits for you on the island."

"Well, if I cannot come with you, then you must tell Timber to bring this Jay here to me instead."

Rose's hand collapsed, and she turned to the window. "He isn't allowed to see you either. Not since you grew up and forgot him."

In the kitchen, in another world beyond Rose's bedroom door, the humming stopped. The wind was too loud, and the water behind the walls bubbled and roiled, giving the plaster a pulse. It wasn't the first Lou had heard of Jay, the boy she'd imagined as a child; he lived in Rose's stories and her own dreams without a voice or a face. She was much too old for such stories, of course, but Rose was still a child. And the longer Lou indulged those stories, as painful as they were to hear, the longer Rose would remain that way.

"Time for sleep," Lou said. "If we are to sneak out before the Rileys leave to explore a new land tomorrow, we must be well rested."

"That sounds nice."

Lou pressed a small smile onto Rose's forehead. "I love you always, little one." She moved to the open window, a chill bubbling down her arms.

"Leave it open," Rose protested. "I like to listen to the singing."

"What singing?"

Her eyes were half-closed, her words slurred. "Timber and the others are lost, but I can still hear them. I like it when they sing."

The stars crusted the sky in a tapestry of jewels, watching over the rooftops of Silverton Lane. Windows were dark, shut tight against the sounds of nighttime. The gardens were blanketed in shadow, tulips swaying softly. Peace fell on the road and in Rose's room, but it could not reach Lou. How many more nights like this remained for her? Surely if the arrangement with the Riley boy was successful, he would insist on moving her far away. She would never need to tend to the perfect gardens or stare at her father's empty seat at the dining-room table again. She would give her mother grandchildren and a legacy to be proud of. The idea should have brought her happiness; instead, dread drizzled down her spine and seized her heart. Because wherever she went, Rose wouldn't follow.

Lou ghosted to the door without closing the window. "Sweet dreams, Rosie."

There was no answer; Rose was already asleep.

CHAPTER 2

LOU

AGE FIVE

Mother hated when I played in the Briarwood. Forests were dirty, and dirt meant smudged cheeks and stained skirts. But Mother wasn't home, and Father had his drink; he smiled while I wove through crooked trunks. I was happy.

My voice was louder in the woods; it bounced off the trees in pleasant waves. There was no one to tell me to keep it down, stop the noise, please, Louisa, *please*. I hummed and hummed, and my heart swelled. Sunflowers, the happiest of all the flowers, painted my skirt. I swung my arm, waving my favourite book of birds by my side. It was a good day. My collar—*too tight, too tight*—was stiff, the cotton biting into my neck. I should have changed, but I was too deep into the trees to turn back.

Twirling was better in the forest too. My skirt fanned out around me, yellow blurring into brown until everything burned like autumn. I spun faster, around and around, feet churning the earth. There was a lake somewhere nearby where the ducks cut shiny strips through the flat surface. How would my voice sound there? I couldn't imagine it, because I wasn't allowed to go to the lake. Not yet. Never ever.

So, I twirled. That was just as fun as visiting a lake, surely.

"I think I know that song. What's it called? I forget."

I stopped spinning. A world dressed in green swam around me. I turned back to the path, ready to run. Careful, always careful. Father trusted me to walk alone, and I would not disappoint him.

"What sort of book's that?" Another question, but there was no one around.

Shadows swayed, birds sang the way they always did. My book thudded to the ground. "Who's there?" I asked.

The bodiless voice laughed, the sound like chocolate cake and toasted almonds—my favourite. "Sorry to bug you. I just didn't expect to hear any singin' today. Hey now, don't look so scared. Hold on—is this better?"

The boy appeared from nothing; there was a brush of bark and a swish of leaves, and he stood in my path, as real as any tree. His clothes were wrinkled, patched, riddled with stains and ripped at the hems. Taller than any of the boys I knew, he wore a crown of bronze hair laced with gold. He had eyes so blue they could have been plucked from the sea. I'm not sure how I knew that. I'd never seen the sea.

Twelve, maybe thirteen—a dangerous age according to Father, and an important age according to Mother.

"My father knows I'm here," I said. "I'm going home to him now."

"I'm not gonna hurt you." His voice was grainy. When he cocked his head and smiled, I found myself moving closer to him. "I only wanted to play. See?"

In one muddy fist, he clutched a toy boat that might have once been red but was now faded to a pale orange. In the other was a hunk of bread. He didn't look like a *deviant*; Father always said those sorts of boys were no good, not good enough for me. But the boy had bright eyes and a smile like the stars in winter. Deviants had claws, yellow teeth, and a snarl for a laugh.

"Who are you?" I asked.

"Just a kid. Like you, only bigger. Nothin' more to it."

I picked up my book and clutched it to my heart, where it belonged. "Can I see your boat?"

He held it out so I could have a better look. "She's not much to look at," he said, "but she sails pretty good. I take her 'round the lagoons where I live all the time, and she holds her own. You ever sail?"

When I shook my head, he furrowed his brow in thought.

"Well, that's a shame. Every kid should have a boat. Or a sword. Do you have a sword?"

Again, I shook my head. Silence was safer than admitting my life was so dull.

"Don'tcha talk?" he asked.

"Yes."

"So . . . talk."

"What's the bread for?"

The boy shrugged. "I like to feed the birds. Sometimes they're not hungry, but I like to try anyway."

Birds. It didn't matter if he was a stranger. No one who liked birds could be a *deviant.* "You feed birds? Here?"

"Here and there and neverwhere." His grin was wide, crinkling his eyes at the corners. "The birds like bread, but you can't give 'em too much or they get bellyaches. You know how it is."

I certainly did. Mother wasn't interested in the birds, and Father couldn't yet find the difference between a canary and a peacock. I knew more than either one of them, enough to know that bellyaches were a terrible thing.

"How do you get one to come close enough to feed?" I asked. "I mean . . . do they really like eating old bread?"

He blinked. "You never fed the birds before?"

My cheeks burned. I looked down at the boat, his stare making my stomach twist. "Mother and Father say feeding them will make them come back in flocks, and they'll ruin the gardens." How such a beautiful creature could be bad was impossible to understand, but Mother was always right, and Father never lied.

The boy tossed the hunk of bread into the air and caught it one-handed. "Well, sure. I mean, that could be true. But not the birds I feed. The birds *I* like are friendly. So friendly they'll come to sit on your shoulder if you're nice to 'em."

His eyes were clear; my own grew wide. "Could you show me?" I asked.

"If you want."

"I should tell Father where I'm going."

You must not wander, little bird. Stay close. Stay safe.

My stomach hurt. I wanted to go home. But what if the birds left before I got to feed them? "Are you going to hurt me?"

His laughter came in a bright, short burst. The trees became greener, grew taller, the sound of insects skittering across the fallen leaves louder. The boy carried life in his pockets. "Course not! I'm here to play in the forest, just like you. If you're scared to come with me, you can stay here. Or you can go back home to your daddy. No skin off my nose. But I'm goin' to see some birds today." With an elegant flick of his wrist, the boat spun in his palm, around and around on invisible waves. "What's your name, kid?"

Never tell a stranger your name, little bird.

"Louisa."

He nodded. "Lou. I like it."

"What's yours?"

He grinned, revealing a tiny chip on his front tooth I hadn't noticed before. "Jay," he said, bowing low. "My name's Jay."

FEEDING the birds was harder than I thought. Jay and I stayed in the Briarwood for years and years trying to catch one. We called to them, swung the bread around our heads, and laughed into the clouds. By the time the sun had travelled across the forest floor, I was sticky and hot and seeing colours I'd never known before.

But I still hadn't fed a bird.

"Try it again, Lou. Take the bread, and you put your arm out like this—yep, that's good—and you stand on one leg, see? Yeah, yeah, just like—*whoops*." Jay stumbled and sank one foot into the narrow stream behind him. "Well, not like that, but you get what I mean."

The birds were nowhere to be seen, but I heard them cawing and chirping and laughing at the way I couldn't hop on one leg just right. "I can do it! Let me try it again."

He grinned. "All right. Arm out, just like I showed you."

The bread had hardened to a crust, making it easy for me to hold tight. I hoisted my arm in the air, my toes pinching the earth for extra height. "Like this?"

"Yep," he said. "Now the leg. Go on."

Arm up, leg out. I clamped my teeth onto my tongue for balance. Hair fell in my eyes, and I puffed it away, annoyed at the distractions. This was it; I would find a bird to feed. I would finally see one up close. It would be soft. And light. And then I would tell Mother that my books were not a waste after all.

"What now?" I asked. "I don't see any coming."

"They'll come. You just have to say, 'I'll be a kid forever,' three times, and they'll come. Easy peasy, poke your knees-y."

I wobbled but managed to stay upright, hating my shoes and their thin slippery soles. "But I won't be a kid forever. That's a lie."

"It's not a lie if you don't want it to be."

What did that even mean? One day I would be a grown-up with pretty dresses and a husband to hold my hand during thunderstorms. I wanted what Mother and Father had. If I didn't grow up, I'd have none of it.

Jay frowned. "Do you want to see a bird, or do you want to grow up?"

I liked pretty dresses just fine. But I loved the birds more.

"Okay." My leg was an arrow behind me. I was a dancer, a princess in a marble castle. Soon I would touch the leaves high up in the tallest tree, fly away, away, away, and that would be fine. That would be better than anything I'd ever imagined I could do. "I'll be a kid forever."

Jay shielded his eyes against the last blooms of daylight. "That's good, Lou. Again."

"I'll be a kid forever." My fingers tingled until they went pleasantly numb. Colours and sound, flying high, rustling the leaves—it was working.

"One more time, but real loud, or the birds won't hear you. Don't take too long neither, or they won't be hungry anymore."

"I'll be a kid forever!" I imagined a bolt of lightning streaking the sky with gold. I imagined a gust of wind so strong my hair whipped out behind me like a bride's veil, rippling like fire poured from the sun.

Nothing changed.

My leg was tired, and my shoulders ached. I had no balance; I couldn't fly. "Did I do it wrong? Why isn't it working?"

His breath came in shallow gasps, eyes spilling over with tears. "Hoo, you should see yourself!" he said, wiping his face clean. "So serious, like a tribal chief. I didn't think you'd do it!"

A trick. I tossed the bread to the ground at his feet, my cheeks flaming hot. "That was mean!"

His shoulders shook as he stepped toward me, hands held out

in surrender. "I was just havin' some fun with you. You're all right, Lou, you know that?"

"So, there aren't any birds, then?"

"Sure there are. I'm a joker, not a liar; that's bad form."

"Then where are they?" The sting of betrayal mingled with embarrassment, but it was nothing compared to my sadness. "I thought they'd come."

He studied me for a moment, and I glared back. This boy would learn that I did not like to joke about the birds.

"Back where I live," he said, his voice suddenly soft, "there're all kinds of birds: big and tiny, pink and blue, and everythin' in between. Some of 'em talk, and others grant wishes. One even made a whole big world with its beak and one tail feather. A boy in my clan loves 'em just as much as you, 'cause he says anythin' that touches the stars is special. C'mere."

I hesitated before marching forward, careful not to show him how hopeful I still was. "I don't like this."

"Relax," Jay said, eyes rolling to the treetops. "I'm not tryin' to trick you again, promise. Look up."

I did, and so did he.

"What do you see?"

"No birds," I grumbled, arms crossed tight.

He laughed. "What else?"

The sun made my eyes water, but I kept looking. I didn't want to miss it even though I still didn't know what *it* was. "I see . . . leaves. And light. Everything glows." I blinked fast until the little red lights inside my eyes burned out to a pink glow.

Jay nodded like I had passed some sort of test. "The birds can touch everythin' you see. They just glide over the trees, so close the branches tickle their bellies. Can you imagine being one of 'em? Free, just flyin' wherever you want to go?"

Free. I hadn't considered it quite like that before. I closed my eyes; it was easier to feel the tickle of the trees that way. If I were a bird, how would it feel to have nothing under or above me? To inhale the clouds and breathe out stardust?

Something fluttered near my ear, and my eyes flew open.

"Nice job," Jay said. "She's a beauty."

I forced myself not to blink; everything good disappeared when my eyes slipped shut. Wings like ink and a belly of purple satin nuzzled against my cheek. Small patches of turquoise peeked out from the folds of its wings, the green of its eyes like summer grass.

"Is it real?" I asked.

Jay smiled and stroked the bird's head with the back of a finger. "Do *you* think it's real?"

"I . . . I think so."

"Then she is."

I looked up at Jay, my heart light but full. "Just like that?"

"Yes, friend. Just like that."

CHAPTER 3

Once upon a time, when Louisa Webber was nine years old, she jumped from the top of a very tall tree.

She could not remember the exact circumstances that had driven her to such an act, only that something was missing. Something important was gone. She could not remember the path she'd taken through the woods or just how she'd managed to scale the tall oak by the hollowed-out log. She only knew it had not been an accident or mistake. It had not been an act of rebellion, and it most certainly had not been a game of pretending. Louisa Webber had jumped simply to experience the fall.

That was the day the colours had begun draining from the world. Her home had once been painted in vibrant colour. On that day, those colours flickered and disappeared until there was nothing left but the hazy sorrow of storm clouds and the water brewing behind her bedroom walls. That water would pull her under if she stayed in her room any longer, she knew. Her home would kill her.

Perhaps if she fell, the colours would return.

Very little about that day was left unclouded by the protective quality of her memory. She remembered only that Mother hated her and wished she were someone else. To be hated by the one charged with loving you unconditionally did a very terrible thing to the spirit. Lou's home was parched and cracked, absent of love, and she needed to be free of it.

So, she jumped.

It seemed sensible at the time. The woods had always saved her before.

But when she dangled her foot in the air, in the narrow space of time it took to leave the safety of her perch and tumble down, down, down, fear replaced everything else. Fear so sharp it muted the screaming in her mind, replaced everything—even her sense of loss. Intense, strangling, heart-crushing fear narrowed her mind to a point, and nothing else mattered. Fear wasn't better than the numbness. It was different, and different was something.

By the time her foot left that bough, it was too late to stop. But she didn't want to stop.

Someone told her she was lucky to have walked away with nothing more than a twisted ankle and some bruises that day. For Lou, there was nothing lucky about it; the jump had not worked. The colours hadn't come back, and the walls still percolated with the dull threat of a flood.

Louisa Webber had jumped to escape the grey and had returned to it just as quickly. Nothing had changed.

Preparing for tea with the Rileys was like stepping off the bough of a tall tree. But this time, instead of tipping toward the forest floor, she wandered around her room, which was filled with an assortment of rejected dresses. The fear, however, was the same.

"You look ridiculous."

"That was unnecessary." Lou winced as lace scratched her wrists, the high collar of her gown a noose under her chin. "Rosie, instead of making fun, would you please be encouraging? I'm nervous enough as it is."

Rose pulled at Lou's elbow until they both stood before the full-length mirror. She observed her own reflection with mild curiosity. "I'm only teasing. You look lovely, Lou. Too lovely for Wet Samuel."

"Rose," Lou said, sighing, "what did I tell you about calling him that?"

Mother swept into the room in a flurry of silk, then, her curls piled atop her head in a crown of gold, a pair of snowy pearl earrings dripping from her ears like tears. She brushed Rose aside and ran a discerning eye from Lou's mane of frizzy waves to her scuffed shoes. "This cannot be your best work, Louisa. What will you do when I am no longer here to fix all this?"

"I cannot seem to get my hair to settle. I tried." Lou stood straighter, her spine cracking under the pressure. Anne Webber picked up a brush and tore through her daughter's hair, the bristles snagging on the tangles that refused to be tamed.

That hurts. This all hurts.

"That looks lovely, Mother. Thank you."

Her mother's lips pressed into a fine line, the ridges in her skin mapping the permanence of a scowl around her nose. Up close, the grey in her hair was like tinsel, a crisp silver lending a soft sheen to her golden locks. Anne Webber had been beautiful once; now she was mostly disappointed.

"The Rileys are due to arrive at any moment," Mother said. "Please, *please* behave, Louisa. I beg you."

"Of course."

"And do not make any of your humorous remarks. Gentlemen do not appreciate a woman with a sharp tongue or an untidy appearance. Remember that."

Rose offered Lou a pained look. "Perhaps it is Lou who will not like *him*."

"There is nothing to dislike. He comes from proper stock and is highly regarded by his father's business partners. This is a match we cannot afford to bungle. After the last two gentlemen, both of whom have already married other girls with better status, *younger* girls, you know—"

Lou's foot slipped off the bough, and her breath caught in her chest. "I understand, Mother."

And she did; she was too quiet, too distracted, *too old*. Samuel Riley was a good match, one Mother had worked hard to secure. They needed the status. They needed stability. And Lou needed to be the one to deliver that to them, to play the role her father used to occupy. It was her duty now.

Anne Webber busied herself with Lou's satin sash, tugging it tight to *give a better impression of a waist*, and put her books away in a desk drawer (*books offer pretty words that will never win a husband*). Lou watched it all as she had watched the trees before she'd plummeted to the ground.

"Now, Rose," Mother continued, "you may join us for introductions, but I expect you to excuse yourself before the tea is served. We do not need Samuel distracted by your charm, dearest."

Fall . . . away, away, away. If only it were as easy as stepping into nothing and walking away with a twisted ankle.

The Rileys arrived promptly at four o'clock, their son sulking at his mother's side. The city had turned Samuel's face harder than Lou remembered it and tipped his nose skyward. Mother made a show of giving them a tour of their home: the new drapes (awful collectors of dust), the antique painting in the salon (a mahogany horse whose legs were too short), the new vase from the city (another collector of dust).

Lou and Rose walked side by side, nodding at the right moments, making as few remarks as possible. After all, Mother often reminded Lou that men did not appreciate women with sharp tongues. The urge to scream at them all throbbed in her throat where it would remain. She pressed her lips shut against the acid behind her teeth. Samuel brooded through the house, offering neither pleasantry nor a kind look in her direction. Her tongue, blunt or sharp, seemed of very little interest to him.

Lou despised him already.

"You have a beautiful home, Lady Webber," Mrs. Riley remarked. She, too, wore a string of pearls, except hers was a pale pink, droplets like candy forming a noose of her very own. "It is so admirable that you maintain this property without a husband."

Rose stiffened at Lou's side, and the sisters reached for each other's hands.

It is only tea.

It is never only tea.

The fall was going to hurt.

"My husband is very much missed," Lou heard her mother say through the fog settling in her mind. "But the girls and I manage quite well. Louisa has learned to cook and sew, and her needle-work is near perfection."

Books offer pretty words that will never win a husband.

Mrs. Riley smiled. Mr. Riley grunted.

"Shall we have some tea?" Mother asked.

Finally.

"That sounds lovely, Mother," Rose said, her smile dripping sugar. "Are there any muffins leftover from breakfast? I'd love a blueberry."

Anne Webber gave her daughter a pointed look. "I believe you have some of your own needlework in your room, dearest."

"I finished that already. I'd like some tea. And the muffins, of course."

Flustered, Mother led them all to the sitting room for the customary shuffle for seating. Mr. Riley took the armchair by the fire, a place that had always been reserved for Father. No one asked him to move. Mrs. Riley steered her son to the couch, pressing him down beside Lou with white knuckles. Rose, oblivious to the etiquette surrounding the grotesque mating ritual at hand, dropped herself on Lou's other side with a glittery smile and a flick of her hair.

Tea was served.

Lou stepped off the branch.

How long would it take to fall to the ground this time?

"Our Samuel signed a new account with a burgeoning diamond miner in the West," Mrs. Riley said.

Mother smiled. "My Louisa can make tea."

"Tea is quite lovely."

"Yes, it is."

The drapes were creased and stained by the sun. Mother should have replaced them long ago, but there was no money for it. Lou smiled at Samuel, but he was busy stirring his tea again and again.

"Samuel," Mrs. Riley continued, "wants four children."

"My Louisa would give him five," Mother said at once. "She has always wanted a large family."

No, she didn't.

Mrs. Riley nodded and smiled and tapped her teaspoon on her saucer in uneven beats. "Children truly are such a blessing."

On and on, and still she fell. A forest without a bottom. Mother's face grew pale, the same colour as the dove-grey sofa. The gurgle of water within the walls grew louder. It was a wonder she wasn't drowning in it.

"Timber told me something amusing last night."

All eyes snapped to Rose, who sipped her tea, eyes like molten chocolate over the rim of her cup.

"Rose, dearest," Mother said, "perhaps this is not the proper time to—"

"What did dear Timber have to say this time?" Lou asked. She slowed, floated mid-air, suspended by the threads of Rose's words.

"He wanted to play horses and bears, and when I tried to make the horse give the bear a hug, he told me bears and horses are free spirits and shouldn't be forced to touch one another. I thought that was clever. Isn't that clever?"

"Yes, clever." Mother cleared her throat. "If I may ask, does your son prefer the country or the city, Lady Riley?"

"And Timber *also* said that no one gets married where he comes from. Ever."

Mrs. Riley set her cup on its saucer with a loud clink. "This is a rather odd conversation, Lady Webber. I certainly hope your elder daughter does not enjoy the same careless imaginings her younger sister seems to."

"Timber is my sister's imaginary friend," Lou said. The tea was warm, and it slicked her dry tongue. "It is common for children her age. Samuel, do you remember having an imaginary friend as a boy?"

Mrs. Riley smiled. "Our Samuel was always much too practical for that. Those sorts of frivolities are what hinder growth, Miss Webber. You would do well to remember that when you bring my grandchildren into this world."

Mother smiled.

Mr. Riley grunted.

Wet Samuel stared at his lap, a vein pulsing in his temple like a worm.

Worms in a fist, worms in the woods, worms underground, deep, deep underground.

"I quite agree with my wife," Mr. Riley offered. "It is likely the girl is suffering from delusions brought about by the absence of a father figure."

"Hmm." Mrs. Riley sipped her tea. "Fathers are so important to a young woman's upbringing. As mothers, we often baby our children more than we should. But it is a *father's* duty to stamp this sort of behaviour out—pull it out, root and stem. Like a weed."

Rose's face reddened. "There is nothing wrong with childishness. Though speaking to you now explains why Samuel is so *wet*."

"Rose!" Mother's eyes were wide. "Apologize at once!"

The lake. How long would it take to run to the lake in the woods and sink to the bottom?

"It isn't Mother's fault Father is gone," Rose said, letting her saucer clatter onto the tabletop. "You growns are all the same, looking down your noses at anyone different from you."

Lou rested a hand on her sister's lap. "It is fine, Rose. Please do not be upset."

"It is *not* fine!"

The Rileys rose to leave, and Lou crashed to the ground. The impact rattled her teeth. She was bleeding, she was broken, a pile of bones and flesh trussed up in pretty silk and lace. Mother raced after their departing guests, leaving Lou and Rose in the sitting room with empty saucers stained with tea.

"Rose," Lou said, "how could you behave that way?"

"What?"

"Today was important to Mother! The Rileys are *important*."

Rage and hurt twisted Rose's features. "The Rileys spoke of you like property! Like you were not in the room!"

"It is the way these things are done, Rosie. You know that."

"What I know," Rose said, her eyes shining, "is that you forgot all about Jay and the island and everything you used to love. For what? Tea parties and a husband with five children and a life without me? Today was important for Mother, but what about what *you* want?"

Her face, Lou thought, the weight in her chest growing heavier. *She looks so much older.* "I love you, sister, and I understand you are upset by all this. But not everyone is so eager to hear about Timber."

"This isn't about him."

"No, perhaps not. But people like the Rileys—like Mother—

do not understand your stories. Sometimes it may better to keep such things to ourselves."

The Rileys were out the door . . . on the lawn . . . gone.

"It wasn't supposed to be this way!" Rose's small fists trembled at her sides. "Father should still be here! You should have stayed with Jay longer!"

"Rose—"

But she was already dashing up the stairs, leaving Lou behind. Their mother was right; books and pretty words did not secure a husband, but what was the point of chasing a new family when it destroyed the one you already loved?

The pain came, just as Lou knew it would.

She ripped through the tie at her neck and let the air back into her lungs.

How many daughters did it take to break a mother's heart? A sister's?

One.

Only one.

CHAPTER 4

LOU

AGE SEVEN

"Last one to the lake's gotta eat a worm!"

"That's disgusting!" I laughed. It was good to laugh. Things at home were always so quiet. But here, in the Briarwood, in a race against Jay, I could holler at the sky until my lungs ached.

I moved like lightning. Green fell behind me, no match for my speed. The trees tickled my cheeks, and my toes never quite touched the ground. I could run, and I could sing, and I could pretend I was in another place.

A *magical* place.

It was spring at last. The new sun thawed the ground and called the birds back to their nests. Worms wriggled in the mud, chewing holes that spotted the leaves. In the spring, a heavy mist hovered over the lake like cotton in the morning. I loved the way the cold puffed a visible chill over the smooth surface of the water before the mid-morning sun chased it away. It was mystical, the way I pictured Jay's island to be.

Mother and Father had warned me about the lake, but like other forbidden things, it was too wonderful to ignore.

Racing Jay to the water was my idea.

It is not proper for a young girl to prowl the woods alone, Mother had told me. But Father said I was strong and fierce and fast. They could both be right, but it was Father's version of me who ran on Jay's heels, gaining ground the harder I pushed. It was the version I wanted to be.

Jay took a turn off the usual path. I stumbled.

"Cheater!" I called, but he only laughed.

"Keep up, Lou!"

While Jay was quick, I was the very best at dares. Shocking people by doing the unexpected sparked a fire in my belly the way nothing else did. And since the race to the lake was a dare of my own making, it did not matter that Jay was the faster one. I would be fierce.

I would win.

The forest rushed by in sweeps of green and bronze, my feet kicking up dust. Jay ran with grace, and I was right behind him, using his footprints as dots on a treasure map. I admired his speed, the way his head shone like spun gold when the sun hit it just right. One day I would be just as quick.

Jay jumped a tree stump, his legs moving like the blades of a windmill. "I'm winnin' this round, Lou!"

"Not yet!" I tucked my chin into my chest and pumped my knees harder. With a scream, I leapt into the sky, the very clouds, and cleared the stump without touching it. I was *fierce.*

Delicate.

No. I am fierce. Move faster.

Jay glanced over his shoulder, his eyes as big as his smile. The lake was close; I could smell the rotten sharpness of it in the heavy air.

Faster.

I was right beside him. Our elbows knocked, and my legs screamed, and I smiled because I was going to *win.*

But as fast as Jay was, he was also arrogant. And as an arrogant little boy, he thought he had already bested me. I lunged into his path and knocked him off course. He cried out, but I didn't care; I was laughing, flying. *Free.* The last row of trees swayed aside to let me through, so I leapt into the open with a triumphant yell.

We had missed the morning fog. White light warmed the surface of the lake, giving it polish, making it glow. I whirled on my heels before my boots could find the edge of the water. "I win!"

Jay puffed up to meet me, eyes like the sapphires Mother wore in her ears at Christmastime. "Only 'cause you cheated."

"I learned from you."

He smiled and dipped his head in a mocking bow, dagger flashing at his hip. "All right. A bet's a bet. Unless we race again?"

"No deal. You'll just try to trick me." I cupped my hands into the water. Cold shocked my cheeks, the back of my neck. What would it be like to step inside and let the water creep up my body until it took over completely? There could be mermaids and other children waiting for me below. So many wonderful things lived in another world—one where Mother asked me questions again and Father was happy. "I hope you like eating your worms."

Jay wrinkled his nose. "I really want another race. If you win, I'll eat *five* worms. How's that for a deal?" His grin sparkled when I said nothing. "Don't you wanna see me eat *five whole worms* instead of just one tiny one?"

The Briarwood grew still. Waiting.

Mother hadn't left her room in days. It wasn't uncommon for our meals to be cold—if they came at all—for Father to sleep in his study, and for the drapes to remain drawn tight across the windows. A heavy, granular sort of darkness clung to Mother whenever she surfaced. Her cheeks were unusually pale, her fingers ghosting to her belly as though expecting to find something there. I didn't understand what she was looking for. While part of me longed to wrap my arms around her like she used to do for me, I never did. Because while the darkness suffocated Mother, Father was busy worrying over a crystal tumbler, and I could roam the Briarwood at my own leisure. With Jay.

"I want to keep playing without you trying to trick me. Do your parents know that you eat worms?" I asked, desperate to keep him talking. I knew everything about Jay. I knew nothing about Jay. Not really.

He picked up a rock and tossed it from hand to hand. "Don't have parents."

"Did they leave you with an aunt or something?"

"Nah." He pulled his arm back, and the stone dropped into the lake with a satisfying thunk. "It's just me and my brothers."

"That sounds nice. I don't have any brothers or sisters."

"You've got me. That's better than havin' a brother."

I smiled. "I know. Do you need to fight for attention or toys or anything?"

"In a way. Mostly we just fight."

I nodded, not knowing what he meant. In truth, I was thankful I had no siblings. But that didn't mean I had no competition; the room at the end of the hall was my biggest enemy. Sometimes I stood outside the locked door, imagining what could be shut inside for Mother to spend so much time there alone. She would touch the closed door, press her forehead against it before disappearing inside for hours and days on end. What was it about the unremarkable wood and brass handle that made Mother cry?

Jay frowned as though I'd spoken aloud. "My brothers are nice mostly. I mean, I get to do what I want whenever I want. If I want to come play with you, I just do it. But I miss bein' on my own sometimes. It gets crowded where we live." He stopped, toeing the mud with his boot. "Maybe you could come back with me to visit."

It was the first time he'd ever offered, and I was suddenly dizzy with unexpected want. "Really? You'd take me to the island with you?"

He nodded. "You could even stay a while . . . if you wanted to. You'd like my friends, especially Benji, I think. He's a big softie. Oh! And the caves by the cove are the best. I know you're probably more excited about the lagoons, but . . ."

I stopped listening. It would be easy to sneak around him now, get a head start into the woods. After all, he *had* wanted to race again. And five worms was quite a lot for him to eat.

I took one step away from the lake. Another. "How would we get to your home?" I asked.

"I'm not sure yet. I never brought any friends back with me before."

I was ready. Without turning at his shocked cry, I launched into the trees. I was flying again, closer to the birds with every thump of my soles. Jay had invited me to his home. Jay was going to lose another race. I was weightless, and today was a good day. There weren't many of those.

"Last one back has to eat five worms!" I called, giddy with the possibility of it all. My laughs bounced off every oak and fir, leaving a trail like fairy dust behind me.

"Cheater!"

"Yep!"

I refused to lose the race; there was no way I'd eat anything that lived in the dirt when all I wanted was the sky.

My hair fell out of the braid I'd fumbled over that morning. It was far from the perfect plait Mother could manage, but she wouldn't see it anyhow. She wasn't there to notice my yellow skirt, now creased and stained with grass, or the fresh scuffs on the riding boots I'd insisted on buying instead of the silk slippers. I would only ever be in trouble if she noticed those things. And Mother hadn't noticed much for months.

The trees thinned. Sunset bounced off the windows at the

back of my home. The kitchen drapes were open, allowing the darkness to bleed from the house and into the open air, allowing the place to breathe. That should have been my first warning. But as I ran, I cared only that Jay's footsteps were behind mine. When I pushed aside the last veil of leaves, I was gasping for breath, the world swirling in vivid emerald and cerulean blue and everything else that was beautiful and bright.

Jay drew level a second later, rubbing a stitch in his side. "That wasn't fair!"

"Doesn't matter. A bet's a bet," I said, echoing his words. The victory crackled across my skin, moving from my nose to my fingertips. "Do you need help finding your snack?"

Jay started to protest, but his eyes fell on something far behind me. His answer was forever lost.

"Louisa Mae Webber!"

I spun on my heels, the stains on my dress, mud on my shoes, and twigs in my hair an ocean wave threatening to drown me. "Mother!"

Her footsteps ate away at the grass, the pale floral pattern on her skirt a moving garden around her legs. Grease darkened the loose hair around her temples while bruises purpled the rings under her eyes. As her shadow grew longer, the happiness in my heart drained away.

My skirt. My hair. She'll be so upset.

"What did I tell you about playing in the Briarwood, Louisa? It is not safe."

I exhaled in a huff. "I'm sorry, Mother. I did not mean to upset you."

"Get inside. You need a bath." She took my hand without looking me in the eye and pulled me toward the house. Her hands were dry, her nails long and sharp, digging into my skin. "Your father has one of his associates coming for dinner. The yellow dress with the lace trim will be most appropriate, I think."

I glanced over my shoulder, my wrist humming under her grip. Jay lurked at the edge of the trees, a frown darkening his features.

"Can Jay come for dinner?" I asked. "He has nowhere to go, and I'd like him to be there with me." We were still moving. "Mother?"

"What?"

Our home greeted us like the sweep of a scythe from Death's own hand.

"Jay," I repeated a little louder. "The friend I told you about. He's just there, by the forest. Can he come to dinner too?"

Mother stopped, her confusion ripping open a hole in my chest. "Stop talking nonsense. There is no one there."

We were finally in the doorway of our home, my footsteps too loud, my pulse too quick. The vividness of the Briarwood fell away until there was nothing but cold and darkness. I was a fool to think I could be fierce.

Before Mother could shut the door, I glanced back down the hill to the trees. Jay stood at the edge of the light and waved, sullen, a fist full of wriggling worms.

AFTER DINNER, Mother and Father argued again. Tears thickened Mother's words to syrup; I was beginning to forget the times when she laughed and sang as she worked. I stood behind my bedroom door with my arms laced around my stomach. It was impossible to breathe. Still, I needed to hear every word. I needed to understand.

"Anne, please," Father said, his voice coming from the kitchen below. "Louisa is finally asleep."

"Which is precisely the reason we need to discuss this *now*. You are always so careful about what we say around her."

"She is a child, Anne." Father sighed, his voice dipping low. "There is nothing left to discuss. Perhaps we were not meant to be blessed with another child with a mere philosophical notion."

I pressed my cheek to the door. The sheet over my head spilled around me like a curtain, locking in the heat from my face and catching my tears. Moments before, I'd been a mermaid with long hair of coral and mint. Now I was a silly girl with a sheet on her head.

"That is unacceptable, Charles. It is your duty to provide for our family, but it is mine to give you a family to provide for. You cannot simply dismiss my need for another child."

"You *have* a family, my darling. Louisa is our child, and she is enough."

"She is not!"

She is not.

She is not.

Too bony, too slow, a disappointment, not enough, not enough, *not enough.* The darkness of midnight hugged me close. I curled in on myself, allowing it to overcome me. Behind the walls, water churned and churned.

"Anne, that is unfair. Louisa can feel your disinterest in her. I see it in her eyes whenever you turn away from her when she so clearly is seeking your attentions. She needs her mother."

Silence greeted those words. "Every time I look at her, I am reminded that she is all I will ever have. If I cannot be a mother, a *real* mother, then I am nothing. The other ladies, they have large families, so many children—"

"You *are* a mother." Father's voice was a sword in the night. "We may pray for another, but not at the price of our daughter's happiness."

Not enough, not enough, not enough.

A pillow slammed into my shoulder. "Hey, why'd you stop?" Jay asked. "I could have stolen the treasure from you just like *that*." He snapped his fingers, and the sound startled me from my thoughts. I turned, stunned, to my window, where he sat on the floor, bathed in blue moonlight.

"I don't feel like playing anymore. I'm tired." It wasn't entirely a lie. Playing pirates and mermaids had lost its appeal when I'd been cast as the mermaid. Again. The fight on the floor below only reminded me where I was. Who I was.

I truly was so, so tired.

Jay leapt to his feet, quick as a sparrow. "Who cares what the growns are sayin' down there? You have a chest of gold to protect, and you almost let this pirate get it."

When I said nothing, Jay plucked a broken tree branch from behind my dresser and pointed it at my heart.

"C'mon, lassie. The longer ye wait, the worse the punishment."

"I'm not interested in being a mermaid anymore." The words poured from my lips like ink. They stained the space between us, spattering on the clean rug, twisting Jay's features into a frown. "It's boring, and I want a turn to be a pirate."

"But you're a girl. Girls are always mermaids."

"There could be girl pirates too. I'd like that."

"I never seen one."

"And I've never seen a parrot, but I know they exist."

The voices were growing louder, Mother's sobs battering against my door.

"Give me the sword, Jay."

He cocked his head, the moonlight shifting around him like a cloak. "Okay, here's the deal: if you can win this sword from me, you can be a pirate."

Every time I look at her, I am reminded that she is all I will ever have.

Not enough.

How could a mother hate her own blood so deeply?

Boys got to jump. To fight. To be pirates steering ships. Girls were told to return to the watery deep, unseen mermaids doomed to be forgotten to the sea. And even when we did what we were told, we were still never enough. I wanted to be a pirate, and for once, no one would force me back into the skin of a mermaid.

I leapt across the room, and the white cotton on my head spilled to the floor.

Jay was ready for me; he threw himself to the ground, rolling toward my dresser, where my books were stacked in straight piles. Silverton Lane melted away until I was somewhere else—somewhere Mother didn't cry, and my love mattered, and I could be anything in the world.

Even a pirate.

CHAPTER 5

That could not have gone any worse.

"That could have gone *much* worse, Lou." Rose clutched the windowsill by her bed, fingers drumming an uneven beat. "Mother truly has some nerve, though, doesn't she?"

"I would rather not think about it at the moment." Lou settled herself on the edge of Rose's bed and rested her chin in her palms. The house was still, a small reprieve before the storm that was sure to rain down on them. "I do not know what to do, Rosie. We've made such a mess of things."

"Do?" Rose turned around, eyes wide. "We don't need to do anything. We solved your problem. The Rileys will never associate with us after this. You're free of this arrangement, just like you wanted!"

"We needed this arrangement."

Rose sniffed. "The way they were talking—like you couldn't speak for yourself, like you were a prize cow to be traded at auction! It was disgusting."

It was all too much. Lou flinched—not because the words

were untrue, but because of how clearly her younger sister saw the truth. But truth didn't matter. "I'd prefer it if you did not compare me to a cow. And the line of suitors is looking quite thin these days," Lou said. "I have no prospects. The shame this brings Mother—"

"And why is that such a problem?" Rose fixed her with a look loaded with rage and loathing.

She's growing up too fast. A child should not look so angry.

"This is not *her* life!" Rose insisted. "What is so terrible about staying together, just the three of us? What is so awful about being alone?"

Lou plucked Benji Bear from the bed, cradling him to her chest as the wind whispered in from the Briarwood. "Oh, Rosie. You'll have a husband of your own one day, or you won't. You will go off to school, or you won't. You will move to the city, or you will stay here, close to our family home."

"So?"

"So?" Lou looked up, her heart racing. "Don't you see? You get the choice, Rosie. You alone will get to decide what to do with your life when it is your turn to make those decisions. But the only way that works is if money and status are not in question for us. And the only way *that* happens is if I play my role and make Mother happy by marrying well!"

Rose dropped onto the bed with a surly look at the door. "I did not think about all that. It isn't fair to put that on your shoulders."

"I know. But it isn't your job to think about this. It is mine."

Far below, the front door snapped shut. With any luck, Mother would be too upset to face them. With any luck, Lou would have a chance to sleep, a chance to forget her embarrassment, her betrothal, her duty, the gurgling water in the walls.

Lou tossed a plush pig at Rose, earning a reluctant smile. The air between them thawed. "I am twenty, Rosie. A woman. I cannot stay here for the rest of my life, as much as I would love to. Samuel was . . . interesting enough."

"For a wet rag."

"Be nice."

Rose wrinkled her nose. "I don't want to be nice."

There were footsteps on the stairs. Lou turned to the window, unseeing. "I wanted to travel once. See the city, discover the places I've read about so often. Did you know there is a tower that touches the sky at the centre of the city?"

"No." Rose placed a hand over Lou's and squeezed. "You'll take me with you?"

"What?"

"If you go off exploring or find a small apartment on a terrible street somewhere, I want to come too. Do not leave me here alone. Promise it."

Rose's panic was enough to pull Lou from the chaos in her head. The footsteps grew louder. "I will never leave you behind unless I do not have a choice," Lou said. "You are my favourite person in the world. Remember that."

There was no time to say more. The bedroom door swung wide, Anne Webber's form a sinister outline of sharp edges and shadows. "That was a spectacle today, Louisa."

Rose rolled onto her back, arms splayed like an eagle's wings. "Louisa did nothing. I ruined your tea today."

"And I will have words with you about your conduct later." Their mother stopped by the window and snapped it shut.

Too hot, too small, can't breathe.

"It is lucky I managed to salvage the entire affair with some very careful promises in regard to your dowry."

"What do you mean you *salvaged* it?" Lou asked.

"You and Samuel are to marry in the fall. That gives us just over one month to finalize the guest list and details. We will need to find you an appropriate dress, one that gives a better figure than what—"

If I cannot be a mother, a real *mother, then I am nothing.*

The news should have made Lou happy; this was what she wanted, what was needed. And yet her stomach tumbled down to her knees, and the walls roared with the arrival of high tide. There was a hairline crack between the baseboards and the floor, and the wall was bubbling from the pressure behind it. Soon it would buckle. A memory clawed its way from the murkiest places of her mind. It was jagged and raw, a memory of sticks and cotton fabric spilling past her shoulders.

"Louisa, are you listening to me?"

Her head snapped up. "Yes, Mother. I am to be married in the fall. To Samuel."

Wet Samuel.

Stop it.

"And a good thing too," Mother continued. "The Rileys do not come from extreme wealth, but they have more than enough to make us comfortable. Their connections carry much weight in wider social circles. It is the least I can give you."

"This is not for her benefit," Rose muttered, but Anne Webber ignored her.

Mother turned to the sky, her face shrouded in mist. The baseboards buckled, cracked. "Get some rest, Louisa. Tomorrow we discuss invitations and your living arrangements. I'll expect you washed and dressed before dawn."

"Lou takes me to the Briarwood every morning," Rose said, glaring at the ceiling. "We already have plans."

"I've had enough of your childish demands, Rose. Louisa will spend the day with me on matters of actual importance. It will soon be your turn to entertain potential suitors, and an outburst like today's will do nothing to attract an acceptable match."

"The horror," Rose muttered.

But Anne Webber was already moving to the door.

Slamming it shut.

Leaving Lou alone with her thoughts. And thoughts were dangerous when left to chase one another around unchecked.

"We can run, you know," Rose whispered.

Lou strode over to the window, pulled it open, and curled up beside Rose on the bed. "I like the window open too. It seems your preferences have rubbed off on me."

"We can leave together—make our own life."

"We could." Lou's body moulded to Rose's as though they were halves of the same heart. "But we won't. Is it all right if I sleep with you tonight?"

Their days together were numbered, and she was going to enjoy them all before Samuel Riley snatched them away.

Rose pulled Lou's arm around her. "Thank you for opening the window."

"Of course. Perhaps Timber can comfort us both."

IN HER DREAMS, Lou wrestled a crocodile.

The beast swished through black water with daggers for teeth and granite for hide. Powerful claws tore her skin raw, scraping against bone as she floundered. Her lungs burned, and her arms worked, but it was no use. Theirs was a frantic dance, a waltz ending only in blood. Darkness gripped her with both hands.

Somewhere above the water, Rose screamed. The crocodile shattered to smoke.

Lou bolted upright in bed, half expecting to face a jaw lined with fangs. Instead, the room was dark save for the moonlight filtering through the window, painting everything in the softness of dreams. "Rosie? Rose, what is it? What happened?"

Her sister leaned far over the window ledge. Black hair feathered down her back, smoothed by the crisp night air. Her fingers curled over the sill, tears leaving dark drops on the painted wood.

"Rose, get away from there!" Lou peeled the sheets away and lunged for her sister; she should have moved carefully so as not to scare her into falling. But all Lou saw was her beautiful Rose, so small and fragile, tipping over the narrow piece of brittle wood. *Careful. Slow down. Don't scare her.* "You had a nightmare, a terrible dream. I had one too. Come away from there so we can talk about it."

"He's gone." Rose's voice trembled, but she didn't turn. "He's gone, Lou. He said he would come tonight!"

Lou reached tentatively into the endless space between them. "Why don't you come to bed and—"

"He's gone!"

"Come here. Please." Lou sighed with relief as Rose allowed herself to be pulled away from the window. "What are you talking about, Rosie? Nothing has happened."

"Timber. Timber is gone."

Lou towed her sister to bed, anger flaring. How dare a child, real or imaginary, have such a hold on her sister? She had always humoured Rose when it came to Timber, but she only did so because he was harmless—until then. "You're upset because of Timber? Come now, you need some sleep. You will feel much better in the morning."

"Timber is *dead.*" Rose buried her face in her hands, sobs rattling her ribs. "How could this happen? He said no one on the island can truly die, even if they sometimes disappear! He was happy there. He didn't want to leave the island."

Lou didn't understand and was too upset to try. "Rose, that is nonsense."

"It is not!"

"I assure you, with a bit of rest—"

"I don't *want* to rest! We need to find out what happened to him. He should have come, he should have been here, he—"

"Timber is not real!" Lou regretted her words instantly. They were too sharp, too heavy, too—*true*—insensitive.

It was ironic, really; the surest way to appreciate a thing was to suffer the absence of it. Rose stared up at her with her wide dark eyes. But where there had once been love and undiluted joy was now only anger. The force of that anger was staggering, the innocence of the young girl she loved gone. Rose the child had been replaced by an older, hardened version in the space of a blink. Lou's heart ached.

"How can you say he isn't real?" Rose asked. "You've asked about him. You've offered to meet him even. I thought you understood, even if you didn't remember."

Lou couldn't bear being the cause of such unexpected pain. But perhaps to be cruel was to be kind. "I understand you are upset, but think of what this *means*. If Timber is not real, then he cannot die. Don't you see? Everything is fine."

Fury scorched the air between them. "I expected to hear this from Mother, not you."

"You are a child, Rosie. I've always loved your imagination, but if your delusions are hurting you—"

"Delusions?" Rose turned away, and Lou was almost grateful for it. The disgust, the disappointment—it was all too terrible to witness. The rush of water in the walls grew louder. The floorboards creaked. They sat together in the bowels of a sinking ship, waiting for the water to breach. "Timber is not something I've created in my mind, Lou. Jay, the island . . . it's all more real than anything Mother lets us see here. Why won't you believe me?"

"Because I know better."

The wind shifted. Turned cold. The water living in the walls had found its way out, and Lou was powerless to stop it. Salt and brine tinged the air, the floor glistened as though bathed in ink, and a fog settled over the room.

Rose did not turn to the water slithering toward the bed. It was as though she couldn't see it at all. "I need you to leave now," she said, her voice flat.

Lou dropped her hands, unsure what to do with them. "You don't mean that."

"I do. This is your fault, you know. You and your logic and your *duty*. That is what destroyed Jay and Peter, and now everything is *wrong*! If you're not careful, you're going to be pulled back there, but it won't be fun. Timber said so."

Heat flashed up Lou's neck. "What are you talking about?"

"The island!" Rose hurled the words at her like spears. "All the lost end up there. Timber didn't tell me how it would happen, only that you might go there one day because you are just as lost as the rest of them and Jay can't stop himself. You betrayed me. You betrayed me, and I'll never forgive you!"

Ice frosted Lou's toes. The water had made it to the bed, shiny eels curling around her feet. She stood, stumbled, lurched toward the door. "Stop this, Rosie."

"It will never stop! Nothing will be right until you find Jay and remember there are other more important things than you and your marriage."

Jay, Timber, an island for the lost. Lou retreated to the hall, raced down the corridor. Her bedroom door swung open and shut to the tune of squealing hinges. She'd outrun the water, but Rose's wails floated down the hall and battered the door.

I'm not gonna hurt you. I only wanted to play.

I'll be a kid forever.

Another door slammed; Anne Webber's frantic footfalls thumped across the hall. "Rose? Rose, darling, what is it?"

I'll be a kid forever.

But I won't be a kid forever. That's a lie.

"Jay—*find Jay!*" Rose cried. "He knows how to fix this!"

An invisible seam ripped her wall wide open. Water gurgled and hissed, pouring like acid onto the carpet. It was her imagination, a terrible part of her nightmare. Soon the crocodile would return for more blood, riding the waves of the flood around her bed. Lou climbed under the covers and tried to imagine her life in full colour.

Drip, drip, drip.

The crocodile snapped its jaws, but she was still alive. She was going to be a wife. Rose would be free. Mother would be proud. It didn't matter that she wasn't ready or that she didn't want it; the house was drowning, and Rose was screaming, and where had all the colours gone?

The name of a boy who didn't exist chased her to sleep.

Jay.

A boy she didn't remember.

My name's Jay.

A boy from an island of forgotten things.

CHAPTER 6
LOU
AGE NINE

*Captain and his men stole the boy from his
den and took away his gold.
Most of us died, still some are alive, but all
of us sail the sea.
We follow the stars, forever we march, to
eternity we must go.
The island holds still, no matter our will, so
never we die, yo-ho.*

My bed was a ship; I would sink it to the bottom of
the sea.

Jay visited every night through a window I
refused to close, even now that cold shivered through the trees.
Mother never bothered me about it anymore. Instead, she let
Father put me to bed. That was good—it left more time for me to
focus on important things. A pirate had stolen my chest of
Spanish gold, and I wanted it back.

I reached into my belt and pulled my prisoner free, waving the stuffed bear over my head like a trophy. "I've got your best friend here, pirate! I'm not afraid to slice his throat."

"Oh yeah?" Jay aimed a sword at my heart. "Ye wouldna hurt an innocent man, lass. Now just let 'im go, an' we can fight this alone."

"I *will* hurt him if you don't give me my treasure back, you miserable cur!" I clamped my free hand onto the bear's head, digging my fingers into the fur. "You have five seconds."

Jay grinned, tongue fiddling with his chipped tooth. "We can make a bargain," he said. "Negotiate. I'll give ye ten coins o' the treasure fer Benji Bear. A real bargain, lass."

I was winning, and he knew it. "I don't make deals with mutinous pirates. There are a thousand coins in that chest, and I want them all. Now hand it over, or the prisoner dies."

"Never!" He crab-stepped over to my bed and reached underneath. "And mermaids ain't supposed to be so bossy."

Cornering my prey was a simple matter of moving to the opposite side of the bed—no, the *ship*. It gave me cover from any attack, made me untouchable. We were surrounded by crocs; I didn't mind the beasts as much as Jay did, but they were still sharp-toothed and hungry. Being a mermaid made the crocs my kin, and they would help me when I called. I was sure of it.

"I'm a special mermaid," I said. My writing desk sat behind me, papered in sketches I'd rendered of birds from the Briarwood. The charcoal lines were blank eyed and unmoving, made immortal by my own hand. There was power in that. "I don't like it when pirates mess with my things. I want my gold back. Come out and fight me!"

"Well, I guess we got a problem, don't we?" With a snap quick as a cobra strike, Jay's arm swung out from the shadows, launching a pillow across the bed.

I dove for cover. Beaded bracelets, charcoal sticks, and satin ribbons—a storm of my most precious things—rained down from my dresser. I dodged it all, slick as a fish swishing through a pond. My desk took the brunt of the next hit. Scraps of paper fluttered around me; instead of flying into the clouds, my birds were shot to the ground.

"Cannons won't stop a mermaid," I said. "I can slip underwater, and you'll never find me!"

"Not if I take ye down before ye swim away, fish!" Jay assaulted me with a cloud of barrettes next, their sting relentless. "Or I'll just harpoon ye instead!"

"Stinking pirate! You'll need to learn your lesson the hard way."

Benji Bear.

I picked up one of the pins lying by my feet. It shone in the low light of the moon, a dagger in my steady hand.

"No!"

"Say goodbye to Benji." Without blinking, I drove the pointed end into the stuffed bear's chest. Twisted. Grinned.

"*No!*" Jay howled, fists pounding the bed. "Ye'll pay for that, *fish*!"

"I know where your other men are hiding. I wouldn't try anything unless you want one of the twins to be next." We faced each other, straight-backed and tight-lipped. "That treasure belongs to the mermaids of Rainbow Rock, and I *will* have it!"

Jay snorted, and the moment shattered. "That's not the name of it."

"Of course it is. The mermaids live in the diamond water around Rainbow Rock."

"*Soul* Rock sounds better," he said. "Rainbow Rock sounds like candy or somethin'. It's gotta be scary."

"Why does everything need to be scary?"

"Because we're playin' *pirates*, Lou! Do you think any pirate would be afraid of a mermaid living on *Rainbow Rock*?"

I paused to consider it. "Yes, I do. Besides, I like the name."

"Pick another one."

"No."

Benji Bear, now quite dead and fed to the crocodiles, glared up at me from the ground. His shiny black eyes, one hanging on by a delicate thread, were filled with silent accusation. I looked away.

"Boys are such bullies. You always think you know better than everyone. But I'm part of this game too, and I say we call it Rainbow Rock."

"And you girls just want everythin' to sound pretty." Jay turned his back to me and kicked out. His boot struck an old toy ship, and it crashed into the opposite wall.

"Jay!"

"I'm sorry! Think no one heard it?"

A stream of curses erupted from down the hall. The narrow space under my door was still mercifully black, but the footsteps did not bode well. "Now you did it," I said, motioning for Jay to leave. "Why can't you be more careful?"

He rolled his eyes but didn't move.

Please let it be Father. Please let it be Father.

I leapt into bed, pulled the duvet up to my chin, and kicked at the sheets puddled by my feet. There was no tidying the mess, no explaining the open window or the young boy now sitting cross-legged before it. Starlight speckled his cheeks, glittered in the depths of his eyes. I would surely be in trouble. But at least I wasn't alone. The creak of the hinges scared away pirate and mermaid alike. Chests of gold sank to the bottom of the sea, and my bed grew still; it was no longer an enormous ship with pearlescent sails, but a slab of wood with four petrified legs.

"What is making all this noise?" Even pulled from the depths of sleep and with her hair unbound and soft, Mother was a terrifying angel. "You should be asleep. And what did I tell you about tidying your room before bed?"

When I did not answer, she padded over to my bed on bare feet.

"Louisa, look at me."

I obeyed, but only for a second; I would not give her more. "I'm sorry, Mother. We did not mean to wake you. I promise to clean the mess in the morning."

"We?" Mother frowned. "For heaven's sake. Is it Jay again?"

When I nodded, her lips disappeared into a sharp gash across her face.

"This nonsense has gone on for far too long. Your father advised me to let this fantasy run its course. But, dear, aren't you getting a bit *old* for all this?"

I looked at her properly, forgetting my grudge. "Too old? For playing?" I said. Jay unfolded his legs and crept up behind Mother, his eyes hard as stones. "I don't understand."

She brought one hand to rest on the swell between her hips and settled beside me on the bed. "There comes a time when one must leave childish things behind, Louisa. Imaginary friends are one of those things."

I forced myself not to laugh as Jay clutched his own stomach and brushed an invisible lock of hair over his shoulder. Something inside me cracked knowing she didn't believe me, but I wouldn't let her see how much her words hurt. "It does not need to be that way, Mother. Jay is real, and he is my best friend. He makes me happy."

Disappointment twisted her features and struck me in the chest with all its might. I knew that expression well, even in the dark.

"Dearest Louisa," she said, "this is life. The reality of how we must behave is not a punishment of my own making, but a fact of growing up. I . . . I wish it could be different, but this is the world in which we live. Perhaps your father is right and I have not been as present as you have needed. As . . . as you deserve." She swallowed, twined her fingers in her lap. "I alone am to blame for that. But I have been blessed with a chance at reparation, at doing better than I did with you. I am to have another child."

"I am tired, Mother."

"Please, Louisa. You will be a sister in a few short months. What example will you offer to your new sibling if you are to continue to behave so foolishly?"

A sister.

Jay shrank into the shadows and reappeared by my side.

Grow up, Lou. Be bigger. Be older. That's what she wants.

"I truly am tired, Mother," I repeated. "May I sleep now? I promise to be quiet."

Her gaze tried to snare mine without success; I was a mermaid, hard to catch. She busied herself with my covers, tucking them under me, pinning me down.

"I understand," she whispered. "I will see you in the morning, then. Good night, Louisa."

Mother moved like a snake through the brush, lips pressed against the complaints of the mess at her feet. Her footsteps whispered down the hall, taking every drop of magic with her.

I kicked off my duvet and rolled onto the floor in one fluid motion. Benji Bear was still on the ground, so I tossed him onto the safety of my bed. He'd suffered enough for one night.

Jay took a slow step toward me. "You wanna talk about it?"

"Rainbow Rock still needs its treasure," I said. The horse would be next; Jay liked him most after Benji Bear. "The only thing I want to talk about is how you will be giving it back."

Jay grinned, and my last moments with Mother were chased away by the fire in his eyes. "Aye, lassie. Yer wish is me command."

This time we were careful not to make a sound.

SNOW FELL on Silverton Lane the next day. Flurries crusted the road in a sheet of ice, and horses struggled to pull their carriages up the hill. I sat on the hall floor, listening to the crunch of hooves and the hollering of men working to shift the snow. I hid upstairs until the front door clicked, a cloud of snow dusting the hall.

"Father!" I called, taking the steps at a run. He was still in his overcoat, his eyes rimmed in blue shadows, his face sallow. I wrapped my arms tight around his middle, relishing the warmth of the wool against my cheek. "I missed you! Are you well?"

"I missed you as well, little bird." He shook thick cotton flakes off his hat and scooped me into his arms. Jay waited in silence by the stairs, but I could feel his eyes on us. Watching. Making sure I was all right. "I am well as can be. Did you take care of your mother today?"

No. "Of course."

"Good. I have a present for you." He set me down and pulled a cloth-bound volume from his coat. "This is a special first edition of one of my favourite fairy tales. I thought you could add it to your collection."

"*The Boy and the Stars,*" I read, taking it from him with light fingers. "I've never heard this story before. It sounds wonderful."

"It is. I hope you enjoy it."

Mother glided into the room, fingers clutching her stomach as though keeping her insides in place. "Come now, Louisa. Let your father get through the door before you pester him."

"I was not—"

"Why don't you show your mother your newest book, little bird. I'm sure she'd love to see it."

A smile tugged at my lips as Jay peeked over my shoulder for a better look. "It is a fairy tale," I said, turning the precious item to give her a better look. "I have not yet—"

"Darling, you must rest," Mother said. "The weather is horrendous, and the journey must have been difficult. I've made braised lamb for dinner. Your favourite." She set Father's sodden coat on a hook in the hall and headed back to the kitchen.

"Your mother must have had a long day." Father offered me a weak smile. "Would you like me to read some of this story to you before dinner?"

"No, thank you. I do love it, though," I said. Jay's hand found mine, and my stomach settled. The roaring in my ears subsided, so I managed a smile. For him. "Please excuse me, Father."

My room was the only safe place, Jay my only friend in the world. My new book called to me; I wanted to root my fingers in its pages and seep under the ink. Anything to be somewhere else for a moment. Jay threw my window open, and we sat on the sill, our legs dangling outside, side by side. Cold pinched my cheeks, but it was good to feel something besides the stifling heat.

Once upon a time, a long time ago, a boy lived among the stars.

Born without wings but blessed with a soul, the child called Peter was blessed by the sky. Time passed, but to the boy, time meant very little. And so he soared from one star to the next for years and years, simply to taste their sugar and bathe in their light. He was the son of the North Star, grandson of the sun, friend to them all.

And yet he was alone, with no true home.

For many years, Peter thought the sky was enough. Until one day, he changed his mind.

"This story gives me the creeps. Why do you like these books so much?" Jay asked, scowling at Father's gift. "I can't even read most of it."

Mother, the baby, the boy in the stars—it all escaped my mind. "You . . . You can't read?"

He shrugged. "There's nothin' in those pages I want. What's the point of livin' if you have your head down all the time?"

"Stories make living easier sometimes. I can imagine myself as a princess, or a tiger, or a tamer of wild crocodiles. Books are special to me. They give me every life I could want." I studied him, this boy with the tousled hair and chipped smile. He was as familiar to me as my own reflection, and yet there was still so much I didn't know. "Would you like me to teach you?"

He snatched *The Boy and the Stars* out of my hands. "I mean, sure, that sounds great. Except the crocs—I'd steer clear of them personally. But there are better things than flyin' without wings."

"Like what?"

"Fightin' pirates, swimmin' with mermaids . . . sailin' a wide blue sea." He dangled the book outside.

My breath caught at the sight of the pages fluttering over the edge. "Give it back."

"Well, that's where we're different, I guess. I wouldn't want a stinkin' book when I can have a whole island."

I swung my arm out—reaching, grabbing, *mad*—but Jay was quicker than I could ever hope to be. "I said give it back."

"Nope." Jay's nails were caked in mud, dark crescents pinching the cream pages. His heels kicked against the house, and I worried the mud on his boots would leave a mark. "What about that baby your momma thinks she's havin'?" he asked. "You happy about it?"

"I don't want to talk about that." I pulled at my book, but Jay' grip was solid, his grin crooked. "Jay, stop this."

"What if you didn't need stories to see all the things you dream about? We could really *live* it, free as birds, no pieces of paper or waitin' on your daddy to give you a new present. Would you do it?"

"Jay—"

"You once told me you would come visit my island. What if we went together? What if we left and made our own rules?"

How could he ask such a thing when he knew I couldn't leave? Not now. Not yet. "It's ridiculous," I spat. "Those are promises you can't keep, and I don't like that. Now give back my book."

"No."

"Jay, I'm serious."

"So am I." He grinned, tugged a little harder.

Heat pricked my eyes. It wasn't fair; he was older, bigger, so much stronger than me. Yes, I had grown while Jay seemed frozen as he was. But that didn't mean I'd gotten any better at anything. "I'll push you off this ledge if you don't give it to me," I said. "This is not a game. Let go."

Eyes like stones at the edge of a river, smooth, a deeper blue today, settled on my face. "Try it. Come on, get mad. Get mad and take it, or give up and storm off. But *do* somethin', Lou. *Do somethin'!*"

So, I pulled. A great ripping noise sliced through the winter wind. The resistance in my arm was instantly gone, and all I had to show for my trouble were three pieces of paper crumpled in my fist. A jagged tear cut through sentences and illustrations like they didn't matter, like they were nothing more than marks on a page, just like my charcoal birds. Jay bit his lip and offered the book back, but I turned away. It was too late. It was ruined.

A knock sounded on the door. "Louisa, sweetheart, may I come in?"

"Yes!" I called, drying my eyes with my sleeve.

Father's footsteps were silent on the carpet. A pair of grey tweed trousers appeared beside me, and I shivered at the sudden heat against my side. "I'm surprised to see you sitting here."

"Why?"

"You hated the cold as a baby. Your mother and I would wrap you in blankets and rock you by the fire, but you always burrowed deeper into us as though craving our heat." Snowflakes settled like confetti on his beard, but he tipped his face to the sky and welcomed more. "What happened to your book?"

"Jay," I said. At the sound of his name, he hung his head, and I almost felt sorry for telling Father the truth. Almost. The pages, signs of Jay's betrayal, hung from my fingers like deflated sails. I wanted to tell Father what Jay had done, even if he didn't believe me. "He stole it from me, and when I tried to get it back . . ."

Much to my surprise, a smile curved Father's lip. The sweet tang of summer oranges wafted around us, pulling me to his side. "That was not very kind of him. But that does seem like something he would do. You mentioned him being a bit wild before. But he has not hurt you before. Were you two arguing?"

I didn't want to talk about Jay anymore. My happiness at being believed was torn and destroyed, just like the pages in my hand. "Please don't be mad at me. I truly love my present. I should have been more careful."

His answering laugh was a plush blanket during a winter frost. "It is just a book. They are meant to be read and used and loved. Nothing cherished remains perfect. But if you are truly upset, I can fix it for you."

"Really?"

"Of course."

I blinked back the tears. "I'd like that. Just please . . . do not tell Mother about this."

His eyes found mine. "Your mother loves you dearly, Louisa. I . . . I know you two do not always see eye to eye, but the worries of motherhood are many. It is a difficult thing to raise a head-strong daughter who does not share your views of the world. She is doing her best to prepare you for life after you leave us behind. You may not understand her actions, but know they are always bolstered by love."

"I understand." I did not.

"Your mother cares for you, but I regret she does not carry the same affection for Jay. I think you are correct to keep this little accident with your friend between us."

I nodded so fiercely that a lock of hair shook loose from my braid. Father didn't try to replace the strands. He never tried to fix me as Mother did. I looked up at him, at every line and silver hair, and loved him so deeply my heart ached.

"You just make sure Jay knows he is to be careful with your things," he said. "Can you do that for me?"

It didn't occur to me to wonder why Father didn't tell Jay himself. All that mattered in that moment was that Father believed me. Jay was our secret.

A gust of wintry air ripped the pages from my fingers and carried them into my room, where they could rest among my other childish things.

CHAPTER 7

Lou woke at dawn while the rest of the house still slept. For a moment, the events of the previous day—*my engagement, the water, the colours, Rosie, Rosie hates me now*—were no more than a vague memory painted in the steely grey of nightmares. She pressed her cheek into her pillow, wishing she could live beneath the sheets. Her wishes were rarely granted.

Mother's friends called it melancholy: a fleeting state of mind afflicting women who did not marry or have children.

Be wary of the melancholy of spinsterhood, Louisa. It is a terrible thing.

It was only a word; it was also a lie.

True melancholy, the kind that ensnared the mind and plunged it to the bottom of the sea, was a terrifying beast. To be able to speak of it, to warn of it, to *gossip* about those afflicted . . . Well, only happy people could speak openly of a monster with such large teeth.

Cabinets snapped shut in the kitchen below, and muffled voices hummed over the shuffle of feet. The day had begun, whether Lou was ready for it or not. She peeled herself out of bed, cringing when cold water squelched through her toes. The carpet was soaked, the walls still weeping their tears through gashes in the plaster. It hadn't been a dream.

Lou dressed quickly and hurried to the familiar door at the end of the hall. "Rosie?" she called, knocking. No answer. "Rosie? Mother?"

The house drowned in silence. With a sharp crack, the floor shifted, and a fresh wound bled ice water into the hall. The runner under Lou's feet grew cold. Black water pooled against the baseboards, darkening the carpet and filling the hall with the smell of salt and rot. She stumbled down the steps to outrun the building current.

Her home was a ship, and it was sinking.

"It isn't real, it isn't real," Lou chanted under her breath. Icy fingers reached down the stairs for her, washing away the colour for good.

"It isn't real."

Every morning, Rosie was the first one up, the first one dressed, the first to smile and propose a new adventure. Now there was only the deathly quiet of abandon. *Ga-gung, ga-gung, ga-gung* went the blood in her ears.

The current slurped through the dining room, swirling around chairs and gathering on the main floor. Lou bit back a cry; the water had never left the second floor. But now it attacked every corner, the tide rising, higher, *higher*.

"Louisa? Is that you?"

The voice wove through the chaos like gold filigree from beyond the open front door. That spring, Mother had carefully dotted their garden with oranges and pinks, lavender stalks and dancing bluebells. But when Lou stepped outside, Silverton Lane was carved from granite, its perfection frozen and cold. The drive tilted under her. The water slithered past her heels and down to where her mother and sister knelt in the grass.

Together.

"Ah, there you are. We thought we heard you waffling behind the door." Mother plucked lilacs with careful fingers, adding new stems to the wicker basket Rose balanced on her lap.

We? "What are you both doing out here?" Lou asked.

"I thought fresh flowers would make a lovely addition to the breakfast table. We are eating in the dining room to celebrate your engagement."

Her engagement.

Rose clutched the basket to her chest, eyes turned away.

Water rushed into the garden, drowning the tulips. Killing them. Killing all the lovely things. And only Lou seemed to notice.

"Yes, my engagement," she said. "But we have not dined there since Father's passing."

Mother's hand curled around a lavender stem, her knuckles white. "I am not required to justify myself to you, Louisa. I *am* still the lady of this house. Though, given your hesitation, am I to assume you will not be joining us?"

"Rosie and I will not have the time today." *Please, please look at me, Rosie.* "We missed our chance to visit the woods yesterday, so I thought we could—"

"Not interested." Rosie threw the words like poisoned darts. "I'm helping Mother with the garden."

"Yes, I see that. I know you are upset about what happened with the Rileys—"

"I'm not upset about the stupid *Rileys*, Louisa!"

"Rose!" Mother hissed. "Not *outside*."

"Oh, no one can hear us, Mother," Rose said, flippant.

Lou stepped forward, water now rippling above her ankles. "Then why will you not look at me?"

"Because you don't believe me—you never have! I can't stand to look at your lying face anymore."

"*Girls!*"

"That is not true, Rosie. I have never lied to you."

"Call me Rose, please." Finally, she met Lou's gaze with flat disinterest. "Only my best friends call me Rosie. And you aren't the sister I thought you were." She—*Rose*—turned back to her basket. "Mother has offered to take me to market after breakfast, so I'll be busy today."

"Market," Lou said. The water climbed and climbed, and she would certainly drown. "You never had any interest in going to market before."

Mother stood. "Do not pester your sister, Louisa. Market will be a nice change from stomping around that dirty patch of trees. You enjoyed it once too. Your sister will hopefully take more from the experience than you did." She smiled at her youngest daughter, a smile that Lou had not seen since Father had taken breakfast in their dining room. Before the illness. Before the end had begun. "Come inside, Rose. I believe we have collected enough for our table."

She moved like a whisper up the lawn, Rose in tow.

Sweat trickled down the small of Lou's back. Storm clouds lurched across the sky, pressed in low, stamping out the sun. "I should like to take a walk and clear my head," Lou heard herself say. "I must be tired. May I be excused?"

"A sound idea for once." Mother paused on the stoop and laid a cool hand on Lou's shoulder. Rose was already gone, wherever children went when they grew to hate the ones they loved—a bedroom perhaps. Or the woods. "Everything will be fine, Louisa," she said. "Samuel is a good man. He will take care of us."

Lou blinked back the tears. "Father told me it would be fine if I chose not to marry."

Anne Webber's eyes grew soft. "Your father was a good man. What he told you back when we were whole cannot still be true now that we are broken. Besides, it is always the mother's job to council her daughters on matters such as these."

"I do not want it." The words spoken aloud were a release. "We can wait another year. There are so many things I should like to do. Please."

"Louisa," she began, dropping her hand, "there may come a day that women can live out the dreams conjured by their own minds. But today is not that day. Women like you and I do not have the luxury of doing what we like. You must marry Samuel. Do you understand, dear?"

No.

The water reared up like a serpent, and Lou took a step back, back to the garden, back to where the waves could not swallow her. "Yes, Mother," she said. "I understand."

"Good. I am . . . so proud of you, Louisa. You are finally accepting your duty and acting your age. I admit, I had many doubts, but I should have listened when your father told me not to worry so much. Will you reconsider joining us for breakfast?"

"Not today."

With a stiff nod, Mother marched through the tide and into their home, her skirts untouched by the green sea. Lou tracked her movements through the bay window, watched as she dipped lilac stems into a porcelain vase until the table was awash in purple shadows. Their father's seat was a throne at the end of the table, his absence more intimidating than his presence had ever been.

But it was not empty.

A boy younger than Rose sat in her father's place. Bare feet blackened with earth swung under the chair, his frayed shirt a stark contrast to the pressed linens on which he propped his elbows. Bright eyes peered at her through rimless glasses. He smiled. Waved. And vanished.

Lou cried out, but no one turned. The water was too loud; a rising wave forced her back down the drive, pushed her around the house. Her last glimpse of Anne Webber was of her face sparkling under the glass chandelier, polished silverware in their hands. She was was oblivious to the water beating at the window.

To the storm gathering.

To Lou.

✳

"What is wrong, little bird?"

"Rosie. She is different somehow. Ever since the Rileys came to tea, she has been—"

"Different."

"Yes."

Lou stood alone at the back garden gate, the Briarwood sprawling before her. The trees, too, had gone black. The one reliable place of colour left in her world had succumbed to the shadows, turning its wild beauty into a monster with too many teeth.

"And why is different *such a terrible thing, little bird?"*

"I am her sister. I simply know."

"But your sister is growing."

"She is growing too fast. I . . . I think it is my fault. I did not believe her stories. I broke her trust. That cannot be easily mended."

The scent of oranges and cloves mingled with the salt from the water at her back. It was faint, but it was there. Like the lingering memory of her father, so tangible in her mind.

"She told me to find Jay," Lou said. *"But I do not know what that means. He does not exist."*

"Existence is a funny thing, little bird. He existed to you. In many ways, that is more important than anything you can feel under your palms."

She sighed. *"I do not trust my mind to tell me the truth anymore. Everything is so hard."*

"That is the problem with growing up, isn't it?" Father said.

"Growing chases away the innocence of childhood and replaces it with duty. And everyone mistrusts duty."

Movement in the trees shook the shadows in the woods. A slender arm pushed past a tall fern, and a dirty foot sprayed loose earth onto the grass like rain. Glasses. A golden head of hair.

The boy.

"You speak of duty as though it is a terrible thing," Lou said. Should she follow the boy into the woods? He would soon disappear as quickly as he had from her home. *"But you were dutiful to me, and Mother, and Rosie. Duty is what holds a family together. Mother says so."*

"Duty is a pirate, little bird. It will break down your door disguised as love or a rare gift. But if you allow it to enter, it will plunder your home and take everything you hold dear. Duty is the death of pure love, Louisa. Never forget that."

The gate was unlocked. She walked through the swinging iron door toward the trees.

"Where are you going, little bird?"

"Away."

Father was her safety. When he'd been ripped from her arms, she'd turned to Rose for comfort. But now that bond was broken too. Lou had never been any good at mending broken things.

Duty was, indeed, a pirate.

Foamy green water slid down the hill toward the trees, drowning the wildflowers, turning them to salt. The flood charged the Briarwood, pushing Lou into its twisted arms. Mother and Rose were safe; she was not.

A stone flew from the trees, narrowly missing her head.

"What—?" Lou started to protest, but the onslaught continued. Another rock, then another. A pair of glasses winked through the darkness, then disappeared.

The boy was in the trees, and the current was too strong.

Perhaps Timber *wasn't* dead. He had come back to see Rose after all.

You're going mad. Timber isn't real.

"Wait!" Lou called out, but the water was a hurricane, scooping her up and washing her into the trees. She reached for anything that could pull her from the current. Nothing reached back. "Help, please!"

Thorns scratched at her legs, shredding her tights to ribbons. Cold soaked into her bones and made her heavy. Made her sink. Trees rushed past, jumping out of her path as she moved deeper into the woods. She gulped for air and found only salt. Faces leered at her from the shadows, but none were the round-faced boy with the tattered clothes.

"The lake, little bird; water always seeks out its own kind. Mermaids and children wait for you there. They will help. The lake is a safe place—one where Mother asks you questions again and we are happy. Together."

Lou screamed, knowing no one would hear it.

The branches thinned, and the sky opened above her. She'd loved the lake as a child and was almost glad to return to it now. The mirror of black water welcomed the green waves with an open, friendly face. And there, at the opposite bank, was the boy.

He turned to the sky, offering her another benign smile. He had brought the water. She had answered his call.

The boy knew what had gone wrong. He had the answers.

The wave curled, pushing her up, up, up; Louisa Webber fell deep into the blissful emptiness of the lake.

CHAPTER 8

LOU

AGE NINE – THREE MONTHS TO GO

Jay sat by my window, knees tucked under his chin. The sky behind him was a pale blue, untainted by clouds, and full of the heady sweetness of spring. It was a perfect day for collecting swords from the woods, for lying in the grass by the lake and counting the birds as they passed. Instead, I was trapped behind my desk, a pen in my hands, far, far from the Briarwood. It was no wonder birds preferred the sky to cages.

"Whatcha doin'?" Jay asked.

"School work." I glared at the pile of arithmetic Governess Huntington had set for me. "None of the other girls need to solve fractions, but I can't leave until this is all done. I'm sorry, I know this isn't very exciting."

"What's fractions?"

I sighed, ignoring the pulse behind my eyes. "Torture."

"Why're you doin' it, then?"

"Because I have no choice. Don't you ever do anything you don't want to?"

Jay shrugged. "Not really."

"Well, that's lovely for you." I touched my pen to the parchment, and the tip bled black. The pool spread, and I did nothing to stop it; problem number twenty-eight deserved to be obliterated anyway. "You don't need to stay here and watch me work, you know."

I hated the thought of Jay leaving me behind, to imagine him leaping over creaks and fallen saplings without me. But that was the price of growing up, Mother said. Creaks and fallen saplings were for children, and I was to become something more soon. A sister. A *big* sister.

"Nah, I'll wait." Jay uncoiled himself and leapt to his feet in one smooth motion. "So, you don't get to fight or use swords with fractions, then?"

"What?"

"Louisa?" Father cracked open my door and offered me a shy smile. "May I come in?"

"Yes, of course!"

I sometimes forgot how tall Father was. His shadow sent a slice of darkness cutting across my floor, the darkness creeping over my carpet toward my bed. A lingering cough ground like shoes over fine pebbles deep in his chest, his sunken eyes absent of their lustre. Despite that, his presence still battled with the sun for the brightest thing in my world.

"You look rather busy, little bird. I can come back later."

I smiled; it was impossible not to. "I was going to take a break anyhow."

Father squinted at the parchment over my shoulder. "How is the arithmetic coming along?"

"Oh, fine. Just fine."

"Really?"

I dropped my pen and slumped in my seat. Jay wrinkled his nose as Father settled onto my bed. I threw him a silencing look, my patience thin. Jay didn't do well with growns, but Father wasn't a grown like any other.

"If I'm being honest, arithmetic is awful," I said. "I do not mind the reading or languages, but these symbols are giving me a headache. Why do I need to learn this if none of the other girls have tutors?"

"That is a good question." *It is?* "I've always thought arithmetic was a bit useless myself. I was dreadful at it. Couldn't make sense of any equation put before me."

Jay grew still, his features painted with mistrust.

"You certainly hide it well," I said, treading carefully. "I can't imagine you bad at anything."

"But I was. I used to spend hours staring at the pages, but it never made a lick of difference. It was my poorest subject. Thankfully, the print business requires very little talent in solving equations."

Relief washed over me; this was my chance to escape. Father *understood*. "Then I should not need to learn any of it either. It is a waste of a beautiful day."

"I did not say that. I still learned all that was required of me, including the subjects I loathed."

"But *why*?" I turned in my chair to face him head-on. "I want to be an ornithologist, not a professor or a surgeon. And you have done well without it. I can too."

Jay snorted. "You wanna be a what?"

"An ornithologist?" Father's smile grew broad. "I am not sure I have ever heard of such a profession."

My palms were instantly damp. "They . . . They study birds," I explained. "Their flight patterns, markings, migration habits. That sort of thing."

"An ornithologist," he repeated, toying with the bow around Benji Bear's neck. "That sounds rather interesting."

"Why do you have to be somethin' I can't even say?" Jay grumbled.

"Louisa, do you know why the other girls do not learn any of this?" Father asked. When I shook my head, he leaned in close, as though to share a precious secret. "Young ladies are not expected to do much more than marry and have children. And while your mother and I wish that happiness on you if it is what you desire, we insist that you have every option available to you. Studying allows for this possibility."

"Perhaps *you* do. I cannot see Mother approving of anything but marriage and children."

"You are an exceptional young woman, little bird. I'll admit, your mother and I sometimes do not agree on all things. And while I love her and the life we chose to live . . . Well, I must admit your future is not as fixed to me as it is to her." Father patted my hand, and my shoulders relaxed. "You, my lovely daughter, are an intelligent young lady. The other girls can make tea, but you shall study your birds."

My cheeks grew hot. "Perhaps we could alter my syllabus, only a little?"

"Does the study of birds not require arithmetic at all?"

"No."

"Are you certain?" Father asked. He knew the answer to his own question, but it seemed he wished to hear it anyhow. Such was the power of a grown, even one like Father; they were allowed to be indulgent.

"I've never given it much thought," I admitted. "But I do not see how division and equations would be relevant to me."

"Well, I can't be certain, of course," he said, laughing. A cough stole his voice, but he cleared his throat, banishing it at once. "I would assume the study of any animal would require knowledge of their habits. Feeding, flight patterns, vocal cues. You admitted it yourself. There must be some calculation involved in determining those things."

"I . . . Perhaps."

"Well, after you've done your arithmetic, you might consider investigating the matter further. But if ornithology does not work out, birdwatching is quite a lovely hobby."

Hobby. Girls could learn the same subjects as boys—with their parents' permission, of course. But her ultimate place was in the home, where she could observe the sky through a glass window. She would never be taken as seriously as a boy.

"I do not want to be a bored wife with a hobby, Father. I want to work in the city, like you. I want to live on my own, not move from this bedroom to my husband's as Mother did."

Father winced, and the sun disappeared behind a thick fog.

"I am sorry, I did not mean—"

"I know," Father said, oblivious to Jay pulling his dagger free of its sheath with a flash of steel. "You have always been somewhat of a mystery to me, Louisa. Certainly, you would make a wonderful wife and mother should that be your wish. But if it isn't, the birds will be lucky to have you."

"Remind me to puke when we get outside." Jay mimed being sick, tossing the dagger onto my desk during a particularly violent heave.

But Father was still in my room, eyes wandering to the stories I'd lined up on a nearby shelf. "Would you have any books about birds you would recommend to a man with limited knowledge?" he asked. "I would be interested to see what the allure is."

"Of course. But . . ." My heart turned to ice before I could reach the well-worn book on my bedside table—a childhood favourite. "I would start with this one. It has sketches of common birds I've found in the Briarwood. It makes it much easier to learn if you see the real thing. This one," I said, plucking another from the shelf and cradling it gently, "is all about rare and exotic birds. Their colours . . . I've never seen anything like it."

"You seem happy."

I looked up, stunned. "I am."

"Are you certain?"

How difficult it must have been for a great man with a straight back and polished shoes to lower himself into a sea of floral wallpaper and lace dresses, to regard my happiness as worthy of his time. I owed him my truth, all of it and more.

No, I thought at once. *I don't think I'm happy at all.* "Of course."

But the truth, while the noble choice, would inflict pain. I loved Father far too much to be that honest.

"That is good, little bird. Especially with the important changes coming in a few short months."

I frowned as Jay marched up to the window, his shoulders rigid. "Changes?"

"The baby," Father said. "Perhaps you could teach your new brother about birds too."

I turned back to my desk, concealing my own daggers, weapons I kept locked away in my mind, the way a lady was expected to. Feelings and words could inflict pain. Father didn't deserve any more of it. "Oh. Yes," I said finally. "I could do that. One day."

Reduce 8/64 to its lowest term and indicate whether it is proper or improper. Labels and problems, numbers that were supposed to mean something more than the loops and lines on a page. Everything was designed to force me to choose one thing over another, and that choice would define me forever. Was I proper or improper?

I must always choose. That was the rule. I hated the rules.

The forbidden room at the end of the hall stood wide open for the first time in years. Mother, with her growing belly and bright cheeks, visited it daily—a devout worshipper on a pilgrimage to the holiest of places. In the privacy of my own thoughts, I was happy her wish for another child had never been granted. It felt like justice. It felt like freedom; if Mother grieved the emptiness of her arms, that grief would make her forget her disappointment with me.

Being forgettable was a bitter sort of freedom.

"Look at me, Louisa."

I did, and what I saw in Father's eyes threatened to turn my weapons to dust.

"I understand you might not yet have any love for this baby. But your new sibling will be an everlasting friend—someone to stand beside you for the rest of your life. The blood bond is strong and invaluable."

"I already have a friend like that." A warm hand found my shoulder, and I leaned into Jay's familiar warmth. "I do not need another."

"You speak of Jay," Father said. "Is he here right now?"

I nodded, but Father did not look impatient or upset or even frightened of my answer. He simply plucked Benji Bear from his place on my bed and set him on his lap like a child.

"Well, I am glad Jay keeps you company. But hearts can be big enough to carry more than one person in them."

"It will cry," I said. "The baby, I mean."

"Yes."

"Often."

"Very likely, at first."

I glanced out the window; a bird soared across the sun like an arrow released from an archer's bow. "You won't have time for me anymore," I said. "You'll be too busy to tell me stories. You'll love it more than you love me." Silly words for a silly girl.

"That will never happen," Father whispered. "No baby will change my or your mother's love for you. We are a family. I cannot wait to see you become a big sister and, much later, an ornithologist."

I forgot to be angry. Like a drowning girl kicking toward the shore, I fell into his open arms and buried my face in his shirt. "Do you promise you will not leave me when it comes?"

"I swear it. And Benji here will hold me to that promise."

The scent of cloves and oranges overwhelmed my sadness. So close to him, I could almost ignore how the bones of his spine jutted against the fabric of his shirt and into my palms. "I love you, Father."

He smacked a kiss into my hair and patted my back, leaving a trail of warmth down my spine. "Just promise me something in turn. Promise me you will give the baby a chance. And the arithmetic too. Remember, it cannot hurt you to be the smartest girl in the room."

I put my weapons away; they weren't needed here. "I will try."

"Good." Father released and plucked one of the tree branches Jay and I had salvaged from the Briarwood out of the small pile beside my bed. "Swords?" he guessed with an impish grin. "I hope you've been practicing. It is a noble sport."

"How did you know?"

"An educated guess. I was quite the swordsman as a boy, you know." He brandished the stick, curling his free hand behind his back. With a growl, he leapt off the bed into a neat lunge. "Well, come on, little lady. I am the fearsome pirate Blackbeard, and you have my sunken treasure chest."

I could hardly contain my glee as I stood. "What about the arithmetic?"

"Sometimes a break can be healthy. And you cannot ignore a pirate inviting you to a duel."

The clash of swords was my true language. I slipped into a pirate's drawl like putting on my favourite boots. "Ye won' get me treasure, Blackbeard. I got an army o' crocs waitin' to tear ye te pieces!"

I leapt onto the bed and retrieved a stick hidden underneath my pillow. Louisa Webber fell from my shoulders like a snake shedding its skin, leaving room for the fierce warrior and thief I truly was.

I was capable. I was *fierce.*

Mother was in the kitchen below, humming a happy tune. If she could hear our snarls, she did not object.

And so we duelled.

Sometime between the first clash of swords and the last, Jay disappeared. But with Father on my side and a sword in my hand, his departure hadn't been loud enough to notice.

CHAPTER 9

L ou woke with a mouth full of sand.

Face down. Clothes baked onto her back by the heat of the sun. Palms burning with fresh cuts. She pushed herself to her knees, body aching, head spinning, but alive.

Alive and . . . confused.

"Oh. Oh *no*."

Gulls circled overhead, cawing at the blistering sun. The ground wasn't the packed earth of the Briarwood, but a river of sand glittering white under a deep blue sky. A slatted walkway snaked down the coast, littered with wooden carts and swarmed by a thumping, rowdy crowd. Men huddled over black-spattered tables, slopping foamy liquid down their bloated fronts. Women wore elaborate gowns slashed from waist to ankle and revealing smooth planes of sweat-slicked skin, their painted lips pulled into sly smiles as they found laps to settle on. At her back was a sweeping cliff shaped like a horseshoe, its stone edge climbing to the sky and topped with a canopy of trees. Sunlight danced off the rocks and onto the water, setting the beach aflame with tones of rose and periwinkle.

Definitely not the Briarwood.

Lou ghosted over to the boardwalk, drank in the surf with wide eyes. The wood steamed underfoot, but the pain was a welcome reminder she was still in her body, alive and well. Merchants beckoned her toward their carts, waving fish and beaded bracelets as she passed. The ocean was clear cerulean, the dresses and wagons and jewelry a vibrant prism of candied hues. It was a feast of colour Lou had never seen. And if she had, she had long since forgotten. Forgetting might have been a blessing in the past, but as she breathed in the heavy scent of sugared fruits and noted the displays of items smeared in shell pink, bright orange, and pale lavender, forgetting was a terrible crime.

"Fresh codfish, miss! Get yerself some fresh codfish!"

"N-no, thank you." Lou turned on unsteady legs, her head light. When was the last time she'd eaten? Elbows jostled her down the walk, overwhelming in how real they all seemed. Roast meat, cloves, a hint of smoking leaves. The men were everywhere, their eyes raking over her, undressing her, passing her from one calloused fist to the next. Still, the colours were beautiful.

"Pearls for the lady!" another man called. "Pretty as your smooth face, plucked straight from the suckers of the sea beast!"

She had enough sense to shake her head and duck into the crowd before he could say any more. Bearded faces sizzled red from too much sun bared their yellowed teeth as she passed. The sea of bodies pressed in, shifted, brushed rough skin against hers. Vendors called out again and again, but their voices were a distant hum.

There was so much water. Had she ever known Silverton Lane to be close to an ocean? Lou planted her feet on the walk so the sky would stop spinning. There had been water, yes, but that water had come from behind her bedroom walls, a treacherous body of murky green waves, not the infinite blue before her. It had overcome her home, chased her down the stairs, down the hill, into the woods . . . *The woods.*

Her final moments before waking on the beach clawed through the fog and took root behind her eyes. She'd left Mother and Rose at home before the current had swept her into the woods. The trees, the shadows, the lake—the world was a coin flipped to the wrong side, everything familiar but not quite right, not quite the *same*. The last memory was only a fragment, but it was strong nonetheless.

"The boy," Lou said. Thick clouds of white cotton billowed over the water, softening the harsh blues and greens of the sea. But there was no mistaking that she was far from Silverton Lane. The boy, however, had faced the waves without fear. He had seen her, sat in her home, and smiled. He had been there when the wave had buckled, tossing her into the lake. He had watched her fall as though it were the most natural thing to do. "I need to find that boy."

"Did ye say somethin', miss?" An elderly man stacking straw dolls in a canopied wagon raised his wiry brows, pulling her from thoughts of the child and the lake. Varicose veins laced up his ankles, his knobby fingers clutching a doll to his chest.

"I am looking for a young boy." Lou moved under the canopy for shelter from the heat. "Perhaps you've seen him? He is no more than six or seven years old, fair, wearing glasses. He . . . He also may not be wearing any shoes."

He shrugged. "I seen many boys like that here. But none today."

"Right. It does not appear as though the sea has caused any damage."

The man bowed his head. "The sea ain't the monster we worry about, miss."

"Right," she repeated. What else was there to say? Dolls lined the three walls of the cart, straw children dressed in hats and skirts.

"I apologize, but could you point me to the quickest way back to Silverton Lane?"

Eyes like onyx glittered back at her, wrinkles spidering out to his temples. "I ne'er heard o' nothin' with that name on this island. But if it be silver yer wantin', the ship'll be dockin' soon."

Island? The beach. The surf. The endless blue. She expected the sea to rear up over the sand in vengeance, the colours to bleed until everything was dull once more. After all, that is what happened every time her chest got so tight, her legs so unsteady. But the world remained as it was, everything in its proper place. Somehow, that was worse.

"And how does one leave this . . . this *island*?" Silence. "Sir?"

The man crouched behind a weathered chest and emerged clutching a doll in a pink burlap dress. Her woolen hair was the colour of pomegranates, her eyes twin buttons fixed with red thread. With a sad smile, he offered it to her. "There be no way off the island, miss. Not unless ye can touch the stars. Here, take a doll. Ye look like ye need some cheerin' up."

Lou stumbled back, the doll still dangling from his fist. To take it was to accept the man's words as fact, and they couldn't possibly be true. He was confused; they both were. But then, where were the carriages and the neat homes with tidy lawns?

The crowd converged around her, pressing in on all sides. Like the silence between heartbeats, the day went quiet. Then, with a deafening roar, men's excited voices yelled up and down the beach. The last thing she saw before the mob pulled her down to the coast was a ragged doll staring blindly at her with shiny black eyes.

She didn't have the strength to fight the current of bodies. Men jostled her forward, the screams grew louder. While Lou saw only red flesh and open skies, she could make out words if she strained hard enough.

"She's comin' ashore!" The crowd cheered. Fists thumped the

air. "Hurry up and get te the docks before the younger lads get all the best spots!"

"I hears he's got the boy in the brig."

"That don't make no sense, man. Why wouldn't he just kill 'im?"

Tables of cards, half-drunk pints, and conversations were abandoned for the sandy beach by the water's edge. At the eastern side of the coast, a wooden dock groaned under the sudden weight of so many people, the platform lapping at the sea like a scorched tongue. The clouds rippled above the ocean, shifting as though expecting to release a storm onto the world. But the day was bright and warm—not a raindrop in sight.

The crowd spread across the sand, releasing Lou from its grip. In a daze, she followed the stragglers to the dock, her legs leaden. The closer she moved toward the surf, the more solid the clouds became. Air crackled across her cheeks, making the hair on her arms stand on end. The day grew quiet, thick with anticipation of whatever lurked over the horizon. Lou squinted into the distance, where the sea began to roil and froth until the navy depths became a cyclone. Hair whipped around her face, but even through the veil of her frazzled locks, there was no mistaking the sails rising from the waves.

Voices roared into the sky.

"The boy's cursed, Gibby. I'm not sure he can die even if he wanted to."

"Ah, I wouldn't worry. The cap'n don' got 'im. He been tryin' fer longer'n the moons hang over me house, and the boy keeps gettin' away."

Two men idled beside her, each holding a pint, each burnt by the sun and missing a few teeth. "What house?" the older one asked. "Ye live in the crack between two rocks." He laughed, the sound bubbling with phlegm. "I tell ye, I never seen Blackbeard an' his crew so chuffed. If yer not careful, that boy disappearin' might crumble that little cave ye live in. Least, that's what the stories say."

His companion rounded on him, jabbing a dirty finger at his nose. "Watch it. Ye don' see me laughin' 'bout the barrel *you* live in."

This is a dream, she thought. A dream brought on by a lifetime of drowning in nightmares. Even from a distance, she could count the sailors flitting from boom to boom as the ship drifted to shore. The old galleon was intricately carved, with four thick masts and a beaked prow. Eyeholes, empty and watchful, puckered the side of the ship. Her sails rivalled the clouds, except for a black flag attached to her bow.

Closer and closer she sailed until her belly scratched against the rocks in the shallow surf. The waiting spectators shouted, begged for blood, the blood of—"Peter! Peter! Peter!"—a boy she didn't know. With every shout, the men and women transformed, devolved to their most basic urges: greed and hunger, lust and violence, a need for blood that knew no bounds. Lou blinked, and they were nothing more than men and women once more, chanting to the sky. A rope ladder swung down to the dock, then, and sailors took to unloading their cargo onto the sand.

"Kill him!"

"Bleed him!"

"Peter!"

The crowd dove for the chests, pummeling one another into writhing knots of furious limbs. Knives flashed under the sun —*too hot, too hot*—and the stench of sweat bit at Lou's nose. Her stomach lurched. She didn't belong there. She had a family, a *duty*. And she was wasting time. Why, then, couldn't she move? The violence tugged at her heart, called her forward, and whatever was in the chests now floating against the wooden dock was too important to leave behind.

Buried gold. Hidden secrets. She wanted it all.

"Treasure, lads! Get the *treasure*!"

"Aye!"

A blue haze flashed across her vision, and the strange lust in Lou's throat subsided. Sand spattered her face and caked her tongue. She screamed in pain, spitting grains onto the ground as she searched for the person responsible. At first, there was nothing but the roar of men and the hiss of the sea. But then a child's laughter pierced through it all. A blond head wove through the sea of elbows and took off for the cliffs. Bare feet blackened by dirt beat a path through the sand. The child peeked over his shoulder, a pair of glasses glittering under the sun, and smiled.

"Boy!" Lou called, stumbling after him, the wind off the sea beating at her back. "*Stop!*"

"Cap'n on deck!"

"Cap'n on deck!"

"Aye, aye!"

But the captain of the ship was of no concern to her. The boy was getting away. And as the only familiar face in a sea of strangers, he carried with him the explanation of how she'd gotten there. Of where *there* was. Lou chased him up the beach, the docks becoming nothing more than background noise as the cliffs grew taller. Sweat, sticky and cold, trickled into her eyes, but she blinked the sting away.

"Please! I only wish to speak with you," Lou called. But it was no use. The boy reached the foot of the cliff and slid into a cleft in the rock, his smile taunting her.

"Fine. *Fine.*" A crude set of granite steps climbed the narrow passage, up, and up, and up. She followed the trail, a sandy set of footprints her only proof he had been there at all. When she reached the top, the darkness of a forest overtook the sun, and she was left with nothing more than the whisper of trees.

"Are you there?" she asked. "I will not hurt you."

Only the birds chirped back. It was dark, the smell of the sea below replaced by the smell of earth, fresh grass, and . . . honey. Or was it coconut? The trees were too wide, the bark striped with ridges and grooves glittering green under the sun. Leaves like large fans wove together to form a blanket veined in emerald and silver, each as wide as her arm and twice as long. Jade, shamrock, and sage mingled with bright lime and bronze. Yes, she missed the vividness of a world in full colour. But that colour was further proof that she was too far from home. From Rose.

Rose.

The forest, for all its vivid colour, was empty of the one thing she needed: a boy with *answers*. She crouched low, pushing aside ferns, raking the wild grass for any sign of him. Finally, a flash of vivid green, unlike the rest of the forest, the low light in the distance. Lou's heart leapt into her chest as she ran over to it; there, in the trampled blades and thick mud, was a footprint. A thousand bright emeralds clustered together in the unmistakable shape of a tiny foot. The boy's path left a trail of green light through the trees unlike anything she had ever seen. One, then another, stamping a clear trail in the unfamiliar wood.

Relief pooled in her chest, making a warm place for pity to grow. Pity for herself, pity for the boy who was likely in need of her help but too afraid to ask. Children turned fear into games while their elders worried. As much as she wanted to resent him for running from her when she called for his help, Lou couldn't blame him for being young.

Sweat spilled from her brow and down her back. The colours were wrong, the smell too heavy, the sounds too crisp. Still, Lou counted the glowing footprints as though tracing a memory of each one in her mind might save her from losing herself entirely.

This isn't the Briarwood.

This must be the Briarwood.

The boy's tracks came to an end, and there was nothing but stifling, overwhelming green and an absence of light. Lou stopped, panic climbing her throat. Unexpected tears bloomed, but she did nothing to wipe them away. She was tired of pretending the pain didn't exist.

"Well, come on, then!" Lou hollered into the shadows, panic overcoming her. "There is no reason for this sort of game, and I am uninterested in playing any longer. Come out at once!"

He didn't.

Lou screamed into the trees. Over and over, her pleas clawed at her throat, making her light-headed, making her eyes sting. She hadn't cried or yelled to her heart's content in years. Such a luxury showing emotion was. Tears ran into her mouth, and she swallowed salt.

"Don't cry. It makes me sad."

A shape peeled itself away from the shadows.

"You," Lou said over the knot in her throat. "Who are you? How did we get here?"

He shrugged, chewed his bottom lip. Navy trousers cinched his waist, held in place by a braided rope. The oversized shirt on his back was frayed, patched in places and worn straight through in others. Yet when he smiled, it was with the ease and satisfaction she had only ever seen on the richest men. She'd never felt that depth of contentment herself. Perhaps the child knew something she didn't. Perhaps he was simply *that* happy. Either way, his silence was infuriating.

"I do not like being toyed with," Lou said, taking a step closer. "Where is your mother?" Silence. "Or, better yet, I wish to speak with your father."

"Why's that better?"

Lou fumbled for her words. *What a strange question.* "Fathers are harder on their sons than mothers. They hold more authority."

"That don't sound right," he said. "Mommas are way scarier

than daddies. Hey, come catch me!" Quick as a whip, he hopped back into the trees and out of sight.

Lou stood, stunned. A child held her fate in his dirt-caked palms, but to him, she was nothing more than a game of hide-and-seek. Anger, frustration, fear—the dam in Lou's heart burst open, pouring every scrap of emotion she'd kept in check since waking on the sparkling beach into her veins like poison.

Fuelled by venom, she ran. The trees were wild, with vines strung from branch to branch, nets meant to trap or scratch her with their crimson thorns. Lou let them try; they shaved her flesh and took her blood, but she wouldn't slow down.

Three things happened in quick succession.

First, the boy veered off the path and into the waiting arms of a weeping willow.

Second, Lou followed his tracks, his giggles, the golden head past the downy branches.

Finally, she fell.

THE DARKNESS WAS BLINDING.

Lou scrambled to her knees after a long, long fall, wiping the silt and sweat from her eyes with dirty sleeves. Walls of packed earth circled a small underground den, tree roots wriggling across the low ceiling like pale worms. Though her vision was blurry, she could make out a few squat tables surrounded by mismatched stools. Golden light wavered as feet shuffled and chairs scraped against the ground. She wanted to stand, but her legs were weak, and there were hands pressing her back down.

"Do not touch me!" she ordered, her voice cracking.

"Keep those weapons up!" At the firm command, metal winked in her direction. "C'mon, Benji, that means you too."

"Sorry, sorry!"

"Where's Sammy?"

"Do I look like I keep tabs on the kid?"

Lou's eyes watered from the sting of the torchlight. As the room came into focus, so too did the sharp arrowheads nocked in bows and swords trained on her heart. "What—put those things down!"

"No thanks. And I'd prefer it if you didn't give my people orders." He stood closest to her, a dagger in his hand. Delicately muscled but still round with youth, he straddled the line between innocence and responsibility. But the way he angled himself between her and the four others standing behind him, the way *his people* reacted to his commands, made him something utterly unique.

"You are the leader, I take it," Lou said. "What is your name?"

"How about I ask my questions first, lady. Who sent you here? The Reds? Or was it the mermaids? We ain't got their stinkin' silver coins, so they can lay off the attacks."

"I asked for a name."

"So?"

Lou tried to stand, but the weapons pressed closer, forcing her to the ground. "So, it is customary for children to respect their elders."

He wrinkled his nose. "I'm thirteen, not three. But I'll give you one thing: you're *old*. A pirate, then? But you're a girl."

That *voice*. He was a stranger to her; she knew very few boys, and so she remembered each one she'd ever met with vivid clarity. He was not a resident of Silverton Lane, nor a rich man's son who had been offered to her as a suitor. But she *knew* him—not by face or the value of his family name, not by the worth of his accounts or the purity of his blood. Instead, she knew him the way she remembered dreams in the early mornings. She knew him in her heart, her soul, her very blood. And in many ways, that sort of knowing was deeper than flesh or memory.

Lou cleared her throat. "I . . . I was lured here by a young boy. Likely, it is someone you know, given you play in the same part of these woods. There was a flood at my home, and I ran into the woods. Would you all kindly put your weapons down?"

He laughed, and the others startled. The sound was unburdened, conjuring visions of stormy seas and bronze hair twisting in the wind. "Hey, she's funny!" he said. "Hear that, gang? Pirate girl's givin' orders now, and she's already accusin' us of trickin' her."

"Yeah, we heard it," said another boy, as dark as his leader was fair. His voice like silk, a streak of black grease paint slashing his face in two, he squinted down at Lou with naked mistrust. "Boss, I swear, I ain't tricked no one. She's a liar. My money's on her bein' a pirate, not someone who's supposed to be here. We should get rid of her."

"You ain't got no money," said a girl beside him, her face, too, splattered in black paint. "But it wouldn't be the first time someone's just showed up without us knowin'. Maybe we should cut her open and see if she bleeds seawater, just like the other pirates do." She had the same dark features, a crown of delicate braids piled on her head. Siblings, perhaps. But where were their parents? "Kiran, you sure you didn't set no pirate trap?"

"I'da told you, Didi. Lay off."

Didi pulled her elbow back, and an arrow swivelled in his direction. "Don't tell me what to do, or I'll put an arrow in you."

"Hey, I'm not the pirate here," Kiran said. "Turn that thing away from me."

"I will when I'm good and ready."

Siblings. Definitely siblings.

"Enough!" The leader turned to the squabbling pair, a storm in his sapphire eyes. "You two keep it quiet, will you?"

Didi and Kiran lapsed into silence while two other boys shifted uneasily behind them. One was tall, his russet head grazing the ceiling, square frame hunched like a turtle retreating into its shell. The boy beside him was shorter and rather round. While the others carried mistrust in their eyes, he was . . . soft. A tentative smile, a flimsy grip on the dagger at his hip. Of all the children before her gripping their weapons, his were the only hands that shook.

"Please," Lou said, bolstered by his hesitation, "I am only trying to get home. There was a boy—smaller, blond with glasses. I mean you no harm. If you know where I might find him—"

"We don't help pirates," Didi said. "And we'd know if one of ours brought a grown over, so you can stop lyin'."

Containing her emotions was a muscle Lou had strengthened over years of careful practice. But muscles grew tired. She stood, ignoring the blades and the hisses of surprise. "I will not stand to be called a pirate, or a grown, or whatever other insults a group of dirty, unruly children conjure!"

The boy with the kind eyes dropped his blade with a resounding thud. He bent to pick up his weapon, cheeks ablaze, while the others rolled their eyes. "Sorry, sorry! It's just . . . Well, we haven't had visitors in a long time, miss. And none so old as you. Excuse us if we think you're a pirate. We mean no offence."

"At least one of you seems to have remembered his manners." Lou brushed her hands against her hips, but the dirt did not come off. "I am not a pirate. I *am* quite lost, however. Now, if you'll call one of your parents to point me in the direction of Silverton Lane, I will gladly leave you to your little games!"

The room grew silent. A shadow flickered in their eyes as they turned toward their leader. It was the spark of recognition. Of fear.

And it set Lou's teeth on edge.

"Lou?" The boy—the one in charge of her fate—lowered his weapon, brows pulled tight over cerulean eyes. "It can't be. Is it?"

Those eyes. Something about a bird. A fleeting memory,

followed by another, and then it was gone. Yet his acknowledgement of her was thick and soft and more tangible than the ground under her feet. He carried her heart in the rigidity of his stance and the tiny chip in his tooth. In the quiver of his chin as his gaze bore into hers and found something there she hadn't known existed. That sort of knowing ran deep and left a stain. Like blood, but thicker and just as permanent.

Lou swayed on her feet. "Are you . . . Timber? No, not Timber at all. I've never met him. You had a boat. A red boat."

His jaw slackened. "Everybody, weapons down!"

Everyone but Didi obeyed. She held her bow tight, lips pulled back in disgust. "You gotta be kiddin', boss!"

"You heard me, Didi. Put it down."

"But—"

"Now!"

Lou's muscles relaxed the moment the girl complied with the order. "Thank you," she said. "May I stand up now?"

He stood before her, searched her face. "Hold on. How the stars didja get here?"

"Did you not hear me? I thanked you."

"I heard you."

"Then the proper answer is *you're welcome*."

He snorted, replacing his dagger in its holster. "You're taller. And your hair's longer." He bent down to pinch a fold of her dress and pulled it toward him, nodding in approval. "But I'm glad to see your mouth stayed sharp even if you're still wearing these silly dresses. Looks like you been playin' in the dirt. I didn't think you'd be allowed to go in your woods and get so dirty, but I'm glad I was wrong. What happened to you? Why're you even here?"

Lou pulled her skirt out of his grip. "My state of dress is not your concern," she said. "How dare you speak to me like . . . like . . ."

"Like I know you?" he finished. "That's 'cause I *do*. Come on, don'tcha remember me?"

"No."

"Not even a little?"

Rainbow Rock still needs its treasure.

Aye, lassie. Yer wish is me command.

Images like fragmented dreams drifted behind her eyes, but if she looked too hard at any of them, they burst into a flash of diamond light. "I do not have any specific memory of you, yet I feel as though I know you as well as I know my own reflection. Is this what it feels like to go mad?"

"Who knows? I don't think you ever believed I was sane, but maybe bein' crazy's not a bad thing. That's somethin' people in your world think about, but not us." He stepped closer, and Lou scooted back to the far wall. "Relax. I'm not gonna hurt you. I only wanted to get a closer look. You're so . . . *old*."

The words pulled at a loose thread in her mind, and the fabric of memory unravelled in a tangled mess of visions and colours. A boat, a piece of bread, a brush of feathers against her cheek. The vision was real, and yet she had no memory of any of it. Lou blinked, and the children settled around her in the darkness once more. Their silence was welcome and maddening in the same breath. She wanted explanations. She wanted apologies. It didn't seem as though she would get either.

"I'd remember a dirty boy with no manners," she said instead. "I do not know you. I only wish to go home."

"She's right, you know," said the boy with the painted face.

Kiran. Learn their names. You might need them.

The leader frowned. "Right about what?"

"You're lookin' kinda dirty, Jay. When's the last time you took a bath?"

Jay.

Lou's fingers grew numb. "That's impossible."

Laughter tittered around them, drowning out her panic. The children slapped Kiran across the back, appreciative of his quip.

Jay smirked. "Why, Kiran? You don't like havin' some competition?"

Didi elbowed Kiran in the ribs while the kind-eyed boy hid behind the largest one with the russet hair. All around her, the tension broke, and the laughter returned to the children's eyes. How quickly they were distracted. How quickly they overlooked the fact that her reality was crumbling.

Sticks from an oak tree by the lake. Voices arguing somewhere in the dark. A warm hand settling on her shoulder. Lou's stomach rolled while half-formed memories pulsed behind her eyes, begging to be seen. To be acknowledged.

"This cannot be happening," Lou moaned, shaking her head. Still, the visions wouldn't clear. "This is not real."

Jay glanced at her and held up a hand for silence. "Everyone, quiet! This is a lot for her to take in. You really don't remember me, do you, Lou?"

"The only Jay I know is the imaginary boy my sister told me stories of. He was a figment of a child's imagination. And *you* are hardly imaginary."

Jay nodded. "Right, your sister. That'll be Timber's kid. Rosie, was it?"

"Rose, actually. How did you know that?"

" 'Cause you and me were friends, Lou. Once upon a time, before life got messy. Think. Think hard."

She wouldn't. She couldn't.

The races and sword fights, giggles under forts made of flowery curtains and cotton sheets hanging off the back of her head.

Is it real?

Do you think it's real?

I . . . I think so.

Then she is.

Birds on her shoulder and a ship with faded paint.

How many ways can one person go mad?

"Who are you really?" she asked.

"A boy," he said. "A friend. That's all. That's all I ever wanted to be."

Faces turned to her, all patiently waiting for the tower of cards to settle after the magnificent collapse. "It . . . It is not possible," she said. But it was. He was there, flesh and bone. She knew him in her soul and in the dirt caked under his fingernails, in the way the wind would bring birdsong to her lonely window at night. She hadn't always been alone. He had brought the birds to her. He had dug the holes with his hands to plant her favourite flowers by the lake. And he never had a face.

Until now.

"It's been a long time, Lou," Jay whispered. "It's nice to see you again. Never thought I would, but here you are." He wrinkled his nose, and the room grew quiet. "You're probably not gonna like this part, though."

"What part?"

Jay jerked his chin over his shoulder. "Tie her up, boys."

CHAPTER 10

LOU

AGE NINE – TWO MONTHS TO GO

Sometimes I dreamed of blood: blood on my hands, blood pooled at my feet, sticky crimson splatter on the tree trunks all around me. Some nights I woke myself up before I could look too closely at the body on the ground. Other nights, the ground split open at my feet, trapping me in a deep grave along with those I'd killed. But regardless of which version visited me when I shut my eyes for the night, I would think the same thought: the red against the muted backdrop of the Briarwood was lovely.

One July night, I woke in a pool of my sweat, convinced it was blood, disappointed to find it was not. My world was turning grey, and the red of death would have been a wonderful reminder everything around me was still alive. I needed reminding sometimes.

Mother arranged my clothes for me the next morning, as was her way. A pair of snow-white tights rested on the back of my chair while a satin dress hung from a wire on my closet door—a body from a hangman's noose. I could not tell the colour of the dress. I'd never cared about such things. That morning, the blindness terrified me.

My eyes travelled first to my open bedroom window, then to Benji Bear beside me and the weathered tree branches trapped between my writing desk and the wall. Everything was as I'd left it before I went to sleep: untouched, the way my life had been for nearly a month. Another night Jay hadn't visited. Another night of nightmares and blood.

"Louisa? Are you awake, dear?"

I scrambled out of bed and pinched my cheeks for colour. Pain lanced up my leg as my feet hit the carpet, my ankle making me slower than ever before. How had I hurt myself? I wasn't sure if I remembered. Perhaps that was best.

"I will be ready soon, Mother!" I called. But she pushed my door open and hobbled inside before I could say any more. Her first stop was not to bid me good morning with a kiss or a tender embrace, but to shut my window. "Are we to have visitors today?"

Mother sat on my bed while I pulled on my tights and dress and braided my hair. Her mouth pressed into a thin line at my lack of balance, but I ignored the twist of embarrassment at her assessment. Instead, I inhaled the scent of her lavender soap and the floral cream she'd begun using on her hands since the beginning of the pregnancy. She was rounder now, her cheeks like roses in full bloom, her eyes bright yet finely lined at their corners. Two hands clutched at her midsection as though trying to support the weight of it all, and I fought the urge to crawl away. Being so close to *it* made my mind do funny things. And so I focused on the woman she'd been before the changes had started.

"I've cancelled your tutorial for the day," Mother said. "I thought we might spend some time preparing the baby's room together."

Together. My heart fell when it should have soared at the thought. The sun dimmed, and all the hope I'd had that today would be the day the colours returned soured. "I do not know anything about babies. You always told me I am a terrible decorator."

"I can teach you about both." She smiled, and I screamed inside. "Come, Louisa. A quick breakfast, and then we will get straight to work. It will be good for you to see what it is to prepare for the coming of a child. You will have your own to welcome someday."

The Briarwood whispered to me, but there was no time to answer. I followed Mother's shadow through our home, hating the roses on the walls, the way the hinges on the door to the baby's room were flecked with paint, the door handle slightly crooked. My room had been painted by a tradesman, skilled in their craft, but Father had lent his own hand to the child's room at the end of the hall. Despite the cough that continued to rattle his ribs, he had ensured every brush stroke had come from his own efforts. It was a labour of love that I didn't fully understand but wholeheartedly resented. The hinges on *my* door were perfectly absent of any defects. And defects, I learned, were a sign of something special. The last thing I wanted was to watch Mother pour her love into something that wasn't me when Father had already done the same.

When breakfast was done, Mother led me to the room I had vowed never to enter again. "Your father has finished hanging the drapes, so those are not to be changed. But the rest is open to your suggestions." She offered me a delicate smile before stepping inside. I stood in the hall, trying to grow roots.

Somehow, the colours still existed in the baby's room. The paint was still fresh—the same green as the underside of a maple leaf. Lace curtains framed a cheerful window doling sunshine onto a wicker-and-lace bassinet. In one corner was an overturned bucket spattered with paint. In another were dirty brushes drying in a glass jar. The only unfinished room in our home waited not for more paint or a pretty coverlet; it waited for a child that wasn't me.

"It looks so big when it is so empty," I said. *I wish it would stay this way.*

Mother smiled, one hand drifting from her stomach to caress the lace edge of the bassinet. "It will not be empty much longer. But if we are to furnish the room, I believe the elder sister should have a say. I want you to be excited about this as well, Louisa. So, will the theme here be horses or angels?"

Had Jay forgotten me? He spoke often of brothers I'd never met, but they had never kept him away from me before. Did he not want me anymore? I still wanted him. A child would soon fill the room and my life, and I had nothing to offer it but a heart too empty to be of any use to anyone.

Jay was gone. I had no way of reaching him; he never *did* bring me to the island. In the end, I had no one. The baby would likely be no different.

But that wasn't fair. The baby, although unwanted, was innocent. If I did not try to welcome it, to make it feel loved, who would? Mother was fickle, and Father was often gone. The neighbourhood children had no imagination, and the woods kept their secrets hidden, even from me. And Jay . . .

Without a word, I drifted from the room. I could not say how long I was gone or if there had ever been a decision made consciously for me to do it. But when I returned, it was with Benji Bear snug in my arms.

"Bears," I said, placing Benji in the bassinet. He looked at home nestled among the covers. "The theme should be bears, I think. Would that be all right?"

Perhaps it was a trick of the light. Perhaps not. Mother's eyes shone with a smile meant only for me. A true smile. A flicker of love. It was too late for me, but I would never allow another child to live in doubt. I smiled back.

"It would be perfect, Louisa. I like that idea very much."

Jay could stay away if he wished. But I needed to remain where I was.

CHAPTER 11

The boy with the round face and kind eyes is friendliest with the larger boy. They are together often and move in harmony. They seem to be most uncomfortable by my captivity. Win one, win the other.

I have a chance.

Lou's wrists were still bound. Her feet were numb from sitting so long on the ground, her legs dead weight that would be of little use to her should she get the chance to run. Jay and the others sat at a low table, a bowl of nuts shared between them, a handful of walnut shells littering their elbows. The largest boy glanced at her, and she smiled, willing him to see she meant no harm. He turned away, a flush creeping above his collar.

The girl—no, Didi, *use their names, use their names—appears comfortable hosting a prisoner and has not looked up once from her bow. She will be of no use. Her brother—Kiran, yes, Kiran—tries to hunch as his sister does, fiddles with his weapon when his sister busies herself with hers, but his eyes flit from corner to corner. He is restless. He might listen to me if I can ever separate him from his sister.*

Win one, possibly convince the other.

A small chance, but a chance nonetheless.

The packed earth at her back was cold and unforgiving. She wriggled her arms, but rope bit into her wrists and ankles at once, turning her skin to pure fire. "Must these bindings be so tight?" Lou asked. "I've been here long enough to have convinced you I am of no trouble. Can anyone here explain why I am still being held prisoner? Anyone at all?"

All but one ignored her. With a furtive look at Jay, the plump boy with the warm eyes picked up a bowl and a chipped ceramic cup. "Um . . . hello, miss," he said, stopping by her feet. "I was wondering if you wanted some company."

Lou made herself appear as impassive as possible. "Not particularly. Please return when you decide to let me go home."

"I know." A flush swept across his cheeks. "But you've been sitting here so long all by yourself, I figured you might be lonely."

"What I *am* is tired. And I do not require any company offered out of guilt by one of my captors."

"I wish you wouldn't think of it like that. Jay really doesn't want to keep you tied up like this, but he's got no choice. Didi would have kittens if he treated you any better than the other prisoners we've had here."

"So, I am not the first." Lou laughed under her breath. "I cannot say I am surprised, though it does make me wonder where your parents went wrong. When will you finally set me free?"

He flinched. "I . . . I don't know, miss."

"Then, why are you speaking to me at all?"

He offered her the bowl with shaky arms and ignored her question. "I thought you might be hungry too. It's just a few nuts, nothing special, but I shelled them for you. A-and this is water from the fairy springs, so it's nice and cold."

"Are you this considerate with all your prisoners?" she asked, holding up her bound wrists. Her stomach protested her hesitation to accept the food with a furious roar. "Never mind. I cannot eat if I am bound. If you would just untie me—"

"I'm real sorry about all this," he said, "but I can't. Not before Jay gives the all-clear. We're not bad once you get to know us. Honest."

"Oh, yes. All perfect gentlemen truss up their guests and leave them to starve on a cold dirt floor."

He gnawed his lip, and the tall muscular boy hunched farther into himself, their discomfort mirrored in each other. "Jay's just careful is all," her new companion said, condensation dripping over his fingers. "You came out of nowhere, and you're older than we're used to seeing around here. Jay says only pirates are old on the island."

"What is your name?"

"Benjamin. But everyone calls me Benji."

"Well, *Benji*," Lou said, "do I have an eye patch?"

"No."

"What about a sword?"

His answer came slower this time. "No."

"A peg leg? What about a parrot who sits on my shoulder and squawks insults at passersby?"

"No, miss."

"Then how in the heavens could you think I'm a pirate?" She sighed. "To be frank, I have no idea what you all want with me. Let me leave, and I will go home promptly. Or find me an adult who can help. *Please.*"

His cheeks deepened from pink to magenta. "I told you, only pirates are old around here. Jay said to tie you up, so we did. I don't know more than that, and I don't want to know. It's usually better for me like that. I'm sorry. Honest."

Pirates. The children wouldn't stop playing their games, even to help a lady in need. If their parents *were* nearby, she loathed to meet them. "And do you always do what Jay tells you to do?" she asked.

"Well, yes." He rocked on his toes, casting a look at the table, where Jay now peeled oranges, doling out wedges to everyone but himself. "He's our leader. Jay took us away from a very bad place. We owe him. You sort of do too, you know."

"Benji," Jay called. "That's enough. Either she eats or she keeps quiet, but I told you not to stick around."

Lou sighed, defeated. "Let's have it, then."

Benji brightened, obliging at once. The liquid was cool and clean, hints of peach and apricot bubbling across her tongue with every sip. She fought a small moan of pleasure as she took a greedy swallow, pulling more down her throat. Walnuts came next, small morsels dissolving quickly on her tongue.

"Good?" he asked.

She swallowed, disappointed to find the bowl empty. "Very," she admitted. *Win one, win the other.* "Thank you, Benji. That is a lovely name."

He grinned. "Thanks. My mama gave it to me before she gave me up. It's the only thing I have from her. I like my name."

"Oh." Lou blinked, and Benji was no longer her keeper, but a boy. Thirteen or fourteen, with the trust of a child. A child like Rose. Suddenly, the thought of manipulating him seemed wrong. "I am very sorry. When did she leave you?"

"That's *enough*, Benji." Jay stood, chair scraping the dirt. Anger made him taller, carved angles in his cheeks and lit flames behind his eyes. "She's a prisoner, not some dinner guest. Time to say good night."

Benji frowned at the ground. "Sorry," he whispered, turning away. "I'll check in on you as soon as I can. I won't let you go hungry."

"That's all right. What woman needs her freedom when she can sit still with nothing to do but eat and be silent?"

Benji's shoulders went rigid, and the den fell silent. Every face turned, etched in hurt and ill-concealed pain. Regret burned in Lou's chest; her words had been harsh, unnecessarily so, and they were only children after all. Children like Rose.

"I apologize, Benji. I truly do appreciate your kindness. My sister believes in the importance of her games as well. I'm sure if she were here, she would tell me children will be children and to leave you to your play."

Benji heaved a mighty sigh. "We're kids," he said, "but that doesn't mean we're playing."

And with that, he joined the others, leaving Lou with her bindings and her shame.

All right, think, she instructed herself. *There must be a way out of here.* With a quick glance, she could make out cots on the floor with leaves and old clothes for blankets, and a smattering of mismatched furniture. A chute hung above her like the bottom of a well, too far to reach. Unless there was a hidden door under one of the rugs or carved within the dirt walls, there was no way out.

Time moved in jagged leaps and stutters in the underground den. When the children played jacks or sparred with wooden sticks, it hopped forward in a way that was very nearly bearable. But when there was nothing to do but stare at the walls or count the roots in the ceiling, it lagged. Stalled. Became a fingernail scratching the delicate flesh of her wrist—annoying at first, then quickly rising to the level of agony reserved for tight slippers and forced engagements.

So, when the ceiling began to rain dirt and the children abandoned their hushed conversations, it was a welcome relief from the monotony of her captivity.

"Hey, you babies hear that?" Didi asked, getting to her feet. "I think he's back!"

"He's back, he's *back*!" Kiran cried. "Took him long enough.

Think he found the new huntin' grounds those pirates were talkin' about?"

"Quiet," Jay instructed. "Stand back and give him some room."

A large object slid down the dirt chute, spraying loose rocks and earth onto the ground. The others cheered, Lou shrank back, and time leapt forward once more.

"Sammy!" Jay gathered the new boy into his arms. "C'mere, have an apple. You okay? Didja get into any trouble?"

"He'll eat later, boss. I wanna know about the pirates. Can we kill any of 'em?"

"Shut it, Didi," Kiran moaned. "Why you gotta think about killin' all the time? The treasure's worth more than a couple pirate heads."

"You." Lou's voice cut through their arguing. A blue shirt. Bare feet covered in mud. Glasses. "He's the boy who was at my home! He knows something about how I came here. Go on, tell them! Tell them the truth so they can free me!"

The child only tucked himself closer under Jay's arm, beaming through dirt smudges and pink scars. "Hi, Jay. An apple would be real nice."

"Is she tellin' the truth, Sammy?" Jay asked, a new softness in his face. "Didja bring Lou here, where we live . . . in *secret*?"

"Course not," Didi said, ruffling Sammy's hair with a grimy hand. "He wouldn't be stupid enough to go against Peter like that."

"Please," Kiran scoffed. "Peter's as good as gone, and so's the island. It's only a matter of time before we go belly up with it."

The muscular boy stepped closer to Benji, the worry plain in the creases of his sunburned skin. He shook his head and gestured around the den with a sweep of his thick arm.

"What's he sayin'?" Kiran asked.

"Henry thinks we shouldn't be talking like this," Benji replied.

"He says we're not gone yet, so we shouldn't be talking like we are."

Jay patted Henry's arm, and the muscular boy settled at once. "Henry's right. We don't know how this'll all shake out, so we stay sharp, all right? Sammy, I still need to know how any of this happened. She's a grown. No one but Peter can go to their world and come back with one of them unless they got permission. Especially after what's happened."

"I know."

Jay handed him an apple and considered as Sammy crunched his first bite. "So . . . explain."

"I can't," Sammy said, shrugging. "I was out in the woods, trackin' a fresh trail west near the Red camp, and I just heard cryin' and water, like there was a storm comin'. Then I was just *there*."

"In her woods?" Jay asked.

"At her house." Sammy tossed the apple core to the ground and took Jay's hand. "Maybe she called out. Maybe not. I know how much you missed her. You said the barrier's weak, so maybe—"

"Stop!" Lou cried, slamming her heels on ground. "I did not ask for this, and nothing anyone is saying makes sense to me! I would never consent to leaving my home. I have a family, responsibilities, a *life*. Someone explain what is going on so I can go home!"

Didi scoffed, shattering Lou's confidence. "You can't go *home*, pirate. Didn't you hear? Peter's gone. We're all stuck here 'til we die. I say we take down some pirates and have some fun before the island disappears for good."

"We can leave the same way I got here," Lou said, her tone measured. "There must be a way. Your parents—"

"Crickets, this grown is thick," Didi said, lips pulling back from her teeth. "We told you, fancy lady, there ain't no parents here! No one knows how you got here, and no one gets off the island unless Peter says so. You're just dead weight to us now. If we're lucky, Jay'll order us to feed you to the crocs, and we'll get a nice show before we go."

Kiran grinned. "That sounds fun."

"No one's feedin' anyone to the crocs," Jay said firmly. "And you don't give orders here, Didi. I do."

"I mean, I was only kiddin', boss."

"Hey, all this fighting is making Henry really upset," Benji said, edging closer to the trembling boy. "Can we keep it down?"

"Enough!" Jay ordered, and a hush fell over them all. "Sammy was there when the grown came over here, so I'm gonna find out everythin' I can before I decide what to do with her. If I like what I hear," he continued, turning to Lou, "I might be able to get you home."

Didi sniffed the air. "I liked it better when we thought she was a pirate. Well, this ain't no fun no more. What good is she if we can't play with her?"

"Jay, if it's all right with you, could I untie her?" Benji was already halfway across the room, his fingers twisted into a knot. "If she's not a pirate, then she's a friend."

"No." Jay glared at them all in turn. "The pirates are back at the cove, in case anyone was wonderin'. If we're not careful, they'll be comin' for us now that Peter's out of the way. We need to be ready. C'mon, Sammy. Let's eat."

While memories were measured in moments and lives were marked by years, the wait for Jay and Sammy to speak was to be measured in millennia. They sat together, elbow to elbow, golden head to bronze until the candles sputtered out. The others fell back to their places, dice rolling across the dirt and throwing up dust like smoke. Darts shot into the walls while cups hid coloured pebbles and the outcome of ridiculous wagers: *It's the one in the middle, I'd bet my mermaid fin on it. That's my mermaid fin, you idiot. I won it in a game of fairy dust, remember?* The hum of conversation chased away her cries, and no matter how hard she kicked the earth or called their names, only their backs replied.

✖

SHE WAS DIRTY. Tired. She'd yelled until her throat was raw.

And the children played and played.

"Try harder, Benji!" Sammy whined. He and Jay had left the table long ago, but instead of announcing Jay's decision regarding her fate, they'd joined the others at the centre of the room for another game. Sammy sliced a wooden stick through the air, forcing Benji back. "You're goin' too easy on me."

"I don't want to hurt you."

"Geez, Benji, I can handle it," Sammy insisted. "Jay said so. Come on now. Hit me!" He sank into a lunge, his body whip-thin and painfully unsteady.

It was soon clear that Benji, while lacking in confidence, had a significant size advantage over his opponent. With a reluctant thrust, Benji landed a blow on Sammy's shoulder, knocking the boy to his knees. "Sorry, sorry!" Benji moaned. "I'm really sorry, Sammy. You know I didn't want to fight you."

"It's all right," Sammy muttered, handing his stick to Kiran. "I'll getcha next time. Sticks are not the same as real swords anyway. I'm pretty good when I get to use a real sword."

Swords. They were playing at swords while she sat in the dirt.

Win one, win the other.

Unless there was another way.

"Okay, try that exact move again, Benji," Jay said, circling, muttering instructions while the others watched. "But this time you don't need to apologize. Makes you look weak, and no Red, Blue, or pirate'll care that you're sorry before slicin' your guts open."

"Sorry, Jay." Benji winced. "I mean, I'm *not* sorry. Right?"

Jay smiled. "Right. Go on."

Kiran tapped his stick to the ground. "Just like I showed you, Benji. Stick the pointy end right at me, and try not to drop your sword."

"It's a stick," Lou said through clenched teeth. "Not a sword."

Jay glared at her. "It's a sword, boys. Don't you forget it, or it'll get you killed."

"Because if you lose focus, the pirate wins," Benji said, face screwed up in concentration.

"Again with the pirates." All eyes turned to Lou. Heat flashed in her face as she spoke; confrontation was terribly unladylike. But she would never be free of her bindings unless she learned to speak a language her captors understood. "Those are silly little sticks, not swords. If you ever *do* face a pirate, they will make quick work of you."

Benji dropped his arm, and Kiran threw his own weapon to the ground in frustration. "She's right, Jay," Benji said. "I only won against Sammy because I'm bigger than him. I'll never be good enough to face a pirate."

"She's not right about anythin', Benji," Jay said firmly. "She doesn't know what you can do."

"It's true," Kiran said. "Benji's no fighter, and I'm tired of swingin' branches around. Now, if you put me against my sister with a blade, I'll show you what fightin' a pirate looks like." Sweat turned the paint around his eyes to tears streaking black tracks down his cheeks. "Let me get my sword."

"Benji just needs practice," Sammy said. "Besides, we could save the island on our own, Jay. Me and you. And now you know that Lou's all right, maybe we can ask her to—"

"No." Jay threw him a silencing look. "That's not happenin', Sammy."

If I could push him, just a little, just enough . . .

Lou leaned forward, measuring her voice, weighing her words. She needed to get it right. "Of course you would never allow someone younger than you to give you orders, *Jay*. Are you afraid Sammy will have better ideas and make a fool of your leadership? As though I needed any more proof that you are lacking."

"Watch it," Jay said, fists pressed to his sides.

"Or what? You'll whack me with a stick? It doesn't look like any of you know how to do more than swat at flies with them."

"Don't listen to her!" Jay said. "She's just makin' trouble."

Lou ignored him, and so did the others. Taunting felt wrong, felt sour on her tongue, but she'd been underground for what—a few days? Longer? There was no way to be sure. She'd eaten and slept, but those habits were usually dictated by the predictable guidance of the sun and moon. There, on the dirt floor underground, she saw neither. Hunger made her delirious, and fatigue made her reckless. She needed to get loose. To do that, she needed to push Jay hard enough to let her fight.

"In fact," Lou continued, "you could likely be beaten by someone without any skill whatsoever. And how embarrassing would that be?"

"That so?" Didi asked, an arrow already nocked in her bow. "Permission to test that myself, boss?"

"I'm more than up to the challenge." Lou tread softly, registering the pink flush tinging the tips of Jay's ears. "But I cannot do a thing in these bindings."

"C'mon, boss, let me have a go," Kiran said, dark eyes dancing in the low light of the torches now lit and buried in the dirt walls. "She's just a girl. I'll bet she goes down in a second."

Didi punched him hard on the shoulder. "Watch your mouth, or I'll show you how much a girl can do, brother."

"Stop it," Benji said, his sword clattering onto the ground. "You're getting Henry all upset again!" Sure enough, Henry was crouched in a corner, his thick arms wound tight around his knees. "You know he doesn't like it when we fight. Lou's just tryin' to get free. Can you blame her? She's been like that for weeks!"

Weeks?

"I'm sorry, Henry." Jay rounded on her, the colour high in his cheeks. "Look what you did. Why can't you just sit there and stay quiet?"

"Because I cannot waste another moment watching such a pathetic sword fight!" The girl with a sheet draped off the back of her head leapt out to face Jay with a gleaming sword, a beautiful pirate free of her own shackles. "Benji is right. I do wish to be untied, and if you do this for me, you'll have another opponent. A change from the usual. An actual challenge. Wouldn't that be nice?"

"Don't talk down to us," Kiran said. "We're kids, not stupid. And you're a *grown*. You probably never even touched a sword."

"And I would best you regardless," Lou said. She was thirsty, her throat raw and throbbing. The only way to be free was to combat insanity with insanity itself.

Kiran and Didi broke out into raucous laughter, but Benji, Sammy, and Henry simply looked toward their leader with apprehension. Jay approached silently, a predator stalking its prey, his young face much too hard. At that very moment, he was not a boy or a man. He was only terrifying.

"You want to make a wager?" he asked. " 'Cause that's the only fair way to let you go."

This is it. "Fine. If I win whatever petty little game this is, then you must not only let me go but help me return to Silverton Lane yourself. I know nothing of this place, but you seem to. I would require a guide."

To her surprise, Jay smiled. "Sounds like a big prize, but I think I can make that happen. What do I get if you lose?"

Good question. Lou floundered. "I . . . I have no money. But once I am home, I can speak with my mother about offering you compensation. I have a dowry. You can choose whatever you like from there."

She hoped it would be enough.

"Your money's no good to us. Nah, if I win . . ." Jay considered for a moment, one finger tapping his pointed chin. This was just another game—a new and very interesting game. "If I win, you stay here with us for good."

Lou's heart—and confidence—stuttered. "That is an unfair wager. I belong back home; you would only be ensuring I return to my rightful place. What you're asking for is my entire life. That's not equal."

"You didn't say the prizes had to be." His grin spread, the tiny chip in his tooth creating a window into his smile. "You set your terms, I set mine. That's just good form."

"But—"

"Sammy mighta been at your big fancy house, but no one asked you to follow him. As far as I can tell, you came here on your own since the barrier between the island and your world is not what it was when Peter was in charge. Nah, I like this deal: fight and win, we take you home; fight and lose, you stay. Or we just keep you here all tied up 'til the island goes belly up and you die with us anyway."

Lou's mouth went dry. What choice did she have?

The answer was always the same: none. She had no choice at all. She never had. What she would give to rot in a hole under the earth if it could only be a fate of her choosing.

"Deal," she whispered. "Now untie me."

"Hear that, everyone?" Jay asked. "Little miss perfect's gonna fight me!"

While the children whooped and jumped and beat spears against the dirt, Jay lowered himself before her. He tucked his blade under the ropes binding her wrists, and they fell like snakes into her lap. Another swift motion, and her legs were free, insects swarming her feet as blood flowed to them once more.

Lou stood. A wooden stick lay under a fine blanket of sand, speckles of crimson dried with the bark's grooves. She bent to retrieve it, but Sammy touched her elbow first.

"This one's yours, Lou," he said. He handed her a sword of true steel, the edge of the blade polished to a shine.

"What is this?" she asked, backing away from him.

"Your sword."

"You were playing with sticks that you *called* swords!" Lou said, panic rearing its ugly head once more. "We did not agree to use actual blades."

"You agreed to fight," Jay corrected her, retrieving a curved sword with a hilt wrapped in leather from underneath one of the nearby cots. He tossed it from hand to hand, testing the weight with easy dexterity. "When we fight, we use these. Sticks are only for practice."

"I'm sorry, Lou." Benji's hands were knotted against his chest while Henry laid a reassuring hand on his arm. "I should have said something! I thought you knew, but how could you?"

"Stop apologizin'!" Kiran and Didi cried in unison.

"Go on." The chip in Jay's tooth turned his smile into a leer, a black hole that would consume her if she didn't remain strong. "Unless you changed your mind?"

"Of course not." She took the sword in both hands, sagging with the weight of it. With the death of it. With the thirst for blood heavy in the air.

Jay bowed low, his sword-free hand flourishing behind him. "It's just you and me, Lou. Except I've been doin' this a really, *really* long time. Didja wanna give up now? The island's not a bad place when it's not goin' all funny."

"No." Lou dragged her sword behind her, scratching a deep track in the earth. "But if we're to continue to be around each other, I'll be insisting you learn to speak proper English. *Didja* is not a word."

"And frilly dresses make you look like a sailboat," he retorted. "So, stop complainin' and fight me."

"Whoop, whoop!" cheered the others.

The dirt under her feet quaked with their stomps, sending dirt hailing down on her head. The room was too small, and there was dust in her nose, and her opponent was already brandishing his weapon like he knew how to use it. She did not; she should never have pretended any differently.

"Do we fight until one of us surrenders?" Lou asked. She hoisted her sword, skin stretching tight across her knuckles.

Jay shrugged. "Sure, if you want."

"That might be too dangerous. What about the first cut wins?"

"That works too."

"Just fight already!" Didi called.

"Whoop, whoop!"

Jay grinned, the point of his sword weaving between them. "Good luck, *little bird*."

Lou's heart sputtered behind her ribs. She swallowed bile.

Oranges and cloves and a warm hand on a cold shoulder.

Metal hissed.

Lou threw herself to her knees just as Jay's blade sliced by her ear. Hands—she didn't know whose—shoved her down into the bitter earth . She spat, clambered upright, her sword swinging aimlessly at the pulsing wall of bodies closing in.

"That was a lot of big talk if that's all you got," Jay said, circling, prowling. One foot, then another, his arms steady, his steel searching for the softest parts of her. Another slash. Lou dodged to the right, narrowly avoiding the blow. "I remember you bein' better than that, but age made you slow. I think I'm gonna like havin' a prisoner around all the time. You can cook our supper and wash our clothes."

Of course that was what she would be best at—washing and cooking and looking a certain brand of pretty. "Be quiet."

A deep lunge, a quick jab through the air. Jay pushed her back, and back, and back. "I'm gettin' kinda worried you won't win."

Lou ducked, shuffled to the left, her shoulders screaming under the weight of her weapon. "I'll be fine."

Jay swooped his arm in a wide arc and slammed the flat edge of the sword against her arm. He shook his head, tracking her fall with naked disappointment. "You made it sound like you knew what you were doin'. Like this was gonna be a fair fight. You know . . . *fun.* But it looks to me like you're just small. And you don't remember anythin' I taught you."

Her palms were slick and cold, her forehead beading with sweat, but it was the lava bubbling in her chest that pushed her back to her feet. She swung and missed.

"Whoop, whoop!"

Not enough, not enough, not enough.

"Looks like you still waste your time with your face in those books," Jay said.

Once upon a time, a long time ago, a boy lived among the stars.

"I thought you wanted big things."

Born without wings but blessed with a soul, the child called Peter was blessed by the sky.

"To study birds and be a pirate."

"Whoop, whoop!"

"But I just see a weak little mermaid."

When his next blow came, she spun on the ball of her foot and out of reach.

One part of Lou—the familiar part that loved her beautiful gowns and worked to make her hair sit right—went quiet. Her breathing slowed, and she raised her arm, bringing her sword around her head like a lasso. A calculated step forward, a heel planted just so. Her blade biting through the air beside Jay's ear. Because there was another part living deep inside, ravenous after being caged for so long. And it was fierce.

She set that part free at last.

Jay leapt away, the soles of his feet barely kissing the earth. But this time was different. This time his face registered something other than arrogance. The part of Lou that belonged to the Briarwood with a stick in her hands smiled.

"I'm the mermaid, I presume?" she asked, pulling her sword from the ground with a grunt. Jay stabbed the air once again, but she hopped back, bringing her sword down on his, trapping him. He was practiced, but she was bigger. Older. And while her mind remembered little, her blood carried a song of forgotten memories, its tune as chilling as it was familiar. "Which means all I know how to do is look pretty and sing. Is that right?"

Jay kicked her blade off his with his boot, and she stumbled back. "That's what I said. You're no pirate," he said. "You're a scared old woman. A pretend fighter. A lost little bird."

"Stop calling me that!" Undiluted rage ran through Lou's veins, the rapid beating of her heart pushing it into her skin, her bones, her very soul. "You have no right to speak those words. Understand?" Lou crouched low, swiping her leg around. Her shin connected with his with the delicious burn of bone on bone. With a cry of surprise, he came tumbling down, face connecting with dirt. *More.* Her sword was an extension of her arm, visions of pirates and buried treasure spurring her on as she leapt to her feet. The others were finally quiet—only she and Jay existed in the silence.

More.

Jay thumped the hilt of his sword into Lou's ribs. Air rushed out of her lungs, and stars filled her vision, but she wouldn't stop.

She would show him how much of a pirate she truly was; he would regret assuming she was nothing more than a weak woman.

Jay came in for the finishing blow, the final strike to keep her captive forever. Sweat burned her eyes.

Inhale, exhale, focus. She was back by the lake in the Briarwood, water lapping at the sandy bank with a delicate tongue.

A boy. A boy with worms in his fist.

She had won then too.

How *had* she won?

Lou swung her leg back and drove every ounce of force she possessed into the ground with the toe of her shoe. Dirt, rocks, and roots sprayed into his face.

Jay cried out, crumpling to his knees.

Dust everywhere.

He reached for his fallen sword, but Lou crushed his fingers with a stomp of her foot. The tip of her blade pressed into his chest, a drop of crimson beading around the puckered flesh. "I win," she said.

The den grew still. She expected him to protest, call her names, or pull a hidden dagger from his boot and impale her. But he didn't.

The iceberg in Jay's eyes thawed as he stood. They faced each other, past and present colliding with the crash of thunderclaps.

"You cheated," he said, chest heaving. "You . . . You actually cheated."

One appraised the other. She never dropped her sword. "What of it?" Lou finally asked.

"Nothin'."

"You're smiling."

"I can't smile?"

His mockery stoked the flame in her chest. "You lost our wager, so it seems to be a rather strange reaction."

He brushed dust off his knees and looking up at her from under a fan of golden lashes pearled with tears. "It's really you."

"What are you talking about?"

"Lou, it's *you.*"

"I know my own name!"

What's the point of livin' if you have your head down all the time?

Lou dropped her sword. "What is happening to me?"

Rainbow Rock still needs its treasure.

Jay reached for her, but she wasn't ready. Not yet.

A bear in a basket, beaded eyes of onyx blinking from the folds of a soft blanket.

"*Stop!*" She ran back to her familiar spot on the ground, but Jay was right behind her. He sank to his knees. Tears pooled in the sand between them, turning it to mud, blackening it with despair and memories long forgotten.

"What's happenin' to her?" Didi asked from somewhere in the haze.

"She's rememberin'," Sammy whispered.

Lou focused on the boy who had cracked open her world and laid her memories bare. He knew who she was—they all did. And somehow, she found she could no longer hate them. Jay wasn't lying.

"She's finally rememberin' who he is," Sammy said. "And now she can help us fix the island."

CHAPTER 12

R ose had spoken of a magical island, a home to fairies and
pirates, a place of adventures and gemstones hidden at the
bottom of the sea. It was the motherland of eternal
friendship, offering the freedom of an unsupervised existence.

The place of her sister's dreams was quite different from Lou's
vantage point underground.

In the den, there was no beautiful lagoon, no beauty or
whimsy. Her once-fine clothes were now crusted with mud, the
fabric thick and stiff against her skin. The children were loud,
obsessed with their games and the arguments resulting from them.
And worst of all, she was never without supervision.

She's finally rememberin' who he is.

They wanted her to remember them.

Memory was a dangerous thing. It could unite as much as it
could strike a blow. She often struggled to remember her father's
smile the smoothness of his laugh before illness had shattered it to
small pieces with sharp edges. In the end, Lou had resolved that
some things were better left buried far underground where no one

would find them—somewhere like a den, far, far underground with the rest of the dead things.

Lou stood, wincing at the ache in her neck and legs. She longed to run untethered and breathe clean air. Everything about the den and the children in it had grown stale. "I'm ready to leave," she said. "I'd like to know how you plan to get me home."

Jay looked up from his game of jacks, twisting a rubber ball in his palm. "What, you mean now?"

"Of course I do. I've been here long enough."

"You really haven't been here long, Lou. Time works different for us on the island. Plus, you remembered me. That changes everythin'."

"It changes nothing."

Jay launched the ball into the swarm of wooden spikes, scattering them like shrapnel. "I was fine to let you go back when you were just a borin' old lady. But now you're one of us. You'll like it better here."

Didi grabbed her bow and stomped over to her cot. Jay let her go, but something in Lou's heart twisted at the sight of the girl's rigid shoulders. It was one thing to want to escape, but to be so blatantly *unwanted* tugged at some dark part of her deep inside.

"I want to go home," Lou said, tearing her gaze away. "I do not belong here. My mother and sister will be frantic. I have a wedding to plan. My family's future depends on me."

"Don't know much about your sister, but I think *Mother* will be just fine." Jay bit his lip and abandoned his game, closing the space between them in a few quick paces. In her memory, he was a wild man, an explorer, and a force almost as impressive as her father. But age brought clarity; what had once been mighty and great, important and immortal, was only a small unremarkable boy drawing in the dirt with sticks. "Sorry if that was harsh," Jay said. "But don't you remember how happy we were together? We played mermaids and pirates. We looked for gold and treasure."

"No."

"I showed you how to feed the birds."

"*No.*"

"C'mon, Lou, stop *fightin'* it." His attention commanded hers with unexpected force. He wanted to connect, and she despised him for it. "You were my best friend," Jay continued, "and I can tell you remember enough about me, even if you can't remember it all. I'm in your brain, with my own little spot buried somewhere deep. But I'm there. I never left."

His voice rustled the branches in a quiet forest where children waited at the bottom of lakes. The birds, the races through the woods, the pirates and treasures . . .

The laughter. How long had it been since she'd smiled with her whole heart?

"We met in the Briarwood," he prompted. "You loved those stupid birds. And your books—I couldn't get you away from 'em."

"Jay." She weighed his name on her tongue, finding it strange but natural nonetheless, a habit formed with time that her body would remember when even her mind refused him. "I know you exist, but I cannot understand it. You won't explain it to me."

"Can't explain what I don't really know. So, you can trust me, okay?"

Lou probed his arm with one finger. Solid. Real. "No one else could see you when I was a child. The only reason I remembered your name is because Rose would talk about you and Timber often. I imagined you the way she imagined Timber . . . That's what children do."

Jay smiled without a drop of humour. "The growns can't wrap their brains around things they don't understand, so they call us *imaginary friends*. Stupid name since we all had lives before we came here and are as real as you are. And growns . . . Well, when you become one, the stuff you loved as a kid sort of disappears to make room for the other stuff. You can't be both a kid and a grown, so somethin's gotta go. And it's always the kid parts that go first. That's how I understand it."

"But this boy—Peter. How is he in charge of an entire island of people? He cannot impose his will on you this way."

"He's not a normal boy," Jay said. "Peter's the oldest kid on the island, and he calls all the shots. Now that Blackbeard's got him—"

"Blackbeard, the pirate captain?"

Jay nodded. "That's the one. Now that he's got Peter, the whole island's been actin' up. I figure that's how you crossed over here. It's never happened before."

Surrendering logic was easier than Lou had thought it would be. Perhaps Rose's stories had left a mark, or she wasn't as adult as she thought she was. Either way, Jay's logic made sense. If the pirates had captured the ruler of a magical island, that ruler would take his magic with him. And if the barrier between worlds was compromised, the strange colour disturbances and water in her bedroom walls could have all come from the island itself.

"That might explain how I made it to your world," Lou said. "But who are you all, then? Did you come here the same way I did?"

A game of jacks, siblings wearing war paint to bed, a den of their very own. The children stood in silence before her, perfect children carrying the weight of being stranded in a forgotten place in the curve of their shoulders and the distance in their eyes. Lou considered them all in turn.

Jay dropped his head, and a part of her broke for him without knowing why. "The island takes kids who run away, or get a little lost, or have parents who don't want them," he said. "It started off with just Peter, and then he found a few more. And now look at us; I guess there are more parents out there who regret havin' us than you thought, huh?" He laughed, but Lou couldn't.

"I'm very sorry," she said. "I was so insensitive before. I . . . I had no idea."

But Jay shrugged her apology off with a wave. "You weren't supposed to know, Lou. That's the point. You forget, you move on. That means you're one of the heaps of growns who go on to have a life. Grow up, grow old, move on the normal way. But us . . . Well, we get a second shot at a better life than what we had before. See, we all got dealt a bad hand back in your world, but here, all that goes away. Besides a couple monsters and some devil flies gettin' in the way from time to time, it's a pretty solid deal."

"This is an improvement?" Lou asked.

Jay grinned. "Once you get used to sleepin' on the floor and dealin' with pirates, sure."

"Some of us like the pirates, boss," Didi said.

"But this is not a life," Lou said softly. "You are the same boy I knew as a girl."

"So?"

"So, you are unchanged! This island has doomed you all to a life lived standing still. You cannot have any ambitions that mean anything because each day is more of the same. Don't you have dreams?"

"Here we go," Kiran said. "It's time for the speech."

"You all could have become mothers and fathers, had warm homes to go back to every night," Lou said. "Are you not saddened by the fact that you will never have any of it?"

Didi stepped forward, her eyes black with hate, but Kiran held her back. The air in the den grew thick with emotion: hers, theirs, the possibilities that could have been but that never would be. Jay's answering smile, however, was patient.

"It's not *your* life, Lou. But for us," he said, gesturing to the others, "gettin' to be a friend to a kid in your world, even for a little while, is better than what we had. We get to help someone who's got no one, and we finally get the chance to come and go off this rock whenever we want. See, unless we have a charge in the Land of the Grown, we're stuck here. But that doesn't erase that we're all the family we need. Who're you to say that's not a good thing?"

"But I *forgot* you," Lou said. "Does that not become painful, to be invisible to people you grow to care for?"

"Lou—"

"And Rosie! She was destroyed because Timber left her. She is not yet grown, but he is *gone*. You leave heartache in your wake when you leave!"

"Hey, that's not fair," Jay said. "We don't leave because we want to. We never have a choice!"

"My sister was so overcome with grief when your friend Timber decided he'd had enough of their friendship that she has become inconsolable! She will not speak to me! She is going to market and picking flowers and—"

"And growin' up?" Didi finished. "Sucks bein' left behind, don't it?"

Lou pressed her lips together, her words failing her.

"Look, Lou," Jay said over Didi's rage, "I don't know what's goin' on with Rosie, but we only leave when a kid grows up. That's Peter's biggest rule. Timber didn't abandon your sister on purpose."

"Then *where* is he?" Energy coursed in her limbs, and she itched to move, to strike, to get back to the sister who was grieving a boy who'd done to her what he'd undoubtedly done to thousands before her. A sister she'd refused to believe. "My sister thinks he is dead. He owes her an explanation before he moves on to another child, Jay."

"You growns are all the same," he said, a new edge to his voice. Eyes that had once been warm frosted over to chips of ice. "Thinkin' the world owes you, but it doesn't. Where was the love our parents owed *us*? You think that was fair?" He spat on the ground, and the others muttered their approval. "None of us would abandon our kids. They're the ones who abandon us. Timber was part of Peter's circle, but I knew him well. If he stopped visitin' and your sister says he's dead, then the island got him."

"Jay," she said, forcing calm into her voice, "an island cannot kill a person."

"This one can. And the longer Peter stays gone, the more of us will go. Until there's no one left."

The ground under Lou's feet quaked, but there was no water creeping through the cracks in the dirt. Mother had put her faith in the wrong daughter. Rose's trust had been misplaced. She would let them both down if she couldn't get back, and what would her troubles mean then?

"Could I be trapped here?" Lou asked under her breath. "For good, I mean."

Jay sighed. "That's what I'm tryin' to tell you, Lou. You're already trapped here. It's done."

"We had a bargain. I won our fight."

"You cheated, and I lied," Jay said, shrugging. "I needed to see if you'd remember, and you did. There's no actual way off this island without Peter."

"You . . . you lied?" Heat flashed across her face. Benji and Henry moved aside as Lou drifted across the room, weightless in her fury. "You made a bargain without ever intending to honour it. Mother warned me about the empty promises of men. But I never thought children capable of such deceit."

Benji groaned. "Aw, Lou, that's not fair. We didn't want to do this to you. It just sort of . . . happened. At least you found us before the pirates got you. That would have been a lot worse, you know."

"I understand, Benji." She turned away and pressed her palms into the wall, slid them up the rough dirt until her fingertips grazed the ceiling. The docks and the market and the elderly man selling straw dolls drifted behind her eyes. Flecks of earth came free under her touch, raining down on her head like stars. Stars. Lou's pulse quickened at the sudden surge of hope in her chest. "I cannot believe I almost forgot. There was a man by the docks. He said something—oh!"

"Crickets, what's she goin' on about now, boss?" Didi asked.

Lou turned to six pairs of eyes blinking up at her. "How do you touch the stars?"

Jay's brows shot into his hair. "What didja say?"

"A man selling straw dolls said the only way off the island was to touch the stars. It sounded like nonsense, but that was before I found out my imaginary childhood friend was flesh and blood. But it seems as though you may already know something about this."

Jay dropped into a chair and buried his face in his hands. "Well, sure. It's a story Peter tells all of us. Touch the stars, and you can get off the island. Touch the stars, and you can go home. It's a load of crocodile dung, if you ask me."

"Why?" Lou asked.

"From what I can tell, only one of us has ever touched the stars and come back to talk about it, and that's Peter. Tons of us have tried, but none of 'em ever came back. They just disappeared, poof, easy peasy, like they never existed. Only Peter knows how to do it, and sure, he tells us to try, but he's never given us any way to actually *do* it."

"Then we free Peter, and he will help put the island right. If he cannot help us touch the stars, he can secure my passage home at the very least."

Jay laughed. "Oh, sure. Let's just storm the ship and break Peter out of the brig. The only time the ship's docked is at night, and the pirates patrol the cove to keep us all out. Then there're the tribes, the fairies, Blackbeard—"

"I did not ask for your assessment of the difficulty of the task," Lou said firmly. "Only if it was a possible way to return me to my home."

The corner of Henry's mouth twitched, and even Didi grinned. "You know, boss," she said, "the fancy lady's growin' on me a bit."

Blue eyes peeked out from between Jay's fingers. "Peter found a way off the island by touchin' the stars. It gave him a lot of power, but instead of usin' that power to leave for good, he decided to stay here forever and torture us. So long as he got to bring others back from the Land of the Grown and could move between worlds whenever he wanted, he was happy. See, the island made him king. He makes the rules. I don't know what's possible if we get him out. Honest, I don't."

"We can ask him," Lou said. "How difficult can it truly be if you've all survived here, alone, for so long?"

Jay slumped further in his seat. "The pirates raided his den a couple moons back and took him prisoner. He's gone. Done for. Ever since he got grabbed, nothin's gone right; we've been gettin' storms, things are disappearin' and changin' place. The sea monster's gettin' powerful again after years of bein' controlled by Soul Rock, and the mermaids lose their temper more than they ever did. Everythin's upside down, but the pirates won't give him up."

There they were—the creatures from Rose's stories. Sea monsters. Pirates. Mermaids. All spoken about as though they were as commonplace as cats . . . or birds. While Jay defended his choices, seemed to relish them, even, Lou's heart broke at the life he must have led to accept an empty existence surrounded by monsters.

"Peter was pretty nasty," Jay continued. "He lied, he stole, he killed when he could. He got what he deserved, no matter what price we need to pay. I'm just sorry Timber's gone. He was a good kid."

"Who cares about Timber?" Didi plucked a peach from Benji's hands. "He chose to stay with Peter instead of joinin' us. If you ask me, he got what was comin' to him too."

"Do you understand what you are saying?" Lou asked. "You're dooming yourselves by leaving Peter with the pirates. You're dooming me."

At that, Sammy detached himself from the shadows, greeting Lou with eyes brimming with tears. "This is my fault, Lou. I didn't mean to make so much trouble, but Jay missed you a lot, and we all just want him to be happy. I don't know how I did this."

One of the lanterns spluttered into darkness. Shadows crawled over the den, stretching and shaping themselves until they were taller. Leaner. *Older.* Trapped in a place with no way out. Doomed to immortality. And now even that small prize of eternal life had been revoked.

"I am not upset with you, Sammy." She sank to her knees so he could see her sincerity. "I cannot blame you for doing what you thought was right. My sister, Rosie, often leads with her heart too. It is a gift," she said. Sammy offered her a quivering smile, and she patted his arm. "You can help me, if you like. I do not know this place or the people who live here. If we are to free Peter, I cannot do it alone."

Jay laughed. "I told you. The pirates have Peter on their ship in the cove. After the sun goes down, they hold the beach. If they catch us on their land, they'll slice us to ribbons. And that's before we even get to the ship."

Kiran looped his arm around his sister's shoulders, pulling her close. "Yeah, and then there're the guards patrolling the deck, the patrols down in the brig, the locks with no keys, and the sea monster that can swallow us up anytime she feels like," he said. "We can't take all of 'em at once."

"I dunno," Didi said under her breath. "I'd risk it to get *her* outta here."

"That all sounds quite troublesome, to be sure," Lou said, refusing to be deterred. "But as I see it, we are doomed if we do nothing."

Silence was louder than the constant arguments and cheers over simple games. Jay marched toward her and gathered Sammy into his arms. "Lou, you're not stormin' Blackbeard's ship."

"I agree, I do not have a hope of succeeding on my own." She addressed him alone; the others would stay behind at his say-so, or they would join her in any reckless plan she proposed. If she was to return home, it was only with Jay's approval.

Win one, win them all.

Her vision blurred, and her throat grew thick, but the truth was a slippery thing. "I do not know this place or any of these people. If you break your bargain with me, I cannot hope to succeed."

"You growns break bargains all the time," Jay said, shrugging.

"And I did not take you for a pirate whose word is worthless."

His lips peeled back from his teeth in a wolflike sneer. "I'm no pirate."

"Breaking a promise to me is bad form. And *that* is what a pirate does, is it not?"

The air drained from the room. Jay's mouth hung wide "Where didja hear that?"

"It is an expression. It means you have no honour."

"I know what it means."

A pregnant silence fell between them. But, as an eternal child with the eternal openness of childhood, emotions sat plainly on his face, unburdened by deception and embarrassment meant to twist them into something appropriate. The children pressed in together, hands finding hands, and their shadows shrank away, shifting back into reflections of the innocent youths she'd first met. If it weren't for the fear of never seeing Rose again and disappointing her mother in the most profound way, Lou might have succumbed to guilt over forcing them all to follow her into danger.

"All right," Jay said, breaking the quiet. "What's the plan, *Louisa*?"

Relief eased the pain in her chest, and she smiled at him. "How many swords do you have?"

CHAPTER 13

LOU

AGE TEN – ONE MONTH TO GO

My birthday was three days ago. No one remembered it.
I'd made the mistake of imagining their smiles as I
threw open the door and raced down the stairs.
Father would tell me how much taller I looked, and Mother would
insist on making roast chicken for dinner, no matter how sore she
was from the baby's terrible weight. Roast chicken was my
favourite, and Mother had never ignored a request for it on my
birthday. What I found instead was an open door at the end of the
second floor hall, light dripping through the new lace curtains.
Mother and Father laughed together, their heads bent over a
polished dresser, one of Father's hands warming Mother's belly.
The room, now with its careful arrangements of fresh flowers on a
side table, a hand-knitted blanket draped over the armrest of a new
rocking chair, and freshly laundered clothes piled on an armoire,
was ready. And it was uglier than any pirate.

I'd waited with impatience for my birthday to come. I was glad
when it was over.

The house was heavy with the first whispers of autumn;
burning leaves, cinnamon, and the tang of pine mingled in the

stale air. Father was still at work while Mother tottered around the gardens, trimming the very tops of the rose bushes, her midsection much too round and cumbersome to allow her to tackle anything lower down. Every one of her groans, every caress and hidden smile, registered like a blade cutting fine slices in my flesh. What lurked beneath that taut pink globe of skin would soon sleep in the gauzy bed by the pretty window and call me sister.

It was a good thing, then, that pirates like me knew the importance of guarding their treasure.

I stomped up and down the upstairs hall in bare feet, knowing it mattered little to Mother if I made any noise. The door to its —*no*—his or her room stared back at me, daring me to step inside. I didn't have to like the baby to protect it. That door was a portal to the sea monster's home, a barred gate into a pirate's brig. Benji lived there now, a sacrifice made in the spirit of a truce. A prisoner. He was lost to me, but he still called my name from within that awful room. Sometimes, in the night, when Jay was away and water dripped behind my walls, I could hear him. I regretted his pain at our separation. Perhaps I would take him back one day. Until then, he was a sacrifice I needed to make.

I ran my fingers over the floral wallpaper in the hall. Every so often, my hands paused over a rosebud; I pressed my fingers down the dark centre, the curve of my skin aligning perfectly with the soft print. The day was quiet, as every other day was.

I was bored of it already.

"Hiya."

I pulled my hand back and turned toward the voice. My nails raked the wall with the swipe of a wildcat, carving one of the buds in half. "Jay! You're back!"

The brim of a straw hat buried his eyes in shadow. "Who'd you expect? Of course I'm back. I never really left."

"You haven't visited me. I wasn't expecting to see you anymore." I tried for accusatory—outraged, even. But when I spoke, the crackle in my voice betrayed me. "Why did you go away?"

He shrugged. "I been busy. Plus, you know how it gets on the island. There're pirates to fight and kids to raid with."

"Of course." I winced at the sting of his words.

"I have other friends, you know. Good ones. Ones with the time to have fun with me instead of playin' pirates with their daddy and followin' their momma around the house like some baby bird."

If I were older, I might have been strong enough to tell him I was hurt. That was one of the things I wanted to be as a grown: strong. I wanted to tell him I missed him and not be embarrassed by it. Older me would be strong and powerful and speak everything she thought. But I was still too small despite having just had a birthday, and no one listened to me. Later I would understand that no one listened to older women either. But in that moment, I could only worry about Jay and his other friends living a life without me.

On an island without me.

Playing games . . . without me.

"But you don't trust some of the boys you play with," I said. "You said Peter is the worst boy of them all. You said he makes you sad sometimes when he leaves you behind and keeps his secrets. I never keep any secrets from you."

"At least he's always around if I need him."

I contemplated my toes: too bare, obscene against the plush cream runner down the upstairs hall. "Oh. Well, I'm glad for you, then."

"You are?" Jay picked at a worn spot on the banister, the wood chipped from a previous encounter with a pirate's sword. "Why?"

You look older, I thought. *Why do you look older?* "Because you seem to have had a nice time," I said instead, making myself bold. "And I only want you to be happy."

"Coulda fooled me. You're always busy now."

"I'm not! And even if I was, you didn't have to leave for so long. I left my window open for you every night."

He leaned far over the rail and looked down to the main floor, then back at long corridor caging us in together. Yes, I had missed him—but I'd also survived without him. I'd lived without the constant distraction and safety I'd come to expect from him. My heart still ached, and the colours continued to bleed from our home like a wound that would never heal, but I'd *survived*. And that was something. That was something real that I could hold on to if he ever left me again.

"Well, I'm here now," Jay said, smearing dirt from the sole of his boot on the pale runner. *I'll have to clean that.* "And I have an idea, if you're up to it."

I grinned. "Do we have some pirate ships to raid?"

"Nope."

"The Briarwood, then. It's so nice out today. We could walk down to the lake, and you could show me how to skip rocks."

"I already tried that. You never get it right."

"All the more reason to practice. I can do it; I know I can." I wanted to rip the hat from his head just to gaze into those eyes and see how thick the frost was. "What do you say?"

"I got a better idea." Jay's smile was wicked, and I couldn't help but take a step back at the changes in him. His shadow was longer, his legs thicker in the same linen pants he liked to wear, with more ankle to show below the hem. There was still a familiar roundness to his cheeks, a golden tan hinting of summer days spent in the sun, but the angles had changed. To another, the changes were insubstantial. But I knew better, and I didn't like it.

"What kind of idea?" I asked. It was better to speak of games.

"It's a new adventure—unless you're scared." There was a challenge in his tone that set my teeth on edge and roused the slumbering tiger in my belly. "You probably are. Never mind."

"No, I want to play."

"Where are your parents?"

Strange question. That never mattered before. "Out. Why?"

"Let's go." He slipped past me, his steps soundless as they pressed deep imprints into the rug. *How long will it take to get the mud out of the runner?* We slunk away from my room, past the linen closet with the slightly off-centre door on bright brass hinges, all the way down to *the* room. My feet stalled, and my stomach tightened.

"Jay, what game is this?"

He twisted the knob. Errant drops of dried paint crackled as the door peeled open. "Just explorin', for now. Come on."

"That's the baby's room." I hovered in the corridor, heart racing. "There isn't anything fun to do there."

"Oh, that's right. Your momma's havin' another kid."

"You knew that already."

Jay disappeared inside, and I had no choice but to follow.

"We shouldn't be in here. Mother only just finished decorating."

"Then we should see how it looks, don'tcha think?"

I hated admitting to myself that the baby's room was prettier than mine. I wanted it to be ugly, but the dust ruffles were soft, the dark wood of ornate tables stacked with jars and stuffed toys pristine and untouched. A vase of hand-painted porcelain held a bouquet of daisies. I had been there when Mother had carefully placed it to hide the hairline crack on one side. She had chosen the vase from among her own mother's old belongings, a family heirloom passed from her to the precious new baby.

It should have sat on my dresser.

But then again, I should have had a birthday.

Our presence was a violation. If anyone was going to defile the room, it should have been me. Alone.

"We should leave," I said.

He snorted. "Why?"

"Mother won't like it."

"You can wait outside if you're too scared." Jay pulled aside the lace cover of the baby's bed and flipped it back.

"Don't touch that!"

A flush painted his cheeks as he lifted Benji from his nest of blankets. "What's he doin' here?"

"I gave him."

"You . . . gave him."

"To the baby." The room grew warm. "It's a gift."

"But he's yours."

My palms grew slick, my mouth dry. "He was mine, and now he isn't. He doesn't belong in my room anymore."

Jay ran a thumb across Benji Bear's nose and stared intently into his shiny black eyes. His chest heaved, ribs straining against the already-struggling buttons of his shirt. The quiet had a pulse; it was heavy, laced with blood and life and hate, all things that moved a heart to beat. He pulled his elbow back and thrust Benji at the wall with a deafening scream.

The carpet. The footprints. There is going to be such a mess.

Benji crashed into the vase, knocking it to the floor. If it had been whole, the thick carpet might have saved it from shattering. But the tiny fracture on the body—though fine and easily disguised—was a weakness, and weaknesses were easily exploited; the heirloom shattered to dust and sharp edges. A white shard rested beside the bear's loose eye, and I bit back the tears.

"So, my game is called Save the Mermaid. You know it?" Jay flipped a picture book onto the floor, the thud followed closely by the loud bang of a drawer opening and closing with abrupt force.

"Please, Jay. Stop."

But he ignored me, prowling the edges of the room like a caged panther. A stack of neatly folded pajamas crumpled at his feet, arms and legs woven of fine cotton twisting at unnatural angles. "Well, do you? It's not my favourite game, but I thought it could be fun to play in here."

I followed him closely, replacing the book, picking up the clothes, righting the pillows he'd knocked off the wooden rocker.

"Let's go back to my room and play your game," I said. "I don't mind a mess in there."

"I'm bored of being in your room all the time." He rounded on me. Hate. That was what hate looked like. "You wanna start hidin' me from your parents?"

"I do not." Do I? *No, not really.*

The air between us reeked of the sea gone bad: rotten fish baked in salt and left to fester in the sun during low tide. I could hear the sea if I strained my ears. It was a soft wash of waves hidden within the walls. It was awful.

"You can be the pirate, and I'll be the prince tryin' to get back the mermaid you stole," Jay said. "Fun, huh?"

"You . . . You want *me* to be the pirate?"

"I'm givin' you what you always wanted." He faced the window, letting the gauzy curtains drip through his fingers like water. "Now you give me what I want. The mermaid—give her *back*."

"Jay, you're ruining the room."

The room.

The carpet.

Benji, Benji covered in broken pieces, my poor Benji.

Jay tore the curtain off the wall, flooding me with light. I couldn't overcome him if I tried; he was already by the door, twisting a sconce off the wall and letting it sail to the ground.

At play, I was a pirate, a mermaid, a ruler, and a conqueror in one. At home, I was a girl. There was no greater gap between those worlds.

My heart jackrabbited behind my ribs, daylight making the room too warm. "Jay, please—"

"I said give her *back to me*!" His anger was real, solid enough to touch, untamed by the rules she followed. Anger was always more powerful in the hands of those unburdened by those rules.

"You're ruining everything!" I cried. "I'll get in trouble!"

With a wicked grin, he popped the top off a pot of petroleum jelly, dipped four fingers inside, and smeared a thick greasy streak across the newly painted wall.

Father's work, all his hard work from his own hands . . . ruined.

"Just give her back, and I'll stop."

A girl, just a girl.

I jumped, itching to hit him, to pummel him with my fists until he cried—until he *screamed*. Not because of any sense of duty to the baby; I couldn't stand to give Mother another reason to hate me and Father another reason to worry about Mother hating me. But Jay was too quick, and I knew better than to try. "You're scaring me," I said instead, trying and failing to still my bottom lip. "I want you to stop."

"I will as soon as you let her go."

"Who?"

"My friend! You have her tied up in a cave on Soul Rock, and I want her back!"

I'd never seen Soul Rock. I didn't know any of his friends. Right then, all I knew was terror and rage and how small I truly was. Mother was right—I wasn't enough. "I'm tired of this game. I . . . I don't want to play anymore."

Jay's hand stilled over a stack of cloth diapers for one blissful moment. Could I walk out of the room and leave him behind? I could tackle the carpet first; the stiff brush was in the linen closet, the tap on Silverton Lane brimming with clean water. It was still possible to erase the muddy boot prints and reverse any trace of Jay's destruction. Of his existence.

I would make it right.

I needed to make it right.

And if I couldn't, I would take my punishment and be glad.

"Fine, I'll leave you alone," Jay said. But he didn't move; both hands gripped the side of the bassinet. "*Pirate.*"

Jay pushed—hard. The bed capsized, spilling fragrant blankets of the softest muslin over the wreckage. He stepped onto the lace canopy, a delicate piece carefully chosen by Mother now rendered a common scrap of fabric marred by sandy footprints.

Picture frames rained to the floor, each one snapping off its nail—*tic, tic, tic.*

More clothes, more toys, all settling around us like ash from a bonfire.

I fell to my knees as Jay made a plaything of Mother's favourite room.

I'd spent so many terrible years wishing for a friend to understand me. Years of hope and sadness and monstrous darkness that only Jay had managed to keep at bay. Years of Mother longing for another child, then putting her entire heart into the possibility of every memory she could have with it. I'd been there through every moment.

It took only minutes to destroy both the room and the sanctuary Jay had always offered. Minutes. And all I could do was watch.

CHAPTER 14

It was easy to convince a group of children to play with knives.

The den was absent of any timepiece, so minutes were measured in snack breaks while hours were marked by supply replenishment runs and turns with the sword. Lou was allowed brief stints above ground, always supervised, never left in peace with her thoughts.

As much as she hated to admit it, the island truly was beautiful. Lights flitted from branch to branch—fairies, Sammy said. Pests, Didi complained. But to Lou, they were pinpricks of hope in an emerald world marked by pastel blooms and soothing bird-song. If it weren't for Rose and Mother, she could imagine the appeal of living there forever. While she hadn't understood it before, Lou recognized the children really were free—a sort of freedom she never had on Silverton Lane, even as a grown woman.

One disadvantage to their freedom, other than being limited to exploring the land assigned to them by Peter, was that the children viewed sleep as a supreme waste of time. The prospect of an upcoming battle with the pirates fuelled them into a frenzy, making it impossible for Lou to rest for very long. Instead, she sharpened knives, reviewed strategy, and memorized maps while the children played, and her bedding grew cold.

Lou's only reprieve was the time she spent in *the circle*. The game was simple: face your opponent while the others watch, a wooden sword in hand, and do your best to cut down your foe. Slash, lunge, attack.

Lou forced her arm forward into a direct strike. Didi's sword slammed down on her wrist.

"Ow!" Tears sprung up in Lou's eyes, but she bowed to the girl who'd landed the blow anyway. Jay said that was good form. After all, she wanted to do well if that meant finally leaving the den. "That was quite good, Didi. I cannot seem to win against you."

"I know." Didi twisted the blade in a wide arc before settling it comfortably over her shoulder. "Wanna go again?"

I'd like to sleep. Her wrist stung; her pride stung worse. "Yes, of course. Can you teach me how to block that sort of attack? You seem to use it quite a bit."

"It's no fun if you know how to stop me."

"I thought the purpose was for me to learn," Lou said through her teeth. *Be kind. They're only children. Think of Rose.*

"I think you're doing great, Miss Webber," Benji offered. He stood at the outer edge of the circle, waiting his turn with a swollen lip from the constant gnawing. "I'm worse than you, if that makes you feel any better."

Lou smiled. "It does, Benji. That is very sweet."

Didi scowled. "*Miss Webber?* Who is she, your schoolteacher? Just call her Lou. Or grown, for all I care. Pretty soon, that's all she's gonna be."

Benji's face reddened. Lou gave Didi a silencing look, but her voice was even with forced calm when she turned back to the boy. "I don't mind either name, Benji. Call me whatever you like."

"Crickets, can we get on with this already? And if you're gonna make this any fun for me, you might as well gimme a little challenge. Keep your knees bent, like this." Didi bounced on the balls of her feet, boots grinding the dirt. "Makes you quicker. Gives 'em less of a chance to stab you."

"I'll try that. Thank you."

"And quit dancin' around like you're runnin' away from a swarm of bees. I swear, if I gotta do another round fightin' a ballerina, I might as well touch the stars myself and end it for good. Plus, it makes you look like you don't know nothin' about swords or fightin'."

Lou suppressed an unexpected smile. "Well, I don't."

Didi frowned, black paint shining around her ebony eyes. "Yeah, butcha never let 'em see it. You got me?"

"I do." *Smile. Bow. Repeat.*

And around went the wheel once more.

They all had a chance to practice, Lou's turn coming up more often than the others. Jay disliked the idea of her in the fray—she was an unwanted distraction—but the risk she posed by being unarmed or helpless was worse. Jay arranged the pairings, swapping fighters for those sent to gather food. While Didi favoured the bow, she handled a sword with confidence and agility. She would be hard to kill. Benji's idea of sparring involved regular fumbling of his sword and apologetic hugs, but he was eager to improve. Henry, however, watched in silence from his cot, eyes never leaving the fight, with Sammy curled up beside him.

"Okay, boys, bring it in!" Jay called. When Didi struck him with an icy glare, he corrected himself with a roll of his eyes. "Right, boys *and* girls. I want you to quit what you're doin' and get some sleep. We move tomorrow after dark."

Everyone cheered but Lou. Her legs were numb, her hair matted with sweat and oil. She longed for a bath with some lavender soap, but the most Jay could muster was a few pails of water from a nearby creek reeking of sulphur. The clean water was to drink, and both the lagoon and fairy stream was off-limits until they could ensure there were no pirates around. Only Henry remained stoic throughout; when Lou's eyes met his, she recognized her own worry curled up there like a poisonous snake.

"Here are your posts," Jay said, pointing to them each in turn. "Sammy, you'll be our runner. The Blues move fast, and you're our quickest kid, so your job's important. Henry, you're the lookout. You'll stay up the cliff in the trees and signal Benji, Didi, and Kiran when the fight's about to start. When it does, I breach the ship. Easy peasy, poke your knees-y."

Benji lifted his arm. "Sorry, Jay. But do I have to fight?"

Jay frowned. "You're a fine swordsman, Benji. You just need a bit of confidence is all. You'll do me proud, I know it."

Didi snorted. "He can't even hold a dagger without droppin' it, boss. Benji stinks."

Benji flushed but did not argue. "I'd only make a bigger mess for you, and the twins will have to save me."

Kiran groaned. "Don't call us that, Benji! We got names."

"Sorry, sorry. Look, would it be all right if I stay with Henry at the lookout point? I mean, I can understand him even when he can't talk. If something goes wrong, I can let you know quicker."

Didi huffed and kicked her toe in the sand. "For what it's worth, I'm with Benji. How's Henry s'posed to let us know a Red or a Blue or a stinkin' peg leg is on our tail after dark? Smoke signal? Do a dance in a big tree and hope we see it before we get our throats cut? Kiran and I can handle the fight on our own."

Henry's head dropped. Sammy leaned into his side, leaving the boy's other side free for Benji.

"Fine," Jay said at last. "Benji, you can keep watch lower down on the cliff while Henry stays up in the trees. You can keep contact and cover more ground."

"What about me?" Lou asked, willing herself to look away from Henry's slouched form. "Where should I go?"

Jay marched to his usual seat, took a swig from a cup, and tore a piece of stale bread off an old loaf. When the silence was swollen enough to burst, he pulled out a whetstone and set to work sharpening his dagger.

"Jay," Lou prompted, "what is my role?"

"You'll be stayin' here," he muttered, never meeting her eyes. "You can stay in the den and wait for us to come back. Guard the place, the food."

"Excuse me? You brought me here against my will, tied me up, and let me live in absolute squalor, and you expect me to trust you'll set me free once you get your hands on this boy? What if you change your mind once you're there? Or if you make a deal with Peter? Or—"

"Lou, stop." Jay looked up. "I wouldn't lie to you. On my honour, I'll do everythin' I can to get Peter out and send you home. Don't know why you even wanna go back to that place, but—"

"Your *honour* is precisely the reason I doubt your intentions," Lou said, cheeks burning. "I do not trust you to keep your word."

"Well, my word's all you got and it's all I can give. What more do you want?"

"To not have been kept prisoner by you, for starters."

Jay's hand stalled midway up the blade. "This mission is ridiculous, but I told you I'd help. I'm lettin' my boys—"

"And girls!"

"Ugh, yeah, Didi, *and girls*, take a big risk for you. I'm this group's leader, so we do things my way, or we don't do them at all. Get me?"

Lou curled her hands into fists. "I insist on being there when you rescue Peter."

"I don't—"

"If you leave me here, I will simply follow you."

"I'll tie you up again."

"I've gotten good enough with a sword to make you pay if you try."

Didi arched a brow and let out a low whistle. "I like her style."

The blade and stone clattered onto the table. "Fine, you can come!" Jay said. "But you follow *my* lead and do everythin' I say. I say run, you run. I say be quiet and stop being a pain, you—"

"Punch you in the nose." Lou glared at him openly while Kiran crowed with laughter. "We have an understanding, then. Now, I'd like to get some rest before you change your mind and have us sparring until morning. Good night, everyone."

She should have eaten, but her stomach was in knots. The arguments, their voices, and the way the children slopped food down their fronts and never wiped themselves clean was all too much. They were only children—innocent abandoned children who didn't know better—but they were a reminder of Rose, and she couldn't bear to be near them another moment.

Lou lay down on her bed of palm leaves and old clothing. The makeshift bedding reeked of pipe smoke and sweat. The scent sticked to her skin, giving her a headache. But it was better than the ground. Marginally.

"Uh, Lou? Sorry to bug you, but I'm just bringin' you these." A pile of clothes fell into her lap. Sammy stood over her, bare toes wriggling in the sand.

"What is this?" Lou lifted both items, black stains caked into the cloth. "It smells awful."

"Pants and a shirt. I lifted them off a pirate a few years ago. They're too big for any of us, and you can't be wearin' a dress durin' a fight."

A few years ago. Lou dropped the clothes beside her. "I don't suppose any of you thought to wash these."

"Not really."

"I see."

Sammy peeked over the rim of his glasses. "We can wash them tomorrow, if you want. I'll bring you to my favourite place. The water's clean, and the crocs don't travel that far from the swamp. It's not close, but at least the pirates won't be there. Jay might let us go alone."

He really was small, a willow branch waving in the breeze. Lou buried the borrowed clothes under some leaves to muffle the smell. "I would appreciate that very much, Sammy. Thank you. Won't you be in trouble if Jay sees you being so courteous? I *am* still a prisoner until tomorrow after all."

"Jay asked me to get them to you. He wants you to be okay."

"I'm not sure that will be possible. Not until I get home." *Perhaps not even then.* Lou smiled, pushing the thought deep down with the rest of the bleak grey things. "These clothes will do just fine once they are washed. It will give me a chance to clean my dress too." She leaned back on her elbows, waiting for Sammy to return to Jay, where he always went to sleep. But the boy stood still, toes burrowing deeper. "Was there something else, Sammy?"

"I really didn't think you'd get stuck here. I only thought that you could visit. Maybe."

She smiled; she couldn't help it. Sammy was a reminder of better things, of how Rose used to be. "I forgive you, Sammy. Besides, I'll be back home tomorrow."

Still, he didn't move. "Jay's happy you're here, you know. I'm sure he'd be okay if you stayed, even if you *are* old."

Jay crouched on the ground, picking his teeth with his dagger and staring sullenly at his boots.

"Oh, yes," Lou muttered. "He looks ecstatic."

"He missed you. That's why he broke off from Peter, you know. He was Peter's right hand his whole life on the island until he got separated from you."

Lou stifled a yawn. "He never mentioned that."

Sammy shrugged. "It hurt him pretty bad when Peter ordered him to stay away."

"Why would Peter order that? Did I do something wrong?"

"Oh, no." Sammy toyed with a loose thread at his collar, glasses sliding down his nose. "You grew up. It was quick too; I don't think Jay expected it."

"That sort of thing does have a way of creeping up on you."

"I tried to make it better for him, but it never helped. *You* help. You were his best friend," Sammy whispered. "I was too small to be allowed a friend in the Land of the Grown, but Jay had tons. And you were his favourite."

"Is that right?"

He nodded. "Try not to stay too mad at him, 'kay?"

Lou smiled despite the heaviness of sleep. "I'll do my best. Is that all right with you?"

"Yep." Sammy bit his bottom lip, swinging his arms at his sides. "Can I sleep here with you tonight?"

"What?"

"I mean, if you don't want me to, I'll understand. But I like you, and I never had a big sister. Didi doesn't count. She don't like sharin'."

A sister. She was already a sister to someone who needed her. She'd made a commitment long ago to be an anchor for Rose, an oath so important it had left a permanent brand on her memory. Once, not too long ago, she'd thought her heart too full to welcome any other love. But the boy before her chipped away at that conviction with his eyes as kind as Rose's, his acceptance of her a balm on her anxiety. In that moment, she might have liked to be Sammy's sister and live in a home strong enough to keep the water at bay.

"Get in, then," Lou said, shifting to make space. "The leaves are quite comfortable."

Sammy climbed in, curled up on his side, and slid his hands under his cheek. "Thanks, Lou. That's real nice of you."

She smiled, laying herself flat. "You know, I can see why Jay loves you so much."

"Yeah, me too."

She laughed, her muscles easing. Sammy's eyelids drooped. His mouth fell open. His breathing slowed. "Sammy?" Lou whispered.

"Hmm?"

"What you said . . . Is it true that Jay was not allowed to see me anymore or is that just something you imagined?"

It was a moment before Sammy answered, his words already bleeding together. "That's the rule of the island. But Jay said you grew up too fast. You weren't s'posed to. He didn't get to say g'bye, and it made him so sad."

The roots on the ceiling twisted, and a quake shook the earth. A fissure divided the ceiling into halves, giving the earth a wide snarl. A low moan vibrated in the walls. No one paid any of it any mind. After all, it was no secret the island was crumbling.

Kiran and Didi shared a cot of twigs and moss beside Benji and Henry. Jay settled his back against a wall and pulled a patchwork quilt over his knees. His eyes met Lou's over Sammy's head for the briefest second before he turned away.

"Do you think Jay would have rescued Peter on his own?" she asked. "To save your lives, do you think he would have done it?"

Sammy's eyes fluttered open. "Him and Peter . . . It didn't end too good. I'm not sure he thinks he's worth savin' anymore. But he would try to help you." He sighed. "I'm sorry again, Lou. This isn't a place for someone like you."

She nodded, grateful for the darkness. "Go to sleep. Tomorrow I'll be gone, and Jay can go back to being miserable. But at least you will all be safe."

Sammy buried his face in her arm, nestling deep. The warmth

of his cheek seeped through the sleeve of her dress and warmed her blood. It was the heat of comfort and trust and absolute innocence. If she could carry a small piece of that trust with her tomorrow, she might not be so afraid.

If.

It was a small word for something that filled her with so much dread.

Tomorrow they would face the pirates together.

Tomorrow the strange children with their childish games would be a dream once more.

Tomorrow she would go back to her duties and the family she left behind to . . . what?

I can go back to forgetting any of this exists.

Lou found Sammy's hand and gripped it tight. When he squeezed back, eyes shut to the world, she knew that this time, forgetting might not be so simple.

CHAPTER 15

LOU

THE DAY

Broken things sometimes could not be fixed. I used to think they could be. But then I recalled Mother's face the moment she saw the baby's room the day it was destroyed. She hadn't laid eyes on me since then. Being ignored for a week was awful. Forgiveness, like love, was conditional. She couldn't give me either thing unless we were whole. And something between Mother and I was the bad kind of broken.

It had also been a week since I'd last seen Jay. He'd left the mess to me, a thousand scraps of Mother's greatest dream scattered across the carpet. I couldn't say I missed him.

Earlier that summer, the clouds had converged over our house like an omen, grey and purple ripples sitting so low I could feel the moisture feathering my skin. The storm had a texture, a fragrance, a blend of colours so unique I remembered it still. Now Silverton Lane was as quiet and drab as one of my charcoal drawings. I paced the edge of the Briarwood, hoping to catch any sign of life, but it, too, was curiously grey; the leaves were the colour of storm clouds, the bark carved in strokes of coal. Even the birds had sensed the plague settling over my world and abandoned our little corner of it for something better.

A rumble sounded overhead. The sky shattered, and a billion raindrops like glass shards fell to the earth. The thick scent of earth and pine rose from the forest, riding the hazy waves of humidity. The trees provided enough cover from the rain, and I waited out the storm under their protective arms.

A twig snapped behind me. I sighed, recognizing his presence. I'd know him anywhere—the tentative steps usually reserved for visits after dark, the way the scents of the wind and forest clung to his skin. Jay had imprinted himself onto my heart and soul. His shame became my guilt, his sorrow my forgiveness. Forever we danced. Forever I would love and resent him.

"Sorry I took so long to come back." Jay leaned against a walnut tree, his eyes trained in the direction of my home across the yard. With one foot crossed over an ankle and his arms laced across his chest, he was the picture of ease. Except for the tightening around the eyes, a slight pinch that spoke louder than any words, he might have been coming for a regular visit. I knew better.

"I called for you, Jay."

"I know."

"I left the window open for you every night. I needed help cleaning the room, dealing with Mother. You've always been there when I needed you before."

He looked away. "I *know*. I wanted to come."

"But you didn't."

Silence. There was nothing for him to say. Perhaps nothing was better than a lie.

"Didja get in trouble?" he asked, fingers toying with a fold of his shirt.

"What do you think?"

He toed the earth, uprooting rocks and sending them skittering across the dirt. "I thought that's what you wanted, you know. I thought I was doin' you a favour."

I frowned. "You thought I wanted you to destroy the baby's room? You ruined everything! Mother and Father were so upset; they thought I'd done it, no matter how much I told them I didn't."

"But you don't care what *she* thinks, and your daddy'll forgive you." He pushed off the tree and circled around until we stood face to face. My head came up to his chin, higher than it had before. I hadn't noticed it before, but I was catching up to him in more ways than one. "I thought you don't want that baby to come anyway."

"I *don't*," I said. He didn't understand; that was happening too often now. "But that does not give you permission to break things and get me into trouble."

"Maybe she'll believe it was me if we go see her together."

Lou snorted. "Mother doesn't believe you exist, Jay. You know that."

"Right. I forgot." He stared at his shoes, puckering his lips, and the rain fell and fell. "I'm sorry, Lou. Really. Please don't be mad."

I crossed my arms, my heart thawing as I knew it would. "Promise me it won't happen again. Promise me you won't make a fuss like that when Mother and Father come home today."

"Deal," Jay said at once, his grin dazzling. The air between us cleared, and I imagined us running through the woods, finding new branches to spar with, and forgetting the world.

Forgetting what day it was.

The day.

Today.

"So, what's special about today?" he asked as though my thoughts were etched on my face. The storm clouds rolled and thumped, unleashing their sorrow on the forest, but we were safe.

Together. "You have some special knittin' to do to win back Mommy's love?"

"Don't tease. My brother will be coming home today."

"So, it's a wittle baby boy, huh?"

My cheeks grew warm. "I don't know. Mother always says that God will answer our prayers if we pray for something enough. And I pray for a brother."

"God don't owe you a thing," Jay said. "No one's listenin' to you but me. Are . . . Are you jealous of the baby?"

Yes. "No." The truth was rarely a pretty thing, and mine was the ugliest of all. "What if it *is* a girl and she takes my clothes and ruins my things?" I asked, willing him to understand. "If it's a boy, he won't like my things and I can keep them for myself."

"And Mommy won't have to pick the best sister, right?"

Yes. "That isn't what I meant." But it was, and the quirk of his lips told me he knew it too. "What if I *am* a little jealous? Is it so bad to want some attention? I hardly get any now, and if it is a girl, she might be prettier, or smarter, or have better needlework, or—"

"All right, all right, I get it." Jay's smile was warm, a drop of sunlight pushing against the rain. "I seen some babies on the island once or twice, and it was so much work. They don't sleep, they slow you down, they make you sloppy. I'm tellin' you, babies ruin everythin'. No one will love it more than you. Got it?"

I frowned into the woods. With Jay beside me, the *pat, pat, pat* of raindrops was almost soothing. "I hope you're right," I said. "I'll be better, I think. I'll be good to the baby. A good big sister."

"I'm always right, *little bird*. And I know you will be."

"I just don't understand why they needed another."

The faint *clop* of hooves pulled Jay's gaze away from me. A thin veil of leaves separated us from my home, ensuring the small bubble around us remained intact. If I could stay there a little longer, I could almost convince myself that my aunt and cousin weren't in the house readying the room at the end of the hall. I could imagine bathing and eating and brushing my hair before bed and bidding Mother and Father a stiff good night. The routine didn't always make me happy, but it was a known unhappiness— and there was something beautiful about a predictable future, even if it was flawed.

"Growns are never happy with what they got, Lou," Jay said. "They could have the world, and they'd still want more. Your parents bringin' another baby home's got nothin' to do with you and everythin' to do with greed. Growns kill magic like a dagger to the heart."

I nodded, wishing I could believe his words were enough to make me feel better. They weren't.

The carriage pulled up to our door, two black mares huffing into the sandy walkway. Father stepped out first, patting his jacket before pulling a keyring from his trouser pocket. He ran to open Mother's door, and I looked away.

"I have to go," I whispered. "They'll wonder why I am not there to greet the baby. Will you come with me?"

Jay wrinkled his nose. "I dunno, Lou. I don't like babies."

"Please. You owe me that much after what you did."

He sighed, staring past the trees. "You sure?"

"I don't want to be alone. Just come in for a little while, and if you don't like it, you can go. It would mean everything to me."

He grumbled under his breath. Wheels creaked into motion behind us; there wasn't much time left to decide. "Fine," he said. "Let's get this over with."

I grinned, and he could never help flashing his chipped tooth when I was happy. I clasped his hand in mine, our fingers twined together, and we climbed up the sloping lawn.

Neither of us knew how little time we had left together. If we had, perhaps we would have stayed in the woods a little longer.

CHAPTER 16

The plan was simple. Then again, everything seemed simple to Jay.

Benji drew a map of the island. He was the best at that sort of thing, according to Kiran.

With only a stick pulled across the den floor, Benji outlined the land, tracing the path to the pirate cove and marking key locations along the way with confident strokes. The island sat in the sea like a horseshoe. Tunnels burrowed below ground, one of which ran from their den on the northeastern shore to the pirate cove to the south. The sea monster ruled the waters by an outcropping of stone due east called Soul Rock, prompting a western detour to avoid alerting her to their presence. While a longer path, it was the safest. The Red, Blue, and Gold tribal camps were unavoidable, however. Scattered throughout the island and forever shifting locations, the forbidden pockets of land most likely to house them were protected by spiked fences and unmarked traps. So long as they answered when Peter called, the tribes were granted their absolute privacy, and Jay wasn't about to upset that truce.

The trek went smoothly, the tunnels lit by torchlight. Ceilings were low and jutting roots made the underground road dangerous, but the path above was worse. Finally, after what seemed an hour, Lou tasted clean air again. Just as Jay instructed her, she knelt in the brush midway down the cliff by the cove with a sword on her hip, wearing a strange man's clothes and hoping this would be her last night on the island.

"Is it time?" she asked.

Jay shook his head and placed a finger to his lips.

The pirates' cove stretched below them, a white beach hemmed by tall rock and dense forest. It was the beach Lou had first woken up on, but it was unrecognizable at night. The merchants were gone, and the boardwalk was clear. It seemed too big. The cliff to her left dropped off in a steep slide toward the coast, smooth rock shimmering faintly. A blanket of leaves as large as watermelons folded around them, painting the ground in darkness. The water ebbed and rolled, foaming against the belly of the only ship docked against the sand.

A root slithered over Lou's leather boot, and she kicked out and swallowed a scream. As though sensing her fear, the branches rustled, dipping closer to her, closing in. The island had a pulse, a heartbeat, a rhythmic tune. It had no fear of her fear. Not one moon, but two. Not a navy sky, but a sweeping expanse of the same emerald peeking through the cracks in the land and tree bark—another effect of Peter's absence, it seemed. The island bled green. That night, it would bleed in other ways too.

"Get down. Someone's gonna see you." Jay jabbed an elbow into her ribs, forcing her lower into the branches. "Don't make me regret bringin' you up here."

"Who could possibly see us in the dark?"

He sighed. "Trust me. Pirates might be dumb as dirt, but they know how to patrol for threats. Plus, Sammy'll be comin' through those trees over to the west. We don't want the Blues thinkin' we tricked them."

"But we did trick them."

"But we don't want them to *know* it."

Lou lowered herself into the brush, her chest tight. The ship bobbed like a cork in the high tide, a great beast of wood and steel. Lou scanned the deck. A dozen men scampered from rail to rail, lashing cargo down with thick rope and tossing weapons into a gleaming pile. On any other night, the soft lull of the waves might have been calming; tonight it was like the tick of a pocket watch, counting the seconds until the ground swallowed her.

"It's not too late to back down, you know," Jay said, eyeing her evenly. "You were never the best at swords, and I don't care what Sammy says—practice hasn't made you much better."

"I'm coming with you."

He peered out the corner of his eye. "I can get Peter on my own. It wouldn't be the first time I've raided that ship on my own without gettin' caught."

"I *said* I'm coming with you. Now be quiet."

"Whatever you say, Miss Webber."

Lou wrinkled her nose. "Don't call me that."

"Why? That's your name, isn't it?"

"It's much too formal. There is no need for that here."

It was more than that. Anne Webber clung to titles and found safety in them. She wore her status as a married woman, first like a crown when parading her happiness on Father's arm, and later as a shield against the pity in the other ladies' eyes. Titles could liberate one second and shackle the next. Titles were fickle. Being attached to them one way or the other made Lou uneasy, and there, buried in the shadows, any added discomfort to her was unnecessary.

"When I marry, I will take my husband's name and be glad to be rid of mine," she said. "Until then, I'm only Louisa."

"Marriage, huh? You'd be tradin' one cage for another." Jay

was quiet then, and when he next spoke, his voice was soft. "When did your daddy pass?"

She tore her eyes from the ship. "How did you—?"

"I remember him. He wasn't doin' too great when your sister was born. It's somethin' in the eyes; they get flat and sad, like they know it's comin'. It never takes long after that."

Lou turned away. "It was a cough," she said. "He took ill with influenza the winter Mother was pregnant with Rosie. He recovered mostly, but the cough never left his lungs. By the time the infection set in, the surgeons were not able to help."

"I'm sorry."

She nodded, a small jerk of the chin. "Father once told me, when he was near to the end, that death is the price of life. I think he believed those words, but to me, I always knew he only wanted to ease my pain."

"Did it work?"

"Not a bit," Lou said. "If death is the price of life, living is a terrible business."

"Unless you never die." Jay cleared his throat, his gaze fixed on the pirates on deck. "You can stay here. You'd never have to die either."

"I—do you hear that?" The cliffs rumbled, shaking the trees so their leaves scrubbed the sky. A sky speckled with stars. A sky that was deep and soft and endless. To the west, a piece of the cliff disappeared, throwing rubble onto the beach. The ground vibrated under Lou's boots, the sound slowly overcoming the low hiss of the sea; it was almost time. "Jay, we need to hurry. If we take Henry as another fighter—"

"No. Henry won't fight, and I won't make him. He's big, sure, but you should know by now nothin' is exactly what it looks like. He won't fight, and that's final."

Lou grew still, her face warm in the light breeze off the sea. The air buzzed, and the rumbling grew louder, a million hooves pounding the earth in the distance. A flash of violet lightning set the world ablaze in a wash of colour; another tremor shook a nearby boulder loose from the cliffs. Lou dragged the sword from her belt just as three whistle bursts pierced night.

It was time.

"That's Henry, right on cue," Jay whispered, reaching for his dagger. "Keep your eye on the western end of the beach. Sammy should be comin' around those cliffs."

No sooner did Jay speak the words did thunder tear down the coast. Shadows shifted and twisted, growing solid as a tidal wave of bodies poured onto the sand. Sammy raced ahead of the Blues, bare feet kicking up sand, something mangled and round clutched in his fingers. "Come on, you hyenas!" Sammy called over his shoulder. "You gotta move a little faster than that. I got your best girl in my hands!"

Arms roped with muscle and slathered in bright blue paint lifted weapons into the sky. The boy was so small, the Blues quickly closing the gap between them. Lou's fingers prickled around the hilt of her sword, the urge to vault off the cliff sparking through her like lightning.

"Easy," Jay said, urging her lower into the brush. "Kid's gonna be fine. He's done this loads of times."

"What did he do to upset them?"

"See that thing in his hands?" Jay asked. When Lou nodded, he let out a low laugh. "The Blues really respect the females of their tribe. When one of 'em dies, they chop off her head and leave it in the sun. Then they can keep a piece of their loved one forever."

Her stomach rolled. "So, he's holding a human *head*?"

"No better way to get a Blue mad."

Sammy led the stampede down the rocks, through the brush, and across the beach. The pirates swarmed the upper deck in time to greet the Blues at the base of the ship. A dark shape—Didi—let fly an arrow from her place in the shadows. Surprise, pain, rage—the night exploded with screams as one of the Blues caught the arrow with his chest.

"Grab yer swords, mates!"

"Tribe's attackin', Cap'n! All hands on deck!"

Pirates clambered onto the main deck, daggers trapped between their teeth and swords lifted to the skies. Kiran and Didi skulked out of hiding and broke into a run once their boots hit sand. Within seconds, they had joined the fray, slicing at pirates and Blues alike.

"Didi killed a man," Lou said. Blood spattered the pale strip of sand lining the cove, making the land shimmer. "She killed him so easily."

"He was just a Blue."

"He was a person!"

Jay turned to her, cheeks bathed in the green light of the sky. "You want to get home real bad, right? The Blues, the pirates, even the mermaids—none of 'em just get out of their camps at night if they don't have a good reason. A missin' female head and a fallen tribal man near the ship was the only way to do it. The island doesn't make things nice and pretty for you just 'cause you're a lady, *little bird*, so get your head straight, or stay behind."

War spread across the sand. Blades crashed against blades, and water beat against the ship, bubbling with anger. The stream of pirates off the deck of the vessel slowed to a trickle until, finally, an orange flame flickered to life below them. The signal: Henry's was to alert them to the tribe's arrival, Benji's to give the all-clear on the ship.

"It's time." Jay moved toward the stone chute beside them. "I promise I won't give you a hard time about it if you bow out."

Lou gripped her sword tight and followed him down the cliffs. The rock at her back was weathered smooth, the humid air smelling of salt and copper as she rushed down, down. It was a straight line to the ship, the battle raging at the stern, where Sammy had led the Blues. The sea was restless, the waves churning and moaning against the hull.

Moaning? "What is that sound?" Lou asked. They slipped into the shadows by the dock. There was blood, so much blood, and the screams were too loud. *Everything* was too loud. Where were Didi and Kiran? Had Benji made it back to the den with Henry? They were close to rescuing Peter and securing her way home, yet she hesitated to leave the others behind.

"The damn crocs never miss a chance for blood. Never know if they're gonna save your hide or eat it."

"There are crocodiles here?"

He nodded and motioned for a rope ladder swaying over the rail of the ship. "A kid rules a whole island and we're goin' to free him from pirates, but you're surprised at the crocs in the water." Jay chuckled. "You growns are funny. All right, listen. They're probably keepin' Peter in the brig way below deck, far from the stars. We stay close, we stay armed. And if it comes to a fight, you use that sword just like I showed you."

Swords meant blood, meant death. Death by *her* hand.

It was easy to be confident when practicing with a stick.

Jay bit down on the steel of his dagger and scrambled up the rungs like a squirrel up a tree. She had a brief flash of Rose hanging upside down from branches in the Briarwood, and her heart sank; Lou could hardly manage a climb up a familiar tree, let alone a stealth crawl up a swinging ladder.

"Hurry!" Jay whispered from over the rail.

"Right." Her confidence was back in the den with its dirt walls. "Rosie could do this. I can do this."

The rungs were carved of wood and softened by the slow rot of salt water. Taking them one at a time, Lou inched toward the sky, her palms slipping. Under her, water lapped at the ship, dark shapes lurking beneath the surface. The wind rushed past her ears, and for an endless second, she was a bird learning to fly.

"I'm going to fall!" she called. "Jay!"

"You're doin' great, Lou. Come on, grab the next one!" Jay stretched over the rail with the sky seething green, then violet, then green once more behind him. Her fingers burned with fresh splinters, and the world tilted, her head too light on her shoulders, the waves stinging her nose, roaring too loud, too *loud*.

"Up here," Jay called. "Look at me. See my face?"

The water, the sky, the lightning, so much green, too much green. But Jay's eyes were blue, deep and steadfast, and that was good, because that was *real*.

"Good, that's good, Lou. One foot at a time, and just keep lookin' at me! That's it, a little more."

The birds can touch everythin' you see. They just glide over the trees, so close the branches tickle their bellies. Can you imagine being one of 'em? Free, just flyin' wherever you want to go?

Her palms hit the upper rail, and Jay pulled her over the edge. "This way," he said, leading her across the deck. The ship lurched with the waves, kicking them back from the steel trap door cut into the wood slats. "Got your sword?" he asked. When she nodded, he gave her hand a reassuring squeeze. "It'll be all right. Just grit your teeth and do what needs doin'. You can't feel bad doin' somethin' bad so long as it's for a good reason, right?"

"I don't think that's—"

An arm swung out at them from the shadows. Lou screamed and fell back, but Jay ducked the blow as though he'd felt it coming.

The pirate was tall, thick, stinking of sweat and spirits, and grunting with effort. Boy and man twisted together, a knot of rage. Jay was quick, but pirates were *men*. What the brute lacked in coordination, he made up for in raw force; each jab of the sword whistled through the air, and the wood planks groaned underneath him as he came for Jay again and again. The pair moved together in a deadly waltz of flesh and steel, and the glint in Jay's exposed smile told her he enjoyed it.

Metal clanged, sharp and chilling. Bone thumped against bone, and they went down in a knot of limbs.

Jay.

A fist slammed into Jay's jaw. The pirate straddled him, pinning him down, a blade held to the sky. Ready.

Move.

I can't move.

He needs to move.

Lou melted into the floor, pinned down by fear.

The pirate was big, bigger than Jay, bigger than them both.

"Argh!" Jay wriggled and shoved until one of his legs slipped free. He kicked out at once, his boot sinking into the pirate's soft belly. Seizing his advantage, Jay twisted away from the man's greedy fists, a minnow flitting through clear water.

A blade flashed under the moonlight and quickly disappeared. The night went still. The pirate's eyes flew wide as his skin dripped in fresh blood.

The noose unravelled from around Lou's throat. She screamed into the night, the burning of her voice searing her, tearing her apart. The pirate's eyes rolled to the sky, reflecting the eerie light of the island sky lit by two swollen moons. As blood pooled across the planks, that light dimmed.

Not a pool—a lake.

A lake without a bottom.

A lake in the woods behind her home. With mermaids and children and cold fingers pulling her down, down to the end of the world.

Lou blinked, clearing away the thought. A smooth red line of blood crept toward her toes, kissed the worn leather of her boots, warmed her feet.

"Lou?"

She looked up at—*a lake, a lake, the children waiting to play at the bottom, bottom, bottom*—Jay, and the night snapped into focus.

"Lou!"

They were not by the lake. They were on a ship. A pirate ship that never should have existed.

"Is he dead?" she heard herself ask. "He . . . He isn't moving."

"Don't look at him. You okay?"

"Yes. No." She frowned, taking him in for the first time. "Are you?"

He grinned, fiddling with the chip in his tooth with his tongue. Blood spattered his cheeks and clung to his clothes, but his eyes were wild as he pulled his dagger free from the pirate's neck. With quick efficient motions, he wiped it clean against his hip and replaced it in his belt. "That was fun, but we need to move." Jay crossed the deck and grabbed a rusted brass ring with both hands. The trap door squealed, releasing a gust of stale air.

Jay disappeared in a flash, his bronze hair painted red by the dead man's blood. Shame flooded her; she'd called him a child, thought him impulsive, untrustworthy even. But he *was* a child, she an adult. And between the two of them, she was the coward.

"Jay?" she called. "Are you all right? What do you see?"

There was a pause, then, "It's clear! You can come down!"

Lou took a final gulp of fresh air and followed Jay's voice down the ladder. The ship was a crocodile lying in wait, biding its time until it would snare her in its jaws, but the vessel's belly was darkness made solid. It gurgled and rumbled, hungry for her. The ship had already swallowed Peter. Now Lou was its next meal.

She stepped off the ladder into a pool of cold water. Something heavy skittered over her boot, and Lou swiped her sword at the invisible enemy.

"Easy!" Jay grabbed Lou's arm, pulling her from the shadows

and into a narrow passage lit by rusted lanterns. "They're just rats. You better get used to it; pirate ships are crawlin' with them. And you better be careful with that sword. You almost stabbed me."

Shame burned her cheeks. "Where do we go now?"

"The brig's down this way. C'mon."

They moved down the corridor, orange torchlight reflecting off the wet floor, turning it to glass. Left, left, right, deeper and deeper through the belly of the beast. The walls were close, the ceiling low. "What do we do if Peter is not being kept here? Do you have another plan?"

"First plan's gonna work."

"Jay—"

"Sh!"

He stopped abruptly behind a stack of empty crates. The passage curved up ahead, hiding two new sets of footsteps, two distinct grunts muttering curses into the darkness. Lou wasn't ready. The sword was heavy and foreign in her unskilled hands. Did she truly think she could fight for her own freedom? She'd never fought for anything in her life. The men's voices bounced down the corridor, pinning Lou to the spot, making it impossible for her to move or speak or think.

"Would ye hurry up, mate?"

"Shut yer face."

The first man laughed. "A bum leg don't make yer hands slow, do it?"

One pirate was tall and lanky with a rim of hair around his ears spilling down past his shoulders. He looked on as the second man wrestled with a pile of wooden crates, a hoop gleaming in his crooked nose, ink swirls branding him from shoulder to wrist. Cells lined both sides of the corridor, dirty holes with rusted bars and heavy brass locks.

"You ready, Miss Webber?" Jay asked.

"No."

He offered her a smile, his teeth bright against his blood-smeared cheeks. Scooping dirty water from the puddles at his feet, he wet his hair, darkened his skin, then did the same to her. In the dim light, he was a different boy than the one living in the den. Jay enjoyed his games, but pirates and blood were more than simple play. She could see it in his eyes.

"Aye, lass," Jay said, pulling Lou down the corridor. The men dropped their crates, glass tinkling inside. " 'Tis a mighty shame about the gold they took! So much gold, spoils o' war an' all, but the lads up on the beach took most o' it."

"Wha's he sayin', Wormy?" the tall pirate asked, reaching for his sword.

The one named Wormy waved a finger at Jay's nose, his ruddy cheeks webbed with blood from broken veins, the jewelry in his face gleaming as he moved. "Who're you?"

"Deckhands," Jay said. "New. Who're you?"

"What?"

"Ah, never mind, I like the look o' ye." Jay clapped the pirate on the back, his head barely reaching his shoulder. "I just came down 'ere to get me some whiskey. I was hopin' fer some o' the gold the Blues brought with 'em too, but that's all gone."

"Gold?"

"Whatchu mean gone?" Wormy asked. "Nobody told us 'bout no gold."

"Aye, mate," Jay said, giving Lou a subtle nod. She peeked into the first cell as the men discussed treasure, then the second, then the next. *Empty.* Lou lurked in the shadows, letting Jay play his game "There was so much o' it. But me, I just want somethin' te drink now."

"How much gold?" the tall one asked.

The next three cells were dark, littered with straw, dripping in seawater. Empty. Lou's pulse quickened. If this didn't work, if Peter wasn't there . . .

"The boys got at least five chests full, from what I could see," Jay said. "Coins as big as yer hand, mate. And gems too. Rubies. Diamonds. Vials of *fairy dust*." The pirates lapped up his words, the crates of liquor long forgotten. "Too bad ye missed it all. Maybe the other lads'll share?"

Wormy growled low. "Those slugs. I knew it. Didn't I say I sniffed a mutiny, Eli? Didn't I?"

The taller pirate—Eli—shook his head. "Dunno. I canna hear out me left ear."

The cell at the far end was submerged in darkness, but a slice of light from a nearby lantern cut a bright strip across the floor. Lou moved closer, pulled by invisible hands.

"You two should try gettin' yer share," Jay said, steering both men away from her. "Ye know how priceless fairy dust is."

"Lad's right!" Wormy said. "Eli, let's go."

"I don' know. Cap'n told us there were hundreds o' bottles o' whiskey down 'ere."

A cough like dry leaves blown across rocks startled them all. A shape moved in the cell at the end of the corridor: a pale foot, a thin leg, then nothing but darkness once more. The ship groaned; it was as though ghosts wailed behind the bars, rattling their cages.

Peter was there. She was certain of it.

"C'mon, Eli. If those bilge rats don't hand over the loot, I'll skin 'em all. We deserve our share, don' we?" Wormy grinned, revealing a mouthful of silver-plated teeth, gravestones in a barren yard of blackened gum and yellow saliva. "We'll be up and back 'afore the cap'n even gets wind o' it."

If Eli had a choice, it didn't take him long to make it. The taller pirate lumbered after his companion, his right foot scratching against the ground as he dragged his stiff leg behind him.

"Fairy dust, lads!" Jay called. "Look for the fairy dust!"

"Aye!"

Clomp-scratch, clomp-scratch.

They couldn't leave the brig fast enough.

Jay burst into a fit of laughter. "Good job, Miss Webber. I thought you bein' a girl would give us away, but they didn't even notice you."

Lou swayed on her feet. "It appears our worlds are quite similar in that regard."

Another cough cut them short. Jay turned, his shoulders growing rigid at the sound. "Who's there?" he asked.

They stepped closer to the rusted bars; a single lock snaked through the seam between two gates, a dark keyhole sinking into its centre. The stink of rotten food and urine oozed from the cell like an infection, making Lou's stomach roll.

"I asked a question," Jay called a little louder. "That you, Peter?"

The days since her feet hit the island were a fog, the border between truth and fiction, dream and nightmare, terrifyingly thin. But the briefest moments often held the greatest weight, leaving imprints on the heart and mind. The moment when a hunched figure peeled himself away from the shadows on hands and knees, his green eyes bloodshot but alert, was one Lou knew she would take with her to her grave. It was one of those moments. She simply wasn't sure if it was a pleasant or terrible one.

He was small. Painfully so. The musculature of his arms and legs was coated with the smoothness of childhood. Reddish-brown hair lay matted against his forehead, his cheeks sallow and smudged with grime. The boy sported cuts and bruises on every inch of exposed skin, his clothes torn and stained with sweat and dirt. The only boy to ever touch the stars was unremarkable in every way Lou could see. He held more power than grown men, *capable* men. She understood that while her home and the island had their similarities, this was one difference she couldn't ignore.

"Jay?" The boy squinted through the bars. "Why?"

"Nice to see you too, old friend." Jay's voice was flat, his jaw hard. He reached for Lou's sword and wrapped both hands firmly around its hilt. "We came to get you out of this hole. You better stand back."

Peter nodded, sitting back on his haunches. "You gotta hurry. They won't be gone long."

"First, we make a deal," Jay said. "Me and you, no tricks."

"Whatever you want."

"I get you outta this cage, you get all three of us outta this ship alive."

Torment flashed across Peter's hollow face. "I don't know if I can do that, Number Two. I been down here too long; the island's magic isn't as strong in me anymore. I don't even think that fairy dust you were talkin' about would help me. I'm done."

"So, what?" Jay asked, his sword stalling mid-air. "You tellin' me we came down here for nothin'?"

"I mean, if you can get Bell or any of the other fairies down here, it could be enough to get us above deck so I can see the sky again. But unless you got one of 'em stashed in your pocket, I'm pretty useless."

Jay laughed, the sound bitter. "You know I don't trust fairies. Me and my people started a war between the Blues and the pirates to get here. It's gotta be enough."

"Please," Lou said. "I'm told you are an exceptional boy—a king on this island. They tell me you found a way to touch the stars."

"I did."

"And certainly that is a much more difficult task than getting us off a ship alive."

Peter squinted at her, a pale light flickering behind his eyes. "You're Lou Webber."

The hair on her arms stood on end; of course Peter would know her. He and Jay were friends since she was nothing more than a child. Peter had ordered Jay away from her. Their history was complicated, made more complicated still by the fact that she remembered very little of it. Being recognized by a stranger was unnerving. Then again, it might simply have been his eyes. The age he carried there. The *knowing* that had no business existing in a strange child's face.

"My name is Louisa Webber, yes. Will you help us?"

To her surprise, the boy laughed. "Guess it makes sense you're a stuck-up pain since Jay liked you so much. He always wanted his kids with fire in 'em. You're not supposed to be here, though. Why are you here, Louisa Webber?" He turned slowly to Jay as footsteps echoed down the passage. "You finally did it, Number Two. You got what you wanted."

"Peter, I swear, this isn't what you think," Jay said, a new edge to his voice. "I didn't mean for it to go this way."

Peter shook his head. "The stars are the only thing keepin' us alive now. She needs to get there if she wants to go home. She needs to get there if you've got any chance of gettin' away with what you started. No way I can do it from in here."

"If we get you out, things will return to normal," Lou protested. "And you have the power to take me home. Jay and I . . . Well, we do not know what you did or how you did it. We need your help if we're to survive. Peter, this is your island. Please."

Clomp-scratch, clomp-scratch.

Fear pinched Peter's features. "You can't get me out. It's over."

"Let's open these doors and figure the rest out later." Jay hoisted the sword over his head. "Get outta the way." With a grunt, he drove the blade home. Lou closed her eyes and clamped her palms on her ears, praying the pirates wouldn't hear them, wouldn't check the brig until Peter was free from his prison. The thick padlock gonged with a sound that vibrated in Lou's bones and sent the walls into convulsions.

She forced her eyes open. The lock was still intact. Above,

gruff voices began to argue, a swarm of angry wasps returning to their nest.

"Try again," she said urgently. "Jay, do it!"

Another swing, another growling effort, another surge of hope.

Again, the padlock did not budge.

Lou lifted the lock into her palm; the metal boasted a thick coating of rust but was otherwise untouched by Jay's efforts. "Jay, how is this possible? Why isn't your sword working?"

"I tried tellin' you before," Peter said. "Unless you got some special magic or can find a way to touch the stars, I'm not gettin' outta here, and you can't go home." He sighed. "And the lock's laced with mermaid hair."

Jay cursed under his breath. "You're kiddin'."

"Well, I wasn't sure until you tried breakin' the lock, but yeah."

Clomp-scratch, clomp-scratch.

Lou rounded on Jay. "What does that mean?"

"Mermaid hair is unbreakable," Jay explained. "It's hard to get and super valuable. I had no idea this ship would have any of it, but I'm guessin' you don't take any chances when you catch the boy who controls the island."

The lull of the sea below her feet rocked her back and forth, making her ill. "So, what now?"

"Now you go," Peter said.

"No!" Above, the buzz of pirates' voices paused. Soon, those men would find two intruders in their brig, a discovery that was unlikely to end in Lou going home. "I was lured here against my will," she said. "I've been *held* on this island against my will. You are somehow the ruler of this prison I am in, and I refuse to believe you cannot help me. So, *help me.*"

Peter said nothing. Jay said even less.

She was wrong. The ship wasn't a monster. The true best was

defeat; it feasted off her anger, revelled in her nerves. It picked her bones clean and left nothing to the vultures. She was doomed.

And they were out of time.

"Down there, Cap'n! They told us there was gold! Are . . . Are ye sure there ain't no gold at all?"

Before Lou could react, a pair of strong calloused hands gripped her around the waist and pressed her against the bars. Rough metal raked her cheek. She bit her tongue to keep from screaming.

CHAPTER 17

"Look what we have 'ere."

Lou struggled against the meaty arm pinning her down, the pirate's rancid breath rustling the hair at her ear.

"Let go of me," she commanded, but her voice shook against the bars. She was weak. She had always been weak.

"You smell nice," he muttered, nuzzling her neck. "Like flowers."

Hands travelled around her waist and down her arms. Men claimed to be the superior sex, marked by intelligence and gallantry. They were the keepers of an elusive protection women required from the misfortunes of the world: marriage. But all Lou saw with her face pressed against the unforgiving metal was a hungry beast who cared little for the tears snaking down her cheeks. The protection of men was selective, it seemed.

Jay bucked, butting his captor in the chin. The pirate bellowed and staggered back, his blade clattering to the ground. Within seconds, the man was back in position, his fist connecting with Jay's gut before he could reach for his own weapon.

"Bad idea, boy. You'll be leavin' that there blade alone so's we can have ourselves a nice chat, understood?"

The new voice echoed from the far end of the hall. Strong hands spun Lou around and pressed her back against the bars, forcing her to face the tall figure moving within the shadows. Each heavy step filled Lou's mind with visions of crocodiles and her heart with steel, the tang of salt and mulled wine choking her. The shadows shrank away from the moving shape, revealing square shoulders and a black coat with matching britches, both free of wrinkles and dirt. Whereas every pirate Lou had seen wore their rags like a badge of honour, this man shimmered with gold buttons and jewelled rings, his buckled shoes polished to a shine. He locked eyes with Jay and smiled, the movement of his sharp features revealing a smattering of shell-pink scars across his cheeks.

The pirates pinning them to the bars dropped their arms, and Jay shook himself free. "Don't ever touch me again, you stinkin' monster," he said. "This is how you teach your men to treat guests, Cap?"

"It's Captain Blackbeard, lad. Mind yer language on me ship, if ye don' mind. Especially in the presence of a lady."

Blackbeard?

Jay moved to Lou's side, his dagger forgotten on the ground. "Since when do you poke your head out of your quarters for a friendly visit from me?"

"Since the visitor in question is lurkin' 'round me prize prisoner. I thought we had an understandin', boy." His eyes turned to Lou then. Something cold oozed down Lou's spine, a slug tracing the most intimate places of her body, leaving them dirty and wet. "And *you*, little lass. I don' reckon I ever seen somethin' so pretty walkin' this island on two legs before."

"I'm new," Lou said.

"I can see that." Blackbeard stepped closer, his gaze probing her with new interest. She wanted to recoil, but there was nowhere to go. There hadn't been anywhere to go for days. "An' what are ye doin' on me ship with wee Jay?"

"I require assistance to return home to my family. I've found your island by accident, and your prisoner seems to be the only one who can help."

"That so, love?"

Lou nodded, earning matching grins from Blackbeard's men. The captain, however, nodded slowly, his expression carefully blank.

"And ye'd like me te hand the boy over to ye," Blackbeard said. "Is that right?"

"It is the right thing to do. But if appealing to your morality is the wrong course, then perhaps your sense of self-preservation is stronger. Keeping this boy in your custody has somehow compromised the integrity of this island. Children are disappearing, and the same may happen to you if you do not let Peter go free."

"Sounds terrifyin'."

"It is." Lou held out a hand, hoping she appeared as steady and confident as her father had whenever he'd bound his word with the touch of his palm to another's. "Give us the prisoner, and we will ensure none of your men are hurt. Do we have an accord?"

Blackbeard cocked his head, his breath smelling of apples and rot. "Ye be a wee thing. Not many o' me men have the nerve te strike an accord with me directly."

Lou dropped her hand. "I am flattered. Is that a yes, then?"

In the cell beyond, Peter gripped the bars, his forehead pressed against them as though he were lost in prayer. The two pirates flanked their captain like grotesque bookends, their breathing heavy.

"I been huntin' that there boy since this island became home," Blackbeard said. "He been a scourge on this place, takin' what ain't his, fancyin' himself a saviour when he be just another pathetic soul lost in a place that don' belong te him. I'm takin' it back, love. I'm takin' it all back. No boy is goin' te decide what happens te me."

"But that boy is the reason you are still *alive*!" Lou said, heat climbing the back of her neck. "You will surely die if you do not release him."

And I'll die with you.

I cannot die here.

Blackbeard smiled, serene. "I don' see the problem, little one."

"But you are not alone!" Lou retorted. "There are children whose lives depend on Peter. You cannot be so selfish as to condemn everyone here to a fate of your choosing."

Blackbeard barked laughter, eyes burning like coals. "Livin's a funny thing if it be forced on a man who don' want it. I seen many things in me long life: some good, some bad, most things somewhere between the two. But that there boy has too much control. Havin' him locked in a cell be the only thing that can bring me some peace."

Peter slumped lower to the ground, his hands lingering on the bars. Pity flooded Lou, hot and sharp: pity for a boy, pity for a child, pity for an innocent life taken away simply because he had dared to stretch himself above his world and take more than he'd been given. "Please," was all she could manage. "I cannot be trapped here. I *cannot*! People will continue to die the longer he remains here with you!"

"Perhaps," Blackbeard said. "But I made me peace with that many moons ago, love."

Jay grabbed her elbow, his fingers slick and cold. But Lou had come too far to turn back. She had slept on dirt, suffered bruises and cuts, and endured hunger and sleepless nights waiting for this moment. And a pirate was trying to take it all away.

Men always took what they wanted.

But that was her world. Here, she was a woman with a real sword and the power to use it.

"What if I proposed a trade?" she asked.

"What are you doin'?" Jay asked, tightening his grip.

Blackbeard tipped his face to the ceiling and laughed again, black sludge dripping from the ship and speckling his otherwise smooth skin. Like blood. "And what could ye possibly have to trade with, love? If ye'll excuse me fer sayin' so, ye seem te be packin' light considerin' how much o' ye I can see through that there shirt."

Lou's cheeks blazed as the pirates laughed and laughed. Power. She wasn't a child; she wasn't home living under her mother's rules or her future husband's assessing gaze. And power meant sacrifice. "Let Peter go," she said, "and you can have Jay instead."

The brig grew quiet, with only the *drip, drip, drip* of the dirty water to break the silence. Inside, she was just as unclean as the sludge plinking from the ceiling and into the brig; Jay had been a friend during her childhood and had sacrificed his own people to help her. But she was no longer a child. She could only remember fragments of him, really, and his people had kept her prisoner. And so she repaid his kindness with betrayal. Jay might have been a leader, but he was a child among children. Too trusting.

Lou raised her chin and regarded Blackbeard square in the eyes. A woman did what needed doing. A woman had power too, and sometimes power meant inflicting pain. "Well, Blackbeard? Jay was Peter's closest friend. His second-in-command, by my understanding. Next to Peter, he is the most important child on the island. A worthy prize."

The pirate pitched his voice low, the baritone smooth as a purr. "Yer lyin'."

"I assure you, I am not."

Jay's face grew slack, pale in the wavering light. "Lou?"

"Ye'd be willin' to sacrifice yer little friend jus' to get what ye want?" Blackbeard nursed the reverence in his voice like a tumbler of fine scotch, swishing the words in his mouth to savour the fire a little longer.

"Yes. Yes, I would."

A smile spread across Blackbeard's face. "I could just throw ye both in a cell and call us square."

"There would be no sport in that. It would be more . . . *poetic* to take Jay prisoner and let him live with the knowledge of my betrayal, is it not?" She loathed herself entirely. But Rose needed to be a priority. Being there for her mother and sister was more important than any loyalty toward a child she'd once known.

Why, then, was she filled with such shame?

An eerie grin split Blackbeard's face. "What's yer name, lass?"

"Louisa Webber, Captain."

He nodded. "Captain—polite. It's been a while since we had a real lady on this rock. Well, Miss Webber, I reckon ye'd make a fine pirate."

"More pirate than mermaid after all," Jay muttered under his breath.

But you're a girl. Girls are always mermaids.
There could be girl pirates too. I'd like that.

A conversation bathed in memory and wrapped in a dream.

The disgust Lou felt with herself made her weak-kneed, but she planted her feet firmly and straightened her shoulders. For Rosie. For herself. "I might be willing to do what it takes to get what I want, but I take no pleasure in it. I suggest you consider my offer if you value your life, sir."

The smile flickered and disappeared. "Well, love, there's the problem. This island's a hole no pirate, child, or fish can dig themselves out of. I reckon most o' us would welcome a bit o' rest after a life of fightin' that's gone on for too long. Even the famous Blackbeard knows when it be time to put down the sword."

Realization dawned, slow and horrific. "You *want* to die?"

The tang of soap and seawater wafted off Blackbeard in thick oily waves. He pulled at his cuffs, straightening his jacket with yellowed claws. "I already fought every monster on this island. It'd be a nice adventure te meet the biggest monster of 'em all. And if I were in yer pretty shoes, I'd be gettin' nice and comfy, lass. Yer gettin' no way back to the Land o' the Grown—least not from me. Welcome te the island, Miss Webber. Hope she lasts long enough for ye te enjoy it."

"Please, *no!*" Lou screamed, but her protests cut to silence as Blackbeard's pirates pounced, their leers rimmed in foam, rabid with need. Clammy hands gripped her around the arm, another winding through her hair, pulling her chin up to the ceiling. All the while, Peter sank back into the darkness, his helplessness beating at her back. But she'd been inactive before—a useless, helpless woman in a world made and ruled by men—and it had landed her in the arms of a pirate.

No.

She kicked and writhed, struggling for something to hurt, to maim, to scratch, but the pirates were too big, and she was in the wrong body to oppose such a tight grip. Jay went limp, allowing himself to be led down the passageway, his feet trailing behind him.

They reached the stairs.

Up they went until the air was fresh, the canopy of brilliant stars a welcome sight after the darkness of the brig. Had it not been for the deck blanketed with bloodied pirates, Lou might have been relieved.

The crowd nodded to their captain, and Blackbeard saluted them with a short wave. "I'm goin' te let ye go. I may be a pirate, but I'm a gentleman first. I can't let ye go easy, though. It wouldn't be sportin'."

"Course not," Jay said, his voice hollow. "Want us to dance for you first, Blackbeard? Ask one of your men to loan us a dress, make it a show."

Growls rippled over their heads, knuckles cracked, and silver teeth flashed green under the eerie sky. Blackbeard moved between them, standing tall. "Peter stays with us," he said. The crew rallied, their cheers ripping through the ship. "But ye both have te get off me ship. Yer a menace, Jay. Yer a thief and a traitor, an embarrassment to yer clan, a—"

"I'm a kid, Beardy," Jay said, glaring up at the captain. "I'm just a kid. Don't try to make me all the things you want me to be when I'm just *me*. A kid got through to your brig. How's that feel?"

Blackbeard bared his teeth, and they were now smeared in coal. "Feels like revenge, lad. Now, boys!"

A heavy hand shoved her forward, and the mass of bloodied limbs crowded around Lou, herding her toward the rail.

"What are you doing?" she called over her shoulder. "We agreed to leave! There is no need for force!"

"Ah, that'll be a problem." Blackbeard sighed. "See, this be a pirate ship, love, not some common canoe. I canna let ye go after ye got some o' me men killed. Ye understand."

"Cap'n, let us play with her a bit. She looks fun." The voice came from deep within the mob and roused a hearty cheer of approval from the others.

"She smells nice."

"Lemme touch 'er face. She got a real sweet face."

Lou pressed in closer to Jay; she had no reason to expect kindness from him after how quickly she'd thrown away his trust, but he stood beside her, firm and warm. The pirates' cheers were deafening, their faces twisting into masks more monster than human. Tongues waggled, and fingers reached, and all the while, the quick *snap, snap, snap* of a creature in the deep below moved ever closer.

Jay did not look at her when he finally spoke. "C'mon, Blackbeard, cut it out already. Just toss us into a nice little boat, and I'll paddle us on back to the island. I'm sick of smellin' your men anyway." He wrinkled his nose. "Seriously, you all live on water. Spring for a bath sometime."

The mask of calm cracked apart on Blackbeard's face, revealing the ugly serpent writhing within. Men roared, waving their swords to the moons. Canines bared, Blackbeard turned to the mob, power rolling off him in thick waves. "Quiet down!" he cried, and the crew grew sullen but silent. "The boy be harmless; nothin' but scraps o' trash Peter tossed away. And the lass be no more'n a child herself. None o' ye will bring any harm to 'em."

Lou exhaled. "Thank you, Captain."

"But we lost lives tonight," Blackbeard continued, "and I still believe in blood owed fer blood taken!"

"Aye!" the crew yelled, fists pumping the air.

"Ye'll be speakin' the name o' Blackbeard 'til the island sinks te the bottom o' the sea!"

"Aye!"

The rail was firm against Lou's back, the chipped wood snagging in her borrowed shirt. The sea opened its jaws wide, waiting for the feast the pirates meant to offer it. Waves churned, and Blackbeard grinned.

Jay twined his fingers with hers.

"This island'll know who *finally* put an end to Peter's plague!"

"Aye!"

Blackbeard's eyes glowed with bloodlust. "Get 'em off me boat!"

"*Aye!*"

"No!" she screamed. But her voice was weak. She was a fool to think it could ever be more.

Pirates charged the deck, swarming like wasps. An arm hooked around her middle, and her breath escaped in a violent huff. A thousand bright red spots bloomed across her vision as the ground lurched away, the sky spinning out of control. For a blissful moment, she was weightless, a bird soaring over the clouds, wings gliding over water, kissing the cool waves.

The water crashed into her like a bed of sharpened knives.

Lou pummelled the wall of inky water pressing in on all sides. With her first scream, the sea attacked her lungs, the burn like hellfire. She thrashed, pushed, kicked, but the black was everywhere. When her head finally burst above the waterline, she took in the most wonderful gulp of air.

"Jay?" Her words were garbled, purring over the water in her throat. "Jay!"

"Go on, get her!"

"Jay's not there, lass!"

"Turn 'round!"

The voices tumbled down on her head. It was too dark. The sea moved, sluggish and heavy, but there was no sign of Jay. Guilt rode the waves, and she was drowning in it. Drowning in all of it. *What did I do?* Lou paddled through the black, struggling to keep her head above water; she might have behaved like a pirate, but it would have been better to remain a mermaid.

Lou looked up at the ship's hulking mass. She was treading water on the side farthest from shore, her path blocked by the immense bulk of wood and iron and a smattering of large logs she hadn't noticed before.

Swim.

"Jay?" Lou pushed against the current. The sea groaned at her efforts, and a nearby log slid past her.

"C'mon, lass. Be a sport and let 'em have ye!"

A flash of yellow blinked from the black mass before her. Lou swam in the opposite direction, careful to avoid it, only to find it following close behind. Panic choked her, making it harder to breath.

Where was Jay?

"The crocs ain't had nothin' as sweet as you in a *long* time!"

"Get on with it!"

The laughter and jeers continued, warbling in the back of her mind. Lou stopped swimming. *Not logs*, she thought, swallowing more water.

Crocodiles.

Her arms and legs flailed, churning the water, making the pirates laugh harder. By her count, there were three. Their tails swished through the surface of the sea, their veined yellow eyes unmistakable. They moved with slow deliberation, their hide as sharp as their teeth. She was food—delicious tender meat—and this was the easiest hunt they could have hoped for.

She made it around the side of the ship but the current pushed her back and out to the horizon. The beach stretched out ahead of her, empty and pale and much too far away. Still, she swam, searching the waves for a bright head but finding only yellow eyes instead.

Jay.

Gathering her strength, she struck out for land. If she could find the children, they would know what to do. The idea of facing them after what she'd done . . .

"Ah, don't be like that, love! The crocs gotta eat too!"

More laughter. A game—the entire island was built on them. The cliffs grew taller, and she allowed herself to think about how wonderful the warm sand would feel under her palms as she crawled out of the sea. She imagined Sammy's embrace would be warmer still, Benji's kindness softer.

Lou's leg hit something solid. She screamed and inhaled seawater, her tears joining the murky depths around her. A crocodile slipped past, churning the water. The beach was a memory, replaced instead by the snap of mighty jaws. And there, like a flame in the night, was a mahogany head drifting farther out of reach. Crocodile song filled the air, drowning out the pirates, but it was Jay floating in the abyss that called to her the loudest.

He wasn't moving.

He can't be dead, she thought. *Please,* please, *I don't want to die.*

All she saw was the boy she'd betrayed. Lou struck out for that bright spot in the darkness. "Jay? I'm coming!" she called out, but there was no response. The glow of the sky turned his face the colour of ripe limes. "Please hold on! I'm almost there!"

When she finally reached him, the cliffs were a haze of grey and green. Her legs were heavy, her shoulders burning. She would never make it back to the island, but perhaps that was what she deserved; penance was the only thing that could wash her heart clean. Lou gripped his arm and pulled. The waves beat her back with a closed fist, and Jay was too heavy. It was all too heavy.

A growl rumbled underwater, sending ripples into the waves. One of the crocodiles sliced the sea in two, its jaw aimed at her heart.

She was so tired.

"Go away!" she called, but the beast kept coming. Golden eyes fixed on her, swaths of translucent flesh swiped across its irises like silk cloths. Lou gripped Jay's arm and pulled, struggling to escape, but he was a weight threatening to pull her under.

A boulder slammed into her chest. Like a rag doll, she sagged under its weight, her hands gripping Jay's body with all the strength she had left. Water climbed down her throat as she thrashed and fought, but the crocodile was relentless. He had her under his control. This was how the end found her. Closing her eyes against the liquid sky above her, Lou braced herself for the pain.

Rose and Mother were far away, free of the burden of knowing how she'd died. Perhaps they assumed she was already gone. Her family was safe in their ignorance.

Lou clung to Jay with the force of her terror.

She did not want to die alone.

Hitting the ground kicked the wind from her chest. Still, she held on to Jay while the crocodile wrestled with her body, pushing her up the sandy beach with its snout. The sand spread warmth across her back, heat that seeped into her chilled bones and fought the nauseating rock and buck of the waves that had almost claimed her life. Lou braced herself on hands and knees and coughed up water until stars bloomed across her vision. The air was sweet and clean, the pirates' outraged cries a distant song. They were no longer a threat; she and Jay were back on land. The beast blinked slowly, gurgling water on its journey back into the inky black.

Adrenaline made her head swim. Without checking her own flesh for puncture wounds, Lou scrambled across the sand. "Jay," she said, shaking his shoulders. "Jay, wake up. Come on, *wake up.*"

He didn't smirk or grin or twist onto his stomach, spluttering water. Colour didn't bloom in his cheeks. His dagger was gone, and without it, he was exactly the thing he'd claimed to Blackbeard: a child.

A cry of frustration clawed its way out of her throat. Lou punched Jay's chest, beat him with fists too cold to feel the pain. Once, twice, again, over and over. The release was better than the guilt; she may not have pushed Jay into the sea with her own bare hands, but she'd certainly cast the first blow by renouncing him. Her last act was to betray the devotion he'd shown her.

She wasn't worthy of him or Rose or even Mother's approval at having finally secured a match. She was nothing.

Another thump of his chest and water poured from Jay's mouth. Lou turned him onto his side and rubbed his shoulders to free the rest of the black sludge from his lungs. "Sh, sh, it's all right," she said. "You're all right."

When the hacking coughs subsided, he glanced up at her through a curtain of sodden hair. "Lou? What happened?"

Relief flooded her. Then came the tears. "I thought you died! We . . . We both could have died!"

"*Feels* like I'm dead." He sat on his ankles and scanned the sea, his gaze settling on the crocodiles already making their way around the ship. "Those are crocs."

"Yes." She pushed hair away from her cheeks and swiped her tears away. "How do you feel?"

"Those are *big* crocs."

Lou sighed. "You were expecting the less lethal baby variety?"

"How'd we get past them?" Jay patted himself down, searching his body with a frenzied panic. "We're not even bloody or anything!"

"I . . . I believe one of them dragged us back to shore. You weren't conscious, and I would never have been able to swim that distance on my own."

"You . . . *Dragged*?"

"Yes."

"With teeth? And we survived?"

Lou shrugged as Jay rose to his feet. "This is your island. I am only telling you what happened. Jay, what I said on the ship—"

"We got caught. Nothin' more to say." He offered his hand to help Lou up, and she took it, relishing the warmth of his palm and the kindness in his eyes. It was a kindness she didn't deserve. "I don't like it, but I understand it. How about you? Are you hurt?"

"I'm fine. No need to worry about me. We should get back to the den. The others must be worried by now. Especially Sammy."

"Yeah, worried . . ."

Three crocodiles waded like islands on the horizon, their low thrumming calls almost a purr. One poked its head above the surface, a tail swishing to a soundless rhythm. Yellow eyes blinked, water spouting from a smiling jaw before it sank back under the waves. Lou and Jay hesitated on the beach, their gazes lingering on the beasts who'd somehow spared their lives. The pirates' angry voices were a distant echo. Harmless now.

"Thank you," she whispered. But even on the island, crocodiles could not answer back. She hoped they heard her gratitude anyway.

"C'mon, let's get out of here."

Jay helped her up the beach and led the way to the sliver of darkness in the cliffs where Sammy had disappeared upon her arrival. Her strange clothes were heavy with water, and the chill was quickly settling into her bones. The way back was slow and quiet, the events of the night a burden on them both. Lou slogged up the stone steps, each drag of her feet like pulling a stick through mud. The sky turned from green to violet, then back to a proper navy, the world resetting itself on steady legs. The darkness in the forest was absolute, and Lou let Jay take the lead, his own steps careful if not a little shaky.

"They'll want to know why we didn't free Peter," she said when she could no longer hear the waves. The darkness was a veil shrouding her insecurity from Jay's probing gaze, and she was grateful for the privacy. "They'll want to know what happened."

"I'll tell them what happened. Bad news should come from me anyway."

He will tell them we failed, Lou thought miserably. *Tell them Peter is gone. Tell them their world will crumble away, piece by piece, until everything they know disappears.* The low light of the moons filtered through the jade canopy, lighting the emerald veins running through the earth like gemstones. Lou hadn't taken the time to truly appreciate the beauty of the island before, or what it would mean to have all of it disappear for good, or how it would feel to have the children's wonderful faces exist no more.

He will tell them I betrayed him . . . betrayed them all for my own benefit.

Pain, unexpected and sharp, twisted her heart. She shouldn't have cared about them. Only Rose mattered. And yet . . .

"I'm sorry," Lou said after a time.

"For what?"

"You know what."

Jay paused and looked up into her face with those knowing ancient eyes. "You did what you had to do to get home to your family. Like I said, I don't have to like it to understand it." A strange song trilled over their heads, and Jay grinned, suddenly serene. "That's a crimson goldfinch."

"Hmm?"

"The bird. She has a real soft voice when she's lettin' her babies know she's on her way home."

"A crimson goldfinch." Lou opened her senses to the soft cadence of birdsong. She hadn't stopped to listen to the birds in a very long time; enjoying the present was such a difficult thing when there was only worry about the future. "I didn't know you liked birds, Jay."

"I don't. Not really." His cheeks were pink, even in the darkness of the trees. "But you did. You wanted to be an ornithologist, remember?"

Lou laughed at the memory as though it belonged to someone else in some other life. "That's right. I almost forgot about that. Children really do have a way of wanting the impossible, don't they?"

The earth quaked, and the trees shuddered, but they didn't slow or mention the strange rattling of the island under their feet. No speaking was necessary to understand how grave the situation was.

After a long, long time, they approached a black hole in the ground—the same gap Sammy had led her to, the same one she'd fallen into unwittingly. Jay stepped aside to give her the option of falling first.

"Just 'cause you were a kid when you loved the birds doesn't mean what you wanted was impossible," he said. "It just meant you were happy enough to listen to your heart."

She said nothing as she stepped into open air. Her thoughts were too muddy, her nerves too raw to think about the betrayal of hearts when the betrayal of friendships was the only thing weighing on her.

As Lou fell, she closed her heart off once more.

Distractions would only hold her back.

They had failed to free Peter. The children were kind, but they were a distraction keeping her from Rose—her *real* family. Her only family.

The island belonged to the pirates and the children, not her.

It wouldn't be her coffin.

CHAPTER 18

LOU

HELLO AND GOODBYE

ome meant a great many things to me: a place to sleep, a place to play, a place to hide from the ghosts living in the walls. A prison. But the one thing home had never been was a stranger.

Until then.

The wallpaper was the same, the furniture sitting in its usual place. Sitting room, dining room, floral curtains and oil paintings, the oak stairwell to the second-floor landing—everything was as it had always been. But the smell was off, powdery and soft and fragrant, as though a new blossom from a delicate tree in the Briarwood had been plucked free and left to bloom within the house. Left to bloom and then wither. Die. There was something new about my home. And I didn't like it.

We tiptoed down the hall, and Jay's hand tightened around mine. I squeezed back, grateful for his steady presence when mine was shaky at best.

"It's okay," Jay said. "I'll be with you the whole time."

"I know."

"We'll go back to the woods when we're done. That always makes you feel better."

"Okay."

Daylight was banished to the outdoors; curtains were drawn, and the air was cool, the upstairs hall blanketed in darkness. My eyes locked on the door to the forbidden room, the source of all my nightmares. The door was cracked open; a triangle of golden light stretched across the hall, brightening the flecks of dust floating above the carpet. I hesitated outside the room, my legs too weak to carry me.

"Or we could go back to your room for a bit if you changed your mind," Jay said. "They don't know you're out here. They'll be too busy with the little runt to care if you don't go in right away. It's easy."

"Easy peasy, poke your knees-y."

Jay was right; there would be no harm in turning back before it was too late to run free. But pirates were strong, and I wasn't a coward. I lifted my hand and knocked.

"Louisa?" Father's voice echoed from the other side of the door, and before I knew it, I was pushing it wide open. He looked up at me, his eyes rimmed with dark circles over pale cheeks. The hollows in his face carved deeper, and a delicate tinge of yellow had replaced the tan that had once painted his face in gold. His smile, however, was as radiant as always. "There you are, little bird. We missed you. Would you like to come in and say hello?"

He patted the empty spot beside him on the window seat. The rocking chair facing him creaked, its bleached wood rails lurching back and forth, two narrow ships rolling across a soft sea.

"I can come back later if you are both busy," I said. *Please say yes. Please send me away.*

"Nonsense. Come here and let us have a look at you."

I smoothed out my faded skirt one last time and leaned into Jay's embrace for some much-needed reassurance. "Of course," I said. My steps were soft, halting, but Father had already turned away from me.

Mother's hair tumbled around her face. Each strand glowed a different shade of gold, her waves softer than the precise curls she always wore. Her mouth was relaxed, and her arms cradled a bundle of blankets. Whatever lay inside the soft parcel of green-and-silver fleece wiggled, cooed, and sighed. It stretched a pink hand complete with five pink fingers above the folds to grab blindly at Mother's chin, the sunlight setting each fingernail aglow. After an eternity, Mother looked up from the child in her arms and smiled, truly smiled—at *me*.

"Hello, sweetheart," she whispered, wide eyes brimming with tears. "Lou, meet your sister. Rose."

I tipped my head over the blanket, expecting a pile of skin and drool. A monster. Her eyes were closed, her mouth puckered into a shiny bow, and for a moment, I couldn't move. While my hair was a deep, indecisive blond muddied with brown, the baby's head was crowned in the bluest black down I'd ever seen. A raven's wing. A beautiful bird.

"Rosie," I said, testing the name. My muscles coiled, waiting for the reprimand. Her name was Rose, not Rosie, and I was to call the infant by her proper name. I knew that.

But Mother's brow softened. "Rosie. I like that."

Jay's hand fell out of mine. I didn't mind.

In fact, I didn't mind if he was happy or scared, if he was waiting patiently beside me or if he was preparing the swords for our next game of pirates and mermaids. I was too busy reaching into the blankets to place a finger into my sister's reaching fist for the first time.

Jay had many friends he called brothers, but they were not connected by blood. With Rosie's small fingers curled around one of my own, I knew that if he had any true siblings, he would never spend so much time with me. He had never known the bond of blood. For in that moment, I hardly knew Jay the way my soul knew the child before me.

The boy with the chipped tooth slipped from my mind. I never said goodbye.

Then again, I couldn't prove he had ever existed at all.

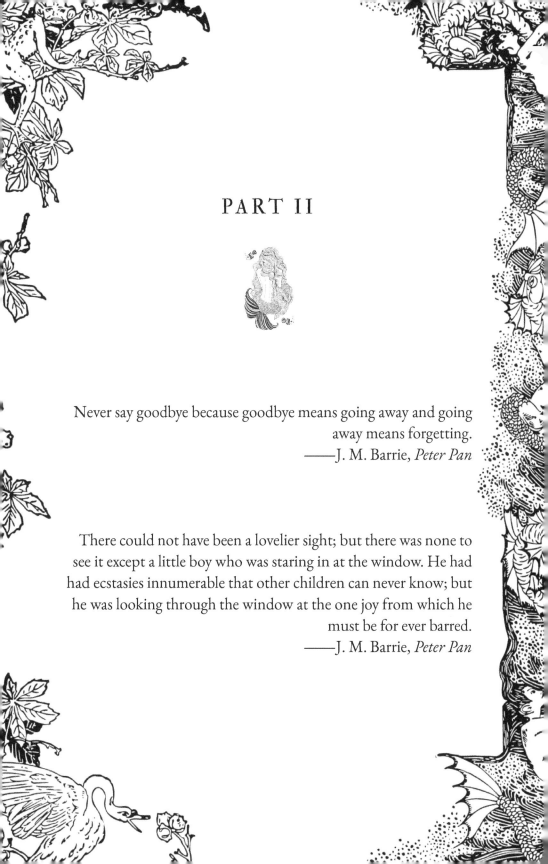

PART II

Never say goodbye because goodbye means going away and going
away means forgetting.
——J. M. Barrie, *Peter Pan*

There could not have been a lovelier sight; but there was none to
see it except a little boy who was staring in at the window. He had
had ecstasies innumerable that other children can never know; but
he was looking through the window at the one joy from which he
must be for ever barred.
——J. M. Barrie, *Peter Pan*

CHAPTER 19

JAY

Things were always great until a big stinking island dragged you home.

Home. What a joke.

I landed face down in the dirt instead of on my feet, and if that wasn't a punch to the gut, I didn't know what was. My fingers clawed at the earth, and I pushed myself to my knees, coughing, spitting leaves, and just plain dying.

I wasn't supposed to be back so soon.

Why was I *back* already?

And there was no doubt I was back; after a life as long as mine, I could feel Peter's island in my bones and tell the woods out by the Hanging Tree apart from the tribal lands by the way the dirt tasted. It was too bright, and the trees were too big, too twisted, too *green* to be the Briarwood. One sharp inhale told me that the croc swamp was a stone's throw east, the heavy stench of fish and pirate sweat riding the breeze moving in from the cove at my back.

Lou wasn't there; she couldn't be. There were rules and barriers to keep those things from happening. There were reasons the mix of the lost and the grown was so limited. They just didn't matter as much as finding out why I wasn't back in that house with Lou.

The *baby* . . .

Something about that wriggling bag of snot and spit had played with the way of things. *I always knew nothing good came from babies.* Pain lanced through my chest at the memory of Lou's eyes softening over the stupid pile of blankets, the way her fingers trembled over its small hand.

I folded over and retched into a pile of leaves, grateful the direction of the wind kept the smell out of my face. No one saw me empty my stomach onto the ground. One of the perks of being lost was the ability to suffer in peace.

It took a while before the heaves stopped. When there was nothing left inside me, the ground under my hands and knees stood still. That was good. That was the first step to figuring out how to get back.

All right, this is a mistake. Just a mistake. I'll open my eyes and see the useless basket in that room that looks like a croc threw up everywhere. Picturing the familiar turns of the halls in Lou's brick tomb was easy. I had walked those halls for years, memorized every loose floorboard and curtain flutter. It was as much a home to her as the island was to me, but it was the only place I was allowed to see her, so it was enough, especially since Peter let me visit as often as I liked. A perk of being his number two.

One of the *only* perks.

I let the vision of Lou's window fill my mind; she kept that window open for me, and it was the place that called my name into the wind, even in the dark and from the greatest distance. I was ready. I was there.

I opened my eyes.

I was still sitting near a puddle of my own sick.

The parched ground sucked up the vomit, and I pushed another wave of nausea aside. "You gotta be kiddin' me!" Palm leaves swayed around me, flicking aside my outburst. Birds squawked—*Hey, don't yell at us, kid*—and the rest of the island spasmed with my rage.

Good. Let it suffer.

Judging by the growth pattern of the ferns and the three-legged chipmunks nestling in the hollows of the ancient maples, the Hanging Tree was almost an hour's walk north. That was good too. My legs were jittery, needing the exercise, so the long trek through the never-ending mess of fruit and forest would be a good way to vent some of my energy before I had to face Peter.

Peter.

Not yet. One thing at a time.

I stumbled to my feet. Blood pooled in my legs, throwing a thousand daggers into my starved muscles. With Lou, I could never stay upset. Not really. After the mistake with the baby's room, I knew I had to keep that side of me bound and gagged unless I wanted to lose her. That kid had enough to worry about without me adding to her misery; I was supposed to take her burdens away, not give her more trouble. But she was far away, beyond the veil, and I let my anger fly.

Not anger at Lou for touching that damn baby.

Anger at Peter.

He was probably back at the Hanging Tree, eating our food and skinning our kills while calling them his own.

The distance between us was keeping him alive.

Him.

Peter. This was all *Peter's* doing.

Lou was still young. Sure, her momma was a loon, but her daddy seemed to get it, to really remember what it meant to swing from trees and have a laugh or two. He was a grown, so there was only so much he could understand of the things that were meant to disappear when childhood trickled away. Lou was leagues away from having her momma's worries and her daddy's haunted eyes and letting her own kids swing from trees. That time would come, but it wasn't now.

She still believed in magic. In *me*.

Or at least, she should. Truth never changed that quick. Not even on the island.

The trees bent to my rage; vines slithered away from me, but the thick branches and heavy flowers of gold and orange and mottled blue lurched into my path, blocking me from getting to *him*. Everything on this spit of dirt was there to protect him, and I was tired. I slashed away at every living thing trying to keep me away from the Hanging Tree. Green, gold, orange, and mottled blue littered the forest floor like dead bodies after a pirate fight.

I would sink the entire island to the bottom of the sea if it meant getting the truth out of Peter.

Sunset was the most beautifully dangerous time of day. I looked up in time to see the heavy sun drip like egg yolk behind the trees, spilling the land with the last warm rays of day.

Red sky at night, sailor's delight.

Red sky at morning, sailors take warning.

I'd heard the saying once or twice in the Land of the Grown. Sure, it made sense for them; everything changed so fast in their world—too fast, even. But on the island, where the sky at sunset always bled with the sorrows of kids who suffered a thousand cuts every day, nothing ever changed. There was too much bloodshed and cruelty to turn the sky to anything purer than the thick ooze of sin, and so the sailors and pirates were always happy.

Red sky at night, pirate's delight.

This island was for them, no matter what Peter said.

The croc swamp followed me north, the rumbles hidden behind a thick patch of sycamores. I never went close to the infested waters if I could help it and had learned to pick their rough bodies out from an outcropping of rocks from a safe distance away. Since the pirates had banned hunting the beasts in their burrows, the island crawled with the damn lizards. Still, I'd have rather faced one of the crocs than see Peter's grinning face.

I heard the Hanging Tree before I saw it. Every kid who'd ever touched its roots and nestled in its belly whispered through the branches. If they toed the line, they were allowed to stay. If they didn't, their bones were buried, making the soil fertile. At least that was one of the stories Peter told us. Then again, Peter lied. A lot.

I tried not to think of their voices swarming around me as I marched over the roots, but they were everywhere, warning me to stay away, just like they always did. Just like they hadn't. And they'd paid the price.

"You'd better be here." I found the sliver of darkness cutting through the trunk and slipped inside. The hard-packed dirt sloped under me, and I navigated the path without a thought. It had been years since I'd needed to feel my way down into the den.

Too many years. Too long.

And I was always the freaking same.

Instead of the usual clang of steel and jeers of a game gone too far, the den was quiet. The boys were gone, probably off pillaging a camp for supplies or trying to lure a princess away from her tribe so Peter would have a prisoner to humiliate around the campfire. The mix of relief and anger wasn't something familiar to me, and in a way, I was almost grateful for the strangeness of it. It was different, and different never happened to me anymore. Not unless I killed something.

But that was before Lou; she wanted to touch the sky when her parents wanted her to stay on the ground. If she could dream, so could I.

Blankets, broken dolls, cracked dishes, and rusty knives littered the ground. I made sure not to disturb any of it as I moved deeper into the den. The far wall was dotted with hooks, every spear and crossbow gone. A raid, then. Peter wanted us armed, sure, but we never touched the long spears and crossbows unless we were hunting big game.

I stopped under the hammock where Peter slept and counted the knots in the tough rope; I could cut it down if I tried hard, but my sword was too dull and too short. If he slept on the ground with us, it would have been easy to take him out in his sleep. But he was the only one with a proper bed; the rest of us slept on the ground, ate in the mud, and cried in silence.

"Look who's back."

Goosebumps exploded down my arms. I dropped to one knee and hated myself at once for the habit he'd built in me. "Hey, boss."

"Ah, you don't need to do that. Get up." Darkness clung to Peter like a second skin, the whites of his eyes watchful and much too bright as I pushed myself off the ground. He was a full head shorter than me and had the roundness of a kid still ripe in him, no older than ten, maybe eleven. But if Peter and his rule had taught me anything, it was the sure truth that looks were deceiving. "So, you're back."

"I am. Where is everyone?"

"Out by Mermaid Lagoon. We're tryin' to get one of the fish to come back with us, but some of the pirates gave 'em swords a couple days ago. They're not comin' easy." His muddy green eyes rarely blinked; I'd never noticed that before. Probably because I never looked him in the eye if I could help it. I could stab him in each eye with one quick move, but he'd see me coming and make me pay.

Patience. Just like he taught you.

I offered him a smile instead of ending his too-long life. Because that was good form.

"Why would the pirates give them weapons?" I asked.

"Beats me. Anythin' female drives 'em nuts."

I nodded. "I hope our boys don't have their hopes too high. Those fish'll never leave the lagoon."

"They will if I make 'em." Peter stepped around me and made his way to the far side of the room, where Slightly and JinJin shared a pallet of straw. He peeled away the mess of blankets and pulled out a small bowl of fresh berries. "Those boys should know they can't keep anythin' from me. Guess I should show 'em what happens if they try, eh, Number Two?"

"Sure, boss."

Peter tucked into the bright blue and red fruits without offering me any, the deep red juice running from the corners of his mouth, staining his teeth and chin. "You can go join 'em if you want, you know. They could use the help. 'Specially Benji. I made a big mistake bringin' that one here."

"Maybe I will." *Not a chance.* "Benji's all right, though. I like him. He keeps the others straight."

"Others like Slightly, right?"

I shrugged. "I guess."

"You never liked him much."

"Doesn't matter what I like and what I don't." I didn't want to talk about Slightly or even Benji. Peter was stalling; his eyes flashed, and his smile spread, and I could have throttled him with my fists. "You're in charge," I said. "You make the rules, and if you say Slightly stays, then he stays. Speakin' of your rules, I had a bit of a problem comin' back from the other side today."

"That so?"

"The island pulled me back when I wasn't ready to go. That never happened before. Any idea what could have done it?"

Peter pushed another helping of berries into his mouth, dark nectar dripping down his chin and staining his clothes. "Ah, Jay, I'm sorry." *You're not.* "I figured that was gonna happen soon. It's why I came back here, to see if you were all right."

Relief flooded over me, and I forgot I was supposed to be mad at him. "So, you *do* know somethin'. Man, does that make me happy."

"Sure I do. It's my island."

"So, tell me," I said. Lou was probably looking for me in that jail cell of a room, trapped with her parents and the baby she hated so much. "Boss?"

Fire blazed behind Peter's eyes. "Nothin's changed, Jay. Nothin' went wrong."

He wiped his dirty hands on a blanket crumpled at his feet. Not *his* blanket—Sammy's. The kid never left the den without that old thing unless we were on a mission, and he would come back to it soiled and violated. Peter always claimed a token, something we loved and kept in our pockets when he took us away. I never knew what he did with any of it, but he'd let Sammy keep the blanket, only to destroy it, thread by thread, whenever he felt like it. The need to drive my blade between Peter's eyes until his screams ran dry thrummed in my blood, but I kept my hands still. *For now.*

"I'm tellin' you, somethin' went sideways," I said. "I was right there, then I wasn't. I always get a warnin'."

"You were pulled out 'cause Lou's grown-up now, just like every other time you've had a kid on your watch. Tick-tock, Number Two. She don't need you anymore, you come home— that's the law. Seriously, you sure you don't wanna join the others? There's plenty of mermaids out today; I'm sure you'll spear one easy."

My fingers twitched to the hilt of my dagger. "Lou's still a kid. She needs me. I've spent years with her; I would know if the change was comin'."

The rest of the uneaten fruit was tossed to the ground, sand coating the berries until they were nothing but soft pebbles on a dirty floor. "Jay, listen," Peter said, raising stained palms. "She grew up. That's it."

"That's not possible. It *never* happens that fast."

"Sometimes it does," he said, shrugging. "Count yourself lucky. You always said you wanted to stop takin' on kids. Now you're free."

This wasn't freedom; this was a game.

Peter swiped the back of his hand across his nose, and his dirty fingers left a red streak across his face. "All right, listen to me. If somethin' big happened to Lou, somethin' that forced her to feel like she had to grow up real quick, then you'd get no warnin' at all before the island brought you back."

That stupid baby. "How do I get to her, then?"

"Get to her?" He looked up, the berry juice already dry. Later he'd have one of us, the smallest of us, run over to the closest stream to wash his clothes. If that boy became croc meat, that was part of the fun. Peter would just replace him with another. "You don't *get to her*. It's over. Be happy, brother. You're home for good."

"Happy." The word was completely at odds with my heart, the syllables jarring to my ears. "I . . . I didn't get to say goodbye."

"So?" Peter snorted. "Who cares? She's one of them now. She's boring. Got no magic, no imagination. Just forget about her. If it means that much to you, we'll find you a new toy. I mean, I thought you wanted to be done after this one, but if you like playin' dollies with the snotty kids so much, then fine."

A new toy. Some other kid who needed a friend, someone to pass the time with until they *moved on* and away from me. Someone lost, someone in pain. Someone who wasn't Lou.

I'd grown up in an overcrowded building that was home to as many rats as kids. Daddy had too many mouths to feed, so he fed the ones that mattered most to him. Momma was too afraid to argue, so she let him do what he wanted. Maybe that's why I was the smallest of my four brothers. Maybe that's why I was the weakest, too. Or maybe Daddy was right, and I was just a runt and a burden. Once Peter found me hiding in my bedroom closet, though, none of that mattered. I was thirteen and had been sitting in my own filth for a long, long time. Daddy had laid hands on Momma again, and while the others had fought back, I, like a weak runt, had hidden.

I didn't remember much more, and the more years went by, the less I could keep straight. Even if I tried real hard, I still couldn't say for sure how long Momma and the others had been quiet before Peter had opened that closet door. He was so real, the hand he offered me solid and soft all at once. At that moment, he'd been my saviour and my forgiveness, leading me out to the window while blocking the bodies curled up on the floor.

I owed him my life, and I had given that to him without argument every day since.

Except now, it wasn't only my life he was taking.

The sting in my eyes blurred the room. "Let me go back and explain why I need to leave her. Let me say goodbye."

Peter's laugh slapped me across the face. "Did you hit your head on a tree on the way back? Lou won't *remember* you. She probably don't realize you're gone or that you even exist! She don't care if you say goodbye or not. Let it go."

I gritted my teeth. "Lou wouldn't forget me. You don't know her. I'm her only friend—her brother."

"You were her friend, but *I'm* your brother. Lou's got a little sister now, don't she? A real sister, flesh and blood. You're nothin' to her."

There was a reason Peter was the unchallenged leader; he wasn't the fastest or the bravest or the strongest. There was something missing in Peter, something that made it easy for him to steal, and maim, and bleed, and kill.

Kill our bodies.

Kill our spirits.

Kill our hope until all we had left was him.

"I wanna go back."

"No." He drew level with me, and I could smell the sweat baked into the folds of his dirty shirt.

The word hit me in the chest, overpowering my will. And the harder I tried to stand against him, the quicker my resolve drizzled through my fingers, like sand held too tight. "She can't think I just left her. You know how that feels; we both do. I owe her that, Peter."

Peter's grin flickered and died like a campfire doused in cold water. His eyes were flat. The first and most lost of all the boys stepped closer to me, his movement across our den making no sound. "You and me ain't the same, Number Two. Don't be makin' the mistake of thinkin' you can tell me what to do on my island. You're never gonna see Lou again. It's forbidden. Understand?"

Yeah. Yes. Yes, I understand. But I didn't. "C'mon, boss. I won't tell anyone you let me go back. Promise. Can't you just do me this one favour?"

The blade came from nowhere. A sharp point pressed into my left shoulder, forcing me down to my knees. It snagged on my shirt and kissed my skin, the steel moving slow. "You're my favourite boy, Jay. You're here to make sure the others follow my rules, not bend them when it suits you. If you don't stand by me . . . Well, what's the point of havin' you around?" The dagger moved through my shoulder, deeper, pain, so much pain. I gritted my teeth and met his glare. In the space of a breath, Peter's grimace twisted into a smile. He lowered his hand and took a step back, wiping a drop of my blood on his knee. "Enough of all the serious talk. The mermaids won't spear themselves. Come on, Jay. Let's just get back to our family."

I didn't need the thick panic in my throat to tell me I was standing on a narrow plank on the deck of a very big ship over croc-infested waters. Something hot and miserable trickled down my cheek, but I wasn't ashamed. The tears came, and I let them flow while the boss had his fun. "I'm goin' back, Peter. With or without your say-so."

Peter sighed, relaxed his shoulders, let pity colour his eyes. "None of you boys had a good daddy. That's why I gotta show you what's right and how the world really is, even when it's cruel. Love and respect take work. Sometimes that means makin' the tough choices to keep you in line. That takes work. I don't like to work."

His arm swung out over his head and slammed down hard, the steel hissing by my ear before sinking into my shoulder. Blood pooled around the deep gash, and with every sharp twist of Peter's wrist, more crimson soaked into the dirt under me.

Still, Peter didn't blink.

I never let him hear me scream.

CHAPTER 20

The den was a different place after she'd been caught by pirates and swarmed by crocodiles. The chute twisted down and left, up and right, with only her breathing to mark the journey. Lou wanted nothing more than to find her spot on the cold ground and sleep until the acidic smell of the pirates' brig no longer haunted her memory. But when the narrow passage gave way to the familiar room with weapons and warm rugs on the floor, the fear of never seeing her own room again overcame her relief at being safe.

A blond head jumped into the darkness, small arms wrenching Jay's middle. Sammy's shoulders shook, and Jay squeezed him back, burying his face in the boy's hair.

"Sh, it's all right, buddy. I'm okay."

Lou looked away, hurrying into the den to leave the boys to their reunion. Sammy, at least, had survived the battle on the beach; she dreaded learning if any of their party hadn't.

"Lou! Jay!" Benji bounded out of his seat, scratches on his cheeks still dripping blood. "We were worried you never made it off the ship. What happened? Did you get Peter?"

"Crickets, Benji, give 'em some space." Didi grabbed for the last apple sitting in the wooden bowl before her, but Kiran swiped it first. "Looks like you finally took that bath, Jay."

"More like a swim." Jay towed Sammy into the den, the boy still clinging to him in a way that made Lou's heart ache. "What did we miss?"

Bandages, cloths, and bowls of water littered the tables, blood colouring it all red. Henry moved from Kiran to Didi to Benji, checking compresses and offering aloe leaves, their healing jelly oozing over parched skin. Once satisfied with his work, he reached for Sammy next, but the boy only tightened his hold on Jay.

"It went down just like you said, boss," Kiran said, tossing the apple core to the ground. "We took down a couple pirates, but the Blues did the most damage. When the tribe saw their female's head in the water, they started killin' anyone they could get their hands on. Win-win."

Jay dropped into a seat, and Sammy sat on the ground between his knees. "And you? Was anyone seriously hurt?"

"Nah," Didi said. "Just some scratches and bruises. I know I was complainin' about helpin' the grown lady, but this was kinda fun. We should start some raids like this more often. Maybe we can use her as pirate bait."

"I am standing right here," Lou said, towering over Didi. "And I have a name that is not *the grown lady*."

Didi's face grew dark. Her chair scratched against the ground in her haste to stand, and Kiran joined her side at once. Both children, faces dripping in black paint and boasting twin scars across their brows, united against her. But Lou's patience had expired the moment she'd been pushed off the ship, and the flippant discussion of future raids and wars stoked a new flame in her belly.

"Whatcha gonna do?" Didi asked. "You can't fight. You can't survive in the woods. Didja even get Peter back from the pirates?"

Jay frowned. "Didi, stand down."

"She's trouble, boss! This is *our* island, not hers! She don't belong here."

Benji sidled up beside Lou, the warmth of his body giving her courage.

"You are quite right," Lou said. "I belong somewhere else. And I would be more than glad to leave this place and never return. But we did not get Peter off that ship. You will need to endure my presence a little longer, I'm afraid."

"We tried," Jay said. "But there was mermaid hair in the lock. Then the pirates tossed us to the crocs."

"What?" Sammy glanced up, eyes wide. "How'd you get away?"

"They were huge, at least twelve feet long," Jay said, settling into the story with a soft smile. He reached for his dagger, slashing it before him. "But I fought 'em off one by one."

"How big were their teeth?" Benji asked in a whisper.

"Bigger than your head. And ugly too. Me and Lou managed to take two out with just our blades, and then we rode those crocs all the way back to the beach."

The pride shone through the gravel in his voice. As quickly as they'd been overcome by pirates, Jay swung the pendulum the other way, giving in to the thrill of a fight existing only in his mind. While Lou saw only the leers of greedy, hungry men and the endless yawn of the sea, Jay saw more. He gestured and mimed an epic tale of monsters struck down by the tip of his blade, a show the others drank in like sweet wine.

Lou stepped forward and cleared her throat. "There is nothing more we can do tonight, but we will come up with another plan to get Peter back. I already have an idea."

Silence fell like a guillotine. Benji squinted at her, his lips deep red against the pallor of his skin. "You . . . You want to try again?"

"Of course. You cannot expect me to stay here and wait to

either die or remain trapped on an island away from my home. I am betrothed. My sister—"

"Yeah, we heard enough about your sister," Didi said. "Sure, it don't matter to you that the rest of us could die 'cause your sister needs someone to brush her hair for her."

"Of course I care!"

"Then show it!"

Jay spun his dagger in his palm and plunged the blade into the tabletop. "Didi, lay off; it's been a long night for all of us. Lou . . . that's not happenin'. We almost died tryin' to get Peter out of that mess. If it weren't for some luck with those crocs tonight, we'd be dead. I won't be puttin' my kids through that kind of danger again, even if it does mean we go down with the island. It's done. We're done. Might as well enjoy the time we got left. Everyone agree?"

Lou moved closer. "We had a deal, Jay. We need to find another way to get Peter off Blackbeard's ship."

"*Need* to? The only thing I *need* to do is look out for my kids."

"That is not what—"

"Peter's cell is unbreakable, Lou! And now that the pirates know what we're after, they're probably gonna move him somewhere else or double the guard. We had one shot, and it didn't work. It's over." He sighed, deflating before her eyes. "We *tried*, okay? I really wish it had worked, but it didn't."

Her eyes burned, and her tears blurred the curved lines of his face. "This cannot be the end."

"I think it is." Jay flipped his palm up, and Sammy took his hand. "Maybe things'll work themselves out on their own. Peter touched the stars once before. Someone else could do it before the island's destroyed. I just know I won't go back to that ship. Not for Peter."

"Not even for them?" Lou asked, gesturing around the den at the other children.

He looked up, and his features were unreadable. "You don't see it, Lou, but I'm doin' this for all of you. Trust me." Jay reached for the empty bowl on the table and frowned. "What I know for sure is if we don't get some supplies, we'll starve before the island goes down. Any volunteers?"

Didi and Kiran stepped forward together. "We'll go, boss," Didi said. "I need to do somethin' more than just sittin' around listenin' to all this garbage."

Kiran gave her a silencing look. "She just means we need to stay busy. I'll go with her to scout the area. See if any of the pirates or tribes are movin' against us."

"Good idea. You two go on up. Sammy and Benji need some rest, so try to be quiet when you get back. Lou, you'll stay with Henry. He might not talk much, but he's pretty good company when things get tough."

"Actually, I'd like to go with Didi and Kiran." Lou ignored the hiss of irritation escaping Didi's lips. "I need some air as well."

"Boss—" Didi began, but Jay plucked his dagger from the slab of wood, and her protests evaporated into the air.

"That's fine," Jay said. "But make it quick. They'll be makin' sure you don't get into trouble. Right, Didi?"

Didi scowled, but Kiran handed Lou a basket of woven palm leaves with a meek smile. "For the fruit," he explained.

A second tunnel out of the den sat behind Jay's sleeping quarters. Kiran and Didi moved silently, navigating the sharp twists and steep climbs with their fingers as their guide. Lou clutched the basket to her chest, the leaves trapping the warmth to her body as her clothes dried. The rumbles of the earth grew louder until they broke the surface, the air heavy with the scent of lavender and copper.

In truth, Lou had more than a need to come above ground to clear her head. She tipped her face to the sky and scanned the slivers of light between the thick branches. Pale green clouds curled across the sky like a road map, the stars a million tiny stops on the way to nowhere. She'd imagined what it would be like to tickle those heavenly gems since she'd learned there was more to the world than the rocks and the trees and her small home at the top of a hill. But reaching that far above her had been impossible then—how could she hope to climb so far above the ground now?

You need to figure it out somehow. You have no choice.

No choice.

Didi pushed a heavy blanket of leaves and twigs off the mouth of the chute and struck out first. "It's all clear," she said, "but you better stay out of the way. Me and Kiran, we got a good way of workin', and we don't need to save you if you get in trouble. Got it, lady?"

"I understand." Lou's relief at being above ground, surrounded by green and breathing in clean air, overwhelmed any aggravation she might have felt toward the girl. They filed out of the tunnel and onto a narrow path leading due south, deep into the heart of the trees.

Hisses and cracks snapped out at them in the darkness. Didi held her bow above her shoulders, tracking the sounds with a practiced ear. Her feet found the flat spots on the path, pivoting through the trees and allowing her to crouch, to lean, to move out of the reach of branches clawing at her. Reaching for her. Reaching for them all.

"It's like the trees are alive," Lou said, suppressing a shudder. "I've never seen anything like it."

"They are." Kiran moved beside her, matching his steps to hers. "The whole island smells us. It fights back when it needs to . . . and it's strong enough to keep us here or make us disappear when it feels like it." At his words, a vine slithered off the frond of a nearby palm tree, a smattering of violet thorns scratching across Kiran's shoulder. He didn't seem to notice.

"I still don't understand how dirt and rocks and bushes can

keep you all trapped. There is a ship. There are sailors. Perhaps it is enough to leave."

Kiran sniffed the air and motioned for Didi to step off the path and follow a trail of fallen berries pointing due west. "Some of the pirates tried to leave. Us kids . . . Well, most of the island's loyal to Peter. Most of us ain't got nowhere better to go. But the ones who did try to sail off only ended up gettin' turned around. Any direction they went, the island found 'em before they could go too far. Like it was waitin'."

"Unless you can somehow touch the stars." Lou laughed bitterly at the notion, but Kiran's nod was solemn. Respectful, even. "Do you truly think the story is true?"

"It's not a story, lady." Didi whirled around, her arrow aimed at Lou's heart. "It's the way it is. And if you two don't quit chattin' soon, I'll take all this food for myself and make sure you get none of it." She stopped beside a thick trunk, pink blossoms with ripe fruit hanging low over their heads. Didi picked a half dozen peaches and filled a hemp bag with practiced fingers. "Kiran, keep a lookout."

"Yeah, yeah." He cast a dark look into the forest, the drip of face paint oozing down his upper lip. "Everythin' looks quiet, sis. Plus, it's the fairies' night to keep watch."

A rumble sounded deep in the forest, followed closely by a flash of lightning bathing the trees in pale violet light. Didi sighed. "First Timber, now the sky. I wonder how much more's gonna happen before we all disappear."

Lou sat down on a soft bed of leaves, grateful for the break. "What was Timber like?"

"Quiet." Kiran chuckled low. "When Peter and Jay split, Timber stayed with the other side. But Jay never held it against him, you know. We all gotta survive the best way we know how."

"Did he and Jay know each other well?"

"Oh, sure. They were together in Peter's clan for a long time, and there was never no bad blood between 'em. But Timber wanted to keep seein' the Land of the Grown, and Jay wanted out." He glanced over at Lou and gnawed on the inside of his cheek. "He really loved Rosie, you know. She was his favourite friend out of all of 'em."

Lou smiled. "He had good taste."

Once Didi's bag was filled with the peaches, she handed the contents to Kiran and moved to the blueberry bushes with Lou's basket in hand. It was strange to hear her sister's name spoken on foreign lips, but for a moment, and despite it being the furthest thing from true, Lou felt closer to home.

"May I ask you a question, Kiran?" Lou asked. When he nodded, she lifted her fingers to his cheek and allowed her fingers to trace the edges of the slick paint. "Why do you both cover your faces in this mask when the others do not?"

He looked down at his feet. "The others don't got ugly scars like ours."

"I see nothing ugly about them."

"Lucky you."

Lou frowned. "I'm sorry. I did not mean to upset you."

Didi towered over him, blocking out the moonlight. "We don't need no sorries. What we need is to get this food back to the den. You think your soft hands can handle some work?"

"I would be glad to help," Lou said, getting to her feet. "I have had my struggles as well, Didi. It is not entirely fair to assume my life has been simpler than yours."

"Look at my face and tell me it wasn't."

Lou looked into the darkness between the trees. "My cage being prettier than yours makes it no less a prison."

Kiran's blade swung into a wide arc over their heads, singing past Lou's ear. He faced the path they'd left behind, his shoulders rigid, sword steady. "Quiet, you two." Whatever retort Lou had on her lips withered to nothing at the sight of Didi's terror, the way she joined her brother's side, her arrow pulled tight on its string. They knelt in the dirt, squinting through the swaying branches, hair standing on end.

It was then that Lou heard them. The wind softened the gruff voices of men, their muffled footsteps riding the sway of golden light from handheld torches.

"Ye sure this be the way?"

"Aye. He said te take the path by the peach trees and look down. This be the biggest crop o' peach trees on this damned island."

A pause. A heavy cough. The light rattled to a stop. "I don't trust the boy."

The second man laughed. "He got no reason te lie. Boy's weak, and none o' his friends came to get 'im. If he knows what's good, he'll be steerin' us straight."

Lou crouched low on Kiran's opposite side. "What are they talking about?"

Kiran shook his head for silence and motioned for them to move closer to the edge of the path. Together, they followed the trail of torchlight in the direction of the den, their collection of fruit forgotten under the peach blossoms.

Pirates. By her count, there were five of them, scouring the ground as though looking for fallen coins. They split up in the trees, overturning leaves and pushing away vines.

No. No, no, no.

"We must warn Jay and the others!" Lou hissed.

Didi shook her head. "It's too late. There're only two ways in and out of the den from the outside, and they're close to both. We can't get through."

No way to warn them that the pirates were swarming. No way to get the children to safety.

"I think I found somethin'!" The call came from behind a

mulberry bush where two palms stretched through the greenery like signposts. "Looks like a rabbit hole, on'y bigger."

"I don't like it," one of the pirates said. "Peter'll say anythin' to get us killed. We set fire to that den, the others'll come down on us like locusts."

"I say we do it and run," another one muttered. "If those rats are keepin' the key to the stars in their nest, we needs te get it. I'm not ready te die."

Lou shifted in the shadows, straining to listen to the mounting argument.

"Jus' think. We get te the stars before Blackbeard, we can take over this whole island. I'd be king!"

"Who made *you* king?"

A laugh. "It ain't gonna be you!"

The pirates collapsed into angry curses, pushing and thumping one another with the entrance to the den not five feet away from their feet.

Kiran shifted, and a twig snapped, sending a crack like thunder sailing over the pirates' heads. Wind- and sunburned faces swivelled in their direction, blades shining as though they'd recently been sharpened.

"Ye hear that?"

"Aye. Check those trees."

"Why do I gotta check 'em?"

"Why you gotta fight me all the time?"

An arrow whistled through the weeds and planted itself in the nearest pirate's chest. Blood blossomed across his shirt, marking the place he would collapse with drips of liquid fire. The men around him froze, scanned the trees, and waited. Waited for death. Waited for their wits to catch up to their shock.

Waited too long.

Didi let another arrow fly, and it split the bark of a nearby palm in half. "That's a warnin' shot! Next one goes in an eye!"

Didi's voice echoed around them, roaring in the night, thrumming with power. The four men huddled together, scanning the sky and finding nothing but the stars.

"Forget this!" one of them cried. He made for the trees without a glance at his comrades, his torch bouncing over his head.

One by one, the pirates scattered.

One by one, the trees collapsed into darkness.

Lou counted her heartbeats before Kiran and Didi got to their feet. When none of the pirates returned and the sky had shifted from green to deep silken violet, they moved into the open and straight for the den. Lou's mind was alight, crackling with energy when only moments before she'd been ready for sleep. She had it —a final decision. And while she should have felt afraid, there was only room for one dominant emotion, and that was excitement.

"Jay'll wanna move out before daylight," Didi said. "We'll set up a watch 'til we can pack our things."

"You're leaving?" Lou asked.

"*We're* leavin', lady. Jay made it pretty clear we're saddled with you 'til this thing ends, so we can't stay here. Ain't no one gonna defend you *and* the den and live to talk about it."

Down the tunnels, into the black, winding deeper into the earth they went. Lou kept her silence, holding it to her heart like a talisman.

Peter had a key to the stars and a way off the island. He knew where it was; he had tried to barter it for his freedom.

And she would get it before anyone else could stop her.

JAY SENT Henry and Benji to collect the fruit from the forest. By the time the boys returned and food was divided among them, Lou had retreated to her place on the ground, her mind a hurricane, her body calm. Jay laughed at the pirates' threat on their den and busied himself with a new bandage around Benji's finger, twisting the bindings until they lay flat. The children moved in a slow whirr of beautiful colour and renewed calm.

"We'll stay," Jay finally announced. "Those pirates came here without Blackbeard knowin' about it. They won't come back now they're scared they'll be shot, and they can't go back to the ship without admittin' where one of their men went. The tribes'll get 'em before we even have a chance." He tossed a peach from hand to hand, satisfied with his choice.

"We can find another den." Sammy straightened his glasses and stepped closer to Jay. "It won't be so bad."

"We won't run from our home," Jay said. "They can't force us out. But if you wanna put it to a vote—"

"Those men were promised a key to get off the island. By Peter." Faces turned to Lou, a mixture of disbelief, confusion, and irritation landing on her like a hammer. "Didi and Kiran heard it too."

"You never met Peter, lady," Didi said. "He'll say anythin' if it means gettin' out of that cell. Even turn us in."

"And what if Peter told them the truth? Is it not worth considering that an answer to freeing us is hidden somewhere on this awful island? We wouldn't even need to free him to set the world straight. We could do it ourselves without risking any lives again!"

Jay touched the tip of his dagger to the ground and spun it around on its axis, orange light reflecting off the blade in blinding shards. In her anger, the rapid shift of light and dark was an unwanted distraction meant to blind and distract. She lurched to her feet and crossed the den in three quick paces. And when she kicked his dagger into the far wall, she unleashed every frustration she harboured in her heart. He gawked at her, his hand now empty.

"Tell me," she demanded. "Where does Peter keep his valuable belongings?"

"How would I know?"

Benji tiptoed to the edge of the room and plucked Jay's dagger from the dirt. Jay bestowed a smile on the boy when his blade was finally back in his palm and sheathed it at his side.

"You were his closest friend and his right hand; I've heard it many times," Lou said, "including from the boy himself. Number Two, is that right?"

She had met a stray dog in the Briarwood once; while she had still been small at the time, the mutt had been smaller. Patches of missing fur had revealed red skin, its ribs standing out against the fur. It had cowered, baring teeth. Afraid. She'd approached, ever so slowly, but the dog had never relented. And had never looked her in the eye.

Jay stepped away from her, busying himself with his shirt sleeves, tongue swiping across his upper lip, pink on pink. And like a stray dog with no home and a heart full of fear, he never met her gaze when he spoke. He was cornered, and they both knew it.

"I might have been Peter's second-in-command, but he kept his secrets to himself. All I know is he found this island in a dream, and it never let him leave. He became one of the trees, just movin' along with the wind and the tides, all on his own. It was fun at first, but there's only so much explorin' you can do before you get lonely and want to go back."

"But he couldn't."

Jay shook his head. "Took him a long time to figure out how to touch the stars. All that time, livin' alone . . . It's no wonder he turned into a loon."

"I thought he was your leader? A friend, even?"

Jay drew Sammy closer to him, as though conjuring a recollection of Peter would be enough to rip the boy from his side. "Peter became more than a friend. We listened to him like a kid listens to a father. But you know what happens when a kid does somethin' wrong to a parent, right?"

They're forced to marry. "The child is punished."

Jay nodded. "When Peter was good, we would ride the wind with him. We loved him. But when he was mad . . ." He stole a glance over to Didi, who was busy mending a hole in a pair of socks, and sighed. "Well, his bad side was as scary as his good. Power does that to a person."

"I'm not interested in the boy's temper," Lou said. "You mentioned he kept tokens of all the children he took in. And, from what I understand, he kept a token of his trip to the stars—a key to doing it again. It makes perfect sense, really."

"No one knows exactly how he did it, Lou. The story changed each time he told it, just a little every time. The only thing that ever stayed the same was that he found the farthest part of the island, thought about his momma, and jumped. When he came back down, the fairies wanted to serve him, and the sea and sky opened up to let him through. He decided he wanted both worlds, so he got it. See, Peter didn't wanna change or own this place alone; he wanted to make it bigger, bring *more* of us here. He's the one who lets us in and out. The only one who knows how to pass through the veil. I doubt he'd leave a trace of how to do it behind for someone to find. Peter was jealous of the things he loved."

Henry sat down next to Benji and offered him a slice of mango. Children—they were nothing more than *children*. And yet the course of her future depended on the information they offered and the will of one very damaged, very disturbed boy.

"What is the farthest place on the island?" Lou asked. She expected Jay to rebuff her and bury the question with the other details of their past together.

Instead, he laughed. "In case you didn't notice, nothin' around here really stays the same. And with the barriers comin' down and Peter gone—"

"I understand things are changing quickly now, but there must be a place you know of that Peter would have gone."

"What about the Mountain of Regret?"

Jay looked down at Sammy and patted his hand. "Your guess is as good as mine, buddy. And before you jump on me about it," he said, giving Lou a withering stare, "the Mountain of Regret is the tallest place on the island. But it comes and goes, never settling in the same place twice. It's impossible to find without Peter. I don't think I've ever heard him talk about the entrance to it, come to think of it."

"Well, of course he would have you believe that," she said, ignoring their doubt. "Peter was jealous of the things he loved, right? But it's been proven he has a weakness for trophies. If there is a key to finding a way off the island, wouldn't it stand to reason it leads to the place closest to the stars and it is still in his possession?"

"I never seen a floatin' mountain," Kiran said uncertainly.

"Oh, it exists," Jay said. "It's just pretty impossible to find."

Lou grinned. "Unless you have Peter's key. Tell me, where does Peter live?"

Jay frowned. "Why?"

"It's as good a place as any to start. He might have some information hidden about the mountain's location."

"We can't go back there," Kiran said. "Nuh-uh."

"Peter banned us from the Hanging Tree when we followed Jay out," Benji explained softly. "We can't go back there."

"Maybe you can't," she said. "But I can."

"What?" Jay's body stiffened. "You're an outsider. You probably can't even get into the Hanging Tree if you found it. Plus, you probably won't make the journey there alive."

"I'll be fine."

"You could die."

"I'll die if I do nothing," Lou said.

Sorrow curved Jay's spine. He turned back to Sammy, clutching the boy close. "We can get you goin' in the right direction," Jay muttered, "but that's as far as we go. I told you, I'm done with Peter and all his trouble."

And while she had anticipated the answer, the blow struck just as hard. She smoothed the frayed, limp ends of her hair, the flyaway strands refusing to cooperate. Rosie's locks always settled so beautifully across her cheeks; she hoped to see that face again.

Jay's eyes swam. "I'm sorry."

"That's fine." It wasn't. "I understand and respect your loyalty. I truly do, but I am tired. It's been quite a day. I think I will get some rest before I head out at first light."

She returned to her makeshift cot before Jay could say another word, curled herself into a ball, and pressed her face into her arms to stem the tears. Around her, the den quaked and bucked as another tremor rippled through the island, reminding her how little time she had left.

Someone spread a blanket across her legs and tucked the edges underneath her. *Sammy*, she thought. *Or maybe Benji.* Lou was much too tired to thank them. She pulled the blanket up to her chin and burrowed deep into its warmth, a line of stitches at one corner pulling her eyes away from the dirt floor. *Property of Henry* was stitched crudely into the wool in pale green thread. The tears came in a fresh wave.

Henry sat between Benji and Kiran, hands loose in his lap. The children's easy chatter skipped over him like stones over water, his gaze drifting somewhere too far for any to reach. He might not have been able to speak, but the blanket warming her chilled bones spoke louder than any voice.

That night, Lou slept fitfully despite the knowledge that a lonely journey to the Hanging Tree waited for her on the other side of her dreams.

CHAPTER 21

JAY

The Reds' camp usually appeared a short walk west along the northern coast. The friendliest of the island tribes, they nurtured a healthy respect for us kids in that they didn't often kill us if we accidentally stepped across their border.

Mostly. There had been some accidents.

When both moons cut silver hoops above the trees, I knew it was time. With the tribe too busy preparing for the ancient sacrifice to the island, no one would think to look behind a couple old evergreens for me. Their best fighters would be sharpening their knives, their children cleansing the ancient bowl ready to receive the blood from one of the rarer island birds. I'd never understood why a couple drops of blood were so important, but the Reds came together under those same strange moons and bled a life dry for it every month.

Peter said blood brought life; maybe the Reds figured spilling some would save them from death. I knew different. There was no saving us. There was no god listening. And every soul on our damned island had already been bled of everything it was worth.

I pressed my back against a wide fir and counted the orange

blossoms on a nearby shrub. I had lived an eternity, but I still hated waiting. The forest made me restless, so I wriggled and twisted, scratching my scabbed shoulder against the bark to relieve the itch and pass the time. The longer I sat, the louder the voices in the camp became, the more the shapes between the trees called out to me. The temptation to listen had long since passed; those voices never had anything good to say.

Relax. You're safe here. Peter would never think to look for me among the tribes. But then again, I'd never expected him to stab me.

Twelve, thirteen, fourteen orange blossoms. Where is he?

The crackle of a newborn bonfire popped over the trees, and I gripped my old sword tight. It was heavier than a dagger but still sharp. My fingers fit naturally into the soft dents in the leather.

Twenty-five, twenty-six. Come on, kid, hurry up.

An orange blossom snapped off its branch and fell to the earth. It was an offence, really. I'd been counting the stupid things, but I guessed everything on the island got destroyed even when it was supposed to last forever. A hand rustled the branches, and I shot to my feet, the sword light as a whistle in my hands.

"Ouch!"

"Sammy?" Behind me, cheers from a spear-throwing contest overpowered the sound of my thumping heart, and I'd never been so glad for a bird to just die already. "Sammy, that you?"

Sammy scrambled out of the branches, glasses sliding low on his nose, his hair a mess of twigs and leaves. "Yeah, Jay, it's just me. I got a bit lost, and then there was a pirate, but he didn't see me, don't worry. I think I got a splinter—these bushes are the worst, don'tcha think? Why do they gotta line the camp with 'em?"

I groaned. "Probably to keep us from doin' this. Did anyone at the Tree see you leave?"

"I don't think so."

"That's good. Tell me you've got good news."

The bird squawked from its wooden cage, the panic scratching at my skull. I couldn't see it, but I'd seen it enough times before to imagine the bloodshot eyes, the spreading of its wings. Sammy glanced at a gap between firs and shivered.

"There's a way back," he said. "It ain't gonna be easy, but you can go back without Peter knowin'."

The words were like a harsh shove off a high cliff, sending my stomach into my throat. "You sure?" I asked. Sammy nodded, and I let out a loud whoop, not caring if anyone in the camp heard it. "I knew it. I *knew* he was lyin'! You're a genius, Sammy, you know that?"

Sammy's chin trembled. "But you won't like it."

"I'll do what I gotta do to get off this island. Go on, spill it."

Sammy fiddled with a loose button on his shirt, looking everywhere but at me. And that's when I knew I really, *really* wasn't going to like it. "I mean, it's not permanent or anythin', and I got no clue if it'll work right, but she told me she could give you a couple hours."

"She?"

"Yeah."

"But it'll work?"

"Yeah. For a bit." Sammy pressed his lips together, suddenly unsure. "Promise you won't get mad, 'kay?"

I'm in trouble. Heaps of trouble. "Just tell me, Sam."

The bird was out of its cage, but it was anything but free. I could tell exactly when it started to fight against the hands holding it in place, when the struggle of trying to escape snapped a wing. When it saw the knife. I'd never actually seen the whole sacrifice through to the end, but panic and death had a similar stink about them, much different than the smell of the woods. I'd pick up on it anywhere. And that bird knew it was going to die.

"You can come out now," Sammy whispered into the shadows. "I promise he won't hurt you."

My heart stuttered. "Who are you—*oh*."

The dark wasn't as solid as it seemed. The shift was small at first—a pinprick of golden light weaving through the tangled branches. It lolled through the air in lazy circles, and the closer it came, the more convinced I was that I'd weep just to be in its presence. Not a star, not a flame, not a spark of angel dust; the beam spiraled around leaves and flowers and slanted trunks, feathers of lilac and red flame swirling within it.

A spare sword lay under a pile of leaves ten paces to my left, right where I'd planted it in the event I was disarmed. I could spring for it to have two weapons instead of one, but my movement now would be too noticeable. No, not the sword, then. I could fight my way out, but with my shoulder on fire and that ball of light burning my eyes—

"It's okay, Jay, you don't have to worry!" Sammy threw himself to my side with open arms. "She won't hurt you. Just hear her out."

"You know you can't trust the fairies!"

"Trust me. Listen to the plan first, and then you can say no."

The light grew brighter, whiter, filled the air with a high-pitched cry that shook the trees. I stumbled back and forgot where the sword was, where the sky sat, where my fists were clenched. This was how I lost—not at Peter's hand, not because the Reds had caught me hiding on their land, and not because I'd found some way to go back and grow old like I should have.

Because I'd let myself get caught by a fairy.

"You can open your eyes, Jay."

She was taller than any pirate, hair like a veil of fresh strawberries cascading down to her knees and framing a heart-shaped face. A dress of leaves and rosebuds hung off her narrow shoulders and fell just above her knees, her bare feet blackened by mud. I'd never seen a fairy dressed as a human; the creatures preferred to avoid the bloodshed on the ground by keeping their own brand of savagery closer to the sky, making themselves small enough not to spot. To see one as a human was to see them either weak or voluntarily vulnerable. And fairies liked to be neither.

"You try anythin' funny, I'll fight back," I warned, holding my sword level. "But you leave Sammy alone, understand?"

The fairy smiled. "I did not come here for violence, Jay. Sammy thought it would be better if we met in this form. My magic is much weaker, you see. I suppose this is an exercise of trust on both our parts."

"You're a fairy," I said, never slackening my stance. "You can trick me in any shape you take. Sorry if I don't buy the act, devil fly."

"It saddens me you feel that way, but I cannot blame you after all you have seen from my sisters." She turned to Sammy, who hugged my waist until it hurt to breathe. I didn't mind that pain so much. "Do you wish me to leave?"

"No, stay!" Sammy said. "Just tell him what you told me. Go on."

"Listen," I said, dropping my arms. "I don't want any trouble. All I wanted was to go back and see my friend, to make sure she's okay before I take off for good. I don't need a fairy goin' back to Peter and snitchin' on me."

The fairy nodded. "Lou is lucky to have you. I always thought the bond you two had was written in fairy dust. He feels terrible about the injury to your shoulder."

My stomach dropped. "How do you know all this?"

"Peter tells me about all his lost boys' friends in the Land of the Grown. I also heard you speak so highly of her—much more than any of your other friends. It pained Peter to enforce your separation from her."

Realization dawned, hot and prickly. *Not just* any *fairy, then. This is bad.*

"You're Lilith." I scanned the sky, the treetops, the shadows cast in the crevices of old bark. "Where is he? Where's he hidin'?"

"Peter does not know I am here, and I do not plan on telling him." She tucked her hair behind her ears, their tips a soft lavender. "I snuck away while he was planning an assault on Blackbeard's ship. He should not notice my absence for some time. You know how he becomes before a raid."

"Don't talk to me like we're the same, you and me. I'm human, and you're—"

"A devil fly."

Yep. "Why would you help me?" I threw Sammy a glare worth a hundred daggers, but the kid looked unfazed. "He's your boss. Why would you go behind his back to help me break his law?"

"I might be Peter's link to the fairies, but I am not beholden to him," Lilith said. "The rules have their purpose and their place, but they are not without their flaws. In this case, I believe he should have granted you some leniency. He loves all his boys, but his anger has a way of making his actions . . . less than noble. It is an unfortunate result of a life lived too long without love."

My shoulder growled the longer she spoke. "So, he stabs us, but he still loves us, and we should forgive him?"

"Lilith says she can give you some fairy dust to get back to the Land of the Grown." Sammy looked up, the hope so vivid in his face that it almost hurt more than my shoulder. Almost. "It's worth a shot. I know the fairies can be trouble, but I trust Lilith. She's been nice to me. Real nice."

I paused. A way back was all I wanted. But fairy dust?

"Is that true?" I asked.

"Yes. I have plenty of it. No one would notice a pinch or two missing from our stores. Only Peter can make the return permanent, but our dust should grant you passage long enough to make your peace." Eyes of bright violet, deeper than a bruise and refracting light like matching amethysts, probed the darkness.

"You must follow the brightest star in the night sky, and your heart will do the rest."

Cheers rang out in the camp. I couldn't hear the bird anymore. It was gone, a thing made of bone and blood and feather without a name.

"What's in it for you?" I asked.

Lilith twirled her hair, the strands catching the firelight drifting through the trees. "You're Peter's best friend."

My shoulder throbbed. "Not so sure you can say we're *friends* anymore."

"You have his ear, then. He respects your position in the clan. My sister is young. Impulsive. She has a terrible temper but a kind heart, I promise you." More fidgeting, more shifting of naked feet in the soft earth with toes curling into the ground like she was trying to grow roots, make a solid place for herself in the ground.

"And?"

"Peter wants to get rid of her." Emerald tears swam in her large eyes. "She's easily managed, but Peter thinks she is a distraction. That if she were gone, I would have more time and attention for him."

"*And?*"

"Convince him to keep her," she said, tears spilling freely. "If you do what you can to convince Peter that she is no threat to him, I'll provide enough fairy dust to get you to the Land of the Grown and back to see your friend. And I'll keep your secret."

My shoulders eased, and Sammy nestled deeper into my side. Knowing what Lilith wanted was a comfort—no one gave something for nothing. "You want me to talk up your sister. That's it?"

"It is enough." Her fingers twisted together into a knot of supple pink skin and snowy knuckles. "His mind is set, and you know how difficult it is to change a decision once he makes it."

"Yeah, I do." I tossed the idea around in my mind, not daring to believe my luck. "I wanna go tomorrow. Can you get me the dust by then?"

She nodded, beaming. "Does that mean we have a deal?"

Chants echoed in the forest. I took Lilith's hand, trying not to let on how much I hated being anywhere near a fairy. The last bargain I'd made was a promise to Peter out of loyalty to him; it had led me to Lou. It was funny to think that the next bargain I'd make would turn that loyalty to ash. I sent a good thought up to the clouds, hoping that bird could hear it. It was the least I could do.

"What's your sister's name?"

Lilith smiled. "Her name is Bell."

CHAPTER 22

"Got your dagger?"

"Yes."

"Waterskin?"

"Yes, Jay."

Sunlight clawed the darkness from the clouds and blew a kiss into the trees. The Hanging Tree waited somewhere beyond the green and blue and never-ending heat; dread coiled in Lou's belly, a snake with sharp fangs, twisting to bite at the very thought of it. So, she let Jay fuss over the blade strapped to her hip and the crude pack swinging off her shoulder to keep herself busy.

"You sure you wanna take those clothes with you?" Jay asked, casting a look of loathing at her leather bag. "They'll be real heavy to carry, 'specially with the heat."

"It's one of my best dresses. Mother will be upset if I come back without it."

"I like to think she'd be more upset if you don't come back at all."

The tattered linen britches and shirt—a reluctant gift from

Didi, who'd pilfered the clothes from a raid of the market by the docks—were too scratchy, the leather boots too heavy. The pants and shirt were an unwanted second skin, but she simply couldn't let the familiar dress and slippers go. They were a link to her sister and the home she longed to return to. While she resented the fitted dresses and the tight shoes, losing them would be a deeper pain than that.

"I will be fine. Just point me in the right direction."

Benji edged past Jay, a roll of bark clasped to his chest. "Henry and I drew this up for you," he said, offering her the curled shaving of tree bark. "The island is small, but it's easy to fall off course. Follow the line from the little house at the bottom—see, that's where we are—and past the crocodile swamp up to the biggest tree in the forest. If you hit tribal lands, you drifted too far west."

"And how do I get inside?" Lou asked. Henry leaned over Benji's shoulder and traced a finger up a slash of dark coal smudging the only tree at the top of the map. "Is this a gap in the trunk?"

Henry nodded and gave her hand a squeeze. Unwanted tears sprung into her eyes, and she looped her arms around Henry's waist, offering the only thanks she could manage with her chest and throat so tight. Henry nestled his cheek into her hair, the thrum of his heart a lullaby to soothe the nerves.

"Don't make any trouble, all right?" Jay said. "We won't be there to help you if things go sideways. The trees are as dangerous as the crocs and pirates, so keep that sword close. And please, please ditch the clothes if you can."

Lou nodded. "I promise to be careful."

"Hanging Tree should be empty; his boys wouldn't stay there without him to protect them. But if you *do* see someone—"

"I should tell them I've come from the market with news of Peter's state from one of the ladies who entertains Blackbeard."

Jay raked his fingers through the mud. With quick efficient moves, he smeared the dirt into Lou's hair, across her cheeks, and down her arms. "Here. This should make you harder to spot. Best I can do on short notice."

No wonder these boys never look clean. "Thank you—all of you. Goodbye, Jay."

A sharp jerk of the chin, and Jay nudged Sammy toward the burrow. Kiran and Didi disappeared into the shadows, their heads bowed in either grief or relief—she could imagine which emotion belonged to which child. But it was Benji and Henry who lingered, offering her watery smiles before leaving her to her task.

Jay was the last to slip away. Through the night and into morning, the boy had shrouded himself in silence and hooded his gaze under heavy lashes. There, at the mouth of the burrow, the mask slipped to reveal his years—his true age, in all its pain and sorrow and weariness.

He nodded, a last act of farewell.

And then he was gone.

The pain was immediate and unexpected and *real*.

She'd thought the den a prison. But prisons, it turned out, were sometimes a simple matter of perspective.

INSECTS BUZZED IN HER EARS—*TOO loud, too loud*—and the land rolled and dipped until there was nothing but green pressing in on all sides. Sunlight sizzled overhead and dripped heat through the trees like acid. Lou took a deep drink from the waterskin, relishing the prickle of ice on her tongue until it was quickly burned away.

Lilies and dandelions swivelled on their stalks, laughing as she picked a clumsy path north. Ferns and evergreens turned to palms and bamboo shoots, greenery to flecks of red and violet, the plants splattered with colour. Lou doubted she would know the Hanging Tree apart from any of the rest; the island shifted, changed, breathed with the strange new species of life she'd never seen. Everything was new; one tree would hardly stand out. She grasped the map with sweaty fingers and prayed Benji's skill with charcoal was better than hers. She hadn't drawn anything in a very long time.

Plink, plink, plunk.

Water trickled behind a patch of palms, and Lou's heart stuttered. There it was: a chance to stop and drink and splash water on her heated neck without fearing the depletion of her resources. Lou stumbled toward the sound of water slapping against rocks.

At nighttime, the crocodiles were dark and ridged, moving stones in the deep black sea. Under the unforgiving sun, they were boulders. Bodies of grey and green and brown slid through the murky swamp dotted with lily pads, some warming themselves among the reeds. Honey eyes roved lazily over the bank, their rumbles sending tremors into the trees.

Lou stepped closer, Jay's earlier warnings forgotten. The nearest crocodile gurgled, its eyes carved in half by a fine sliver of black. She searched the darkness in them for any sign of danger, but there were only whispers, whispers carrying her name and promising her release—release from what, she didn't know.

She didn't understand the children's fear of the beasts. Despite their massive jaws and tough hide, they hadn't harmed her when given the opportunity. When she returned home, she might tell Rose about them. Perhaps she would draw them before they were swiped from her memory for good.

"Beautiful, ain't they?"

The voice came from behind her, at the place where the swamp curved around the trees. Lou's hands went to her blade, but the man was unarmed and offered a kind smile riddled with holes. *Don't stop. Trust no one.* Jay's warnings were clear, but they'd come from a place marked by isolation and mistrust. Politeness was a sign of maturity, as impulses were often rude and better stamped out. Or so she'd been told.

"Yes, they are quite lovely," she said. "Much less terrifying than I once thought."

"Ah, but beautiful don't mean they ain't dangerous. Best te respect a power like that." He stopped an arm's length away, his hair a patchy frazzled brown, lifeless in the way it hovered around his peeling scalp. The shirt on his back may once have been white but was now a deep copper in many places.

"Well," she said, "perhaps it is best to let them be."

"Their meat makes a great supper, if ye knows how te catch one."

Her stomach lurched, and she finally found her legs. "Pity I'm not particularly hungry." She took a step back. The man reciprocated with a step forward of his own. "Good day to you, sir."

"Not so fast, girlie."

It had taken years for Mother to invite Lou to the market. Every week, Anne Webber would disappear on a cloud of skirts and perfume, returning with fresh fruit, warm baguettes wrapped in butcher's paper, and some scraps of silk and lace for her sewing. Often, Lou had imagined the market as a place of lustre and fine spices, the vendors' stalls draped in jewel-bright tents. To attend was a rite of passage into womanhood, and she'd taken extra care with her hair the day Mother had finally called her to come along. But instead of a magical market, there had only been many eyes on many bearded faces lingering much too long on her body. Mother was brave enough to cast them away with the power of a glance, but Lou had never forgotten the hunger so easily stoked in even the gentlest of men.

Mother wasn't there to ward away the pirate.

"I could cook for ye." He swiped his tongue across his teeth. "Girl like you deserves it."

"As I've said, I am not hungry. But thank you."

"Aye." His eyes travelled down her neck. "Yer well-fed, but ye can never have enough food."

"My men are waiting for me in the forest." The lie felt strange on her tongue, but he scanned the trees quickly. She reached for her sword, fingers slipping over the hilt.

"Yer lyin'. There be no one comin' close to this here swamp with all the crocs in their burrows." His movements were quicker now, the colour high in his sunken face. "Yer alone. With me."

Lou ran for the trees. Sobs, *her* sobs, rattled out in time with her racing heart—*ga-lug, ga-lug, ga-lug*. Despite the pirate's wasted body, he was faster. When his hands found her, twisted into her hair and forced her to the ground, his laughter was bitten down to ragged breathing.

She was slow, stupid to think she could make her way to the Hanging Tree without Jay's help. He'd warned her. He'd told her to move and take only what she needed, but her pack was an unwanted weight, the soles of her slippers digging into her spine as the pirate pressed her down.

He turned her until she faced the sky. His breath was hot on her face. Dirty hands pulled at her shirt, fumbling and clumsy with excitement. She kicked out, flailed, pushed, bit, but he didn't slow. He was a pirate, used to fighting for his dinner.

"The mermaids be pretty, but yer a fighter. I like it."

"Get off me!" Lou bucked, and he drove a knee into her stomach. She thrashed, and a belt buckle came loose, flashing silver in the sun. He was strong, and his hands were on her bare flesh. There, with the sun and crocodiles to bear witness, she crumbled.

She and Rosie had watched the clouds when they were children. Rabbits, puppies, a strawberry, a top hat—each tuft of white wore a different face. They would lie in the tall grass and name them all, the sky an endless stretch of blue and marshmallow. No one had lain above her then, pressing her into the grass until she couldn't breathe.

But Lou focused on the rabbits, the puppies, the fluffy strawberries far above as calloused hands found her stomach. Scratching her. She closed her eyes, offering her tears to the earth.

The roar came from somewhere far away. But then his hands were gone, her lungs pulling in air. Clean air. And the clouds were beautiful once more.

"No!" Lou cried. "Get off! *No!*"

Lou sat up, fingers already fumbling to fasten the buttons of her shirt. Her britches were intact, and she sobbed in relief for the woman she might have become if the pirate hadn't been pulled away.

By a crocodile.

He lay on the ground, his lower half clamped in the crocodile's jaws. Man and beast were knotted together by blood, every jerk of the croc's jaws drawing a fresh scream. Her pulse slowed as blood spurted from the pirate's stomach, crimson snakes pouring onto the grass, staining it red, staining it in sin.

Somewhere, sometime, the screaming stopped. Torment twisted the man's face one moment, and then his eyes turned to glass. Empty. The crocodile helped himself to the remaining flesh, making a feast of the pirate who would have made a feast of her.

It blinked. Their eyes met, and a sense of knowing replaced her terror.

"You saved me," she whispered. "Twice. Thank you."

Lou found her map by the swamp's edge and followed the stream north, leaving nature to take its course.

BENJI WAS RIGHT: the Hanging Tree was different from the rest of the woods. Dense growth carpeted the island, but Lou's first clue she was getting close came when the trees thinned away and the sunlight turned to brass. A large sequoia spiralled up to the sky and sat on thick tentacles. Gnarled fingers pushed back the clouds and kept the rest of the trees at bay, claiming that piece of the island for itself.

Lou's mind whirred to life, when only moments before it had been a pool of mud and misery. As the first cricket chirps put the birds to sleep, she stepped up to the moss-covered bark, eager to get inside. There could be others like the man by the swamp lurking in the forest. Waiting. Waiting for her with their own calloused hands and slippery tongues.

But she wouldn't make the same mistake again.

Just as Henry had indicated on the map, a long gash ran down the bark on the eastern side of the tree. Made for children, the fit was tight, but Lou managed it just the same. She could still feel the pirate's fingers on her stomach, but it would be easy to forget he'd ever existed once she was home and the wall between worlds was solid once more.

At least, that's what she hoped. The ghost of his breath still lingered on her skin. Lou doubted she would ever be properly clean again.

Down the tunnel, into the darkness.

The dirt path gave way to a large circular room lit by a single lantern. A hammock swung overhead, the remnants of a miniature dollhouse splintered in its belly. Blood spatters stained the earth where shredded blankets and rotten food littered the dust. It was as Benji and Kiran had described it would be, save for one important detail: it wasn't empty.

There was a girl sitting on her heels in the dust, lank blond hair veiling her face. Mud smudged her mottled, bruised skin and threadbare dress. She wore no shoes, no ribbons, no frills. It was as though the child had been assembled from the dirt itself.

"Hello there," Lou said, but the girl didn't look up. One finger traced circles in the dirt, loops and whorls a language all her own. "I . . . I'm sorry. I was told this den would be empty. Do you live here?"

The girl's finger moved faster, and she turned her chin away as Lou knelt before her. *Who are you?* she wanted to ask. But no question on the island offered a simple answer. But as she watched the drawings take form on the ground between them, the young girl's appearance changed; her dress, once faded and stained with sweat, became a soft cornflower blue trimmed in lace. Pearl buttons travelled like ants down her front, disappearing in the folds of her skirt and throwing swirls of colour across the faded edges of the den. Hair that had appeared lank and dirty was now a thick sheet of silken gold falling in waves around a pink face. The pirate in the forest was gone, and the island had sent Lou an angel in disguise as penance for its sins.

"My name is Louisa. You can call me Lou if you like. What is your name?"

No answer. *She's afraid. Poor child.*

"Are you alone?"

The girl nodded, her pale finger stilling in the dust.

"Can you speak?"

A small shake of the head this time, a sad and reluctant *no*.

"I know how it feels to be frightened. Do you live here?"

The child nodded.

"Where do you sleep?"

The girl pointed above her head to the hammock, and Lou wondered how she ever managed to climb that high.

"That's the nicest spot here," Lou said. "A proper bed far off the ground. Peter must value you quite a bit. You *do* know Peter, I presume?"

Finally, the girl looked up. She nodded vigorously and reached for Lou's hand, urgency crackling between them in waves. If the child lived with Peter and was in his favour, she might know his secrets. With any luck, she might know exactly where he kept his most precious belongings.

"I'm here to help," Lou said. "This island is falling apart because Peter was taken. I've tried to free him with his old friends, but the pirates have him caged in an unbreakable cell. I want to make things right again, but I'll need help. Would you be able to help me?"

Her lips pulled down at the corners, her brows knitting together.

"You can trust me, little one."

"My . . . name . . . Bell." A soft smile revealed a row of small white teeth, and the girl's voice shone like a drop of starlight piercing a black winter night.

Lou grinned back, melting into the child's warmth. "Bell. That is a pretty name. Is there anywhere you think Peter would have hidden things special to him, Bell? Maybe a secret nook, or a spot he likes to go alone? Perhaps something from the Mountain of Regret? A map or a key or . . . anything?" She waited while the girl's face worked, the grinding of the cogs over one another almost audible between them. *Please. Anything at all.*

"You help Bell. Bell help Lou."

"A trade." Lou's heart soared; the girl *did* know something. "That is quite fair. What did you have in mind?"

"You help Bell," she said louder. Her eyes winked as though lit from within. Their brightness tugged Lou closer. They sat nose to nose, trapped in a cocoon of light and warmth and trust. "Bell help Lou."

The familiar scent of grass, peaches and oranges, and lemon-blueberry scones drifted around them. *It smells like home.* "I'll do what I can to help you, Bell. You can count on that."

Bell's eyes were deep and inviting, water churning and bathing her in their light. "Bell take you to key. Lou get treasure for Bell."

"There is a key to the Mountain of Regret?"

This time, Bell nodded so vigorously that her hair flicked between them, spilling the lavender and blueberry moss into Lou's mind. It was toxic, and it was beautiful, and she couldn't breathe.

"I can do that." Lou sank into Bell's scent and let the sound of the girl's steady breathing calm her mind. She had been so lonely, but no more. Rosie lived in a distant place, but Bell was her new home, as familiar as a beloved childhood toy.

"I will help you."

She would give anything to have Bell curl up in her lap and comb her fingers through the glowing strands of her hair. To be there for her. Always.

"Lou say yes? Lou help Bell?"

To love her like a sister.

"Lou, stop!" The light in the den grew brighter, but its warmth couldn't touch them. Nothing could as long as she and Bell remained together.

I have *a sister.*

Not anymore.

"Yes," Lou whispered. "I say yes."

Bell smiled. The apples of her cheeks flushed pink as she lifted her palm, reaching into the safe space between them. Lou lifted her own fingers, a moth drawn to Bell's flame.

Safe. So safe.

It was right to reach for a comforting hand in the darkness.

"Don't touch her!"

Footsteps pounded, voices cried out, but it didn't matter because Bell's hand was warm. Their fingers twisted together, inseparable. Faces swarmed around them in a strange current, but Lou's palm was fused to Bell's, the connection a steel cord twining them together at the wrist. And anyone else didn't matter.

Lou was happily trapped with the sweet girl in their own —*prison*—world.

What is happening?

Bell let go of Lou's hand, and her beautiful smile turned to a mouthful of fangs dripping with poison.

Strong hands clamped down on Lou's shoulders and pulled her back. The spell was broken, shattered around her like glass. She pulled away from the grip on her body; the pirate from the swamp was back, his hands all over her again. Her screams ripped through her with the force of a thousand knives.

"Lou, take it easy! It's just me!"

I know that voice.

"Lou? You okay?"

"Jay, c'mere! The beast is puttin' up a fight."

I need to find Bell. They cannot take her from me too.

Blue eyes broke through her panic. They held hers firm, pulling her away from the forest, from the leering pirate with the belt buckle heavy against her stomach. Bit by blissful bit, she came back to herself, and her limbs relaxed. The eyes had a face surrounded by a cloud of bronze hair and a chipped smile.

"Jay? Why are you here?"

"Figured you'd get into some kind of trouble. Don't worry, the devil fly can't hurt you anymore. I'm just glad we got here in time."

"She isn't a devil fly!" Lou cried, ripping herself free. "She's an innocent child who needs my help."

The den went quiet save for the scratch of feet against the rough ground.

"Please tell me you didn't make a deal with her," Jay said. "*Please*, Lou."

Henry and Kiran grunted with the effort of wrestling a wretched creature to its knees. A twisted face grinned with a smile lined with fangs, its toenails curling into the packed dirt. Didi's aim with the bow never wavered from the monster's chest, and with Benji consoling Sammy at the farthest corner of the room, there were no free bodies to search for Bell.

She got away.

The creature shrieked, and acid-green spittle flew from her lips. Jay dragged Lou back before the droplets could touch her, his face a mask of disgust.

"What is that?" Lou asked.

The shrieks whittled down to a predatory growl. She was a thing of nightmares, her movements sharp and quick, her hands too long, fingernails tapered to claws, gums swimming in saliva, red and swollen. But the eyes were grey as storm clouds.

"That's Bell. She's supposed to be a fairy, but I think she's more demon than the devil himself."

Bile rose in her throat. "No. I met Bell; she looked nothing like this creature."

Jay sighed. "Yeah, that's what they all say. This," he said, jabbing his thumb over his shoulder, "is her real form. You saw what she wanted you to see. It's a neat trick she has, tinkerin' with people's memories 'til she finds what makes you tick."

"Rose," she said, tears thick in her throat. "The girl I saw . . . She reminded me of my sister."

"She probably saw that in you. Listen to me now, Lou. When we came in here, you two were holdin' hands. Why?"

Lou waded through the rapidly fading memories. "She told me she could help me find the Mountain of Regret."

"But we don't even know where the entrance to it is," Benji said. "Even if we knew where it might be, there's no way to get from the island to the mountain before it disappears again."

"But it exists," Lou said. "And Bell knows how to find it."

"I guess anythin's possible." Jay's face grew pale. "But it won't be easy. Pirates are one thing, but whatever Peter's keepin' to himself has gotta be protected by a lot worse. If Bell's willin' to make a bargain for it, chances are we don't wanna go anywhere near the key to the mountain or whatever door it unlocks. Did the devil fly say what she wants in return?"

The fairy gave up her struggle and sagged in Henry and Kiran's grip. Her breathing came in rapid, hungry bursts. "Bell get treasure. Lou get key, go home. Easy peasy, poke your knees-y, Jay."

Jay and his crew wore equal looks of disgust. Bell's laughter was a rough, gravelly sound grating on the inside of Lou's skull.

"A kay. That true, Lou?" Jay asked.

"Yes."

"Crickets, she's dumb!" Didi said, prowling the den like a caged animal. "Boss, I say we kill the devil fly and cut the old lady loose. She's bringin' way too much trouble on us."

"I'm sorry," Lou said, looking to Jay for support. "I didn't know what she was or what trouble she would bring. I thought it was a fair deal in the moment, and I never thought for a second of bringing any trouble back to you all."

"Dammit." Jay pulled his fingers through his hair, kicking rogue pebbles across the room. "Dammit! And you bound your promise. Your palm. Look at your *palm*."

She lifted her hand, and her stomach lurched. The line was a thin slash veined in yellow and green, a festering wound with the pulse of infection. Lou stared at it without blinking, the ground swaying under her. "What is this?" she asked.

"It's a binding promise," Jay said, averting his eyes. "But it's more like a curse. You get the key, and she gets Peter's treasure."

"That does not sound so terrible." The slash on her hand thickened, spreading outward like a spider's deadly web, and she knew she was wrong. "Does this curse get worse?"

"Until you die." Didi's words were as firm as her jaw, and she didn't look the least bit saddened by the thought. "That was a seriously stupid move, lady."

"Cut it out, Didi!" Jay rounded on her. "She didn't know."

"Not my problem."

Kiran frowned at his sister. "So, what do we do now, boss? I mean, I know you told us to back off this whole Peter thing, but I don't feel too good about lettin' her die like that."

The others nodded in agreement, and Lou felt the treacherous spark of hope once more. She didn't deserve their help; this mess was hers alone to fix, and Didi knew it. But Lou was so tired of being alone.

The vision of the beautiful, vulnerable girl had been a balm after the savagery of the island, the pirate and his sticky hands. But that illusion had been ripped away, leaving only the truth behind: that everything beautiful held ugliness in its roots, and the only way to fight it back was with ugliness itself.

"I would have helped you if you had only asked," Lou said. "You did not need to trick me."

Bell fixed her with a glare of naked hate. "Bell eat Lou's corpse if she fail."

Lou lunged, her fists pounding the air, her feet kicking up sand and dust and anything standing in her way. She'd allowed men to throw her to the crocodiles, crumbled under the hands of a terrible pirate, but no more. Her fist bit into Bell's sneering face, and the fairy laughed as green blood spurted from her nose. Jay grabbed Lou around the waist, pulling her back with a shout for help.

"Don't be stupid!" Didi cried. "You can't kill that fairy before you get her treasure unless you wanna die too. That's how this whole thing works. But if you wanna fight, I'm itchin' to have some practice."

"Shut it, Didi!" Jay said, and the girl went quiet. "Where's this treasure you want us to find for you, Bell?"

Blood ran freely into her grinning mouth. "Mermaid Lagoon."

He nodded. "What part of Mermaid Lagoon?"

A laugh like nails over stone replaced the snarls, and Lou shivered.

"The bottom, bottom, bottom," Bell said. "Lou get treasure for Bell from the fish, fish, fish. Or big girl dies."

CHAPTER 23

JAY

I'd never been so happy to see the house on Silverton Lane.
The gutter crawled with dried leaves and other unclean
things. I sat there with all the filth and waited for the
window to swing open for me.

The window right under my feet.

Lou's window.

Somewhere beyond the layer of shingle and wood and perfect
white paint, Lou walked and played and breathed. The night was
cold as most nights at the end of summer tended to get. The
crickets chirped, and the Briarwood swayed under the invisible
hand of the wind. It was nice to be back. It was home.

Lou was home.

I leapt down from the roof and hugged the thought of Lou's
happy face close to my heart. It was a funny thing, to be weightless
and worried at the same time. Like jumping from a cliff but never
landing. If this was the power Peter got from the stars, I couldn't
blame him for wanting to keep it all to himself.

The window was still closed. It was cool, but not freezing. I hadn't been away *that* long. Still, shame gripped my gut with both hands and twisted. Waiting was hard.

And I'd waited two whole weeks to get back. That was long enough.

Warm air vented through the crack between the two white panes. One small push, and the glass swung open, blowing the scent of lavender and vanilla into my face.

"Lou?" I whispered, stepping inside.

No answer.

She's probably sleeping, you idiot.

But instead of a small hill where she'd be curled up under her blankets, sheets tucked under her chin, the coverlet lay perfectly flat. Something was wrong. Lou should have been in her room. It was where she hid from her mother, where her plush animals slept, where we played every day . . .

Where we *used* to play.

I scrambled to the door and into the hall. I'd always hated the horrible floral wallpaper and the runner like a ship's plank stretching from one end of the house to the other. The corridor twisted with the vines and roses, the effect bringing me back to the island and the smothering way the trees pressed in on me.

I had to find her.

The door to the baby's room was open.

A voice floated out into the hall, low murmurs humming in my ears.

Huh?

The room at the end of the hall breathed me in. Light filtered over the carpet through a crack in the door—Lou's mother, taking care of her precious baby the way she never had with her first child. Was that why Lou's bed was empty? Had she run off in the night, trying to get away? To find me?

Panic, hot and thick and choking, grabbed me with both hands.

The walls were green, and I was nauseous. Shadowed corners and strange smells smacked me in the nose, and the barbs of a baby's cries pierced my skull. Bells from a music box tinkled by the window while a small dancer turned perfect circles on a faded gold disk. Everything was back the way it had been before I'd destroyed it all. Like I'd never been there at all. Maybe it was immortality that finally hit me. Maybe it was the fact that I'd befriended the most powerful being on the island and hadn't a thing to call my own. Or maybe I'd finally found a heart buried somewhere behind the flesh and calcified bones that carved me in stone. Whatever the reason, I was overwhelmed with the need to leave a mark that was mine and mine alone, a need so great my gut rolled and my chest squeezed. I wanted my time to mean something. It had never occurred to me that, immortal or not, nothing I ever did had ever mattered. Nothing until I'd met Lou.

Immortality had its price. I'd never cared about the payment for it. Never found something I wouldn't give in exchange for it. But I'd have given anything to step on the broken glass and soiled carpet I'd left behind.

At least it would have meant I'd left a mark.

Even if it was a terrible one.

Lou's head gleamed a dull gold over the gossamer-and-lace bassinet.

"Hi." I hated how nerves made my voice crack. Lou hummed some sweet tune into the small bed, smiling as she adjusted a blanket. My shoulders relaxed, and I smiled back. "Sorry I was away for so long. I tried to get back so many times."

The baby let out another shrill cry, and Lou reached out with both arms. "It's okay, little girl," she crooned. "Are you hungry?"

She never turned to me. She *was* still upset. I couldn't blame her.

I stepped closer, careful not to look straight at the small body flailing and grunting in that damn basket with the ridiculous curtain. Why did babies need curtains? "Look," I said, "I know you're mad; I get it. But can you just let me explain?"

Lou placed her palm on the baby's stomach and gently rocked her back and forth, hushing the child in little whispers. Still, the cries grew louder, one bleeding into the next until it was a constant stream of ear-shattering despair. I expected Lou to cringe, to back away and join me. Instead, she leaned in further, hands moving like gentle butterflies over her sister's body.

Lou's mother swept through the door, her shoulders hunched and face muddled with sleep. "Is everything all right? How long has she been crying?"

"Not long. I think she is hungry."

Anne Webber lifted the baby into her arms and settled into the rocking chair, lowering her nightgown with fumbling fingers. Lou picked up a book and settled, cross-legged, between her mother's feet.

My mother had had hair like spun gold. It was so pretty; I couldn't help but run my fingers through it, even when she mentioned how Daddy liked it nice and proper. Still, she never stopped me, and I continued to do it—even after she woke up with bruises splattered across her cheeks. Everything else about her was a wish and dream lying at the bottom of a murky lagoon, but I remembered her hair. And that she'd loved me enough to let me touch it, even if it had ended up killing her.

I'd never wanted to go near Lou's mother like I'd wanted to be near my own. For a time, Lou hadn't wanted to be close to her either. And yet there she was, snuggled up to her legs like she'd never been away.

With a delicate cough, my best friend, the sister I never had, opened the colourful pages of her book. The baby nestled against her mother's chest, and the room went quiet, replaced by a soft suckling sound.

Lou began to read.

I'd never heard the story before; a girl who was raised by fairies in the woods drank the dew off the leaves to feed her magic. The words were soft and lulling, so sweet I didn't have the heart to tell her that fairies were demons and any magic in the woods had turned to dust long ago.

"She does love it when you read to her." Anne Webber stared down at her baby in a way that twisted my heart from my chest. "When did you start this new book?"

"Just yesterday. She seems to like fairies more than the pirate stories I had on my shelf." Lou turned her face up to her mother, a smile like shards of diamonds throwing glitter across the room. "I can't say I blame her; they're rather bleak. I'm not sure what I ever liked in them."

It was getting harder to breathe. My hands shook at my sides, and the air grew too thick to do my lungs any good. Fire was a hook digging at my naval, tugging me back, pulling, *pulling*. I dug my feet into the carpet, but the force was stronger, the sound of Lou's voice coming from a great distance.

"What's happenin'?" I asked. "Lou? Why won't you talk to me?"

No one turned—not even Lou.

"I think she's full," Anne Webber said around a yawn. "Would you like to put her back in her bassinet?"

Lou nodded, a flush high in her cheeks. She placed the book on the floor and reached for the baby, cradling her to her chest as though the tiny bundle were made of the most precious and breakable glass. "Come on, little girl. Time for bed."

"I'm here!" I said. "Just turn around, please!"

I clawed at the wall, tried to tip over a basket of washcloths and knock a diaper from the nearby table, to scream and scream and scream. But my hand wouldn't grip the wall, my fingers grazed the washcloths like a feather across a stone, and my voice existed only in my mind.

She can't hear me, I thought savagely, the truth of those words breaking what was left of my heart—that useless, unchanged immortal heart. *She can't see me.*

It didn't look like my absence touched her at all.

The island called me home, and I fell back into its grave.

CHAPTER 24

The northern coast of the island was soaked in heat, but the burn of Lou's palm overshadowed the scalding sun. Bell's curse had spread overnight, festering red and sickly yellow, veins creeping up her wrist and invading her arm. Jay had made camp in the woods by the Hanging Tree to avoid travel by night, and Lou had gone to sleep under the umbrella of swaying palms. Except now she was awake, and a new day brought with it fresh pain. Lou's clothes were stale, her mouth bitter and parched, but the promise of a lagoon was enough to move her through the woods.

Hands on her stomach, pulling at her clothes. The girl wasn't a girl at all, and nothing was as it appeared to be.

His breath was still in her ear.

Panting.

She couldn't get far enough away.

They moved before dawn, but the island never slept. Eyes followed them south, deep into the jungle-like terrain. Hope and stubbornness kept the pack containing her dress and slippers strapped to her back, and no one said a word about it. There wasn't any point in challenging someone edging closer to death with every heartbeat. Instead of withering under the weight of it all, she tracked Kiran's grunts, Bell's heavy footsteps, and the passage of light through the trees, imagining the mermaids and how beautiful they would certainly be.

The shadows ahead of her were thick. Benji offered his hand to help her climb over the larger roots and fallen logs—*hands, hands in my hair, calloused hands all over*—but she didn't take it. The forest sprawled, chirps and caws of the birds mocking her. *Hot, so hot.*

They travelled in silence. Her mind was a mess of visions and colours, her arm burning with every footstep. Still, she couldn't stand anyone helping her—touching her.

On and on they moved.

The sound of rushing water was deafening as they neared a wall of cypress trees. A fine mist floated between the branches, the roar of waves overtaking the call of the larks and the squelch of their boots in the mud. Lou swiped the hair from her forehead and her palms came back slick with sweat and laced with poison. "Are we close?" she called over the noise.

Jay nodded. "Won't be long now. Just keep your weapons up in case we get any surprises."

Bell's eyes traced the contours of Lou's face, her teeth like steel shavings. "Lou no look good," she said with a croaked laugh. "Jay move faster."

"Shut it." Jay turned and stuffed a wad of cotton into Bell's mouth, securing it in place with a rope. With a nod of approval at his own work, he led them on in sullen silence. He hacked away at the vines strung from tree to tree with unnecessary force with Sammy close behind, waterskin in hand. The waves grew louder, and the air clouded with flies.

Lou pulled down her sleeves to hide the infection creeping up her arm. "I . . . I think I need a moment. I don't feel well."

Didi rounded on her, the black paint trickling into her mouth. "No one asked what you needed! We're not stoppin' 'til we get there."

"Let her be, Didi," Jay said, stopping at once. "This is a lot for her. And the curse makes it harder for Lou than the rest of us."

Lou smiled, warmth spreading through her chest at his unflinching defense of her. "I'm sorry. It's just my pack. It's getting heavy."

Didi shook her head. "Not our problem you can't let it go."

"C'mon, Didi," Kiran said, huffing at her back. "Give her a break. This must be rough for her."

"She got herself into all this trouble. Now she's makin' demands? It's hot, we're all tired, and I don't see why we gotta listen to all her whinin'!"

Lou faded into the backdrop as their argument floated ahead of her, the pounding water hammering into her skull. Whether it was the heat or the curse, she was fading.

Jay had stopped behind a curtain of vines draped over a low-hanging branch. "I need you all to be quiet and listen to me. We got an hour, maybe two before the sun goes down. Kiran, is Bell still tied up nice and tight?"

Kiran yanked on the thick rope fastened around Bell's throat, and the fairy fell to her knees. "She's not goin' nowhere, boss. I got her."

Didi turned and aimed an arrow between Bell's shoulders with a steady hand.

Kiran grinned at his sister. "Plus, I think Didi's just itchin' to use that bow."

"Good," Jay said. "Keep her tied up, and make sure that gag stays nice and tight. I don't need her makin' noise and tickin' off the mermaids."

Henry reached over at once to secure the gag, but Bell was

quicker. She lunged at his fingers and laughed through the dirty cotton as Henry stumbled back, clutching his hand to his chest.

"Quit it, Bell," Jay said. "I've got you bound and gagged, but nothin' stops me from stringin' you up by your hair while you wait."

"You're keeping her here?" Lou asked. "How is she going to retrieve the key in this condition?"

"The mermaids hate Bell, and so does anyone with half a brain. You can't trust her to get the key, Lou." Jay sheathed his dagger and glowered at the fairy. "Okay, here's the deal. Peter's got a treasure at the bottom of the lagoon, but he doesn't share it with anyone. The mermaids guard it for him, so don't expect them to give it up easy. Me and Benji'll go in, ask 'em for it nice and polite and hope they hand it over when we tell 'em what's at stake if they don't."

"Easy peasy, poke your knees-y." All eyes shifted to Lou. She tugged on her shirt again, shifting uncomfortably under the burn coursing through her shoulder. "I'm sorry," she said. "I don't know where that came from."

Jay smiled. "They won't make it easy, but we're gonna try to be peaceful about it. They like boys better than girls, at least in the daylight, so don't shoot me, Didi, but you and Lou gotta stay here."

Bell grunted, kicked the ground, widened her eyes.

"She wants to say somethin'," Jay said. "Henry, take the gag out."

Didi's mouth fell open. "Boss—"

"Do it."

Henry reached for the knot of rope behind the fairy's head and pulled the gag free. Cotton and twine fell between her feet.

"No." Bell's voice grated in Lou's ear, lifting bumps on her neck despite the heat.

Didi bared her teeth. "What'd you say, fairy scum?"

"Lou make promise. Lou get treasure. Or no deal."

Jay groaned over the crash of water beyond the trees. "You gotta be kiddin'. She can't go up against the mermaids. They'll never trust us with her there!"

"What is she talking about?" Lou asked.

"You made the pact with Bell," Benji said, handing a waterskin to Sammy, "so it looks like you have to be the one to get the treasure for her to keep your bargain."

"And if I don't keep my bargain, I die." The poison in her skin reeked, the stench of decay sharp in the heat. Sunlight shifted from golden to burnt orange, and thunder clapped between the clouds gathered above the trees. "How long will the curse take to kill me?"

Sammy lowered his sunburned nose to Lou's arm before she could pull it away. "She's got a day, maybe two if we push it."

"Then I'll come with you," Lou said. "If I don't, I'll die anyway."

Jay nodded. "Fine. Henry, Kiran, Didi—you're the strongest. Guard Bell and make sure she stays put. Sammy, Benji—you come with us, but keep an eye out for pirates. Lou, you listen to me. We're a team, and you gotta trust me and do what I say. You think you can do that?"

On the ship, she'd thrown him into the arms of the pirates without a second thought. She'd expected retaliation from the others at her betrayal; what had been unexpected was her sudden and terrible guilt. And yet Jay still stood beside her. Helping her. A constant. She could not leave him stranded again.

"A team," she said. "I can do that. How should I approach the mermaids if they dislike women?"

Jay's eyes flitted to Lou's hand, and she tucked it behind her back. "You just follow my lead," he said. "They don't know you, but I've been around here a long time. C'mere a second." He pulled her away from their party and close to the treeline, carefully avoiding her infected arm. "Do you remember playin' mermaids and pirates together when you were little?"

"It's flashes," she said, probing the dark spots in her memory until they flitted away. "I remember things in flashes of dreams. If I think hard enough, I can remember how I felt when we were together. But the rest . . ."

"It's just a dream." He nodded, and if her words pained him, he didn't show it. "You used to think mermaids were these simple, pretty, innocent things. That's why you hated it so much when I made you the mermaid instead of the pirate. But trust me, the mermaids you're gonna see are nothin' like what you read in your little books. Don't forget that."

Her neck began to itch as the poison crept across her skin. "I have no interest in making this more complicated than it already is, Jay. I will behave. I promise."

"Good to hear it. Don't stare, and don't take anythin' they offer you unless I say it's okay." The light shifted around them, the sky moving from orange to vivid magenta, their faces becoming masks of demons. "There isn't much time, so we gotta move quick."

"Much time?"

"If we wait, you'll see what I'm talkin' about." He gave her good hand a squeeze and turned away, darkness twisting in his eyes.

Lou may not have remembered Jay in solid lines and vivid colours, but the imprint of him had never faded. She knew that now. He was an echo, a spectre that followed her through every thought and decision, an observer and a friend without judgement. She knew when her ghost was in pain, even if he didn't have the words to put to it. She dropped her pack to the ground and followed him into the trees. Followed him anywhere he led her. She owed him that.

Sammy ran to Jay's side, and Benji's hand found hers before

they left the others behind. She smiled, and the burden in her chest eased a fraction.

One day, maybe two, and Rosie would truly be without a sister. Their family would continue to endure the consequences of Father's absence, and her sacrifices would turn to smoke. Her sword was heavy at her side, and she exchanged Benji's hand for the blade. Her pulse slowed, and she focused on Jay's steady back to keep upright.

"Did you want to say goodbye to Henry?" she asked.

Benji smiled. "Goodbye has a way of making something feel final. Goodbye means forever, so I like to say nothing instead. Jay will make sure we all get back."

Jay pushed aside a veil of leaves to let Lou through.

The floral scent of lavender and roses hit Lou first. A current churned at the base of the falls at her left, the water a sheet of pale pink, duck egg, and creamy marshmallow. Magenta sunlight danced off the waterfall, turning the spray to falling gemstones. Rainbow foam frothed and rolled, drifting out to gently rolling shores. By Lou's count, five large rocks dotted the water's surface.

"It's . . . It's beautiful," Lou whispered.

More than the pastel waters or the vast expanse of cliff and trees overlooking the lagoon, it was the mermaids who made Lou take pause. Until then, she'd seen pirates and tribes, all of whom were very much human. Bell was the farthest thing from a natural being as Lou had ever met, but the ugliness in her thrust a barrier between them that she could not overcome. But the mermaids . . .

"Yeah, sure," Jay said with a snort. "Beautiful and crazy. Mermaids are awful creatures. Just bein' this close to 'em makes me wanna hurl."

Heads turned at their arrival. Green, blue, and bronze bodies lounged across the jewel-crusted rocks and wove through the waves like quicksilver. Tail fins fanned the air before disappearing into the depths of the lagoon, silken petals dipped in colour. The sun lingered just over the falls, a blood orange sliced down the centre and squeezed onto the trees.

"Hello, girls," Jay said with a toothy grin. He crouched by the water's edge, dipping his fingers in the waves. "How're we doin' this fine day?"

The mermaids sunning themselves on the rocks ignored him, their long fingers smoothing thick locks the same shade as their fins. Lou flushed at the sight of their bare chests, nipples pale through the gaps in their waist-length hair. Her own chest thumped behind loose clothes, and she laced her arms across herself.

"Hello, Jay. It's been a long time." The mermaid wove seamlessly toward them, her lime-green fins churning the water, jade hair twisting like seaweed behind her. "I missed you."

"Aw, I 'preciate it, Greedance," Jay said. "But you don't have to lie. I know we've never been too close."

The mermaid folded her arms on the sand, water trickling down her light pink cheeks, her pink shoulders, her magenta lips. She shrugged. "Any enemy of Peter's is a friend of mine."

"You're the only one. The others aren't so glad I'm here. Still mad, huh?"

"My sisters have a long memory and a low tolerance for change. Your little feud has taken Peter's attention away from them. But you have such a pretty face, and I am much more forgiving." She moved to assess the rest of their party, and Lou recoiled; Greedance's eyes were a dark molten red. She pouted at Lou, her face falling dramatically. "You should have known better than to bring a girl here, Jay. I don't like it when someone has something I don't."

"Lou's my friend." Jay offered Lou a smile, gesturing for her to join them. "And she came to see you."

I did? "It's nice to meet you," Lou said. Greedance caressed her breasts until her nipples became hard nubs on her otherwise smooth skin. Lou looked away.

"She's lovely." Greedance turned to Jay, tongue flicking across her full upper lip. "Not pretty, but I can see her uses. I don't usually entertain girls, especially when my sisters have different . . . tastes. But this one—"

"Is off-limits, Greedance. I didn't come to bring you a toy."

"Best not to tease me when you're outnumbered."

"Twelve of you against the four of us wouldn't be a smart fight for us to start, it's true," Jay said with a laugh. "So, we're not here to fight at all."

Full lips drew up in a seductive smile. "You aren't a party of four, though, are you? Especially with that abominable fairy hiding in the trees. Now, if you'd *kill* Bell, I'd be oh so grateful."

How did she know?

"You can't kill Bell yet," Jay said. "But once I'm done with her, I don't care what happens."

The pout returned to Greedance's mouth, but she flipped her hair over her shoulder and nodded. "Fine. I'll let the fairy live. But if you would reconsider letting little Lou stay a while, I would be eternally in your debt." Her long green nails pinched the skin around her breasts, drawing blood. "She's pure. Untouched, except for a man who tried to ruin her. He didn't quite manage it, though. I can make you forget about all that, young one."

Lou's palms grew slick, and she ignored Jay's look of confusion.

"We need your help to find somethin' on the bottom of the lagoon," Jay said, "and Lou's gotta be the one to get it. That's all."

"And why would I help you take something that does not belong to you?"

"Because it would really piss Peter off to have his treasure raided."

Greedance tilted her face up at him and flicked her tail into the water. "Does this have anything to do with that poison promise spreading on her arm?" She glanced at Lou, beautiful face suddenly serious. "If you stay with us, you'll never have to die. You can live forever in the lagoon."

The infection was throbbing, pulsing up her arm and creeping across her back, making it painful to stay upright. The day shifted from magenta to plum with the dipping of the sun. "Thank you, but I think I'll take my chances at the bottom of the lagoon," Lou said over the sound of the falls. "If you do not help me, there won't be a lagoon left for any of you."

Greedance's teeth were symmetrical little squares behind her swollen lips. "Peter used to come around here a lot before Blackbeard got him. He left his treasure chest with us for safekeeping and told us never to let another soul near it." She flipped onto her back, the setting sun illuminating the flat planes of her stomach, the curve of her breasts. "Peter's word is law. But since I can still hear his cries echoing in the water, I'd say he won't be back from the ship anytime soon."

Jay exhaled in relief. "Good deal. C'mon, Lou, let's get this over with. Sammy, let the others know Lou and I are headin' underwater. Benji, keep an eye on the other mer—"

"Not you," Greedance said. "Lou has to be the one to get the treasure, but her little curse said nothing about you being involved."

He blinked. "I'm goin' with her."

The mermaid tutted loudly, shaking out her hair. "It would be impossible to keep you both alive, especially if I need to keep Enveer, Rathlyn, and Prideree away from you. They're the worst of my family, you know." Back on the rocks, otherworldly faces with exaggerated eyes and lips and long necks veered in their direction. "You want that treasure, I take Lou. Alone."

Lou's chest erupted into flames; Bell's curse sank teeth into her flesh and tainted her blood, her heart pumping the poison too quickly to stop. She kicked off her boots and made her way to the sandy edge. "Take me there."

"You sure?" Jay asked.

"I don't have time to argue. The curse is spreading too quickly."

A pearlescent hand reached for her, and Lou swallowed a yelp of surprise at the slippery feel of the mermaid's skin.

Greedance tugged.

They plunged into the cool water, the first rush of waves refracting like diamonds around them. The mermaid's hand was a manacle around her wrist, her tail beating them deeper into the abyss. Stone peaks materialized out of the creamy depths, spindles weaving silk into a city under the waves. Closer, she could make out turrets and walls carved out of pebbles, the strange city twisting with roads and peppered with jewels.

Air. She was running out of air.

Bubbles streamed from her lips. She gripped Greedance's hand, dug her nails into the slimy skin with all her force. The mermaid twisted around, her hair green smoke.

Black. Everything was going black.

Cool slippery lips pressed against hers. Lou pulled back, turning her face away, but another hand clamped over her jaw, holding her firm. A gritty tongue pried open her mouth, and Lou released the last of the air in her lungs.

Rosie.

Rosie, I'm sorry.

Rosie, I tried.

A gust of fresh air forced her ribs to accept the sweet breath of life. The lagoon, the green strands floating around her face, and the glowing red eyes inches away from hers all snapped into focus. Lou pulled in another greedy breath, and the mermaid smiled against her lips before breaking the seal.

They floated above the underwater city. Greedance had no

interest in the towers or the marbled walls. Instead, they swam over a courtyard littered with bones. Lou tried not to dwell on the piles of remains, but the skulls were impossible to ignore. Deep black pits leered up at her, a permanent grin flashing in the abyss. But it was those adorned with glittering bows or decaying hats that would haunt her dreams that night.

Another kiss of life, another lurch in her stomach as the mermaid lingered too long, her tongue too insistent against hers. But she needed air, and need was a funny thing.

One long-nailed finger cut through the water. Lou followed Greedance's gaze to where a chest sat covered in seaweed and sand at the tip of a boulder. Carved of wood and framed in steel, the chest sat nestled in the weeds.

Lou struck out for the chest. Her skin was fire, the curse raking a thousand nails across her back. Soon she would be too tired, too far gone. Soon her muscles would seize from the influx of poison, and she would join the piles of bones scattered at the bottom of the lagoon.

Soon. But not yet.

She wedged her fingers underneath the wooden box and gestured for Greedance to do the same. With a sly smile, the mermaid plunged to her side and leaned in close. Lou took another breath, ignoring the swarming mermaids, their eyes a bright crimson, their multicoloured hair forming a rainbow cage around them.

The box groaned loose.

Water pushed at her nose and mouth, but she'd gotten the chest. Greedance's powerful tail beat away at the treacherous waters and mermaids following them up and up and up. First there was only darkness, but a soft light pushed its way into the lagoon, growing brighter with every pass of the mermaid's fin.

Cool air broke over Lou's face. She gasped, blinking away the droplets and shaking her head free of the skulls still lurking under her feet. The movement burned, and when Greedance cupped her face in one of her slick palms, it was agony.

"Poor girl." Greedance wrapped her tail around Lou's waist and the other mermaids drifted closer. "It's gotten to your face."

Lou jerked away from her touch, triggering a flash of pain that blinded her. "It does not matter now. Help me bring the chest to shore."

"Lou!" Jay called, waving frantically. "Hurry up!"

"I'm trying!"

Benji and Sammy were gone. So was the sun. Instead, two moons ghosted above the water, faded by the last dregs of daylight.

Greedance didn't move. The mermaids formed a wall between them and land. Crimson eyes glowed.

"Little Lou." Greedance's voice deepened, rasped, her nails curling around the chest floating between them. "Why would you want to leave?"

Salt filled Lou's mouth as the water grew cloudy. Waves pushed her farther from Jay and land and safety, and she struggled to stay afloat.

"Bring me back," she said despite knowing her words meant nothing to the mermaids. "Now."

Sharp teeth slid out of Greedance's gums, grazing her bottom lip and drawing thin rivulets of blood. "I like you. Not a very pretty face but such a pretty soul. I love the nighttime, but we never get any visitors once the sun disappears. Don't you love the lagoon at nightfall?"

Fins slapped the water's surface, sending sprays of salt water into Lou's eyes, her open mouth, onto her bubbling skin. She gripped the chest and kicked out for the shore, twisting away from the mermaids as they followed. Jay was calling her name. She focused on his face as the claws raked her skin, the piercing call of their siren song raising a chill down her spine. Lips searched for her. Fangs nibbled on her flesh.

She screamed.

The chest. The chest was still in her hands.

With a grunt, Lou pushed Peter's treasure toward the shore, hoping her final efforts would be good enough. "Go!" she called. "Get this to Bell!"

Jay was right; the mermaids truly were terrible creatures, especially after dark. They circled her like hungry sharks, their faces creased and twisted as though gills and scales had replaced their flawless skin. Fangs gnashed, and their voices stitched together in an inhuman symphony of tortured screams. Lou flailed, foot connecting with something hard. She worked to stay afloat, but in her mind, she was on the ground again, staring at the sky as the pirate worked over her.

But the sword was still in her waistband. And she still had one good hand.

In one fluid motion, she pulled her blade free and sent it home above Greedance's naval. It was a second before the warmth of the blood overcame the cool water. The mermaid's eyes flew wide, her scream rattling Lou's teeth.

The sword was smaller than Jay's—a larger dagger, really—and easy to remove from the soft flesh of Greedance's underbelly. Another strike, over and over, and the warm tacky blood mingled with the clean water. More hands grabbed at her, the night filled with outrage, but Lou couldn't quiet her blade and the rage fuelling it. Her lungs filled with water and blood, and the world blurred.

She was drowning.

Drowning in blood.

But she was alive. She let loose a cry of triumph, and her blade sank into a shoulder, a neck, an arm.

A mermaid with pale blue skin and moss-covered teeth dove for Lou's throat, but she was too late. With a sickly squelch, steel sank into the creature's neck. Red blossomed around her, a low gurgle replacing the horrid screams. In and out, over and over.

Lou's arm slowed, heavy with fatigue, but she couldn't stop.

Someone cried out, but it was different somehow. A blond shape swooped over Lou's shoulder and sank its teeth into Greedance's neck. With one backward pull of her head, Bell gnawed the head free of its body. Mermaid Lagoon shone red under the light of twin moons, the screams raising to a pitch as Bell taunted the other mermaids with clicks and screams.

"Bell!" Lou gasped, inhaling another mouthful of water. The fairy's eyes were alight, her smile eager, sharp, dripping with blood as she waved the severed head over the water. "I did what you asked! I got the treasure. Now take the curse off me!"

Bell turned to Lou with a vacant smile. "Done," she said, grasping the back of her collar. In an instant, there was no more air, only the rush of water and salt and Bell's claws raking her skin.

She couldn't explain how she knew it, but this was what drowning felt like.

Light flashed above her, and Lou launched into the sky. A strange glow pulled her with the force of too many hands, and she rode the cocoon of yellow light over the lagoon. If she hadn't been so relieved to be breathing once again, she may have screamed. But the shore raced up to greet her like an old friend, catching her with soft hands as the fairies, now only a pinprick of light, released her into the air.

"Lou? Are you hurt?"

Jay.

She rolled to her stomach and coughed until her lungs burned. Sammy and Benji burst through the trees first, Henry, Kiran and Didi close behind. At that moment, she'd never been so grateful to see the children who had held her captive. "The chest," she managed once the coughs subsided. "Did you get the chest?"

"Sure did." Jay smiled, his clothes dripping, forming a puddle around his knees. "I didn't think Bell was gonna make good on her promise, but she brought you back. You did real good, pirate girl."

Benji offered Lou his sweater, cheeks blanched in the weakening moonlight. "You . . . Your curse is gone." Eyes roved over the bare skin of her arms, searching for the infection that no longer burned her body. "See? Your skin's all nice again."

Lou did nothing to hide her exposed flesh. "I feel much better —like myself. Bell got what she needed, then."

Jay's face went dark, and even Didi wore a mask of disgust. "Oh, she did."

Lou stood on shaky legs. "How many mermaids did I kill?"

"A couple," Kiran said, grinning. "I never saw no one give 'em a hard time like that."

"A hard time." Lou laughed. "That is one way to put it. So, can we open the chest now?"

Didi tapped the heel of her boot into the wooden lid, *thunk, thunk, thunk.* "Don't see why not. Seems like a lot of trouble for a rotten hunk of wood."

"Not a hunk of wood," Sammy said, sinking to a squat before the chest. "It's a treasure. But Bell didn't take anythin' from it. Funny, huh, Jay?"

The night went quiet save the thump of Lou's heartbeat in her ears. "What do you mean she didn't take anything? I was to get the chest for her in exchange for the key."

"Turns out the devil's idea of treasure is a mermaid head," Jay said, nose wrinkled in distaste. "I always hated that fairy."

Lou frowned. "If all she wanted from this expedition was a mermaid's head, she could have attacked them herself. She had no reason to put us through any of that." Anger licked at her belly, giving her strength.

So much fear. So much pain. And for what?

"Aw, don't cry, Lou." Sammy stood and patted her arm gingerly. "It's not so bad."

"We told you," Jay said. "The mermaids hate Bell. She can't go near enough to any of 'em to be able to get their head."

"So, at best, I was a distraction. At worst, I would die, and she would simply try again some other way." She'd been bested by a young girl who'd bargained with her life as though it meant nothing more than a breath on the wind. Lou swiped her blade against her thigh, rubbing the steel clean, and returned it to her belt. She would happily use it again if the need arose.

A quake rattled the island, and the mermaids plunged into the depths of the lagoon. Boulders splintered and tumbled down, down, down, until there was nothing but a gaping hole where the falls used to be. There was nothing for Lou to do but drop to the ground and shut her eyes against the possibility of the end.

It was a long while before the night went quiet. When it did, Lou looked out over the water. The falls had run dry. The flat surface of the water was dark and studded with broken stone. Mermaid lagoon was a graveyard.

Lou tore her gaze away from the wreckage and crawled over to the chest. The lock was rusted and fragile, but after her experience on Blackbeard's ship, she knew appearances were deceiving.

"I need a larger sword," Lou said. "Now."

Someone placed a heavy blade in her outstretched hand. Rage flooded her, and she let it take over. Let it fill her. Let it replace all her restraint and poise and patience. The island was no place for such adult things.

Lou drove the sword home.

The lock shrieked and fell to the sand.

CHAPTER 25

JAY

How many times did life have to stab me in the heart with a rusty dagger before I learned my lesson?

As it turned out, the answer was twice.

Twice now the island had pulled me away from her.

Twice now I hadn't been ready.

Twice I'd been crushed, except this time I'd learned a nifty little piece of information I hadn't had before: Lou really couldn't see me anymore, even if I tried real hard.

Peter was right. I'd doubted him, but it turned out he did tell the truth when it suited him. And making me suffer suited him just fine.

Fairy dust might have been enough to get me back to the Land of the Grown, but it was pure rage that sent me flying back to the island. My hands shook so badly I didn't dare grab my dagger. But this time I wasn't out for blood. With my shoulder scabbed over and tender, it would have been suicide to challenge Peter. No, that could wait.

I'd try again. Fairy dust had helped me once; there was no shortage of it so long as I championed Lilith's sister. I would find a way to get her to understand my need—all I wanted was some more time.

Peter might have been able to touch the stars once, but I was the one who'd found my way around them.

I just need a solid plan, that's all.

My hands steadied, and I slowed down. My feet found the familiar path through the woods, the rumble of the crocs by the swamp a sure guide back to the Hanging Tree.

The way she looked at that kid. Her smile when she leaned into her momma's legs . . .

"Quit it." I shook the images from my head, and they passed out of thought like water over smooth stones. Mosquitos buzzed in my ears, and the air was too thick after the cool night on Silverton Lane. Maybe if I spoke to Peter again, really *explained* what happened, he would understand this was something I needed to do. Maybe he'd finally make an exception and let me fix it.

Not a chance. He'll only think I'm weak. And he'll be mad.

The trees thinned, and the Hanging Tree welcomed me back.

"Jay!" A figure raced out of the shadows, pale blue light pooling on his eager face. I loved Sammy, but I was exhausted, and every time I looked at him, I hated myself for wishing he were Lou. The kid didn't deserve anything less than my whole heart, but I just didn't have enough of it left to go around.

"Not now, Sammy. I don't wanna talk about it."

"Wait!" Sammy's eyes were bright as I hurried past him. Feverish. "There's an initiation tonight!"

I stopped mid-step. "What didja say?"

"He came back with another one just after sunset."

"Why didn't I know about this?"

Sammy twisted his fingers, his chin trembling around his words. "No one knew. He got real quiet after you left and went out into the woods on his own. He . . . He was lookin' for you. And then he went to the Land of the Grown."

Peter knew I'd been gone. *Shoot.* "Didja say anythin' to him?"

"I told him you were off by the eastern coast 'cause the pirates were makin' their way too close to the Hanging Tree. You went to head 'em off. I . . . I'm not sure he believed me."

The strain in the boy's voice broke through my anger, and I rustled up a spare smile for him. "You did good, Sammy. It was good thinkin'. Where is he?"

Sammy wrinkled his nose. "He's off gettin' the kid ready. You should get in the circle before he finds out you're back. It won't be long now."

"Right." After having Peter's island control my every step, the last thing I needed was an initiation bringing another poor kid into this mess. But as I left Sammy and slipped through the crack in the Hanging Tree, an initiation might not have been my worst enemy. An initiation gave Peter something to do instead of thinking too hard about my absence, and if I played my part, he might not pick up my scent.

Peter was smart, but I was smarter. And I had a whole lot more to lose.

The lost boys sat with their backs pressed against the curved wall. The circle was complete, save for two gaps like missing teeth in a monster's jaw, places where Sammy and I should already have been. I moved to the centre, nodding at them as I passed. Benji waved, offering me a weak smile, and Timber gave me a quick salute, but the others simply nodded back. Only Slightly didn't acknowledge my authority as I took the number two position in the den; his brow threw shadows across his cheeks, and light bounced off his dagger and into my eyes.

Don't worry, Slightly. You'll get yours soon enough.

Peter was a fan of grand entrances, always choosing blood and great speeches over compromise and listening. It was something he'd learned after many years as a leader, he always said. But the way I saw it, power was something that burrowed under the skin and raced to the heart, a poison turning even the gentlest kids into pirates. In the end, I had no experience leading a clan, but if I had to, I was pretty sure I could do it without having my people look at me the way Peter's kids looked at him: with disgust and awe and the kind of fear that never goes away but lies dormant until it wakes in a fury of mutiny.

I heard the chains first. Peter stomped on the dirt path, his heavy footsteps echoing down the passage like the giant from one of Sammy's nightmares. Dirt caked into the creases on his face, giving him a permanent sneer. A heavy iron chain was slung over his shoulder, and he tugged once, twice, hard enough to pull his next victim into the fold.

I stepped back to make more room. A loud gasp flitted around the circle.

The recruit was taller than me, his arms and legs roped with muscle. He trailed behind Peter with his nose turned to the ground, feet shuffling, leaving long tracks in the dust. The pirates were our biggest enemies; the combination of size and bad form was always a danger worth looking out for. But a boy the size of a man was a rare gem in a necklace beaded with chipped wood.

"Ah, everyone's here. Good." Peter moved to the centre of the circle and tugged the recruit after him. A pinprick of sparkling white light illuminated the room; Lilith never left Peter's side during initiations. "I got a surprise. Jay, come here. Now."

Not a request. *That can't be good.* "Hey, boss."

"You made it back." Peter stared at me, expression unreadable. *He knows. He's gotta know.* "Glad to see you, Number Two."

"It took a little longer to get back from the coast, but the pirates won't be botherin' us any time soon." It was an easy lie. Too easy. "Guess I lost track of time."

"Still wish you woulda told me your plan. Tonight's special; it woulda been a shame for you to miss it."

"Every initiation is special." I forced a smile onto my face, relaxing the bum shoulder that burned whenever Peter got too close. "Isn't this one too old to be here? He's almost fully grown. I'm not sure how the others are gonna feel about this."

"I wouldn't worry too much about it." Peter poked the boy's arm, looking him over like an animal out for auction. "Maybe there's somethin' wrong with this guy. He won't talk, or can't talk, or I don't know what. Anyway, I'm not complainin'. We could use a big one like this."

"We do just fine on our own," I countered. "But if you were lookin' for more help, I know Lilith's sister, Bell, has her ear to the ground. We could use an extra fairy."

Peter's eyes flicked to mine. "You hate the fairies. Lilith woulda been gone a long time ago if I hadn't ordered you to leave her alone. What's Bell to you?"

Careful now. Careful. "I'd rather a devil fly we know than take on a grown recruit. What good's a big guy who can't talk gonna do for a kid who needs a friend?" *There you go. That's better.*

"I'll think about it. But until I make up my mind, we gotta bring big guy into the fold."

The boy looked between us, then at the rest of the den. Russet hair, a broad nose smattered with freckles. Twice our size and weight, yet *he* looked scared. Well, at least he got the measure of things pretty quick. "Does *big guy* have a name?" I asked.

Peter shrugged. "Probably. If he lives, I'll even find out what it is. First, I got some news. Boys, there's a new kid who needs us in the Land of the Grown. Jay's old charge, Lou Webber, has a sister now. I need one of you to take her on." His smirk twisted his features. "I need someone I can trust. She's important, this one. Special."

"I can do it." The noise fell away. The island fell away. The initiation fell away. Peter had what I wanted—and he knew it. He bored into me, dangling the bait under my nose, and I bit. "Boss, I can take this one. I already know the family."

He laughed. *Bastard.*

"Well, I don't think that's fair," Peter said. "You just got a turn. I'm sure one of the others would love a chance to bounce between worlds for a bit."

"I don't mind," Benji offered. *Thanks, pal, but he already made up his mind.* "Jay *does* know them all, and I don't mind him going."

"I do." *Slightly.* "Jay shouldn't get two in a row. That ain't fair, 'specially since I got passed up last time."

"You got passed up 'cause kids are scared of your face," I said. "Really, Peter. I'm your best bet. Give me a chance."

"Deal's a deal, Number Two. You wanted one more, and I'm keepin' my promise. You won't be takin' on no more kids. Ever." He bowed low to me, every move of his scrawny body mocking me. Taunting me. Begging me to attack and make a scene. I held myself steady. "Timber! You up for a new kid?"

I caught Timber glance in my direction before he nodded to Peter. You didn't deny the master of the island when he called on you directly; I still hated the roar of jealousy climbing up my throat at picturing him in Lou's world. "I can do it. Sure. Sure, Peter. I'll watch over them both, Jay. You don't gotta worry."

"Good. Now that's done, we can get to the good stuff." Peter faced his audience with a spark of delight. "This big lug won't be fightin' no pirate tonight." Another rustle of mutters, another round of whispers. "See, it would be too easy for him to take down a dirty pirate seein' as he's the same size as most of 'em. But I don't just value strength. Sammy! Bring 'em in!"

Peter tugged the chain again, and Lilith disappeared outside. When her light returned, it didn't come alone.

More footsteps.

More grunts.

My stomach bottomed out.

A boy and a girl, both wiry, with skin as rich as the bark of a twisting sycamore, stumbled into the Hanging Tree, Sammy shuffling after them. Their hair drifted over sharp cheeks in tight curls, their eyes almost the same shade of black. Siblings—they had to be. Bound wrists dripped blood onto the ground while gags cut their mouths. The girl snarled as Peter pulled them into the centre of the circle like pigs up for slaughter.

"I found these two spyin' on me when I went to grab the big one," Peter said. "They were in a back alley, stealin' food from the rats. So, I figured I'd make this interestin'."

The girl glared up at Peter, murder plain in her eyes. He pulled a dagger from the armory wall beside him and tossed it at the older boy's feet.

"Kill 'em, big guy."

My mind froze, and no one else said a word either. "What are you sayin'?" I asked.

"I want the big one to kill the gutter rats who think it's okay to spy on me when I'm doin' my work. So . . . pick up that dagger and do it, or I'll get rid of you instead."

"Hey now," I said, "that's not how we do things. We don't kill our own."

"He ain't one of us yet, and neither are they. If you had a problem with this new . . . direction, well, you woulda known all about it if you hadn't spent so much time by the coast."

It was all a game to the boy who would never grow up. And there was nothing more mouth-watering to a kid starving for chaos than a game built around death. He knew exactly where I had been, and the blood of those prisoners would be on my hands. My punishment. Mine.

In a flash, the dagger was no longer on the floor.

"Hold on, big guy," I said with a forced smile. "Whatcha doin' with that blade?"

He loomed over me, steel glinting in his clenched fist. He turned it this way and that, the shifting angles throwing shards of light across the den.

But when he didn't obey, Peter hovered closer, so driven by his anger it practically lifted him off the ground. "Go on, you dumb tree stump. Don't make me tell you what I do to people who don't follow the rules."

"Maybe we should vote on this, boss," I said. The girl growled and pulled at her bindings while the boy sobbed silent tears, but I couldn't care about calming them down yet. Peter always said the best way to stay alive was to keep an eye on the biggest threat in the room, so I was. "They're just kids. They probably didn't know what they were seein' when you went to the Land of the Grown. We should recruit them too and have an even bigger clan to face the pirates."

Muttered agreement greeted my words, but Peter pinned me with a glare. "They're just trash! If they were worth a lick, I woulda felt the need to bring 'em over, and I didn't. They weren't much use over there, but if I can make sure the new kid is willin' to kill for me, then they'll be useful to me *here*."

The rest were talking now. Wriggling, writhing on the ground. On the dirt. Worms. We were all worms to Peter.

"He kills 'em, or I get rid of all three," Peter said easily. "And anyone who argues with me gets the blade next. So, what's it gonna be, big guy? You already got the dagger—let's go!"

"Stop!" I cried, but it was too late.

The boy had already lifted the dagger high over his head, ready to obey Peter's order. Steel whispered through the air. I dove for him, my hands clawing at the thick musculature of his arm.

Instead of sinking the blade into one of the siblings like Peter had instructed, the new recruit swung his arm wide. The ground at his feet swallowed the dagger with a greedy slurp. For a second, every pair of eyes took in the sight of the blade in the ground.

Then, the world exploded with Peter's anger. "Moron!" he cried. "Idiot! Guess you made your choice."

"Peter, wait—" I said.

But the new boy shook his head, eyes soft. *He wants me to let it happen. He wants to die.*

Colour rose on Peter's face. "Stay out of this, Number Two. Tell me, big guy. What's your name?"

We waited, and I wished the giant would say something. Anything.

"His name's Henry." Benji's voice quivered, his eyes darting everywhere except at Peter. "At least, that's what I think he said."

"The big tree didn't say anything," Peter said.

"I know. He doesn't talk, but I can hear him. I . . . I don't know why."

Peals of laughter exploded throughout the room.

"That true? Your name's Henry?" Peter asked. The large recruit nodded, and Peter crowed again. "I wasn't expectin' that. Neat trick, Benji! I picked him up 'cause I figured he was strong, but a strong kid who can't talk is even better. Different."

I released a heavy breath. "So, you'll keep them?"

Peter shrugged. "Sure. I mean, we can try them out for a bit and see how they do. I guess."

My grip on Henry's arm relaxed. "All right, boys," I said. "You heard him. Say hello to your newest brothers and sister! I don't know about you all, but I'm starvin'. Did we get any game from the hunt tonight?"

"Hold on." Peter held up a hand for silence, and he got it. "He's in, sure, but he went against orders. I can't have a kid not knowin' his place." His brows pulled together, mouth puckering into a frown of mock regret. "You gotta take care of him, Jay."

I knew that look—a new game.

"What are you talkin' about? It's done. We can move on now."

Peter's eyes slid down to where the other two prisoners hid behind my knees, a mess of dirt and tears and entwined limbs, and it took remembering my bum shoulder to keep from lunging at him. "It's not done 'til I say it is."

"We got three new bodies to fight the pirates. Henry here won't be any trouble, and neither will they. It's done."

It could have worked. But once Peter had an idea, he wouldn't be distracted. "You're my number two. It's your job to do what you're told. And I'm tellin' you to teach Henry a lesson about who's the leader here. Cut him."

If I accepted, I was as much a monster as Peter. But if I refused, that wrath would turn on me, and I could forget ever seeing Lou again. My loyalty pushed up against my need for survival until I couldn't tell them apart.

My fingers trembled as I pulled the dagger from the ground.

"Cut him!" Peter crowed.

Cut him. Cut, cut, cut.

I didn't want to do it. Really.

You just have to say, "I'll be a kid forever," three times, and they'll come. Easy peasy, poke your knees-y.

But I won't be a kid forever. That's a lie.

But she was a kid, an innocent little kid with a life ahead of her that would eat her up and spit her to the crocs. She couldn't suffer that. Not yet.

It's not a lie if you don't want it to be.

"Do it, Jay!"

I kept Lou's face in my mind. Henry wasn't a boy—he was a way out. A way back to Lou.

"Don't move," I muttered, wishing I could say more. Wishing I could apologize without sparking Peter's anger. "I'll make it quick. I promise."

"Right across the chest," Peter said, his voice too even. Blood made him calm like that. "Make it clean, and he'll live."

"Sure thing, boss." I raised the dagger and pulled my elbow back, twisting to drive the blow with my back leg.

Make it clean.

I would, because no one needed to suffer.

Henry closed his eyes, his chin puckering with suppressed sobs. I inhaled, letting the stale air fill my lungs, trying to keep my arm from shaking. The lost boys stared, but no one stopped me—no one dared, and I didn't resent it. I knew what it took to survive in this world. We might never grow up, but that didn't stop this life from crushing us anyway.

Henry never flinched as I came for him. The brother prisoner screamed, pouncing from the ground with his limbs still bound. His sister followed close behind with a cry of her own, their bodies shielding Henry's. A blink was all it took for my arm to swing too far. I couldn't stop it.

Silver flashed across their terrified dark faces in a clean arc. Henry stood back, mouth hinged open in an O of surprise.

Dark flesh split wide. Crimson droplets flecked the ground, soaking the dirt like rain.

CHAPTER 26

Lou threw open the lid of the chest.

"What is it?" Sammy asked.

Didi shoved him aside. "She don't know yet, dummy. Be quiet!"

"*Everyone* be quiet!" Lou plunged greedy fists into the chest and pulled the objects out one at a time: coins crusted with dirt and mould; a pale yellow blanket, threadbare and stained; a sewing kit with a gleaming thimble; two toy soldiers, one missing an arm, the other in dire need of a restorative coat of paint; and a bear, its brown fur matted down flat.

"Ugh," Jay said, backing away. "He kept it all. Unbelievable."

"You recognize these objects?" Lou asked.

"So this is where Peter keeps all his souvenirs from the kids he takes. This can't be everythin', but there's a good amount of stuff I recognize. I've seen a lot of this come and go over the years."

"So, it's all just a bunch of junk," Didi said, nose wrinkling. "Move aside, lady. If somethin' in there belongs to me, I'm takin' it back."

"Wait." Benji lifted his hand, thick fingers quivering toward the bear. "I . . . I think I've seen this before."

Didi rolled her eyes. "Yeah? Who'd ever give *you* a fancy toy bear?"

"I'm not sure." Benji clutched the bear in his hands, one shiny black eye swinging from a single thread. "I mean, I don't remember much from before Peter brought me here. But it reminds me of something . . . soft."

A single pearl stud, a diamond-encrusted flower, a gold hoop, all mingling in one tarnished silver bowl.

A pacifier.

A lock of hair, sodden and tied together with a red ribbon.

Lou's fingers probed, shuffling the contents left and right. *A key, a key, a key.*

A bracelet.

Shoelaces threaded with gold.

A rock.

"Wait."

Her hand hovered over the stone. It was grey and veined in silver, the edges smoothed and curved into the shape of a heart. Crystals flecked within it flashed in the moonlight as though the stone had captured the stars themselves. She held it up for Jay to see, and his eyes went wide.

"That's it," he said, weighing the stone in his palm. "It's gotta be."

"You're tellin' me we almost died for a *pebble*?"

"It's not a pebble, Didi. It's a piece of Soul Rock," Jay said. "See?"

Sammy wrinkled his nose, inching closer to the heart-shaped stone. "You mean the creepy island where the sea monster lives? Cool."

"Not cool," Jay corrected him. "Dangerous. I'd know the look of that stone anywhere. If Peter's keepin' a piece of Soul

Rock in a treasure chest, there's gotta be somethin' special about it."

Benji pressed his new bear to his chest. "I remember him telling us stories about it. He warned us never to go there, Jay. It's where the dead go."

"Yeah, a perfect story to keep us away from it," Jay reasoned. "I heard Peter talkin' about the hills at the other side of the rock once. Maybe that's the Mountain of Regret."

"Maybe," Benji said, growing paler than usual. "Could the entrance to the mountain be on Soul Rock? I mean, I know it's never supposed to be in the same place, but what if it's the same path each time? Only the destination changes."

"I don't know, but it's the best theory we got." Jay laughed. "Peter only ever gave us stories. I can't wait to shove 'em down his throat."

Didi's face fell. "Well, me and Kiran are out."

"Sis—"

"We can't give up now!" Lou said through tremors of cold seeping into her bones. "We've come so far; we need this key!"

"No, *you* need the key to go back to your fancy house." Didi brushed sand off her pants and linked her fingers with Kiran's. "*We're* already home."

Lou blinked. "There is more to the world than this place, Didi."

Didi pulled her hand out of Kiran's and stepped over the chest until she was face to face with Lou. "You don't get it, lady. We're here 'cause no one wanted us. You got stars in your eyes and a place to go back to, but we don't. All any of us ever had was hate and people who should have loved us but didn't. Nah, we're all the family we got. And if this place goes down, then I go down with my brothers."

Lou expected Jay to intervene, to tell them to be quiet and leave her alone, except he and the others stood aside, letting the storm have its day. She was on her own this time; not even Jay would help her.

"You cannot believe that," Lou said. "This place isn't what you deserve, with its laws created by one boy."

Didi laughed. "You got no idea what we deserve, *Louisa*. As far as I'm concerned, the faster you leave, the better it is for all of us." Her jaw flexed, and she spit on the ground, her hair a wild bird's nest rimming her head like a crown of thorns. She turned for the trees and Kiran followed close behind, leaving a heavy silence behind.

"I . . . I'm so sorry." Lou swallowed bile. "I didn't mean to upset her."

Jay faced her, his features hard. "I know it's not your fault, Lou. But you gotta understand, we grew up different than you. We hate this place, don't get me wrong, but it's the only place we ever felt like we belonged. So, seein' you wantin' to leave so bad, preach like you're better than us . . ." Jay sighed and looped his thumbs into his belt. "It's like hearin' we're not good enough all over again. It's hard to be reminded that you got somethin' we don't."

Pain twisted her gut. "I am so sorry."

"I know." The hard lines of his young face softened. Jay pocketed the rock, leaving the chest by the shore. With a finger, he lifted her pack and handed it to her. "It's late. Let's just make camp on some higher ground and deal with this tomorrow. Sammy, you go find a spot. Henry, Benji, could you find some supplies? Wood, and maybe a rabbit or a couple birds? It's been a long day."

The boys jumped to attention, breaking for the trees and leaving Lou alone with Jay.

"We aren't going back to the den?" she asked.

"It's too late. Forest's too dangerous at night, and we're too far away."

"And the chest?"

Jay regarded the lump of wood and metal with something close to contempt. "We leave it here. If we're lucky, a pirate'll find it and burn it all to ashes. I'd do it, but I don't have the heart."

Once Didi and Kiran returned, Jay led their group to the top of a nearby hill to make camp for the night. Lou prepared a fire while the children fashioned beds from palm fronds and secured the site against intruders with hidden traps. While fatigue made Lou clumsy, Jay and the others shouldered their roles with ease. They moved quietly from task to task until a temporary home emerged from the dirt and branches. Perhaps it was their overlong lives that bonded them so closely. Perhaps it was the sadness and despair of their past that compelled them to cling to one another through hardship. But the more Lou watched them, the more convinced she became that the children were simply a family united by love. She had thought them cursed. She had thought them prisoners. Now, she envied them.

Dinner was picked clean. The fire burned low in the gathering dark. There was nothing left to do but sleep and wait for either morning or death to find them.

"I'll take first watch," Jay said, adjusting the large leaf draped across Sammy's back. He smiled down at the small boy huddled at his feet, affection blazing in his eyes. "Kiran, you okay to take over after me?"

"Sure thing, boss."

Lou rested her back against a rock and tucked her knees up to her chest. The stone was warm, her back moulding to the dips and curves easily. Her muscles ached, but the breeze was soft on her skin, and the sword was solid against her thigh.

Rosie would have loved the island. In another life, she might have been a squirrel or a raccoon—a scavenger navigating the ups and downs of the earth and jumping from tree to tree with ease. Lou had envied the way she could be so free, so alive, so different from everything Mother wished her girls to be. And yet her sister had always been favoured. Had Mother shed a single tear at her eldest daughter's disappearance? Lou was willing to wager a trip back to Mermaid Lagoon that she knew the answer to that terrible question.

She was the last to fall asleep. In her dreams, water poured into her lungs and long fingernails caked in grime pressed into her back, her legs, her face. Those dreams chased her through the night and into the morning. If she'd had more strength left, maybe she could have woken herself up when the visions grew dark. She could have sought comfort among friends. But monsters lurked in the strangest places, and Didi and Kiran's continued distance reminded her that friendship was a luxury she hadn't earned.

When the sun trudged over the trees, Lou decided to abandon any hope for fitful sleep. Her throat ached, and her skin was tight, but she was dry, and there were things to do, amends to be made.

"You're up early." Jay grinned over a shiny red apple, his back up against the same tree as the night before. "After everythin' that happened, I thought I was gonna have to throw some water on you to wake you up."

"Please, no more water."

Someone had removed her boots while she slept and propped them up beside her to dry. Benji lay curled on a bed of leaves, the bear nestled under his chin. Henry—large, muscular, silent Henry —lay sprawled on his back, the frond of a large palm tree barely covering his torso while he dozed beside Benji, both boys reaching for each other, even in sleep. And then there was Sammy; his ball-like figure rested at Jay's feet, cheek smashed into the earth, bottom curved toward the sky. Rosie had slept like that as a young child, and Lou used to place her hand on her sister's back and rock her from side to side. Still, whenever Rosie was uncomfortable, she would lie on her belly and rock herself in the same unconscious way.

Lou swiped her arm across her eyes. "It looks like you haven't moved at all. Did you get any sleep?"

Jay smiled. "I have a hard time sleepin' when I'm not in the den. Somethin' about bein' outside, open and exposed . . . keeps me awake every time."

"I don't remember you ever sleeping in my room. I guess I understand why."

"I did. Your room was as much home to me as the Hanging Tree ever was." He cleared his throat and smoothed a lock of hair away from Sammy's face.

"He is very attached to you. It's a lucky thing, to find comfort in another like that."

"He's the youngest kid here. Sammy was in foster care for a year before Peter found him. His parents took too much medicine; they were on that stuff more than they weren't. One day, Sammy got tired of seein' his daddy put hands on his momma, so he pushed him down the stairs." Jay chuckled. "His momma took him to the orphanage the very next day."

"That's horrible," Lou whispered. "You would think she would have been grateful for her son's intervention, as terrible as it must have been for him to do what he did."

"Growns don't often see things as clear as us kids do. And they almost never know what's good for 'em before the bad things smack 'em in the face." Jay set eyes on the boy, the ice in them thawing to warm blue pools. "For a long time after he got to the island, Sammy hoped his momma would come find him. But she never did. And with Peter bein' . . . well . . . Peter, the kid needs someone to look out for him."

Sammy's back rose and fell with every breath. Lou smiled, reaching for his hand and stroking the supple skin with a featherlight touch. "He is better off living here with you."

Colour pooled in Jay's cheeks. "Never thought I'd hear you say that. Anyway, he likes to take care of me, and I let him, while I take care of him right back. It works for us."

The island came alive in drips and drabs, first with the butterflies floating from flower to flower, then with the louder snap and crunch of invisible paws on the ground. Except for the shifting of the earth leaving fissures between the trees, everything was as it should have been.

Didi and Kiran moved soundlessly away from camp, a jar of oily black paint shared between them. While they reapplied their masks, Lou slid her boots over her dirty stockinged feet, relishing the way her toes slid over the worn leather. She pulled a long stick of half-eaten rabbit off the spit, ignoring the growl of her stomach.

"I'll be right back," she said.

Jay nodded, his eyes following her as she tiptoed away from camp. Rosie was waiting for her, and Lou had every intention of returning to her sister. Her obligations would be waiting too. But in the meantime, there were bridges to be mended.

Didi saw her first. She scowled, wiping the black paint off her palms with a golden leaf. "What now, lady? The rock too hard for your back?"

"You have every right to be upset with me."

"Oh, well, since *you* say I have a right, then I guess it's my lucky day."

Kiran placed the black jar in his sister's pack, his face a fresh oil slick gleaming in the new sun. "No one's mad at you, Lou. Didi just has a bit of trouble makin' friends is all."

"No, this is not Didi's fault. It is mine. Can we start over?"

Didi and Kiran exchanged a glance, and Lou took heart in their silence.

"I've disrupted your life and put your safety at risk. I've taken food from your rations and a bed in your den and have only complained. From what I can tell, you all were rather happy in your ways until I came along." Lou offered the skewer of meat to

Kiran, who took it with wide eyes. She didn't dare offend Didi's pride by handing it to her directly, but she hoped the girl understood anyway. Gestures were all she had left. "I am truly sorry."

"Fine." Didi shrugged. "You're sorry for bein' a pain and distractin' Jay from takin' care of us. We're pretty used to bein' ignored, so no big deal."

Ah. There it was—the fissure in Didi's iron mask. Lou's heart thawed toward the girl, and she was suddenly a woman of twenty faced with a child in pain.

"My mother never wanted me, you know," Lou said. "Did Jay ever tell you that?"

"Yeah, okay." Didi swatted the meat away. "I saw that dress and the pretty little slippers you came in with. I'll bet your momma brushed out that long hair of yours and dressed you up all nice, like a little doll."

"My mother is a very traditional woman. Compared to the other stories I've heard, my upbringing is, by comparison, quite unremarkable. Comfortable, even. But it would be naive to assume that pretty clothes and a fancy dress are equal to love and happiness." It was strange to speak the words she'd always held hostage in her heart but never spoken aloud. Though they were true, truth had never been an acceptable reason to speak her mind. "I wasn't proper. I didn't keep my hair tidy or my dresses pretty. I didn't want to marry or have children."

Didi scowled. "Still not seein' the big problem here. So, you didn't want kids. Big deal."

"She wanted another," Lou continued. "Another *baby*. When she looked at me, I saw only resentment and darkness. By having another, she got a second chance at having the *right* child, a replacement for the daughter who could not bring her the pride she craved. At least, that is what I pieced together."

Images flashed in her mind then of nights swishing tree branches in her room and of her mother, tight curls pinned atop her head, running into her bedroom and reprimanding her for the noise. Of a room at the end of the hall with the carefully selected decor she was never allowed to touch. The room that made her mother cry until she didn't hide her tears anymore.

Because she didn't care if Lou was there to see them or not.

"I think I needed Jay because my mother hated me," Lou said. "Father softened the blow for a time, and when he passed away, Rosie became my light in the darkness. And now I have neither. Jay replaced the love I lacked. You might be the only ones who understand that. My taking his attention must feel like losing a parent all over again. You have no idea how sorry I am for all of it."

Moisture gathered at the corners of her eyes, but Lou smiled around the tears. She'd never been able to fashion a complete thought out of the scraps of emotion she held in her heart. But the island had stripped the noise from her mind and had made room for all the things she'd long forgotten.

Kiran's mouth hung wide, partially chewed meat spread across his tongue. "You really remember Jay?"

Lou considered his question carefully. "In pieces. Mostly, I remember he was my way out of the darkness and into the skies. And that sort of memory lives in the heart, not the mind. It's different from remembering . . . better, even. And if you two did that for other children, then I'm sorry I made you feel anything short of heroic. That sort of existence has meaning."

"I wish someone would remember us too," Kiran muttered.

Lou smiled softly. "It's possible someone already does. But even if they do not, that does not make the life you lead here any less amazing. The bond you all have, the love for one another, is a gift not many receive." She brushed her hands free of the sand stuck on her palms and offered Didi a final smile. "Anyhow, I understand if you wish to return to the den after all this. I simply wanted to thank you for all you've done."

Kiran's head swivelled between them, and Didi dug a trench

with the toe of her boot, eyes turned to the mud. "You're welcome," she muttered. "Kiran, gimme some of that meat."

Lou's heart was lighter on the walk back to camp. Henry and Benji were stirring while Sammy had toppled onto his side, trapping Jay's feet underneath him.

"Kid sleeps like a rock," Jay said, frowning down at Sammy. "I wish I could block out the world like he can."

"Rosie used to rouse if I played with her hair. It is a softer way to wake a child than simply forcing them up. May I?"

Jay nodded, and she bent to the slumbering child, her fingers finding his brow, his hair, the bridge of his nose with the ease of habit. She stroked his face in silence until his eyes fluttered and met hers, a yawn stretching his pink mouth. Sammy's hair was a mess of tangles, and Lou raked her fingers through the knots, teasing them apart.

Mother used to fix her hair in the same way. Lou pulled her hand away.

Benji reached for the waterskin Henry offered him, the pair already preparing to move. "So," he said, "I figure that if we travel due east, we'll get to the beach by midday. That would give us enough time to get to Soul Rock before the sea monster gets too cranky and the sky's too dark to see anything. What do you think, Jay?"

"It's a good idea, Benji. You help Sammy get his things packed up so I can draw out a map of the quickest route. If we can make it before the sun is right over the rock, we'll beat the tribes goin' on their afternoon hunts."

Lou watched as the four boys jumped to action, kicking the ashes of the fire askew, loading their packs, and getting Sammy ready.

"You're all coming with me?" she asked. "After last night, I assumed none of you would want to risk the journey."

"You kiddin'?" Jay asked. "You'd never make it without our

help. Plus, I got to thinkin' while you were snorin' up against that rock. If one of us gets hurt on the way back, we're gonna need an old lady like you to take care of us."

"*Old lady?*" Lou laughed, pulling her heavy strands into a messy knot at the base of her neck. "Well, that is fair. And since none of you have more sense than a toddler, I'd say it would be criminal to leave you alone now."

Didi and Kiran marched back into camp, the skewer of meat nowhere in sight.

"But I think it should be put to a vote," Lou said. "Everyone should be able to decide freely whether they wish to journey with us."

"Yeah, all right," Jay said. "All in favour, spit!"

To Lou's revulsion and amazement, six faces tipped to the ground and let fly globs of saliva into the dirt.

"I'm not sure the spitting was necessary, but I'm grateful to you all," she said. "Thank you."

Benji turned red under his collar and threw his arms around Lou's neck. "Sure thing, Lou. So, we have the key to Soul Rock, but then what? Does anyone know what happens after we get there?"

"Stay alive and hope for the best," Didi said. "All we gotta do is steer clear of the crocs, pirates, sea monsters, and tribes, and we should be in good shape."

The plan was moving from improbable to unlikely, then swiftly into the realm of the ridiculous. Lou rested against a fallen log, and Henry sidled over to her. *It's all right*, he seemed to say, and her sorrow simmered down into her belly. *We won't let anything happen to you.*

"Thank you," she said. "But I don't want anything to happen to any of *you* either."

Henry smiled, and she leaned her head against his shoulder while Jay and Didi made their plans. With a goal, the children were renewed. And when a tremor shook the land, crumbling trees and rock into new cracks in the hard earth, no one looked worried. They were united in their desire to brave a new adventure together.

Lou reached for Jay's hand, the warmth of it having become more familiar as the days had stretched on. In the other hand, she held her sword, a few errant flecks of dried mermaid blood gleaming under the burning sun. She liked them there—proof of her victory. She wanted to prove to the others she was worthy of being there too.

There was something else she should have wanted more than the acceptance of that small band of children. Something familiar. *Someone* familiar.

But as they moved into the woods together, Lou left a piece of herself behind. Suddenly, she couldn't quite think of what—or who—that familiar something was.

CHAPTER 27

After Mermaid Lagoon, the rest of the island was a miserable, unending sea of green. Hair fell into Lou's eyes, stuck to her cheeks, and snaked behind her collar. She never did know how to arrange it properly. The sun baked her face and blinded her. It was slow-moving through the brush, and her pack hugged her back, trapping heat and adding weight to her tired legs. Jay kept pace with her, offering a hand when the path was obstructed and a waterskin when her sweat ran dry. This time, she took it.

After hours in the woods, the waterskins eventually *did* run dry.

Her tongue scratched against the roof of her mouth.

I know my duty to my family.

Benji clutched his bear, and Jay slashed a path through the branches, clearing a way for them. For her.

I wanted to travel once. See the city on my own, discover the places I've read about so often.

It was so hot.

I cannot seem to get my hair to settle, Mother.

Please, please behave, Louisa.

The island had claimed her body but had given her a new life brimming with chaos—and choices.

She heard the words of past conversations in her mind. But they were nothing more than ghosts. They meant nothing—not anymore.

It was so hot.

"This is ridiculous," she said. "I need moment, please!"

"You okay?" Jay asked. "I still have a couple berries in my pack if you're hungry."

Heat crawled up her cheeks while she unloaded her pack and tossed it into the bushes. The only heavy thing she had was her sword, but that was a friendly weight, a cool weight despite the heat, the heat, the insufferable *heat.*

Lou uncoiled the knot of her hair, took the sword in hand, and tilted her head to the side. Damp strands hung around her face, and she gathered it in a tight fist.

"Gentlemen do not appreciate a woman with a sharp tongue and an untidy appearance," she whispered to the dirt. Her blade kissed the tresses she'd tried so long to tame. But none of it mattered on the island, and that insignificance was the most significant thing in her world.

Steel tore through her strands in one swipe. Lou tossed the scraps to the ground, and the breeze carried them across the reeds. Air—beautiful, clean air—feathered across her neck. She could breathe.

"Much better," she said, replacing the blade. "How much farther do we have before we reach the coast?"

"Uh . . . not long," Jay said. A half grin, reluctant and beautiful, crawled across his face. "You wanna pick up your pack?"

"I can tell Mother I lost it or a crocodile tore my clothes to scraps. She'll be equally upset either way."

For once, no one mentioned the state of her hair.

The others converged on her like a shell on a turtle's back; Sammy linked his small hand in hers, the other slipping into Jay's free fist while Benji, Henry, Kiran, and Didi offered her reassuring smiles or a share of their remaining food. Her shoulders were light, and she tipped her face to the sky in defiance of the sun, sweet nectar flowing unchecked down her chin.

Lou had been to the beach by a river once as a child. She'd dreamed of white stretches of glittering sand and an unending strip of blue water brimming with unknown treasures and creatures. In her mind, the sun would have been warm, the beach soft under her too-tight shoes, a flock of happy children building sandcastles and splashing through the surf. Instead, the water had been muddied and grey, weeds curling across the pebbled coast, the rocks too sharp under her shoes. There were no children—only the gulls picking away at fallen scraps left behind by the ghosts whispering over the stones.

The beach across from Soul Rock wasn't the one from her childhood. Grass gave way to pebbles in soft shades of pastel green, buttercup, and blush, hard candies scattered across the shore. The waves foamed white with each pass of the tide, and the rustling of stones tinkled like marbles in a glass jar. Cliffs lurched over the beach, the edges laced with trees and dotted with caves. For the first time since her childhood, she could imagine the existence of a real treasure hidden somewhere within the blue.

"Is that it?" Lou asked, pointing in the distance.

Jay nodded as they all stood shoulder to shoulder before the sea. "That's her."

"It is fitting."

"What is?" Didi asked.

"It looks like a skull," Lou said. "A place called Soul Rock should look terrifying, and it does. How do we get there?"

"This way." Jay headed toward the eastern cliffs, his head bent against the ocean breeze. "Tide's comin' in, so we gotta hurry!"

Ten feet of treacherous cliffside led to the yawning mouth of a cave. Inside, a heap of rotten leaves rested by the far wall, wriggling with insects and stinking of decay. Lou brought her arm up to her nose, preferring the smell of someone else's old sweat to the stink of the sea gone bad—gone *wrong*.

Jay clawed into the hill of leaves. First came a dark brown slat of wood punctured by rusted nails, and then, bit by bit, the side of a small dinghy. They all attacked a piece of the buried treasure until their fingers were blackened and their breaths came fast.

"Is this boat yours, Jay?" Lou asked, stepping aside as the children pushed the boat down the rocks, across the beach, and into the shallow waters.

"What answer do you want?" Jay asked.

"An honest one."

"No, you don't."

Henry and Kiran climbed in first and picked up their oars. When Lou's feet hit the bottom of the boat, the waves roared to life. Green-and-blue water pulled and pushed at them, chopping across the surface of the sea and throwing off a salty spray. Soon the beach was far behind, and the water under them was a deep jewel blue.

Jay shaded his eyes with a fist. "Keep your eyes open! She knows we're comin'!"

"She?" Lou asked.

"The sea monster," Benji said, patting her hand. "She protects the rock."

At his words, a stream of bubbles rippled around their boat. Tentacles snaked through the water, slick and black, lined with suckers the colour of a new baby's flesh. Lou leaned over the side and dipped her fingers into the quaking waves. Hands pulled her back, but the tentacles curled and pushed, and Lou reached for one. Just a touch was all she needed, a stroke of the monster who slipped through the fathomless world.

"Lou!"

The sea monster groaned, and their boat tipped in response.

But Soul Rock was lurching closer, and she'd come too close to the end to die. The sea monster would sense that, just as the crocodiles had.

"Are you crazy? Don't look right at her!" Didi said. "Sorry, Jay, she's not listenin' to me!"

Tentacles reached for them, slapping the sea, kicking up waves. Henry and Kiran swung their oars, but there were too many targets, all too fast for their weak arms.

Lou stood in the boat, her legs working against the violent bucking. "I don't think she's dangerous! Let her be!"

"Crickets, she's gone nuts."

"No, Didi—look!" Sammy pointed over Jay's shoulder to where black arms stretched to the sun and swept back into the sea. Their oars stilled, but the boat leapt forward nonetheless. "She's helpin' us!"

Jay's hair and clothes were sopping wet, and he frowned at the monster through his streaming locks. "Why would she do that?"

Lou grinned. "Because the crocodiles didn't hurt me."

Closer now, the ocean turned from black to indigo to turquoise. Lou let the small dinghy sway and buck on the choppy waters, knowing she would never feel that way again—not by the pathetic lake behind her home that never caught the light of the sun or the place she'd retreated to as a child deep within the woods.

The woods.

What was it called?

It didn't matter.

Their boat thudded against rock, and Jay hopped onto dry land, face pale. "Dock her right over there," he instructed, pointing to a flat peninsula jutting out from the grey stone. "Let's secure her nice and tight so we don't gotta worry about her driftin' off before we get back."

If we get back.

Lightning sizzled overhead, splitting the sky with crimson light. Jay busied himself with the ropes, fastening them to a boulder outside of the range of the waves, swatting Sammy away when he offered to help. Salt water dripped into his open mouth, but he did nothing to brush it aside. Instead, his eyes were cold flecks of ice, wide with urgency.

"What's wrong with him?" Lou asked.

"If this doesn't work, the island's done for, and so are we," Didi said. "Everyone thinks they're okay with dyin' until it's time to actually do it. Come on." She shouldered her bow and picked her way up the steep rocky shore. "We all gotta stick together. Kiran, you comin' or what?"

"Yeah, just helpin' Benji dry off his bear."

Didi rolled her eyes. "We're gonna die, but he needs a dry bear."

Jay marched past, the smooth stone from Peter's chest clutched in his fist. "Who're we to decide what Benji needs or doesn't need, Didi? We're wastin' time arguin' about it. Let's find out what this rock of Peter's can do before the sea monster changes her mind."

Soul Rock was a charred slab of granite in a world plastered with colour. The size of a small island, its rough wind-worn terrain twisted and reached up to the sky. As though hollowed out with cannon blasts, the highest peak of Soul Rock was pierced through; three holes watched their approach, empty eyes with a broken nose warning them away. But the warning was wasted on them; it was too late to go back.

Lou and Jay squinted up at the twin holes in the stone, the grey rock smoother, paler than the ground on which they stood. "This place feels familiar to me somehow," Lou said, shivering.

He scratched his palms up and down her arms, warming her at once. "Peter used to say nightmares are just dreams that got trapped on Soul Rock before findin' a head to sleep in. If you stand at the edge of the beach at night, you can almost hear kids screamin' through the holes in the rock." Jay scowled and held the stone up to the sky. "So many stories, and I got no idea if any of 'em are true. I hope we never see this damn place again."

"Let's hope we do," Lou said. Jay's features softened, and she plucked the stone from his palm. "Do you know what we are looking for?"

"Not really." He frowned up at the watchful empty sockets. "He didn't like talkin' about the place unless one of us wandered off and never came back. He always said, 'The rock saw 'em comin' and took 'em away to the place of nightmares.' After hearin' that, none of us wanted to know much more."

A chill whispered up the back of her bare neck. "It sounds like a fear tactic to me. We should probably scour the island to find a place that fits this stone and forget Peter's ridiculous stories."

"Maybe there's nothing here?" Benji said. *Hopeful boy.* Lou offered him a warm smile, the wind tugging her sheared locks from her cheeks. "I don't like it here."

"Take it easy, Benji," Didi said, clapping him on the back. "Hug your bear and take a breather. We're still all right."

Soul Rock was easy to lap in under one hundred paces. Lou scoured every crevice, kicking at shadows, hoping to unearth the edge of a door or a hole long covered in rubble. The others followed suit, each travelling their own path around and around, the low thud of the wooden boat keeping time in the rising waves. She moved deeper, climbed closer to the eyes that stared and watched and *saw.* Swirls of granite flecked in light winked back at her. Her palm grew warmer the closer she got to the peak.

Her fingers dipped into a shallow pocket in the stone. "Jay?" she called. "Come see this!"

"What is it?" He led the other children up the rock. "You find a door?"

"A hole!"

"What?"

"Crickets, did she say a *hole*?"

Lou waved the stone that was Peter's buried treasure with impatience. "There is a small hole at the centre of the stone. See? Right underneath the nose, between the eyes of the skull."

Jay leaned over and ran his fingers over the surface. "Oh, yeah. So . . . what now?"

Lou sighed. The waves were no longer loud, the sea monster no longer a menace. A shrill whistle sounded in her ears, blocking out the sounds of the island, the children, all her doubt. She lifted her hand to the rock and smiled when the pieces aligned, crunching into place.

Soul Rock rumbled. Quaked. Stone ground against stone. A dark line carved through the dust at their feet, dividing the centre of the rock from the rest of the tiny island. They clung to the stone and to one another while the skull spun around, tunneling beneath the sea.

A heavy darkness soaked in seawater crept over their heads.

Jay whooped, and the children cheered. Rose would have joined them.

Rose.

No . . . Rosie.

She couldn't be sure of anything except for the cavern opening under them and the safety of Jay's presence beside her. Rose was a child in a world far away, but Jay knew her best. He would protect them all.

Peter was gone.

But she wasn't.

Yet.

The platform struck ground. Torches blazed to life around

them, bright blue flames lining a singular tunnel. Underground, the sea was muffled into submission; Lou could hear nothing but the children's even breathing, the soft thud of Didi's bow against her back, and the rustle of clothes as they stepped down the path together.

One cold hand found its way into hers, and she squeezed back, pushing her heat into Sammy's tiny body with sheer will. "It's just a scary tunnel, Sammy. We're here together. No one will let anything happen to you."

Sammy peered up at her, then at Jay, the skin of his palm slowly reaching the temperature of hers. "I'm not scared, Lou. I swear."

"We know you're not," Jay said. Then he looked to the others. "Everyone, get your weapons out."

For a secret tunnel forbidden by the master of a strange island, the path under Soul Rock was peaceful. The silence was a calming relief after the bustle of the waves. They huddled together as they navigated the tunnel, their shared warmth beating back the humidity of the sea. But at the slightest crack or drip of water, Lou would clamp down on Sammy's hand, the urge to protect him overwhelming.

They moved together, taking the turns here and there and neverwhere with no end in sight. A tang bit the air, pinching Lou's nose, but she ignored it. Everything important was clutched in her hands or walking beside her.

Another crack, another soft swish of seawater behind the tunnel walls. Without warning, a roar of fury broke the quiet, echoing around and around. Lou stopped, turned, and pulled Sammy behind her.

"Ugh, I can't stand this!" Kiran growled once more and spat on the ground. "You stepped on my foot again, Didi!"

"That wasn't me, stupid. But sure, keep talkin' loud in the

creepy tunnel so any pirate lurkin' around here knows exactly where we are."

"Don't call me stupid. You *always* treat me bad, and I *always* gotta protect you!"

"Protect *me*?" Didi stepped closer to her brother, and in that small movement, Lou could see that the warmth in the girl's eyes had turned to lava. "I always gotta make all the decisions. You follow me like a little puppy, waitin' for me to get the food and set the traps, and I never complained about it! I'm tired, Kiran. Why can't you just take care of yourself for once?"

"Hey, what's wrong with you two?" Jay asked. "This is a real bad time to fight."

Kiran lifted his sword. "You always thought you were so much stronger than me," he said. "Better, smarter, *tougher* Didi thinks she's the favourite. But you're only alive 'cause I told them to keep you."

"Shut up."

The air around them shimmered and clung to Kiran and Didi like oily smoke. Benji joined Jay in his attempt to step between the two, but the steely cloud surrounded both brother and sister in a terrible and impenetrable bubble.

Kiran's lips pulled back in a snarl. "They wanted a boy. They wanted only *me*. But they got two babies instead of one, and they wanted to throw you away, toss you in the river and pretend you were never there. They told me so."

Didi's lip quivered, but she glared at her brother with a fury Lou had yet to see her wear before. "You're lying."

"Papa told me so. They kept you 'cause they felt sorry for you. Just a weak little *girl*."

"Kiran, stop," Benji said.

But he didn't.

He can't. The thought came unbidden, rolling off the cloud that wrapped itself tighter around Kiran and Didi.

"You ruined *everything*!" Kiran cried. "If you didn't exist, they woulda loved only me, and we wouldn't have been so poor! They shoulda gotten rid of you when you were born."

Didi curled her fingers into claws and lunged at her brother. Bodies and growls twisted into a knot of violence, feet and fists drawing blood. The cloud roiled around them, feeding on their rage, growing thicker as punches were traded for blades.

"Stop!" Lou cried, turning to Jay. "Do something!"

He and Henry threw themselves into the fray. Blood pooled at their feet, oily and slick. Didi and Kiran rebuffed their attempts to break them apart. Shouting echoed in the tunnel. A fist pulled back, and the dark cloud grew still as though anticipating a fatal blow.

The fist held a large knife.

Henry lunged for the arm—Didi's arm—but it was too late. Didi was a child possessed by anger, and the smoke climbed around her, triumphant.

Henry's cheek split open. Blood trickled down his jaw, soaking his collar and spattering his shoes. He grunted and sank to his knees, hands grabbing at his face.

"Henry!" Benji rushed over to kneel beside his best friend. "Henry, you okay?"

The cloud licked at Henry's skin. Didi's molten gaze settled on the blood she'd drawn, and she stilled. Realization dawned, quick and terrible, and both siblings froze over Henry. The fighting stopped, and their faces went slack. Didi dropped the knife, and the strange haze vanished into the cracks of the tunnel wall.

Didi's face dripped blood. She retreated at once, scanning them all for the extent of the damage. "Kiran?" she asked. "I . . . I dunno what just happened."

"Me either." Kiran sat back on his heels, chest heaving. He cradled his left arm to his chest to stem the blood oozing from a deep gash above his wrist. "It's like I was listenin' to everythin' comin' out of my mouth, but I couldn't stop it. I'm sorry, Didi. I didn't mean any of it."

"Yeah, you did. It was all true."

"Honest, that wasn't me!"

But Didi's face was soft as she crawled to his side. "Lemme see that arm." With deft fingers, she tore a strip of fabric from the hem of her shirt and fashioned a tourniquet around Kiran's arm. The flow of blood slowed, but his fingers were pale, and his face was haggard with pain. "Think you can move it?"

"I don't think so."

"Did you see that thing around them?" Benji asked. He rose, taking a shaking Sammy into his arms. His gaze, however, lingered on Henry, whose face still wept blood. "What was it? A cloud?"

"No idea," Jay said, "but I'm sure it won't be the last time we see it. There's a reason Peter says no one comes back from Soul Rock. There's a price for comin' this close to freedom. Who's gonna take Kiran back to the dinghy?"

Kiran looked up at once. "I'm not leavin'. I wanna keep goin', boss."

"Kiran, don't be an idiot."

"I said I can *do* it, Jay!" Kiran turned to his sister. Their faces had been cleared of their painted masks and were mirror images—scars and all. "I need to finish it with my sister."

Didi nodded. "We keep goin' together, then. No one's gonna look after my brother but me."

"Fine," Jay said with a huff. "But no more fightin'. I don't know how much longer we got before we come out the other side of this tunnel. We can't turn on each other now."

"Lou?"

"Hmm?" Lou looked over at Sammy, and her heart squeezed at the desperation etched there.

"Would you stay with us if you could? If we find the stars and you get to stay, just like Peter did, would you stay here?"

She wasn't sure. Even on an island bathed in magic, only one boy had ever managed to straddle both worlds. Could she somehow enjoy that same luxury? The idea, the possibility, however slim, brought her dangerously close to hope.

"That would certainly be wonderful," she said with a tentative smile. "It would make me happy to stay with you, Sammy. But first, we have to make it to the mountain. Are you all right to keep going, or would you like to rest?"

"I'm fine. That cloud won't get me."

As though sensing their need to turn back, the earth shook, pouring sand and rubble onto their heads.

Just another quake.

The ground shook harder. A gash ripped the tunnel open under them, and Lou screamed, reaching for anything that could keep her from falling. But she should have known that nothing in Soul Rock was there to save them. They fell into the dark pit, spiralling into the belly of the island.

CHAPTER 28

JAY

The pebbled beach by Soul Rock was aggravating; the happy colours winked and rattled with the passing waves, thousands of gaudy diamonds on an island of trash. It was all fake. An illusion. There was nothing pretty or happy about the forgotten land, and the damned pebbles were just another thing to tick me off. Sammy and I waited at the edge of the coast in the dead of night, the kid running back and forth, chasing the waves.

"I don't see her!" Sammy kicked a rock into the sea, and the tide swallowed it with a roar. "You want me to run back to the Tree to see if she's around?"

"She'll be here." If I was honest, I had no idea if the devil fly would keep her promise. Lilith had been the one to call tonight's meeting after the botched initiation last week, so the chances were good she'd come through. But the blood from the violence I'd committed was still sticky on my fingers, and I wasn't sure there was any coming back from that. "She needs me as much as I need her. I'd worry more about the sea monster gettin' mad we're so close to the water."

The fairies were tricky. Old as the island themselves, they fell from the sky when the night was too full of stars. The blanket warming the moons got too heavy and shook them loose. The stars shot through the sky and drifted into the tallest tree, making it the hub of their magic—the Hanging Tree. According to Peter, it was the weakest of the stars that were banished from above; the ones with a flaw or two, a paler light, or plain bad luck never stood a chance against the brightest spots in the universe. I'd never asked Lilith why she'd been cast out. Maybe it wasn't about her at all but devotion to her sister that bound their fates. And her sister, Bell, was more than broken.

Bonds had a way of breaking us. It was funny if you thought about it. And I did from time to time. Lilith was a lot like me in that way: lashed to another whose light was darker than hers, her fate messy and tangled and forever doomed. Maybe that was why I stood on that beach, so certain she wouldn't give me up to Peter. She understood what it was like to suffer by someone else's hands and still be so loyal to her captor that she lost a piece of herself bit by bit.

Sammy and I waited, the hush of the surf doing nothing to soothe my nerves. The night was black; the moons were shrouded by the low-hanging clouds. I doubted anyone would see us, save the fairies still blanketing the world above. Still, the beach was exposed, and so was I. Sammy wouldn't stay behind, stay *still*, and if anything happened to him—

"Hey, look!" Sammy pointed to the horizon, where a light whizzed out over the water.

I squinted at the orange glow, the brightness making my eyes water. It lapped Soul Rock once and struck out for the beach, a firefly in the dark.

Lilith took form the same way she had the first time I'd seen her on two legs: with a burst of stars, a shrill biting cry, and a flash of violet that rivalled the petals of the tiger lilies by the lagoon.

"Can't you do anythin' about that light?" I asked. "My eyes burn whenever you do that."

"I'm sorry I'm late," Lilith said, ignoring my irritation. Her bright face was apologetic, red hair spilling over her shoulders. In that moment, I wondered what she had looked like as the moon's neighbour and resented Bell for taking that away from her sister. "I only just got away from the Hanging Tree. The others are having a difficult time . . . adjusting."

"I don't blame 'em. Gettin' the new kids sliced up isn't the best way to make a good first impression." I picked my way down the beach, loose stones grinding under my boots. "Let's make this quick, 'cause I'm pretty sure he's havin' Slightly follow me. I need another round of dust."

"Jay," Lilith said reluctantly, "Peter may not know what your plans are, but he suspects dissent in his ranks. I do not think it is wise to prod the crocodile any further."

"No one asked you for an opinion. It's one more time. Honest."

Lilith glanced at her toes, blood creeping up her cheeks. "I did promise you fairy dust in exchange for help with my sister, but you have not kept up your end of our deal, and . . . and I do not think I can continue to help you unless I am certain she will be safe."

"Our deal?"

The sea monster reached a tentacle to the stars and slammed it back down into the water, spraying the coast with salty tears.

"Our *deal* is you give me as much dust as I want, and I work on Peter as best I can. And I *am* workin' on him, all right? It just takes a bit of time."

"How much time? Only today he went down to the Golds and tried trading her for one of their females. The girl's father thankfully refused, but if he had been tempted by the magic of a fairy, I'd have lost my sister!"

"Peter's been thinkin' about bringin' more help into our

circle. He knows we can't keep protectin' ourselves from the pirates without more hands and some eyes on the ground. He needs Bell, he just doesn't know it yet. I know I can convince him to bring your sister into the fold, but I need to do it on my terms. My word is my bond. You know that."

Lilith frowned. "You promise?"

"Cross my heart." I stood my ground while Sammy lingered in the background, a moving shadow. "So, about that dust . . ."

Lilith toyed with the leaves at her waist. A gust of wind rolled off the sea, rustling her hair and pushing the scent of roses, plums, and salt up my nose. She extended her hand and tipped a pinch of shimmering dust into my open palm. "Please be quick, Jay. I care about my sister, but your safety is still important to me. Each trip puts you and Sammy at risk."

"You'll make sure he stays safe, right? Walk him back to the Tree and cover for him?"

Lilith nodded. "I will stand by his side until you return. Be safe."

The waves called to me, and somewhere in the forest over-looking the beach, an animal rustled through the brush.

I inhaled the glittering powder cupped in my palm. Warmth trickled into my skin, my blood, my bones until hot and cold were the same and the pebbles, those damned little chips of happiness, disappeared. Lilith and Sammy waved, and I drifted away, focusing on Lou's face, the smell of her soap, and the sound of her voice as she read me stories from the books she carried with her every-where. I'd see her soon, and that truth made me drift quicker.

I'm comin', Lou. Just sit tight, little bird.

"Careful, Jay!" Sammy called. "Don't you worry about me!"

I left him and Lilith on the dotted expanse of land. With a whoop that disappeared on the wind, I circled the trees before launching off to the sky where I belonged. Far above the island, all I could make out was a carpet of green and pockets of darkness.

If I hadn't been so distracted, so excited, I might have seen an orange spark of light flitting from branch to branch on the eastern cliffs.

If I'd been more careful, I might have noticed Bell perched in a palm tree, her snowy ears trained on our every word.

If I hadn't been so focused on a world that wasn't mine, a kid who wasn't mine anymore, I might have cared that while I was making my plans, Bell had her own.

CHAPTER 29

They stood at the end of a long hall with a white door wedged into the far wall. It taunted her, that door. The lights were dim, the walls and ceiling a cool grey, but behind that white slab of wood, in that other place, was every dream she'd ever had. She didn't know how she knew it, but she did. They needed to get inside that room. Dread flooded her. She wanted to cross the hallway—*no, it's a tunnel*—if only to prove she could, that she was worthy of what was held within that sacred space. That those dreams were strong enough to beat back the nightmares.

Crossing the hall meant falling farther down and away from the stars, but Lou didn't mind anymore. She needed what was on the other side of the tunnel more than she wanted to reach the sky. And so, with Jay and Sammy at her side, Benji and Henry guarding their flanks, and Didi supporting her brother's weight in resolved silence behind them all, they crossed.

Jay pushed the door open.

They left the hall—*tunnel*—behind.

Lou had never been allowed to attend school. Girls were last on the acceptance list, their chief duties and skill sets putting them squarely in the home rather than at a place of higher learning. But when the tunnel spat them out the other end, she was suddenly certain she hadn't missed anything of great importance.

Three rows of long wooden tables and low-backed wood chairs were arranged neatly in a narrow classroom. One window spilled soft white light across the weathered faces of the tables, a black wood stove burning low in the far corner. A blackboard nailed to the opposite wall displayed symbols and numbers scrawled in white chalk, messages left to an empty room.

Almost empty.

A little boy sat at a far desk, a folded sheet of parchment clutched between his fists. Red welts glared up at them from the backs of his hands, and russet hair fell over his eyes, obscuring the sprinkle of freckles across his nose. Outside, the sun dipped and fell, but the boy stayed firm in his seat, cradling the parchment with a lover's care.

"What is this place?" Sammy asked.

Jay pulled them all close, he and his raised dagger heading their flock. "It looks like a place in the Land of the Grown. We couldn't already be there, though, can we? Seems too easy. Hey, kid. Where are we?"

The child bent over the parchment, his burnt red hair falling across his eyes.

"It is a classroom," Lou said, reading the symbols on the chalkboard with a familiar dread—*problems, so many problems, forcing you to choose or fail; there is no in-between*—and turning away just as quickly. "Quite a well-furnished one, from the look of it. But it still smells like the sea. Can you sense it? I do not believe we have left the tunnels."

"Another trick," Didi said. "Perfect. Why isn't the kid lookin' at us?"

Henry stepped forward, his shoulders hunched, one hand

soothing the other as though he could still feel the sting of those welts across his larger healed hands. Large, strong hands, and shoulders much broader than the average young boy.

"Henry," Lou said, stepping closer to him. "Is that you?"

In response, Henry closed the distance between him and the child sitting in the narrow chair. His shoulders trembled. Quaked. The ceiling cracked, and the wind thumped against the far window, begging to come in.

"This is a dream," Lou said. "An illusion of the past. The child cannot see us."

Young Henry cast a hooded glance over to the door, his eyes piercing through Lou and her Henry as though they might as well have been vapour. Clumsy fingers unfolded the parchment and smoothed the creases across the desktop. He lowered his nose to the page and ghosted his fingers over the signature, reverently tracing the name.

David.

The note was from a boy named David.

And while it was a terrible thing, Lou finally understood why Henry was lost enough to find the island.

Oh, my poor Henry.

Footsteps smacked against the wood floor, and Henry's broad shoulders curled inward at the new sound. The man was tall and broad, a thick mane of blond waves laced with silver framing a pair of narrow amber eyes. Every step echoed in Lou's bones, the straight shot of the man's spine commanding attention the way her mother's hard gaze always did. The man stopped before the chalkboard and clasped his hands behind his back.

"Are you ready, boy?" he asked, his voice deep and smooth, chocolate in a melting pot.

Henry's young ghost covered the note with his palms and glanced up at the man from whom he'd inherited his eyes. "Yes, Father."

"Your mother is expecting us home in time for dinner. She's invited the governor and his wife, so we cannot be late." His eyes settled on the space above the boy's head as though he couldn't find his son's eyes. "Well, hurry up. Gather your things."

"Yes, Father." The child peeked at his father from under a fan of pale lashes and attempted to tuck the note away, but it was no use. The man's eyes were as sharp as his posture, and he caught the motion with a deft eye.

"What is that?"

Both Henrys grew rigid, and Lou resisted the urge to throw herself between the young boy and the man whose sudden attention to his son buzzed with anger. Henry's father grew taller somehow, his imposing presence throwing shadows and releasing poison into the cold room. The walls shook again, and Lou would have given anything for the next shudder to crumble the world and put an end to the vision before her.

She should have known the island wouldn't be so kind.

"I asked you a question, boy."

"I-it is but a letter, sir. Only a note, nothing more."

A pause. "Show it to me." He took the square of parchment before young Henry could offer it willingly. With a flourish, he scanned the sheet from top to bottom, brow furrowing as he went. "Is this David the one Sister Mary spoke to you about?"

"Yes, sir. He is my friend."

The slap came like a cobra strike, swift and precise. Benji went to older Henry's side, but the boy flinched away from the touch, tears staining his pale face and magnifying his freckles.

"Do not lie to me."

"Father, I swear, I—"

Clack. Knuckles collided with the boy's cheek, and he toppled sideways, catching himself on the chair beside him.

The man's eyes were twin flames in a face carved from stone. "I said do not *lie*."

"Please, it is no lie!"

Young Henry's cheek swelled, red and angry, but the blows came down like spring rain.

Another.

Another.

Again.

The image of Henry's former self lay curled under the desk, blood spurting from between his fingers as he grappled with the beaten edges of his face. "I-I'm sorry, Father. Please."

The man ripped the note to confetti, letting the pieces scatter around the boy's huddled body. "That will be your last warning, boy. I will not tolerate impropriety in my house. You will not stain our family's reputation after I've worked to solidify it after your last . . . indiscretion. Do you understand?"

Henry nodded, and Lou's heart shattered.

"Good. Perhaps in future you will learn to be careful with expressing yourself so brazenly. Sometimes silence is best. Now hurry, or we shall be late."

Henry whispered to his feet and staunched the flow of blood from his lip with the cuff of his shirt. A low moan of shifting earth filled the room, closing in with the force of a storm. The scene before them blurred, fading to the brown and gritty darkness of the tunnel under Soul Rock. New fissures splintered the walls, and the black mist crept in once more, an intangible spectator to their suffering.

"Jay?" Sammy whispered. "What's goin' on?"

The island's echo of a younger Henry flickered and shifted. Desks disappeared. The light from the window muted to the deep brown of dirt and sand, and the classroom shattered like most dreams did once reality set in.

All around them, the earth rumbled. A fine black mist curled around Lou's ankles and crawled over to Henry's rigid form.

"That's no good," Jay said. "The damn cloud is back. Everyone, weapons down! I don't want anyone fightin' again. Henry, that means you too. Hey—you okay?"

But Henry's attention was trained far ahead of them. The man who was his father stood silently in a pool of inky seawater now spurting into the tunnel. Jay angled himself between their group and the darkness of the gathering cloud. Didi, too preoccupied with Kiran's injuries, could do nothing more than cover her brother with her own body, her gaze daring the specter to challenge her.

"I hear you there. Breathing." The man's deep voice slithered out of the darkness and caressed her cheek, but Henry staggered back as though hit by the sound. "I have been waiting down here for someone to come along and find me. My son—I've lost my son. Have you seen him?"

Henry's father emerged from the shadows, but the man slinking toward them was not the same who'd raised a hand to his son. This man's face was pale and gaunt, those amber eyes sunken in his skull and rimmed by darkness. The hair and beard were no longer sleek; they grew in long clumps held together by grease and dirt, patches of raw red skin peeking through the nettles.

Lou and Jay flanked Henry, but their presence did nothing to soften the boy's stance. Shock, disgust, terror—she couldn't tell which emotion overshadowed the rest on Henry's face, but there was no mistaking the putrid stench of hate rolling off his coiled body in waves.

"My boy. Is that you?" The man stepped forward and the cloud approached with him. Henry nodded once, a sharp jerk of the chin. "Your mother and I have searched for you for so long. She will be happy to learn you've found us instead."

"Henry," Benji called. "He isn't real. He can't hurt you anymore."

But Henry's body trembled the closer the man came.

"You'll come home with me now, won't you, son? I've missed

you." He reached out and laid a hand on Henry's shoulder, provoking another round of shivers. "Such a handsome boy."

"I don't think Henry's missed you," Didi called. "Don't touch him."

The man moved and spoke as though oblivious of their presence, the strange black mist stretching around his body like wings. Fire lit his face from within, the haunted gaze reserved for Henry alone. "You will come home with me. You will complete your studies as we always intended and bring honour to our family."

Kiran snorted. "Is this guy serious? Henry, let's just get out of here. We know it's a trick. I know it feels real when you're in it, but it's not. Let's just *go*."

"You remember the Huntsteads, don't you?" the ghost whispered. "Mr. Huntstead is the dean of medicine at the university. I have managed to reserve a place for you so that you may begin in a few months."

"Benji, can you tell what Henry's thinkin'?" Jay asked. "Why isn't he movin'?"

Benji's face glistened with fresh tears. "He's getting lost in the memory of his father. Of what he did to him. The things he remembers—I don't want to say it out loud."

The dark cloud was building across the man's skin, creeping out to form a cocoon around him and Henry. If Lou moved any closer, the terrible mist would touch her too, and the thought of it invading her body made her stomach turn. More water rushed into the tunnel, climbing up her legs and chilling her skin.

"You will be a surgeon," the man continued. "You will marry Miss Crawford. We have come to a suitable agreement with her parents and have only the finer details of the ceremony to finalize. The home beside ours is small, I'll admit, but it is a fine space for you to raise a family of your own."

Henry's breathing came faster, and he was becoming more difficult to see through the haze. He and his father moved closer, merging until Lou could see Henry's face reflected in the man's glazed eyes.

"You will make us proud, boy." His voice took root in Lou's heart, where it burrowed deep, stretched its feelers, and twisted. Those words. Those expectations. They were a familiar source of agony that felt disconnected from her now. Still, the urge to bend the knee and accept the man's requests was strong. Those requests had been made of her once. She knew that, but it was all a memory shrouded in dreams. She preferred it that way. "You will do what you were born to do, Henry. And once you've fulfilled your role in this family, all may be forgiven. My *son*." He took Henry's hand, and the poisonous cloud twisted around them while the water climbed higher. Their hands together—one strong and smooth, the other yellowed and covered in scabs with bones twisting like tree roots in arid soil—was an abomination.

Lou couldn't look away. She could only watch, helpless, as the water rose. They all cowered behind Henry, unable to reach him on the other side of the dark veil.

"No." Henry spoke in a whisper, but the sound was as clear as glass breaking. "Leave me alone."

All eyes turned to Henry, the boy who never spoke, the boy who, Lou had always assumed, *couldn't* utter a word. But there he was, a quiet, sweet boy who spoke more kindness in his silence than many could utter in their loudest voices. He had a voice of his own—he simply had chosen not to use it. It must have been a terrible thing to forget his own voice.

"Speak up, boy. I do not believe I heard you correctly."

Careful, Henry. The cloud is growing.

"I said no. I won't go back. None of those things are what I want." The black smoke contracted around them, coaxing more water from the tunnel's cracks. Not much longer, and they would all rest at the bottom of the sea with no monster or crocodile swift enough to reach them. "You can go now, Father. Leave me."

"Watch your tongue, boy."

"I am not trying to be rude. I never meant to dishonour you." Henry straightened his spine and towered over his father. His hands, his shoulders, the entirety of his strong body grew still. "But I must do what is best for myself. I have my own family now."

The man's face twisted. Teeth curled over his bottom lip, fangs dripping saliva into his beard. Twin red pinpricks ignited the coal in his eyes, and he leered at his son, daring him to defy him again. More monster than man, Henry's father revealed the evil that lived within him, and it was ugly. "You are a disappointment, boy. We should have gotten rid of you at the first sign of the disease."

Duty is a pirate, little bird.

Lou had had enough. "Jay, we need to stop this. *Now.*"

Jay nodded and pushed forward at once, but the mist had grown stronger. Lou tried to follow him and found her legs too heavy. *Too weak, too small, not enough.* Water roared in her ears, and Sammy's sobs echoed all around her, pulling her back.

But she couldn't go back. Not yet.

"It is not a disease, Father," Henry said. "It is who I am. It is what lives in my heart. It is love."

"That explains why you abandoned your kin to join a pack of savage boys. Is this where you carry out your obscene perversions, boy? Which one is your favourite, hmm? Show me."

Henry flinched as though struck. "I beg you to stop this, Father."

"He's not your father, Henry," Benji said. "He's just a ghost. A lost soul."

Henry was alone on the other side of the poisonous wall caging him with his father. Words could not reach him. Blades could not help him. And nothing could stop the sea from climbing ever higher.

This is where I die, Lou thought, her toes lifting off the ground with the rising tide. *This is where it ends.*

"A proper doctor would have set you right, but I was too late to see the signs. Your friends will never accept you for the animal you are, boy. An animal that requires putting down."

Kiran hissed as water clawed at his mouth, and Sammy clung to Jay's neck like a babe, his tears disappearing into the sea.

"A monster. You belong in a cage." The man rose above the waves, his hands dripping red. He closed his fists tight, and purple bruises bloomed around Henry's neck, long thin lines that clutched his throat in a ghostly grip of torture long past. "You ran like a coward."

Disease. Coward.

"A man would have taken his punishment and thanked me for it," the ghost whispered. "But not you. You will never be a man. No one will ever love you for what you are, and that truth will chase you no matter how far you run."

The water was black, stabbing Lou's chest with a thousand knives. She tried to swim past, to save—*Rose*—Henry from the agony.

He—*Rose*—was hurting and needed help. *Her* help.

Benji pushed her aside and swam toward the raging cloud. With the stuffed bear in his teeth, he grunted with the effort of moving onward. The black water crashed around Henry's rigid form, but Benji's progress was straight and sure.

"You are not my son."

Why can't you be more like your sister?

"A mistake!"

Not enough.

Lou swallowed water and let it spread into her lungs. The urge to cough it up, to breathe clean air, was overwhelming, but her lungs were frozen with the sea. She'd felt it before, that cold creeping inside her. Pulling her down. Pulling her under. But that was another life. Another place.

Benji reached over the climbing waves. The spectre's eyes slid over Henry's shoulder, blood vessels bursting in his cheeks and streaming blood down his haggard face.

"I'm right here, Henry!" Benji released his bear into the waves to speak over the chaos of the tunnel and the man's laughter. "I'm right behind you! I won't leave you!"

The ceiling cracked, and pale yellow light pierced through the muck. Henry turned, his features twisted in agony, soaked with water and shame.

"Benji." The word was a whisper, but Lou could hear it scream in her heart. Henry stood naked, his soul laid bare. He looked at Benji lashes clumped together by tears. "I'm sorry I never told you."

"I knew, Henry. I always knew." The cloud retreated enough to allow Benji through. He wrapped his arms around Henry, pulling him tight, pulling him into an embrace of love and friendship and acceptance. "It's all right. It's always been right."

The roar of the sea pushed over Lou's head, and they all went under. Henry and Benji disappeared in an explosion of light and water and sound. There were others she should have longed to see instead of the boys clutching each other before her life ended: a woman with hair of spun gold, a girl with the heart of a songbird, free and brimming with life.

Who are you? she wondered. It should have mattered; it mattered to her once, long ago.

In another life.

Two heads—one black, the other gold—disappeared, and all that remained was the sea and the darkness.

CHAPTER 30

JAY

Failure stung every single time.

One second I was sitting on the windowsill outside Lou's room, listening to her read to herself out loud and agonize over long division, whatever that meant. I could tell the pink in her cheeks had faded even through the barrier of the glass, a sure sign she hadn't seen the sun in weeks. But when she put her books down to welcome the baby curled over their mother's shoulder, the glint in her eyes shone brighter than any star.

I was still stuck on the outside.

The window was latched shut, banishing me to the cold. I'd pounded against the glass pane, screamed her name, kicked the ledge. How long I lingered on the perimeter of her life, I couldn't say. And when the island called me home, I didn't have the heart to fight back.

Next time I'd fight longer. I'd pound my fists harder, scream louder, kick through the wall separating us until she heard me, saw me, knew I was still there.

I hated Peter.

I blinked fast, and the stink of the sea stung my nose. The

beach was the kind of dark that existed before dawn, washing the land blue and green, the birds rousing from the nests, the young ones first to crack the silence open with hungry beaks. The water was choppier than when I'd left it, the waves foaming white against Soul Rock and sifting through the pebbles with greedy fingers. A headache slammed between my ears, but it was nothing compared to the pain of being back.

I'm sure she almost heard me that time. The aftershock of the island's gravity faded from my fingers. *Poor kid's stuck with that thing because she's got no one else.*

The sky was navy velvet speckled with white sugar, and I stomped up the beach with a stomach full of acid. It wasn't fair. I didn't want to hurt anyone or cause any trouble. My entire existence was built around need and want and yanking others back from the edges of sharp cliffs. I wasn't supposed to be the one standing in their place, ready to jump.

"Sammy?"

No one answered. The kid was gone, and that was good. Lilith would have taken him back to the Tree before Peter could link him to my disappearance, and that was just as good as fairy dust, as far as gifts went.

I'd thought I wanted to live forever, no matter the cost. As it turned out, what I really wanted was to crawl back to where I'd come from to put an end to an eternity of misery.

Wheeee!

The whistle drifted over the cliffs, and my heart stopped. A branch cracked within the shadows, and a second later, an arrow grazed my left arm. I dove to the ground in time to avoid the kiss of steel, but shock made me slow. It made me sloppy. I reached for my dagger, fumbling with the hilt.

"Who's there?" I called.

Another arrow whizzed past my ear. I tried to jump, to disappear, but the fairy dust had worn off, and I was grounded, a permanent part of the island again.

The palms at the top of the cliff glinted with steel.

"Come on, you cowards!" I drew my elbow back, wishing for a bow and arrow instead a blade. "Get down here so I can see your face when I kill you!"

A war cry pierced the night. A dozen ropes lassoed over the cliff like snakes taking to the beach. Faces stained in red and black paint shimmied down the rocks, quivers bouncing on backs and swords gleaming white in the moonlight.

Not Reds.

Not Blues.

Not pirates, or Golds, or any other enemies the island could have conjured up out of boredom. They were my people.

No, not mine—Peter's.

"Are you all insane?" I straightened up but kept my dagger close. "You almost took my head off!"

Peter's inner circle set foot on solid ground and approached carefully, weapons at the ready. Henry and Slightly led the charge, their cheeks decorated in black slashes, camouflaging them against the cliffs, while the brother and sister combo lurked at the very back. I recognized them by the way they moved: quick and close, their steps pulling up sand in just the same way, their elbows locked. I turned away from them before I could see the bright red scabs slashed across both their faces. Scabs from wounds I'd given them. Twins with twin scars. Lou might have called it poetry. I called it a damn shame.

"So, no one's gonna talk, huh?" I scanned them one by one. *Let them see. Let them see the face of their brother before they attack it.* But something was missing, and that absence was as terrifying as any weapon pointed at my heart. "Where's the boss?"

Benji's voice quaked in the night air. "Peter brought Sammy on an errand, but they should be here soon. We didn't want to come tonight, Jay, but he made us. You've always been good to us."

"Speak for yourself."

Slightly. Course it's Slightly. Before every fight, it was Slightly who tasted blood first.

"You had Peter's ear for too long. It's our turn now."

"Some of us don't want a turn, Slightly," Benji countered, earning him a low hiss. "This isn't right. After Peter, Jay's been here the longest. We need to trust him."

His words settled on deaf ears. I lowered myself into a defensive stance; there was no trace of doubt left that there was going to be a war, and I was at the very centre of it.

"Yeah, I know, Benji," I said. "I don't blame you for followin' orders. So, what am I gettin' punished for doin' this time? Takin' too much food? Forgettin' to clean up the floor I sleep on?"

Slightly lifted his spear. "You'll see."

The clouds slipped away from the moons, revealing the night sky in full bloom. Another whistle surfed off the cliffs and tumbled down to where I stood. Peter shot through the air like a falling star, his movement over the beach casting no shadows—only kids with souls had one of those. In that moment, he was the boy who'd found the tallest mountain on the most magical island and a way to tickle the skies. And when he soared down to face me, the power in his gaze was fuelled by the heavens themselves.

I lowered my arm and resisted the urge to drop to the ground on bended knee. *Every damn time.*

"Hey there, Number Two." Peter's teeth were razors, his dirty fingernails claws. His hair was pulled back and windblown, the glint of gold behind his eyes giving him the look of a predator. "Glad you're back."

"Hey, Peter. Are we goin' on a hunt or somethin'?"

"You can say that. Looks like there's been a bit of a rat problem on the island lately."

A problem. A betrayal. It always started the same. Peter would get that funny light in his eyes, and his body would change from boy to beast with the flicker of the lanterns, a result of being a part of the island for too long. He'd buzz around us, his thirst for bloodshed a thing I could smell and that made me feel like I wanted what he wanted: *I got a hunt for you, boys.* I had always been on his side of every fight, Peter's right hand to wield the blade. I didn't know what to do with myself standing opposite him. I nodded like I wasn't scared for my life; it was what he'd expect any of his best boys to do.

"A problem, huh?" I said, putting on my best look of concern. "Not good. What's goin' on?"

He knows.

He can't know . . .

He knows.

Peter smiled, and he wasn't a kid anymore. He was a crocodile sizing up his next kill, ticking away the last moments of my life with every swish of the dagger he held behind his back.

"See," Peter said, "I know I can be tough on you boys. It's a sad thing to have your blood family hate you so much they get rid of you. But that's why I do all this, Jay. I'm tough 'cause you can do more with yourself than what your blood families thought you could. We're *all* family now. Family don't stab each other in the back, do they?"

I held still—the only way to escape a predator's jaws—and kept my gaze as level as I could. "Why would you ask me that? You know we all look out for one another."

Peter slithered closer, and the others followed, every single one of them connected to the original lost boy by invisible unbreakable strings. "Then tell me the truth, Number Two. Whatcha doin' down here all by yourself?"

I fiddled with the chip in my tooth, the jagged edge stabbing my tongue, keeping me sharp. "That cave over by the eastern coast is deep and high enough above water to avoid high tide. I thought it might be perfect to store some smaller boats. You know, in case the pirates ever take one of us onto the ship and we need to rescue our own."

"Where would we get the boats?"

"Wherever we want. The island's yours, remember?"

"Oh, I know. But what didja need fairy dust for?"

I shrugged because it seemed like the innocent thing to do, but my shoulder was still sore, and every muscle in my body told me to run. "I didn't—"

"No more lies." Peter's eyes flashed with heat, and the crocodile backed me into a corner. "See, I didn't believe it when one of my boys told me you were goin' to the Land of the Grown behind my back and usin' *my* fairy to do it. Mutiny's an ugly thing for pirates. It's even uglier when a brother turns on his family."

Someone spit on the ground, and the shadows grew longer, reaching out to the edge of the sea, where monsters and the deepest of forgotten evils waited to strike me down. Spears and arrows, sabres and daggers, all rounded on me like a compass needle swinging true north. It was over. I should have been grateful for all the extra time I'd gotten—*tick-tock*—but there was never enough time when I still wanted something I couldn't have.

Tick-tock.

Time was my enemy. Any reminder that I had run out of it was a traitor.

I was grateful for the darkness; no one could tell how much sweat was pouring down my cheeks or that I was counting all the ways to take them down. "You know I'm loyal," I said. "I've always been on your side, boss. Hear me out."

Peter shook his head, and fire fell from the tips of his hair like rain, scorching the ground where he stood, turning the world to ash. "I'm done listenin' to you, Jay. I turned a blind eye for weeks, thinkin' you just had to come to your senses. But it's enough. Bell! Come out!"

Whatever I was expecting, summoning Lilith's sister wouldn't have made any kind of list I could scratch together. I searched the cliffs, the trees, the ocean at my back for a bright spot in the dark. But the sky was quiet, the night unbroken by anything bright or joyful. Instead, a young girl trudged out of the shadows on blackened bare feet. She was no taller than my shoulder, her hair brittle as old straw and matted with dirt and leaves. An urchin from the woods, she was barely recognizable from the cliffs, the hard lines of her body and dull complexion that of the bones littered at the bottom of the lagoon. The boys looked away as she took small, deliberate steps to Peter's side, her dress a crumbling burlap sack riddled with holes.

"She's not what I pictured," I said, nose wrinkling at the stench of rotten meat clinging to Bell like a bad cold. "This must be important if you're lettin' a fairy come down here in human form."

"She deserved a reward for bringin' me some new information. Pretty messy business, if you ask me."

"What business?"

"She saw you and Lilith on the beach talkin' about breakin' my rules and goin' back to see your little runt. She *saw* you, Jay. That can't go unpunished."

The world grew still. I waited.

Tick-tock, tick-tock.

This close, I could smell the copper drying on his tunic.

"Sounds like a neat story. I can see why you'd be mad."

"I thought the same," Peter said, his voice even. "Just a story. I was 'bout ready to slit her lyin' mouth open from ear to ear. I mean, how could I believe a dirty fairy over my second-in-command?" He nudged one of Bell's heels with the toe of his boot, ushering her closer to me. I wished he wouldn't. "But it turns out she's more useful than the ones I thought I could trust."

I let out a short laugh. "Don't tell me you believe her. I mean, sure, I wanted to go back. I even tried figurin' out how to do it myself. But look at her, Peter. You can't take her word over mine."

"I didn't. Not at first." The new edge to Peter's voice made my skin prickle. " 'Cause everyone knows how the rules work. Once you're done in the Land of the Grown, you've gotta come back and stay here 'til I tell you different. And even if you . . . *forget*," Peter said, flashing his blade along a shard of moonlight, "there's always someone here to remind you. But I did some checkin' into Bell's story, and she came back clean. You betrayed me, Jay."

I swallowed hard, the disappointment in his voice pulling at the threads of shame in my chest. "What did you do?"

"It don't matter. You *betrayed* me. I'm so disappointed in you."

Tick-tock, tick-tock, tick-tock.

"Lou needs me."

"Not anymore," Peter said. And his words were law. They were true. And they were *wrong*.

My insides turned to smoke. I was empty. Somewhere in a distant corner of my mind, where only the eyes of my brothers existed, I felt myself drop to my knees. My dagger clattered to the ground, and I pressed my palms into the surf, letting the pebbles bite into my skin. Even the obscenely beautiful things on Peter's island could draw pain and blood from weakened souls. "Forgive me."

The lost boys rustled, shifted together like the dozen limbs of an unbreakable monster. The moons painted Bell's grin with the dark red of fresh blood, a low hiss rising in her throat. And while I knew better than to expect anything different, the disgust on Peter's face cut deeper than any dagger.

"I love all my boys," Peter said, "but especially you, Jay. How could you do this to me?"

"Please." *I hate this. I hate you.* "I did it 'cause I love her. That's gotta mean somethin'."

Weapons waited, and so did I. Peter could kill me with a blink, one slice of his arm. But he only stood with a dagger that had already tasted my blood, letting inaction do the brunt of the torture for him. "It does count, and for that love, I'll still let you belong to this family after tonight."

One lunge, one quick swipe of my blade, and Peter's heart would stop beating, stop haunting us all. My eyes slid to the waiting mob by the edge of the cliff, and I swallowed the sticky bile clinging to the back of my throat. "Thank you, boss," I said through my teeth. "That's more than I deserve."

"You know you were always my favourite."

"I do."

Peter signalled for the others to lower their weapons. "Get up, Jay."

I obeyed; I wanted to live. But Peter wasn't done.

"Hey, Sammy! You wanna bring her out?"

Sammy? All eyes slid across the dark beach to where two shapes struggled across the coast. Sammy came first, dragging his feet and letting the tears fall like pearls onto the pebbles. A figure stumbled after him, the gag in her rosy mouth cutting her weak moans to pieces. Red hair, ears tipped in lavender, pale skin painted in bruises.

"What's Sammy doin' with Lilith?" I asked.

Sammy stopped beside Peter, face pale. "I'm sorry, Jay," he whispered, words rattling with terror. "I didn't—"

"Quiet." Peter scowled.

"All right, this is ridiculous. It's gone *way* too far," I said, doing my best to backtrack without falling into the ocean.

"Sammy was just followin' my orders. He's got nothin' to do with this."

"That's the problem. You think you can give orders when this island is *mine*. There's gotta be a price for disobeyin' me. I thought you learned that last time when you slashed open the faces of two innocent kids."

Bell bared her teeth, yellow against deep red gums. Peter set a hand on her shoulder, and the young fairy settled with a quiet growl. "So, here's the thing. Sammy's loyal to you instead of me, but at least he still knows what loyalty means—even if it's to the wrong person. How do you think I should deal with that, Number Two?"

Sammy turned the colour of moon-bleached sand. "I don't wanna die, Jay," he said, whimpering like a hungry pup. "Please don't kill me."

"I ain't gonna kill you, Sammy," Peter said, laughing softly. "That's too easy. But from now on, if Jay gets outta line, you get the punishment." He stepped closer to me until our breaths mingled into one humid cloud. "You run off again without my say-so, Sammy gets a lashin'. You steal some more fairy dust, Sammy gets left on Soul Rock for a week with no food or weapons. Maybe then you'll both learn your place again. You understand, don'tcha?"

"Yes." I couldn't look at Sammy or Peter but fixed my gaze on the swaying trees, the crocodile's tail still counting the seconds.

Tick-tock.

"One more thing." Peter raised his dagger so the pale light bouncing off it illuminated Bell's face to reveal the monster underneath. "Here you go, Bell. A promise is a promise."

The air, the ocean, the rippling trees—all of it stilled the moment Peter removed Lilith's gag and tossed it into the waves. With a smile that chilled the air around us, he then offered his favourite blade to Bell. I'd never seen him without the dagger, even in sleep. It looked out of place, dangling freely without its master to keep it safe. And when Bell swiped the blade out of Peter's palm, a dozen pairs of eyes followed it through the air before the fairy sank it straight into Lilith's stomach.

Sammy's scream slammed into my skull.

The monster swallowed whatever beauty Bell could have possessed. Fairies were fallen stars, and I now knew why she hadn't been allowed to grace the skies any longer: her light wasn't silver, or gold, or a pale, pale blue. It was red. The red of blood. The red of sin. And that couldn't be left to infect the brightness above and darken the world. The crimson-soaked metal struck again and again until a half dozen wounds dripped rivers of blood into the beach.

Thousands of colourful diamonds on an island of garbage turned to rubies soaked in death.

Lilith folded onto the sand, the red of her hair masking the stain of her lifeblood leeching from her throat, her chest, her stomach. "Sister . . ." she gurgled, but the wind howled, catching Lilith's fading voice in its grasp and tossing it aside. "Sister." Her eyes searched the sky before they went blank.

Sammy broke free of Peter. I held him to my chest, knowing the tightness of my arms could never erase what he'd just seen, not caring if I caught hell for comforting the boy without Peter's permission.

"Didja need to do that in front of him?" I asked under my breath.

"Now you know what happens to traitors," Peter said. Fairies are like flies: kill one, catch another, just like that. I can't kill you yet, but I got no need for fairies who go behind my back."

The tide came in and washed the beach clean. Except for the pale body sprawled out on the pebbles like a gutted fish, it was as though none of it had happened. But nothing could wash the horror from my mind, and that was the kind of torture Peter offered: simple and permanent, with his own hands clean.

Peter crouched over Lilith's body and pushed a stray lock of hair off her white face, her violet eyes reflecting the stars. "I liked her, you know. Always did. Kept her around longer than I probably should have, but that's my fault. I'm king enough to know when I'm wrong." He held out his hand, and Bell replaced the knife without wiping it clean. "Come on, boys. We're done. Let's go raid some camps for their canoes. I like Jay's idea about hidin' some in the caves."

Peter didn't look back at me as he moved up the beach with Bell on his arm. The others followed, puppets pulled on invisible strings, with only Benji lingering behind. Tears glazed his eyes before he moved beside Henry and Timber, the last ones to leave me behind. I steadied Sammy, drawing him close enough to share in his tremors.

Following Peter was the only thing I could do. As long as Sammy's fate was linked with my actions, I was bound to the first eternal boy more than ever. The tide climbed higher up the shore, snaking around Lilith's body and twisting her hair like ivy.

"I really liked Lilith," Sammy said.

"I know. I did too."

The image of Lilith's empty violet eyes would stain my memory for as long as I lived. And I planned on living a very long time.

There was lots to do.

CHAPTER 31

link, plink, plink.
Lou walked through a forest, a bird wearing plumes of indigo and apricot perched on her shoulder. The ground sloped softly downward, the elms and willows following her with gentle fingers. She turned her face up to the sky, warmth chasing the chill from her cheeks and coaxing the buds of yellow and blue and magenta from the flower stalks lining the path. Instead of the warm sweetness of spring, every breath raked through her chest with hints of copper and salt. It was better not to breathe.

Plink, plink.

The familiar lines of the trees shimmered, and Lou stopped moving. Still, she didn't breathe; her lungs were caging fire. Best to contain it, especially around such flammable beauty.

Plink, plink.

At the crest of the path, a figure twirled in the chasm between two firs. The strange girl reached for the sky as though to capture the sun in her palms. The bird on Lou's shoulder took to the trees, but she was happy to see it join the girl. Her ebony strands caught the light, flashing red and blue against the sea of endless green. Lou called out to her through a voice thickened by tears, but the girl continued to twist in the wind, a silk gown fluttering around her ankles.

Daylight flickered, pulling the girl in and out of focus, taunting Lou. The young sprite, whoever she was, smiled at the heavens as though their light had never left her, oblivious to the sludge dripping down the bark of every tree. What a wonderful thing, to trust in the heavens so blindly.

For Lou, darkness and light resided on different faces of the same coin. For Lou, dreams and nightmares waltzed together to the tune of her worst fears. For Lou, watching the girl hold goodness in her delicate hands, there was only space to wait for the coin to flip and allow the nightmare to have its turn.

"Little bird."

He was there, lingering in the darkness. Waiting. The bitter scent of spoiled oranges and cloves assaulted her senses. She missed that smell more than she missed regular meals and a warm bath. More than her books and her bed and the stories she muttered to herself in the dark. That scent was a warm hug, a chase through the trees. It was legs dangling over a windowsill, a story shared between friends, and the sweet sort of dream that could flip the coin and banish the nightmares.

"You cannot be here," Lou whispered. Her words shook the trees, but the girl still danced under the sun, daughter of daylight and brightness and everything good. "This is another trick."

A shape moved beside her, but Lou didn't turn to look at what it was. She didn't need to; seeing him would only make his departure more difficult. Because everything she'd ever loved always left her.

You're lost. In a tunnel. Dead and gone.

Jay.

The boy was nowhere to be found. But he would never have

left if he could've helped it. She knew that now. This truly was a trick of the island, a test put forth to her by the tunnel to force the ghosts of her past to claw her deeper underground.

Just one ghost.

"You must remember why you've come to the island, little bird."

"The island is falling," she said at once. "I cannot go home."

"Do you remember your home at all?"

The wind shifted, pushing oranges into her lungs until her chest was on fire. Beyond the trees, the girl spun faster.

"Do you know who she is?"

"It does not matter," Lou said, gripping her ribs. The pain stretched its fingers into her heart, driving her to her knees. "You are not real, and neither is she."

"Tell me who she is," the voice said.

"I will not speak to a ghost!"

Plink, plink, plink.

"Then you are already lost."

Light flickered and dimmed again. The girl began to hum; her song swirled around Lou's body. A fissure split the sky, and water poured down in a storm of despair, soaking Lou, plastering her to the ground. Orange and spice everywhere.

You are already lost.

The sun turned to coal, and the world burned to ash. Lou rolled onto her side and vomited water, her stomach heaving up the remnants of the sea until she was empty of it all. Trees turned to chapped walls crusted with bones and pebbles belonging far away from the sun.

It wasn't a forest after all.

The tunnel yawned ahead of her, dripping with salt and moss. So deep underneath the island, it was impossible to see the sun or the birds gracing the skies. But she was alive, and that was enough. For now.

"Jay?" Lou pushed up to her knees. Shapes stirred on the ground, and she moved to the nearest one. "Benji! What happened?"

Benji groaned and gripped Henry's arm. "Henry? Lou? Are we okay?"

"It seems so." Her clothes clung to her body. Her lungs had been scorched by the sea, but her heart still beat. And most importantly, the air was free of the cloying stink of oranges. "What happened to us?"

"This tunnel's cursed, that's what," Didi muttered, hoisting Kiran to his feet. "First me and Kiran, now Henry. It's tryin' to pick us off one by one. No kiddin' no one ever comes back from this place."

Jay coughed, stood, and shook himself off. "Looks like we're all gettin' a turn with our demons. I wonder who's gonna come back to haunt me."

"Who cares?" Kiran asked, nursing his wounded arm. "Let it try again. We'll beat these stupid ghosts at whatever game they got."

"Easy, Kiran." Jay turned to the only way through the dark cavern in which they sat. "We got lucky the first couple times, but that might just be a warm-up. We aren't at the Mountain of Regret yet, and we don't know what else is waiting for us before we get there."

Sammy nestled into Lou's side, one lens of his glasses lined with cracks. "How are we gonna find the tallest mountain on the island when we're stuck in here?" he asked. "That doesn't sound like the right way to get to the sky."

He was right, of course; children were crude and simple in their understanding of the world. Silence fell over them all at Sammy's question, for it had no satisfactory answer. The only way to move up was to tunnel onward, delving into the bowels of the beast in the hope of one day seeing the light.

"It's too late to go back now," Jay said. "But no matter what we see in here, we gotta remember that none of it matters. We're all still family, and nothin's gonna change that."

A smile broke across Henry's face, his eyes bright with tears. "Do you mean that, Jay?"

"I'm hurt you even asked me that."

A soft breeze rippled through the tunnel, and they came together in anticipation of another hurdle. Together: that was all that mattered. They were one, facing the demons of the island as a seven-headed beast.

Didi glared at the open space. "Never thought I'd say this, but I can't wait to go home and do nothin'."

Kiran snorted. "Not even fire off some arrows at a couple pirates?"

"Nope."

"Home." Sammy sighed into Lou's arm. "That sounds nice."

Home. She was home, and there were ghosts waiting in the wings to prevent her from saving it. Lou followed the groaning caverns and snaking passageway with the rest of their group. Kiran and Didi trudged on together while Benji and Henry matched strides, their grins impossible to hide, even in the darkness. With Sammy tucked safely between her and Jay, it was easy to ignore the distant whispers echoing around the bends.

After a time—she wasn't sure how long—their last waterskin ran dry. The blisters on her feet stung with heat. In the tunnels, there was no game to hunt, no trees to bring fruit, and no cushions on which to rest. A growl rumbled low in Lou's gut, and Sammy's stomach replied in kind. Their progress slowed, and their breathing grew laboured, and death was something she might have welcomed if it meant relief from it all.

They turned a bend and faced a solid wall of earth.

Lou stopped. Looked. Paced the end of the path with a

sinking dread that left metal on her tongue. "No. This cannot be. Is this another trick?"

"Hold on a minute," Jay said. "No way a tunnel exists to go nowhere. There's gotta be a way out. Everyone, take a part of this wall and look for a door, a window, anythin' that can get us *out*."

Kiran slumped to his knees. "Give it up, boss. We're in a grave."

Henry ran his hands along the wall, scattering dirt to the ground like blackened snow. "Our dens have chutes," he muttered, voice gravelly with disuse. "This place needs to have a way out, just like every other den."

"I don't see no chutes, Henry," Didi said from the ground beside her brother. "And don't take this in any bad way, but hearin' you talk is freakin' me out."

Jay placed a palm to Sammy's forehead and frowned. "You need to rest, kid. You're not lookin' so hot."

"I'm okay."

"Sit down."

"I wanna stay with Lou." His stomach gave another roar, and Sammy stood straighter, as though that could mask his body's protests. "I don't know how long we got left with her."

Jay met Lou's eyes, and even in the dark, his fear was a flame with enough heat to scorch the world to kindling. "I'm scared too, Sam," he said. "I wanna spend time with her too. But we all need to be ready for when we get outta here, so I'm gonna need you to take a break. Lou won't be goin' far."

Benji gasped, and the sword was back in Lou's hand. "What is it?" she asked. "What did you find?"

"I nicked my finger." He popped his thumb into his mouth, and his eyes flew wide. "Oh. *Oh!* Look at the wall." Sure enough, a glimmer of light pierced the darkness, carving its way in a sharp arch into the wall. "Is . . . is that a door?"

Benji's blood seeped into the wall, and the tunnel responded to the offering by carving a crude door set on rusted hinges on the far wall. Roots and dirt fell from its face, freeing its edges from the rest of the island's architecture. The grain of it twisted with the cracks in the wall, wearing the dirt like a crown. Lou's heart fell; she was overwhelmed with the intangible truth that to pass through the door would be to accept the good on the other side with the bad. And there would be no way back.

Jay dusted dirt off the door and squinted at the iron bar affixed across the planks like a plaque. "There are some marks on here," he said. "Listen to this: 'Here in the dark, away from the sun, all may pass to the stars—minus one.' What's it mean?"

"It means we can finally get outta here," Didi said. Kiran's breath hitched, and her jaw fluttered with suppressed emotion. "We need to find some food and fresh water, and this tunnel's got neither. We won't last long in this damn place."

Jay shook his head. "Let's think about this for a minute. Just 'cause it's a door doesn't mean we just go through and make it out alive."

Didi frowned. "Are you kiddin'?"

"Jay is right," Lou said. "What lies on the other side may be more harmful than the spirits in these tunnels. And we still have no idea what that written passage means."

"Who cares?" Kiran huffed. "Most of us can't read anyway. And there's a good reason for it too. Reasons like that stupid door tryin' to keep us trapped longer 'cause we're busy worryin' about a couple scratches on an iron plate."

"Doesn't mean we can't be smart about this." Jay probed the place where a handle should have been. A soft *click* snapped within the door, and it swung open, smooth and soundless.

If Lou had any expectations, they were far from what lay beyond the tunnel walls. Snow hurried in on a frigid wind, ice chips flecking off her cheeks and stinging with the bluster of winter. They clustered together to beat back the cold, but their bond wasn't enough to combat the unforgiving storm pushing them back. Snow clotted into the cracks of the tunnel, turning whatever water remained to ice.

And there, underneath the flurries and heavy push of winter, was another sound. It was low at first, the last weak notes of a music box before the key was wound once more. But whenever the wind dipped and twisted, pockets of silence would let the new song through: a humming, like a quiet lullaby.

Kiran ventured to the door on unsteady legs and reached beyond the threshold with his good arm.

"What are you doin'?" Didi asked, rushing to his side.

"I'm the weakest one here. If there's trouble on the other side, it makes the most sense for me to go out first. It's cold, but I don't feel no pain. It's as good a sign as any."

"There could be traps, you idiot. You'll die in seconds with only one good arm to fight with."

"Then at least you'll know not to come after me."

Under the stark and unforgiving sky, Kiran's face was grey. Lou understood his logic was sound—respected it, even—but the need to pull Kiran back to the safety of the tunnel was overwhelming. Still, she couldn't ignore his wishes. She knew all too well the frustration of having no choice as to the outcome of her own life. And one look of fury from Didi meant that she knew it too.

He stepped into the crunchy cotton drifts, his breath coming in white bursts.

"Crickets, I gotta be insane." Didi raced after her brother, and the humming grew louder, as though fewer bodies in the tunnel had made some extra room for the sound to expand, take place, blossom into Lou's very mind.

Baby, baby, wee sweet one,
Ears aglow in midday sun.

Cold bit at Lou's bare skin, and they all huddled together,

waiting for the world beyond the door to accept them or cut their journey short for good.

Except nothing happened. The wind howled, the snow shifted in thick clouds, the siblings stepped farther out into the cold, locked together at the elbows.

Kiran and Didi wore matching looks of triumph, shivering but otherwise unharmed.

"It's safe!" Didi called. She shielded her eyes against the wind, surveying the area from under her one free arm. "From what I can tell, it's a straight shot up the mountain. Steep, but we can do it."

Momma holds you close, my dear,
I'll keep you safe and far from fear.

Henry braved the door next, his bulk blocking out most of the snow. He stepped across without incident and motioned immediately for Benji to follow. Benji, however, was pale, the bear pressed to his chest.

"All right, let's give Benji a minute," Jay said, frowning at the boy's hesitation. "Sammy, you're up."

Sammy glanced at the open door, then back at Jay. "I won't go alone. We go together."

"Lou, Benji, and I'll be right behind you, kid. I promise."

He paused, teeth gnawing on the inside of his cheek. "Okay," he finally allowed. "But don't take too long."

After Henry's exit, Sammy's body was terribly small in the never-ending white. He dragged his feet, thin arms wrapped around his narrow chest. Pale eyes squinted against the flecks of ice assaulting him, but Henry's open arms were a beacon of safety.

And if one day you shall so fall,
I'll crush their hearts. I'll end them all.

The song grew louder. Jay searched the darkness at their backs, blade held tight, but it was Benji who backed away from the door. The storm outside was growing impatient, throwing frozen water like broken glass as punishment for keeping it waiting.

Sammy reached for Jay with both hands. His presence left small tracks in the snow as though he were nothing larger than a rabbit living in—*the Briarwood*—the island's woods.

"All right, Benji," Jay called. "Come on. It's safe."

Benji melted into the darkness. The lullaby began again, low dulcet tones weaving a beautiful melody of warmth and fierce protection. Lou made to follow Benji, but the black smoke was back, slithering across the ground, moving to the heart of the tunnel. She stopped; it was Benji's turn to face his demons.

"Benji, come back here."

Oh, Jay. He won't listen. I'm not sure he can even hear us anymore.

"I see something," Benji called. "I . . . I can't tell what it is yet. But it's for me."

At his words, a figure cut itself from the cloth of the shadows —first a head, then two arms, a full skirt. The shadow had eyes and sat in a chair. And something else . . .

"Do you know her, Benji?" Lou asked. Wind whipped at her back, rolling over her skin like calloused fingers. "Benji, listen to me. We are almost at the end of this mess. You must ignore whatever the tunnel is showing you and you will make it out of this. Jay and I are right here. Remember us. Remember Henry."

But Benji didn't move, because the shadow now sat before them in full colour and living flesh.

A woman sat in a rocking chair carved from solid maple, the swirls of the grain branded deep in the wood. Thick strands of auburn hair fanned across her face, her cheeks rosy even in the dim light. She had no corners, only soft edges and curves that sloped and held on to the light in tentative palms. The chair ground against the dirt floor, low and rhythmic, her feet coaxing it back and forth. As she rocked, she crooned into the crook of her elbow, and round dark pools of wetness dripped down her bosom. Lou fiercely wanted her to be real; the woman was pink while Henry's father had been jaundiced, gentle while he'd been equal parts calloused and slippery. And if there were ghosts in the tunnel, the figure drawing Benji to her with the cadence of her lullaby was an angel.

"What's goin' on?" Didi called, her teeth rattling from the cold. "We're freezin' out here!"

Benji stepped into the light cast by the strange woman. The song fell from her lips like silk across bare flesh. She could have been real; Lou knew better.

"Benji, let's get out of here," Jay said. "That's an order."

But Benji didn't turn.

The melody changed, becoming boots splashing into creeks and black hair reflecting light as skirts of sunflower gardens fanned out over wild grass. Lou blinked back tears. A glimmer of memory sparked, not in her mind, but in a forgotten corner of her heart belonging to tea parties and taffeta.

"Benji, I said *let's go*!" Jay's voice rose to the tipping point between concern and panic. Shadows shifted, the dark cloud puddling at Benji's feet, and the boy became harder to see. "We don't have much time before that thing takes over. You saw what it did to Henry."

"I know her," Benji said. "She isn't the same as the others . . . She won't hurt me."

The lullaby wound to an end. The rocker creaked, and the woman finally looked up from the invisible child in her arm to the boy standing before her.

"There you are," she said. Eyes the colour of rich caramel burned, the exaggerated arch of their brows mirrored in Benji's bewildered expression. "I have been waiting to see you for so long."

"I'm not sure who you are," Benji whispered. Tears choked him, but he stood his ground, his bear trembling in a tight fist. "But . . . But I should. Shouldn't I?"

"In a fair world, yes, you should. But our lives have been far from fair. Still, I cannot be angry when I finally got to see you once more. I've missed you." She reached out to him with trembling fingers. Lou braced herself for the smoke to twist her expression into something dead and evil and otherworldly, but it simply lingered around them like a screen. She stroked Benji's cheek with her thumb, and he dropped to his knees before her. "Oh, you are handsome."

"Mamá?"

She smiled, and Henry called out to him, screamed his name over and over until his voice cracked.

Here in the dark, away from the sun, all may pass to the stars —minus one.

"I know what the passage on the door means," Lou whispered. Jay threw her a terrified look, and she squeezed his hand, hoping to give him a calm she didn't quite feel. "One of us must remain in the tunnel. It seems that was always the price of passage through the door. The tunnel wants Benji."

Jay shook his head. "I'm not leavin' him behind."

"I do not think we have a choice in how this unfolds, Jay."

The woman stroked Benji's hair, straightened the shoulders of his shirt, drank his eyes with hers as though she'd never seen anything quite so exquisite as the wonderful boy at her feet. Benji let her, and Henry called for him once again with a voice that had only just been awakened by another's acceptance of him. He pushed against the open doorway, but an invisible barrier separated the tunnel from the outside world. He was trapped, doomed to watch Benji's fate unfold. They all were.

It was impossible to name the culprit—it could have been the strange cloud in the dark, the love reeking from the woman's pores, the wind clawing at Lou's back with brittle force—but the tunnel shifted. The island drew Benji and the woman who could only be his mother into a corner all their own, the dark cloud now a protective wall. She and Jay stood on one side of the path while Benji remained on the other. Two worlds orbiting each other, two celestial bodies on different paths, circling but fated never to collide again.

All may pass to the stars—minus one.

"I waited for you right here, all this time," she said. "My beautiful baby boy. How I have dreamed of this moment."

"How are you here?" Benji asked.

"I cannot say for certain. Grief is a terrible thing, especially that which comes with the loss of a child. Mine has always been especially difficult to bear, but the flowers made it manageable . . . for a time. Then, when even the spring blooms failed me, the tunnels appeared to make it manageable."

"What happened to me?" Benji asked. "Did you not want me?"

She looked down at her lap and shook her head violently. "I was never courted by any of the boys in my village. We were painfully middle class; money came in, but it was hard-earned and spent quickly. I was lucky to be offered a betrothal at seventeen, an age where my sisters had already married and begun families of their own."

"What is this?" Jay hissed in my ear. "We're wasting time. None of that can be true, can it?"

"Let him be," Lou whispered. The story called to her, the woman's voice a haunted howl in the darkest of winter nights.

She, too, had been left behind once. *Not enough, not enough . . .* It was a terrible burden to bear, that rejection, even with her memories of the past so faint. All the pains of another life she couldn't recall throbbed in her temples and bled the colour from the tunnel, and Lou struggled to find the thread that could pull her memories from the abyss. She was forgetting something. A part of herself. A very large part. And the words Benji's mother spoke called to some lost piece of her heart she desperately wanted to find.

Lou wanted to hear it *all*.

Before she was doomed to become a part of the tunnels forever —a lost soul, a ghost of herself. An unrecognizable shadow of her greatest mistakes.

Benji's mother smiled down at him. "I wanted to keep a nice home, arrange a tasteful garden of tulips and hydrangeas to rival anything my mother had. It was to be a good life—a *full* life— with a devoted husband of my own and a dozen children with rosy cheeks playing with the dogs in the yard."

The woman paused, her eyes misting with the memories of a life unlived. "My uncle came in from the city for my wedding. He was Father's older brother, unmarried, but a successful merchant in his own right. Mother did not approve of him staying in our home, with his room so close to mine, but Father insisted. That was enough to quash her protests. I wish he had let her speak."

Benji's upturned face moved like a flower tipping toward the sun, accepting her words as though needing them to live. But Lou knew the rest of the story; she'd been to market and seen the hunger that desire brought.

"He came to me one evening," she continued, her fingers twisting in her lap the same way Benji's did when he grew upset. "Everyone had retired for the evening, but I was too excited to sleep. I was trying on my veil in my room; I loved the way the lace overlayed my hair, for I'd never liked my appearance much to begin with. I could not know his intent . . . but then, the intentions of men are never the business of women.

"I remember little of the ordeal. Only that I did not bleed again, and when I felt the first stirrings in my belly, I began to question whether the dreams of girlhood nurtured by my parents were a lie. But I carried you inside me until I was round to bursting, my little miracle babe. And when you came, I knew I loved you despite the evil that had placed you inside me." Her hands stilled, and she met her son's gaze with unflinching pain. "You were born, and they took you from my breast and sent me far away. And I never saw you again."

Benji swallowed, and the sound echoed in Lou's bones. "It sounds like I ruined your life. I understand if you didn't want me."

"I wanted you more than my own life." The ferocity in her tone rallied against the winter storm, shook the walls, and drove the rubble from the ceiling and onto their heads. Cracks were forming in the cavern—cracks that grew and twisted and groaned. "I tried to find you, but no one thought to keep a record of where you'd gone. I was just a girl with no family or money. But I loved you every day, missed you every moment." Her eyes were glassy, tears spilling over their boundaries to rest like dew on her cheeks. "My little boy. My precious little one. It is *you* who found *me*. I am sorry it had to be in this place."

Rumbles filled the cavern, and the greater Lou's heart ached, the more the tunnel shook in protest. A mother's grief was the island's grief, and hers held the strength of an eternity of sorrow.

"We need to go, Benji!" Jay called, but the boy didn't move.

"I never knew," Benji said. "They always told me I was unwanted. A bastard. I don't remember much from before this life. But I would have remembered you if I'd met you." His breath hitched, and Lou's heart cracked. The seams of the cavern grew wider.

Benji's mother brushed a tear off her son's jaw. "I managed to give you one thing before they took you from me. A bear. A piece of me to keep until we found each other again."

The rumble climbed to a roar, and the ground quaked with the anger of the island. In that moment, Lou couldn't have moved if she'd wanted to. She and Jay stood shoulder to shoulder, an immovable wall guarding mother and son.

In his grief, Benji bent his head and laid his cheek on his mother's knees, his tears leaving dark tracks on her skirt. "It's really you."

"It's not," Jay said. "Get up, and let's get out of here before the tunnel comes down on us."

Benji sighed. His brow, furrowed from a lifetime of apology and worry, smoothed to the marble of unblemished childhood. He had found the lost piece of his heart: the woman who'd birthed him, who had fought to keep him, who loved him enough to sacrifice her honour to give him life. She was different from Henry's father or the past that haunted Kiran and Didi; they had been unwanted.

"Benji is different," Lou said. "His mother truly loved him despite the sacrifice and trauma of having him. He might have been lost once, but he isn't anymore. We cannot take him away from her now—not unless that is what he wants. It must be his choice."

Benji's mother never let her gaze wander. She soaked in the image of her son on her lap, tears streaking down her face, hands moving across his cheeks like a prayer. What would it be like to be loved so unconditionally?

You know what that is like. You just forgot.

"This place will fall," the woman finally said. "You must go if you are to live, my little boy."

"Come with us!" Benji said at once. "You can live with us in the den. Jay won't mind."

"This is my place, and this is where I will stay."

"No!"

"Do not be upset; this is where I held you in my heart. It is where I got to meet you, even if only this one time. I will always love you, my little one," his mother said. "My little Benji Bear."

"Benji!" Panic made Henry as loud as the crumbling earth. He tried again to push into the tunnel, but it didn't work. Lou knew it wouldn't. The tunnel wasn't meant for him anymore.

Benji glanced over his shoulder while Henry screamed in the cold. "I can't leave her, Jay. I just found her."

The wall of darkness shifted, and a jagged line cleaved the edge of the tunnel in two. Soon that crack would spread, and they would all be lost. Lost to the island in a place too deep to climb out of.

"He's made his decision," Lou said. "I'm so sorry."

Jay shook his head, chin quivering. "I don't leave anyone behind."

Lou pulled Jay to her and let his tears become her tears. "It will be all right. Think of Sammy. He needs you to come out of this place alive. We must go before we are all lost and he is left without you."

Her heart bled for the boy who'd never known his mother and the woman who'd never known her son. She bled for herself and for the children who'd lived a hundred lifetimes never finding a moment of what Benji clung to now. And until the very end.

One more time.

"Benji," Lou said, "we cannot stay any longer."

The boy smiled through his tears. "I know." Benji kissed the stuffed bear with the damaged eye and the matted fur. His tears soaked into it, darkening it, imbuing it with every important part of him. With a shuddering breath, he tossed the bear at Jay's feet. "Give this to Henry, okay? Tell him I love him. And I'm sorry. Just . . . Just don't tell him goodbye. He won't be able to take goodbye. Lou understands what I mean." A hunk of stone cracked off the ceiling and landed the earth between them with a mighty crash. "I love all of you so much. Go!"

And when the earth quaked and filled the air with black dust, Benji returned to his mother's embrace with a happy smile. A peaceful smile.

Henry roared in agony; the wind moaned with him. Rubble fell on them like hail, sticking to their clothes and sweat-slicked skin. Lou and Jay gave a final wave of farewell before racing to the door, their hands linked in grief.

Benji did not scream or weep; he did not call out at all. At long last, he was where he belonged. He was *home*.

Lou and Jay made it out before the tunnel collapsed, burying Benji and his mother together for eternity.

Then there was only dust.

CHAPTER 32

JAY

I tucked my knees into my chest and wedged my hands between my legs. The ground under the Hanging Tree had enough give to keep the bruises away, but the cold was something my blanket of leaves couldn't chase off. I twisted and tossed, digging my good shoulder into the mud for an extra bit of warmth. Finally, I burrowed into a crack in the trunk for better cover from the downpour and resigned myself to a night soaked by the rain.

Figures.

At first, I'd had hope Peter would forgive me. But I'd stopped counting the days when they'd turned into weeks. Hope was for kids and fools, and while I was cursed to live as a child for as long as the island wanted it that way, I was no one's fool. Peter's mind was set, and so I was trapped on the ground, living with the worms, doomed to keep my feet on the ground.

"Jay? You still awake?"

I shot upright, and my back screamed in protest. "Sammy?"

He crept out of the Hanging Tree, his smile warmer than the crappy leaves I hid under. "Yeah, it's me. Hope I didn't scare you."

"Nah, not me. I was just about to go to sleep." I worked hard to give him a smile, because no one needed to feel bad for me, least of all Sammy. "What're you doin' out here anyway? Did Peter lift the curfew?"

"He's already asleep. We had a big day meetin' with the Golds to talk about their borders."

"I didn't know he was doin' that today."

"He wanted to keep it a secret, I think." Sammy reached into the tree and pulled out a crudely stitched blanket of beaver pelt. "It's not much, but it'll keep out most of the rain."

"Sammy . . . you gotta be careful. Peter can't know you're helpin' me." I grabbed the hide with greedy fingers anyway and wrapped it around myself nice and tight. "Thanks, though. I don't know what you had to do to get this past Bell and Slightly, but thanks."

"It's easy to get away with stuff when no one expects much from me." His cheeks flamed, one side of his face darker than the other. "It's not fair, you bein' stuck out here. You didn't do anythin' wrong."

"Oh, I did. I went against Peter. I'm surprised I'm not dead." A shiver rattled my teeth, and I pulled the blanket tight. "Hey, what happened to your face? You fall or somethin'?"

Sammy turned away so the shadows took over. "It's nothin'."

"It's not nothin'. Tell me what happened."

The rain came down harder and plastered Sammy's bright hair to his forehead. "You . . . You ate the last apple today."

"Yeah. And?"

There was a pause, short but loaded.

And then I understood. "Peter wanted it."

Sammy looked away. Acid bubbled up inside me, all-consuming and hot. It spread into my guts, my throat, my fingers and toes until I couldn't tell if I was in pain or completely numb. I slid the pelt around Sammy's quaking shoulders and brought him in closer.

"It's okay, Jay. Really."

"What did he do?"

Sammy's breathing hitched, and he buried his head in my chest. "Not much. Peter just roughed me up a bit. It doesn't hurt too bad. I swear."

I'd kill him. I'd really do it this time. I'd been a coward to accept any punishment that brought Sammy down with me. "It'll be okay, Sam. We'll make this right."

"I'm scared."

I rubbed my palms up and down his arms, hoping the friction from my frozen fingers would chase the shivers away. "I know, but you don't need to be. Say, can you do me a favour? I haven't had somethin' to eat except for some nuts and that tiny apple since lunch. Do you think you can find me a rabbit or quail, maybe? I'm starvin'."

Sammy swiped the back of his hand across his nose and nodded. Ready to help me, as always.

I made a mistake, kid. But I won't make it again.

"Sure thing, Jay. I'll check the backwoods over by the Reds' camp. They usually have lots of small game."

"That sounds like a good plan. Go on now."

With a final nod, Sammy disappeared into the trees. The rain would mask any noise and muddy his footprints, making him tougher to track. I'd left one mess behind just to jump into a bigger one with a bigger monster than my daddy. I was a coward. How many bruises and broken bones had I been responsible for because I was too weak to do anything more than watch or hide?

Peter wasn't the only crocodile on the island. The croc lived in me too. It waited like a virus to take over my body and mind, to make me just as bad as the other monsters. Peter had given himself over to that darkness, but I had to fight. For once in my long, long life, I had to do more than watch or hide.

Throwing the pelt to the ground, I edged into the centre of the giant sequoia. Like the ghost I'd become, my practiced steps made no noise on the way down. Every notch in the bark, every rock and root, was a known and familiar piece of the island. An island that had been my escape but had turned into a prison.

I deserved it all.

The kids were just bodies curled up on the dusty floor, eyes shut, snores escaping slack mouths. Even in sleep, they held their weapons close to their cheeks or gripped in tight fists. My own knife had been stripped of me on *that night*, and while I had no chance of getting to one of the boys' weapons, the spears were propped in a neat row against the far wall. Unguarded. Waiting for me. I helped myself to a sturdy oak rod topped in forged pirate silver and smiled. It was old and splintered, but the arrow was sharp, and the wood was light.

Good enough.

Peter's hammock stretched over my head, the web of tightly knotted rigging rope spanning the entire den. There were no ladders, steps, or blocks to get up to his quarters.

A bird's-eye view is better for watchin' over all of you, the boss always said, but why wouldn't he need a ladder? Because he'd touched the stars once—whatever that meant—and had a fairy to help him in and out of bed every day? To me, he was just a bag of skin curled into the ropes, the pink flesh puckering through the diamond pattern like quilting. See, I knew the truth: No matter how much Peter banged on about us all bein' family, he thought he was better. Above us. And that would never change.

I slashed my spear through the rope. Peter spilled to the ground, and the hammock swung off the wall, a fallen rope bridge. He rolled onto all fours and blinked away the sleep, the diamonds on his back like a human turtle shell. Stabbing him was an option, but I wouldn't kill the boy while he was unarmed. That would be an unearned advantage and the kind of bad form that would strip my victory of everything I cared about.

No, I had to let him try.

Peter stumbled to his feet, his belly soft, his face round and flushed. A boy. Nothing more than—*a lie*—a boy.

"I told you already," Peter said. "Traitors ain't welcome in my tree."

"You hit Sammy, so who's the traitor?"

I drove the spear above his left shoulder, just to tease him a little, and Peter dodged the blow. His eyes grew wide, taking me in with new mistrust. He knew just how serious I was then.

Good.

The others stirred, their bedding scratching against the ground. Soon there would be more bodies to fight, more chances to lose. I'd make quick work of them too. Maybe not Benji or Timber, but Slightly would be my next target after I took Peter down.

"This ain't you, Number Two. Come on. Put the spear down." Peter glanced one way, then another. With a bare foot, he rolled Henry off his bed of mouldering leaves and snatched a rusted sword out from under him. "You can't win this."

"You killed Lilith." My breathing came faster now. I raised my spear over my shoulder and brought the end down with a grunt of power that shocked me. Peter spun out of reach, but it was close. "And don't call me Number Two. You cast me out, so I don't work for you anymore."

Peter struck with his sword, knocking my spear away with the blunt side of the blade. "Lilith betrayed me," he said, the balls of his feet digging in the dirt as we circled each other. "You're lucky I didn't do the same thing to you."

He sank into a lunge, but I sidestepped his blow easily.

"I have a spear, and you have a heavy sword," I said, the grin growing wider on my sweaty face. The boys were circling, their eyes pinpricks of hate trained on my face, my back, my spear-wielding arm. But no one got in my way. They weren't stupid. "That blade's gonna make you slower than me. You'll *always* be too slow, Peter."

"I got fairy dust." He drove the sword down hard, but it fell short, landing in the dirt by my feet. "I can do anythin' I want with Bell's help. You won't last another day. She'll be down to help me soon."

"Sure, if you want our brothers to see what a coward you are. Plus, how easy do you think it's gonna be to think of a way out of this when I'm about to put you in the ground?" I struck out again, and my spear finally found skin, slicing a wide arc across Peter's chest. "You took her away from me!"

"Who? Lilith? You hate fairies! Devil flies, remember? That's what you've always called 'em."

"Not Lilith—*Lou*! It's always been about Lou!"

With fumbling steps, Peter faced me again. "Not this crap again. This is the way it is, Jay! You gotta let it go!"

"But she didn't grow up!" I was screaming, crying, raging at him. Another slash of my arm, and fresh blood streamed from Peter's forearm. "And so what if she *did*? Does that mean I don't get to say goodbye? That we can't still be friends? Why?" Slash, more blood. Peter's arm dropped to his side, and he fell onto his backside with a grunt. "Why do you have to be such a . . . a *monster*?"

Peter's legs pinwheeled out ahead of him, and he backed slowly up to the edge of the room. "Because I want you to feel it too," he said, voice barely above a whisper. Blood streaked the ground, trailing under Peter like slime under a snail. His smile was painted red. "The island found me when no one else wanted me. But I didn't appreciate the gift it gave me. I wanted to go back so bad. So, I did what I could and found a way to see my parents again. You know how it is with kids: they miss their parents first, hate them later. I was no different. Turns out they didn't even remember me when I finally saw them again. They made another one, turned my room into a nursery for the stupid thing, and moved on. Face it, Jay—Lou can't be there for you like the island will."

I laughed, the spear shaking in my fist. "So, your mommy didn't want you, and that means *we* can't be wanted either?" Feet shuffled on the ground, and voices rumbled low through the circle of boys closing in, but I was too high to come down. "If Lou doesn't want me around anymore, fine. But she's gotta tell me herself. 'Til then, I'm still gonna try, 'cause I don't wanna be like you." I lifted my spear above Peter's head, chest heaving, eyes bright.

"She's not your sister." Peter licked his lips, smearing blood around his mouth. "But hey, if you're ungrateful for everythin' I've done for you, then at least have the guts to finish me off. Nice and clean, a good kill, just like I taught you."

We were both crocodiles gnashing our teeth and drawing blood. His pain was my pain; his evil was my evil. In that second, we were the same: unwanted and unloved but for the family we'd made for ourselves. And we clung to that manufactured happiness for fear of losing ourselves to the monsters we were deep down inside. Until we had no fight left in us.

"I should kill you," I said. "I should bury you deep in the island you love more than any of us. And I should take your place just in case your ghost sticks around to watch it all happen."

The muttering grew to protests, cheers, feet stamping the packed earth, shaking it with the promise of death. An island without Peter was something I'd never considered. No one knew if it was even possible. The boy was a cockroach, a being of a thousand lives. Could he even *be* killed? My arm ached, begged to be used, to drive the spear into Peter's heart.

"Finish it," he whispered, blood bubbling in his chest. "You hear them. They want you to make a choice. If you get rid of me, all my rules die with me."

"I could see Lou again."

"Maybe. Or maybe this place will stop existing, and you'll be lost before you can get halfway back to the Land of the Grown. The only way to save the island and get Lou back is to touch the stars, and there's too much dark in you to make you fly that high. If you were gonna do it, you'd have done it a long time ago. Nah, you're stuck here, Jay. You're *stuck*."

I bared my teeth, and the cheering grew louder, filled my mind and my heart until everything was painted red. Were they cheering for me? Probably not.

It was a funny thing, hating the person you'd been groomed to love.

Blood ran down Peter's arms, torso, head. *Drip, drip, drip.*

The mob waited. I still had my spear.

I was better than all of it.

"I'm leavin'," I said, lowering my arm. "I'm goin' out on my own, and you won't stop me." Yeah, that sounded right. A better option than killing him. "You won't hunt me or get in my way. This is where we part ways, *brother*."

Peter's grin remained plastered to his face as he cocked his head to one side. "You wanna start your own clan? Or join the pirates? The tribes, maybe?" He laughed, and fresh blood spilled from the corners of his mouth. "That's not how my island works."

"It works however you tell it to work. I want to be free. Yeah, I made mistakes, but so did you. After all the years I served this place, you owe me that much." The room grew still, and I could feel their eyes on me. "I don't want my own clan. I'll just be takin' Sammy since I don't trust you worth a lick."

Peter frowned. "Drop the spear, and we'll talk."

"Say we got a deal, and I'll drop the spear."

It was a long moment before he nodded in agreement. "Fine. You're free, Jay. But this island is still your home, and you'll respect my territory unless you wanna start a war."

My shoulders sagged with relief. "Fine. But I want your dagger."

Another round of whispers. Bell whizzed into the den and straight to Peter's shoulder, her light a cold spot in the room. "It's all right, Bell," Peter said, eyeing me with suspicion. "He don't mean it."

"Oh, I do. You took my dagger, but I don't want that one anymore. I want *yours*. Call it payment for my troubles."

After a moment, Peter nodded. Bell drifted off, returning seconds later with Peter's favourite blade tucked safely within her light. Careful not to touch any part of her, I plucked the blade out by the hilt, surprised at how heavy it was in my hand. Peter's eyes were on me as I curved my fingers around the supple leather, relishing the win.

"Is that it?" Peter asked. "Or do you have other demands before you get outta my tree?"

I tossed the spear to the far side of the room and backed away with careful steps. "That's it for now."

Freedom—I was dizzy with it. The entrance sloped up and away from the den, and I had no regrets as I took one last look at my home. Saying goodbye to it was easier than I'd thought it would be.

"I'm goin' with him!" The new girl—Didi?—pushed out of the circle of boys, all legs and skinny arms. The slash across her face was still a bright red, almost a perfect match to her brother's, but the puckering skin was closed, healing slow and steady. She towed her brother after her, jaw flickering with the effort. "Come on, Kiran. Let's get outta here."

"Are you nuts?" Kiran asked. "He's the one who did this to us." He gestured to their faces, the scar forever branding them.

"Yeah, and he did it on Peter's orders." They sidled up to me, shoulder to shoulder, and I couldn't think of a single thing to say. "At least he's got the guts to stand up for what he cares about. He's the only one that codfish seems to be afraid of, so if he goes, we go with him. Anyone else comin'?"

Benji shuffled over, his face stricken with the impact of his decision. "Okay, sure. Yes. I'm coming too! I hope that's okay, Jay. I never wanted to do any of that to you. You know I'm really sorry about it all, right?"

"I know, Benji, I know. But I told you, I don't want a clan of my own." My heart pounded as Henry got to his feet, towering over the rest of the boys. Peter shifted on the ground, visibly bubbling with rage; Henry was his biggest prize, his newest asset. He hadn't expected to lose him so soon, and that made me want him more. "You too, Henry? I mean, you know I got no plan for us, right? I don't even know where I'm gonna sleep tonight."

Benji shrugged, one hand patting Henry on the back. "We know. But we don't want to live like this anymore. If you can give us some peace where we can make a new home for ourselves, we're with you all the way."

And just like that, we were divided. Us and them. Those who remained ran over to help Peter up, hands already working to stem the bleeding. Those who'd left his side were a warm presence by mine, and I would never take that for granted. Never.

And if I ever did, the island should let me rot like a stinkin' pirate.

Timber peeled himself away from the mob. "I'm sorry, Jay," he said, casting frantic glances at the boy bleeding on the ground. "I'd come with ye, but Peter'll take me away from Lou's sister if I do. I figure if anyone's goin' te take proper care o' the girls, it should be me."

"It's okay, Timber. You got my blessin', all right? I trust you."

He nodded. "I'll tell Rosie all about ye. It's the best way te get Lou to remember."

I swallowed the tears because crying wasn't how I wanted to start my new life. Freedom would taste of the sky and the spring, not of the sea.

"That's it, then," I said, standing guard while the others filed out of the Hanging Tree. "Let's move out."

CHAPTER 33

There was much to be said in a heavy silence, but none of them said a thing. Not about grief or blame or the natural questions following the death of a loved one. Snowflakes rode the bite of winter as Lou climbed the Mountain of Regret. Their shattered hearts heaved with the weight of their loss. The chill was fitting that way.

Benji was gone. In all her time on the island, Lou had thought each of the children unbreakable and eternal. But she should have known that nothing was permanent, not even when it should have been. She'd learned that lesson before, sometime long ago, but couldn't remember how. All she knew for certain was that one of their own had ceased to exist, and the ease with which his light had been snuffed out forced Lou to wonder what would happen should any of the others fall too. Tears froze on her cheeks and formed crystals in her lashes. Her heart was outside her body, back in the tunnels with the boy who'd been the first to show her kindness.

Henry clutched the only thing left of Benji under his chin, trapping his tears where Benji's had soaked through the bear's fur.

In that way, they were one, together even in death. But it wasn't enough; Henry had returned to the silent tomb he'd lived in for years, lapsing into silence as they stomped up the mountain path. But this time, no one questioned the heavy quiet. Instead, each of them found something to keep themselves busy to avoid speaking the truth. Kiran and Didi searched the path for animal tracks while Sammy fiddled with the crack in his lenses. Jay's soles left gaping wounds in the crisp blanket of frost, his tears long since run dry. Lou couldn't bear to look at him; what words could ever be enough to comfort a boy who'd lost a friend and a brother to another's cause?

My fault.

It was hard to breathe. While she couldn't fully understand the thought, she was certain the forest far below her would now be painted in grey. Colours were reserved for the living, and death was closing in on them like an avalanche.

"Jay?"

"I don't wanna talk about it, Lou. Not yet."

They continued up the narrow path through barren trees. The climb was steep, the wind sharp as knives, but Lou's boots were warm, and the heat of Jay's body was enough to keep the chill at bay. One look over the edge, and nausea overtook her; the Mountain of Regret floated above the island, looming over the trees and sweeping across the clouds. The sea was a swatch of blue under them, the crocodiles like pebbles circling the pirate ship in the cove with its belly cooling in the high tide. Instead of joy at having made it to the end of their journey, Lou felt nothing. She couldn't remember what they'd hoped to gain by finding the end. The price had been too high.

"It was Benji's choice." Her voice was hushed, but Jay flinched as though she'd screamed over the wind. "You didn't do anything wrong. You couldn't have stopped it."

"I don't know if the snow's a normal part of the mountain,"

Jay said, "or if the island is finally givin' up, but we better hurry either way. I can't feel my fingers anymore."

They climbed for hours, eating snow to soothe their rumbling stomachs and resting on the rocks to catch their breath. Anything worth speaking of was buried back in the tunnels under a pile of rock and broken bones. But it was getting harder to speak, even if they wanted to.

"The air's gettin' thin," Didi said, shedding her sweater and wrapping it around Kiran's trembling shoulders. "We should be close to the top. And look."

Lou followed her finger up to the sky. Sure enough, the deepening blue of the heavens was crusted with silver specks. Stars flashed above them, winking with a promise of glory in the weakening daylight. They were so close. Why, then, did she want to turn back and live out the rest of her days with Sammy's hand in hers, Henry's shoulder to lean on, and Jay's heart to live in? Didi and Kiran would teach her how to hunt and trap and speak her mind. It would be a good life. It was a life she should've wanted.

But there was something she needed to find, and it rested at the mountain's peak.

And so they climbed.

"I don't want you to be disappointed if this doesn't work for you," Jay said. "I still have no idea how to reach the sky, even if we do make it all the way up."

"That is unnecessarily kind, Jay," she said, meaning every word. "This isn't only my fate—we all live or die together if the island does not survive. We do not need this land to exist to know we be united forever."

An odd look flashed across his face. "That's what you think this is about? The island's survival and what'll happen to us?"

She shrugged. "That is the entire reason for this journey, isn't it?" Something sharp within her twisted, her stomach bottoming out. She did not understand the sensation, nor why Jay remained silent and apparently baffled by her answer.

"Boss!" Didi called, pulling Lou from her confusion. "I . . . I think we're here."

The crest of the mountain glowed white under the rising moons. Lou sprinted to the top with every shred of energy she had left. The stars were out, a blanket of them, millions of watchful eyes in varying hues of the rainbow. They breathed and whispered, oozing light onto the world. Lou tipped her face to the sky; the only thing between her and the souls dotting the heavens was endless open air. She imagined passing her fingers across the universe, rustling the flecks of pink and green and forget-me-not. Each star held a story; each sang its own lullaby.

"Peter always said that star over there was his," Jay said, pointing to the brightest jewel above them. "He told me he stretched out his hand and listened to the wind and grabbed hold of it."

Lou smiled. "Just like that?"

"Yes, friend. Just like that."

You just have to say, "I'll be a kid forever," three times, and they'll come. Easy peasy, poke your knees-y.

She could live with him forever on this mountain, far from the destruction below. She would be happy. It's all she ever wanted. That, and to be a kid forever.

But that's not true.

Think. Think hard.

The stars called out to her, and she looked back, trying to find the one belonging to her.

She's rememberin'.

Yes, she was.

The sky shuffled the stars, and they settled into a new pattern. Lou squinted just like she had when she'd read the clouds in some other time, giving them shapes and names. Up above, there was a face, a watchful eye brimming with tears and a hand curled over a plush doll.

Remember.

The girl that had twisted between two trees in a vision almost forgotten now watched from the sky. Lou let herself fall into the memory that wasn't quite a memory but a song. A race, a book of stories, and pretty shoes banished to the back of a closet in favour of scuffed boots.

"There's a girl in the sky," Lou muttered. "I've seen her before."

Jay wrinkled his nose. "Where?"

"She . . . She's meant for me. I know her."

His face drained of all colour, but it was Didi who took her hand this time. "Maybe you should let her know you can see her. Try lettin' her in. That's what I would do, if I had the chance again."

Opening her heart to the sky was as easy as falling.

A girl moved across a dark floor littered with toys and spoke tales of a young boy. That boy had brought the sky down to her by luring the birds to her shoulder. That boy—Jay—had smuggled pieces of the woods indoors, had played games with her while angry voices raged around her.

And that was when Lou really remembered it all.

Jay had been there for her through the fights and the tears, the twisted ankles and adventures through the Briarwood. *The Briarwood*. She knew the name like she knew Jay had always been real. To Jay, she had always been enough. He had never given up on her, even when her own father had been selfish enough to die and her own mother had been selfish enough to grieve. But she had wanted more than her mother and father. Lou had wanted to keep Jay to herself, to play in the woods, to live in her home, unchanged. Forever.

She was selfish too.

"I don't want it to happen like this," Jay said, but his voice was far away. "Lou, I gotta tell you somethin'."

How long do you think it will take your cousin to eat her fruit, Louisa?

One hundred years, Mother.

A giggle echoed off the snowy banks, and starlight flashed with the brilliance of rainbows.

Mother.

Lou's world constricted to a sharp point. The stars shifted above her, constellations taking shape before her very eyes. The wind brought with it the chill of snow and the scent of oranges, lavender, fresh peaches, and the clean tang of soap. Each sound and smell was a note in a familiar song, and all Lou had to do was listen. Jay tugged on her hand and called her name, but she could hardly sense his touch anymore. She floated above the island, her mind whirring to keep up with the memories crashing into her.

Silly girl. We will not be alive in one hundred years.

Summer on a porch, and two grubby hands shining with the rush of melon nectar pouring down her wrists; a baby, no older than two, gripping the fruit like it would last forever; a head of golden curls bent over the kitchen table where a ripe melon waited to be sliced.

A sob escaped Lou's lips, and she floated deeper into the chaos of light above. In the distance, voices called her back, but there was no room for them and the beautiful visions to exist together. She had to choose one over the other. In the end, she always had to lose in order to gain.

Perfection couldn't be preserved. Things did not last forever, and neither would she. While she never wanted to accept those truths as a child, when the stars spoke to her, Lou finally listened.

Remember.

Remember what brought you back to Jay.

Cotton sheets draped across her head; a boy fading to black as a baby girl took his place in her heart; a woman in a chair by the window offering a smile brimming with love and hope. That smile would soon sour, but she hadn't known it yet.

Salty tracks burned Lou's cheeks. The wind mounted to a crescendo, holding her close like a mother to its bosom. She remembered now.

"Mother," Lou whispered. "I remember Mother. How did I forget her?"

Wide skirts and rigid spines; a moustache combed and waxed; a room trimmed in ivory lace. Lou's feet left the snow, and she spread her arms wide, welcoming the stars into her heart. The girl in the sky showed Lou's past to her in the curves of a constellation, and Lou watched it all unfold with open arms.

"What did I do?" Lou whispered.

The Briarwood; chasing a girl with raven-feathered hair through the trees; longing for the birds, the streams, the feel of cool spring water rushing over her toes in a place where no one would tell her to straighten her dress or comb her hair.

Rosie. The lake.

No. Not yet.

The shades of grey painted over the colours in the girl's vision, and a familiar headache pulsed behind Lou's eyes.

Blue skies stretched left and right and straight on to forever while the smell of ripe melon on a warm summer day and lavender shampoo snaked down her throat. Still, she remembered Jay's eyes: two drops of ocean that reminded her of home, but it was the sky that called her name.

Lou doubled over in agony.

Melancholy had never been permitted to be anything more than a forbidden string of syllables attached to the reputations of sad, sad women. Except the pain of Lou's sadness was alive. It was a poisonous weed, germinating in her mind, growing roots—

agonizingly deep roots that stifled her joy until the world was flat and grey. It was Death waiting over the edge of a steep cliff.

It truly was a monster with large teeth.

Anne Webber had fought with melancholy herself. Looking back, Lou understood just how difficult it had been for her mother to never be the same as the other ladies—not when the babies she wanted would not come, not when her first daughter had an embarrassingly unconventional character, not when her husband passed away well before his time. If she was a stronger woman, Anne Webber might have recognized her daughter's melancholy sooner. She might have given Lou permission to face her monster head-on. Instead, Lady Webber passed her own pressures down to her daughter, hoping to give her what she lacked, succeeding only in throwing her before the monster without a single weapon.

In the end, both women were so alike in their loneliness, yet neither knew how to build a bridge to reach the other.

"I must speak to my mother," Lou told the stars, suddenly frantic. Guilt choked her with thick fingers, and her heart raced. "I've taken too long. I need to go back, to apologize!"

At her words, the stars shifted, a new constellation taking the place of the first.

Jay. He was her freedom, her spear to face the monster in her mind. An open window; leather boots racing through the woods; a hand on her shoulder when Mother ignored her. When she was a child, Jay was a pair of arms holding the broken pieces of her heart together. But his arms had grown tired, and she had replaced him.

"Jay," she whispered. "I'm sorry I couldn't remember you."

Jay didn't turn. No one noticed her tears in the snow. It was as though she existed in another world, watching the children but never part of them.

She had been deluded. The island could never be her home; it was a stopping point, a lesson to learn before she could return to her real life. She'd do better; perhaps she wouldn't marry or have children, but she would have more patience for her mother's expectations. She would take Rose with her to the city. She would live.

The stars moved.

Look, they whispered.

Lou obeyed.

Rose, no older than a few months, lay beside her on a large duvet. The child gripped Lou's finger with her whole fist, a grip like the brush of a feather to a grown but containing the force of a baby's whole heart. *Come home to me*, the baby whispered. *Come home.*

The darkness in her mind receded as she stroked the peach and cream of her sister's round face, the baby's eyes still a muddled grey that would one day turn black. But that baby grew and grew, and within seconds, the bedroom melted away to another scene. There were hands on her face and whispers in her ear. They'd buried Father two days prior, and she'd been a prisoner in her bed ever since. Outside, the light brightened and waned, the moon and sun creeping across the glass in turn. But they offered no colour anymore. No life. For Rosie, she would find her feet again, but it would be years before she could step foot into the Briarwood once more.

Lou turned her head, and a comet rushed past, calling her attention to another cluster of stars. Faster now. The images were urgent, just like Jay's voice beyond the veil.

Age twelve, Lou toyed with the blades of grass by the Briarwood. She counted the trees along the edge of the forest, practicing the numbers Father had taught her long, long ago. Birdsong erupted over the trees, and Lou caught a glimpse of her mother. Anne Webber's brow was lined, her eyes vacant as she rearranged Rosie's blankets around her in the tall grass. Their eyes met over the bundle of cotton, and the darkness Lou held in her heart was mirrored in her mother's face. And when Anne Webber looked away, it would be years before she would return her daughter's gaze again. The darkness would be there on birthdays and at Christmas, during every fever, and any time a couple would walk past, arm in arm. Lou would only see joy in her mother's eyes when she turned sixteen and the Rileys mentioned what a lovely match she'd make for their son. From that day forward, Lou would strive to bring that look of happiness back to her mother's face, even if it would mean her own misery. It was funny, how complicated love could be.

The stars shifted, and so did the fog of her forgetting.

Each vision was a starburst of clarity pushing away the spell the island had cast; memory by memory, her ties to the island—to *Jay*—were snipped free. She was floating away and away. Part of her wanted to stay with the boy who'd been the only light in a world oozing with darkness. But there was another part to over-rule the rest—a part that needed her to fly. And to reach the stars, she needed to be free.

Remember.

"I'm sorry, Jay," Lou whispered. "I shouldn't have forgotten her. I shouldn't have forgotten *you*."

She didn't know if he could hear her, but the stars did. Their bright hands pulled her close, and the truth buried deep in her mind shook free, every moment of it sprawling out before her in terrible detail.

Lou was back in her room. It was dark, the window trimmed in familiar gossamer and lace. The bed sat beside her white wooden desk while books stood at attention across a handsome dresser. A girl—*Rosie*—burrowed deep into a pillow, the plush comforter hiding most of her face. What was visible was red and puffy. A woman—*Mother,* she remembered—stroked Rosie's hair over and over, smoothing the strands away from her cheeks. Dark patches spattered the sheets like rainfall, spreading puddles of sadness in a permanent stain across Lou's bed.

"Sweetheart, you must eat something."

"I'm not hungry." Rosie stared ahead, unseeing. Beside her, a book of exotic birds peeked out from under small hands, the nails chewed raw.

Mother sat beside Rosie on the bed, her curls unbound, dull in the low light. It was unlike her not to carefully wash and style herself, to be anything less than perfection. And yet there she sat, her nightdress stained with tears of her own, her fingers trembling as she stroked her daughter's hair. "You should get back to your room. Get some rest, Rose."

Rose's fingers clamped down on the book, her eyes growing wild with fear. "Do not make me leave. I cannot be away from her."

"Dearest—"

"No." The hard edge in her sister's voice was new, the tone of someone much older—someone who'd seen loss and grief and hardship. What had happened to the girl dancing through the trees and singing to the sun?

You know what happened. Think.

Rose's eyes swam in an ocean of despair that spilled its tides over her pale face. "I can still smell her, Mother. The pillows and sheets, her clothes. This whole place reminds me of her, even if she did not belong here."

"This was her room, sweetheart. She always belonged here."

"This was her prison. Lou belonged with the birds."

Anne Webber's face crumbled. Red blossomed in uneven patches across her cheeks, her bloodshot eyes pressed tight in a web of fine lines, and a thread of saliva snapped between twisted lips. One hand went to muffle her cry, but Lou could see the motion was one of habit and not of concern for being heard in her grief. Anne Webber's sadness was thick and palpable in the dark room, laid bare for Rose to see. But instead of seeing anything at all, Rose's attention continued to trail in the abyss.

"Do you think she is with Father?" Rose finally asked.

"I . . . I think you were right before, my darling. She is with the birds. And I believe Father is with them too."

Mother and daughter huddled together, the window dressings, white desk, books, and dolls all in the same place Lou had left them. Anne retrieved a cardigan, bright yellow with embroidered periwinkles and cherry blossoms, and brought it to her nose. Inhaled deep. She lowered herself beside Rose and swung a free arm across the girl's shoulders. Her daughter. Her only remaining daughter.

Away, away, away.

And then they were gone.

Lou blinked, drinking in the blue skies once more. The storm had stopped, the snow reflecting bright white under the new light filtering through the barren branches. Her chest throbbed in the place where her heart should have been. She was hollow, her heart back in her bedroom with her mother and sister.

She was no longer, and would never be, a woman. She could not exist in both places after all.

"Lou?" Jay was beside her once more, but he was solid when she was only part of the wind, part of the sky. Soon the breeze would take her away.

Not yet. You must accept what you did. Why you are here.

"Lou, you gotta fight it," Jay said, his cheeks sheening with tears. "Didi and Kiran did it. Henry did it too. You can beat this. It isn't real."

But it was. She could never have forgotten her mother and sister, the only family she had left. And yet she preferred a pirate's attire to the strange dress she'd held on to for so long, preferred the hair now brushing her shoulders in jagged sweeps to a familiar weight down her back. She had never loved her hair as much as she'd admired her sister's, had never liked the skirts or tight shoes that pinched her feet, but how easily had those familiar pieces of herself been banished from memory? The island had a way of making one forget, but only because she wanted so badly to leave that piece of herself behind.

Jay opened his mouth to speak again, but his eyes grew wide, and the others crowded around him, guarding him with their lives.

"You're too late, Number Two. I told you, rules are rules." Peter approached through the trees like a ghost, but his voice carried clear through the mountain. "Lou's almost there, but she needs to accept the rest of the truth if she's gonna make it. Are you gonna tell her, or should I?"

CHAPTER 34

JAY

It was tough to climb a tree with a blade in each hand. No matter how many years I practiced, Peter's dagger—my dagger—never got easier to handle.

These branches were my home away from the new den. Sure, I'd finally gotten away from Peter, but the den was too noisy, too busy, and sometimes I couldn't bother pretending to care. There was something about being far above the ground, between the sky, the earth, and the sea, that made me part of all of it and none of it at once. It was peaceful. It was quiet. It was the only way the voices faded, and I could imagine seeing Lou again, hear her voice reciting a line from some book or humming a lullaby to that baby. But the baby wouldn't be a baby anymore, and I could only hope Timber had kept his promise. That was all I got for all my troubles: another kid keeping watch over my lost sister and a few moments of peace up in the boughs of some tree Peter hadn't thought to look for me in.

Lou lived at the back of my mind always, but there was a more pressing problem. Peter had kept his word and let us live, but that didn't stop him and his boys from raiding our traps to steal our kills and pick the trees around our den dry of fruit. With the attacks coming every other day, the den would never truly become home, and I'd need to live in the tree just to get away from it all. I wondered how the pirates lived on that ship, so close together, a dagger stashed under every sleeping head, just waiting for an assault, and the pity I felt for them was sudden and unwanted. I knew them. Felt sorry for them, even. I would be paranoid too—I already was.

The sails of the pirate ship billowed like black clouds, and they followed me everywhere. I liked this spot best; the view of the island beside me was as good as any to alert me to any oncoming threats, and the ocean stretched out across the world ahead of me. That was a lie, though. I had tried to leave by boat and ended up right back where I started. The joke wasn't lost on me; I just didn't think it was very funny.

My stomach gave a rowdy growl, but the stink coming off the sea was doing nothing to help my appetite. The ground crawled with pirates, but I let them be. For now. They sang while they worked, loading trunks and baskets of food onto the ship, moving like ants through the trees. It was always the same tune, and after all this time, the words were etched onto my brain like a treasure map.

"Captain and his men stole the boy from his den and took away his gold," they sang, and my mouth moved with theirs. "Most of us died, still some are alive, but all of us sail the sea."

I closed my eyes, and the song vibrated through me, my fingers tapping the hilt of my dagger to count out the beat.

"We follow the stars, forever we march, to eternity we must go. The island holds still, no matter our will, so never we die, yo-ho."

I breathed, the gruff voices reaching into my soul, twisting the strands of the boy I was into the man I'd never become. Not here. Not ever. Peter had taken that from us all.

The island holds still, no matter our will, so never we die, yo-ho.

Pirates were scum. But they sure could sing.

I opened my eyes, and the sky was the deep magenta of a setting sun. Both moons were shadows overhead, glowing above the trees. And below me, footsteps pattered and thumped, the heavy breathing of struggling pirates cutting their song short.

"I tell ye, he be gone." The pirate grunted under the weight of a dead deer, blood dripping from the lifeless carcass slung over his shoulder.

His companion dragged two swords and a crossbow behind him and snorted. "Peter's not left this cursed place fer longer'n a day since I known 'im. I'd wager he be 'round here somewhere, hidin' in some den, waitin' te slit all our throats."

"Blackbeard said no one's seen the boy for near a week, ye maggot. The clan's gone too—took to the forest and left it all behind. There be no trace of the stupid urchins s'far as I can tell."

"Well, yer dumber'n a toad in a croc swamp, so I'll be takin' me information from better sources." The pirate scratched his beard with the arrow of his crossbow and cocked his head at his blood-soaked comrade. "Peter canna be gone fer good. Who'd take his place? You?"

"I'd do a better job'n you. Now quit blabberin' an' get out me face!" His own cheeks purpled under the deer's weight, and the pirate staggered out from under the trees. "Peter's gone! Next ye know, that Jay lad'll be in charge, and we'll be after fresh blood. 'Bout time too—the island's goin' rotten. Too much o' the same fer too long. S'not natural."

Peter. Gone. It had never happened before. The island needed a leader, or it would fall to pieces. Peter had always said as much, a nice little bedtime story to give us nightmares.

But then again, Peter lied. What if he'd abandoned the island to live in the Land of the Grown? No, it couldn't be. This place was an extension of him, a world made in his image. He'd never leave it in the hands of a pirate.

"Only one way to know the truth," I muttered to the leaves. The sea roared back at me in approval.

I tucked my weapons into my belt and monkeyed my way down to the ground. There was no point letting the others know where I was going. If the pirates were right, then the Hanging Tree would be empty and harmless. If they were wrong . . . Well, I would just make sure to stay hidden where Peter's boys couldn't see me. Plus, I missed it. It was tough to let go of the place that had been a piece of my life for years, even if it was a piece I hated.

The light slipped away, but I didn't need it to know where I was going. My heart drummed behind my ribs, the forest unfolding, letting me pass, letting me through. Without Peter, the entire land and every creature in it could be mine. I could go back and forth between worlds, quit waiting for the dagger to slice my throat while I slept. I could do anything I wanted. All I needed was to figure out how to touch a star or two.

If Peter could do it, so could I.

The Hanging Tree was a silent monster in the low light. The branches were longer and the roots more twisted since the last time I'd visited. But that might have been because the Tree was dark and barren without the fairies to light the boughs.

No fairies? I stepped out of the cover of the forest, and no one attacked me with an arrow or tried impaling me on a rusty sword.

They could be out huntin', findin' new blood, or raidin' a camp . . .

No.

The pirates were on board their ship where I'd left them, and the woods were too quiet for war. The ground was rough, and the grass stuck up straight into the air like no one had trampled it flat in a while. No footprints, no singing, no *thwip, thwip, thwip* of arrows cutting through the air. The opening to the Hanging Tree was black and hollow.

All right, just a peek. I didn't need backup for a short poke around. After all, even if someone was inside, they wouldn't kill me. We had a truce, Peter and I. I'd just tell the truth: I'd heard a rumour the place was abandoned and came to lend a hand to any survivors. I slid into the darkness, and the cool air washed over me. It was like slipping on my oldest and best pair of leather boots; the fit was perfect. With any luck, all of it would be mine.

Stale air and the stink of food gone bad hit me first. The cots were bare, littered on the ground like garbage tossed aside for the rats. Some of the blankets were still folded up, nice and neat, but most were gone, along with the pillows, tastiest food, and weapons. Bell's house hung like a quiet bat from the ceiling, and Peter's hammock hovered beside it, empty. He'd stitched it up since the last time I'd been there. I wished it didn't leave a knot in my gut, but there I was, trying not to vomit on the dirty floor.

A small rectangle sat on the main table at the centre of the room. The shape was too perfect to be anything made by the hands of an island resident, but something about it pulled me close. And I let it, my mind swiped blank by panic. Bright colours flashed at me from a smooth cover so new it might have never been touched. But that wasn't true. I knew what it was, and it had been touched many times before, loved and cared for like a beloved pet. A bright yellow beak, deep red feathers striped with blue and green along the wing, one solitary branch sitting beneath the tropical bird . . .

A book. The weight of it was a phantom in my palm, but it was like coming home. I couldn't find my breath.

"Too bad I can't read, eh, Number Two?"

I wished I were surprised when Peter and his clan materialized behind me. "Where didja get this?" I asked.

"I remember you tellin' me how much Lou loved birds. Guess she still does. Either that or she has a tough time gettin' rid of old things. But seein' how fast she forgot you, I'm guessin' she just loves birds a whole lot."

I saw red and blood and death. *His* death. "*Tell me what you did!*"

Peter shrugged. "Timber mentioned his girl Rosie was worried about her sister. Somethin' about gettin' married soon to some grown. Their momma has a plan, but Rosie don't wanna admit it to anyone but Timber. I figured I'd check it out, see what was goin' on. She had this right next to her bed. The colours looked so nice next to her plain face, I thought it'd be a shame to keep a pretty book like that trapped there with her."

Red. Blood. Death. "Is she okay?"

"You mean did I hurt her?" Peter laughed, and Slightly followed on his heels. "Nah. She's all grown-up and has no idea who we are; there'd be no point doin' her harm." His smile widened, and I could have sworn his teeth were fangs. "Timber told the younger sister stories about you, you know. But Lou . . . She don't believe 'em."

And while I still wanted to squeeze his scrawny neck and watch the light leave his eyes, there was still enough space for the pain. I knew the kids didn't remember us; it was all part of the deal, making space for grown-up worries and grown-up things by getting rid of childish attachments. But hearing Lou's name, hearing she had no idea who I was despite me carrying her in my every thought for years, cracked my heart open and spilled everything I had left onto the ground.

"I thought it was against the rules to go see a grown once they grew up," I said through clenched teeth. "Those are your rules, aren't they?"

"I make the rules; I can break 'em." He stepped closer, and I could smell the sweat rolling off him. "This game of cat and mouse, attackin' each other back and forth—it's no fun 'cause no one ever wins. And it took me some time, but I figured out why. I love our little games, but your heart's not in it, Jay. You don't care about anythin' but that girl. And if you don't care, I can't hurt you. Then I got the idea to hit you straight where it hurt. Get 'im, boys."

Four bodies broke away from Peter's side and launched themselves at me. I didn't fight it; there was no point. They were on me, twisting my arms behind my back, pulling rope around my wrists, and taking my knives from my belt. They didn't go for the blindfold this time, probably so I could see the exact second Peter cut me down. That was fine; I didn't care about what they did to me anymore.

"I've been goin' to visit Lou a lot," Peter continued as the boys dragged me across the den and up the path out to the woods. "She's bigger. *Loads* bigger. And she loves that sister of hers more than anythin'. I wish I had a real sister to love that much." Peter's eyes locked onto mine, greedy, not wanting to miss any of my pain. "I like to play with her hair when she sleeps. Touch her cheek. Her lips. Makes me think growin' up wouldn't be so bad sometimes, you know?"

Metal clanged on metal, and the boys breathed onto my neck, their stink heavy with death. They were beasts. *Crocodiles.*

Tick-tock.

Their steps counted down my patience.

"You won't touch her again," I said.

Peter's voice drifted on the wind, and I twisted to look him straight in the eye. "See," he said, "all I had to do was get you when you were all by yourself in that stupid tree you think no one knows about and wait. Pirates'll say anythin' I want if there's some gold in it for 'em."

"So, you bribed some rotten pirates to get me out here all by myself?" I asked, blood pumping in my ears. "Whatever. You win. Nice job. Now what?"

"Now I let you go."

A trick—it's gotta be.

Tick-tock.

Letting me go would be a big mistake.

"Why are you goin' through all this trouble? You coulda just told me to come meet you here."

Peter turned to the sky, starlight dancing off his smooth skin. " 'Cause I win at all my games, and now you know it." He nodded, and his clan moved back to the Hanging Tree without him, swords and arrows tucked safely in belts, boots, slings, and holsters. "I can get to Lou any time I want. Touch her things, sleep in her bed, hear the stupid stories she tells her sister. Pirates do what I want, just like everyone else on my island. So, we can keep dancin' this dance—I sure like it, don't get me wrong—but I see the look you're gettin', Number Two. Just know, this is still *my* land. There's an order to things and a reason I do what I do. You might not like it, but it's not your place to understand. All you gotta do is play the game."

My breaths came in sharp bursts. Peter knew what fate was worse than death for me. He couldn't imagine the pain of losing a sister, but Lou was as good as blood to me. I suffered the loss of her every moment of my doomed and overlong life, but knowing she was still alive was as close as I was going to get to her. And now he was willing to take even that away from me.

I backed into the trees, my hands still knotted together, until the forest blocked Peter from view. It was clear now: I would never get the best of him, and I'd never be free of him for good.

A boulder jutted out of the ground a couple minutes' walk into the woods. Crouching low, I sawed the rope against a sharp edge until my bindings snapped loose and the blood rushed back into my fingertips.

Red.

I didn't need a trail of breadcrumbs to bring me back to my tree by the pirate ship, my sanctuary that wasn't a sanctuary anymore. Because Peter had known about it all along. I'd been able to go on so long thinking it was my own secret because *he* had allowed it.

Blood.

The giant boat swayed on the gentle ebb and flow of the waves. Its sails were down except for the one black flag billowing out from the nose, the rowdy talk of drunken pirates wafting out on the quiet breeze. I followed the trail of black blood dripping from the mouth of a dead deer through the last few trees and crossed the wooden path down to the dock.

The pirates saw me before I saw them. Sabres attached to thick, hairy arms attached to grubby, stinking men greeted me on the main deck. But I'd stopped caring about my life a long time ago.

"Evenin', boys," I said brightly. "I wanna see Blackbeard."

They laughed, the sound oily and caked in grime, but I didn't move a muscle. It was the tall one on the left who spoke first, spit flying from the gaping holes in his mouth where teeth should have been. "How's about we kills ye righ' where ye stand, boy?"

"I wouldn't." I stepped forward and grabbed his blade in my bare palm. Squeezed. The steel bit into my flesh, and I bit right back, daring it to sink deeper. It took a second for the blood to make its way down my palm, but by the time it snuck past my wrist, the red was flowing in thick streams. "I got nothin' to lose, so my life isn't much my concern. But I'm here to change that. Make a bargain. Tell Blackbeard I can give him Peter, and we'll see if he won't see me."

They exchanged a look of mistrust. I didn't blame them; the boys and I had cost them gold, food, and a few girls from time to time. But they couldn't pass up an offer like a map to the king of the island without running it by their captain.

"Yer one o' *his* crew," the one-armed man to the far right finally grunted. "Why would ye give 'im up? He was yer boss, wasn't he?"

I smiled. "I'm my own crew and my own boss. And I can lead *your* boss straight to Peter . . . on one condition."

One-Arm grinned at me and lowered his sword. "Gimme yer terms, an' I'll see if it be worth passin' on te Cap'n Blackbeard."

"I show him exactly where Peter lives and how to get inside. I bring you all there, and you can take whatever you want from his home. Includin' his pet fairy."

"And what's yer price?"

"The key exists, and I want it. But I'll share. Tell your captain that—he'll know what that means."

Steel flashed, and boots shuffled on the aged wood. "Yeah? And then what?"

"Then," I said, tossing the sabre aside with a bloody hand, "he's gotta get rid of Peter. For good."

CHAPTER 35

The boy who ruled the island was just that: a fragile young
boy. Lou's only memory of him was coloured by steel
bars fastened together by an unbreakable lock, a handful
of thirsty pirates, and the heave and swell of waves underfoot.
He'd been dirty and weak, nothing more than a prisoner on a ship.
But as Peter moved through the snow in the brilliance of daylight,
his eyes gleaming with menace and his jaw set, he was much more.
Others followed close behind, their hair swaying in the wind, their
weapons lowered to their sides. His steps left no tracks in the
snow, each footfall bringing his mob closer. She couldn't have
looked away if she'd tried; such was the power of a king certain of
his crown.

"You look different from the last time I saw you, Lou." One
corner of Peter's mouth lifted in a lazy smile. "Like you're one of
us. I'm surprised you made it this far."

"Bring her back down to the island," Jay commanded. "I can
hardly see her anymore."

When Peter dressed her, Lou came back to herself, her feet

hovering over the snowdrifts, the stars far above her once more. "Peter. How did you get free?"

"Bell." Peter said the word carelessly, like brushing lint off a sleeve. "And you, in a way. You helped her get that mermaid head. See, only fish hair can saw through a fish lock. I knew you two would cross paths if you decided you wanted to go on your big adventure, but I couldn't be sure you'd go the whole distance. Lots of 'em never do. Guess that's where faith comes in, huh?"

Bodies swarmed around her—the familiar arch of Henry's shoulder, the sharp glare only Didi could manage. Peter waved at them in greeting, and a dozen more children wandered out of the trees, gathering around him, flies to honey. Their eyes were sad— too sad to belong to ones so young.

They aren't young. Not really.

"If you escaped the pirates," Lou said, her voice barely stronger than a whisper, "then you're in charge of the island again. Take me home."

"But you forgot about it. You got so deep in your new life on the island, you forgot all about your real home."

"I . . . I do not understand how I could have forgotten, but I remember now. I remember it all."

"We'll see." Peter turned to Jay. "I warned you to stay out of my business. You had your shot to get off this island a long time ago, and you chose to stay with me and serve. You made a pretty big mess of this."

"You didn't give me a choice!" Jay cried.

Peter shrugged. "If that's what you think, then I can't say nothin' to change your mind. But I do what I do for a reason. I always told you that, but you never believed me. You fought to save a dying girl your whole life. Now that you got her, you won't even tell her the truth that could save her 'cause it might hurt *you.* That's not love."

"Stay out of it, Peter," Jay said. "I was gonna tell her after I took the island from you. No reason I can't have Lou *and* every-thin' you love. You deserve to lose everythin'." Jay lifted his blade, and Sammy did the same.

"So, that's it. You were gonna keep Lou from havin' peace and risk your kids' lives, all to make me suffer?" Peter shook his head and refocused on Lou. "The stars showed you things, right? They showed you things you forgot, little by little, the longer you stayed on the island."

Lou clamped her jaw firmly shut. Black hair swung before her as the outline of a girl hung from a nearby tree. Beside her, a boy in the woods held wriggling worms in his fingers, his laugher rustling the jade leaves, the chip in his tooth a soothing point of familiarity. Her friend. Her life. But those were only memories, and Lou still didn't understand it all. Not yet.

The trees were blurring, and Jay seemed so far away. There was only Peter and the blanket of jewelled dust above him.

"I want to go home," she whispered. "Please. Can you help me?"

"Ah, Lou. The minute your feet hit island soil, there was never a way to get you home. Not in the way you think." Peter's brow furrowed, and he drifted closer. She searched for any sign of deceit in his face but found only pity. And it burned through the last of her patience.

"But you said if we found a way to free you or touch the stars, I could go home to my real life!" Lou protested, tears springing free. "You said it! I *remember*!"

"That was the only way I could get you to take your journey seriously," Peter explained. "Every soul who comes to the island hears the story about the stars. Every soul gets an equal chance to touch the stars and leave this place."

"Tell that to Benji," Didi snarled.

"Benji found his own path, and he's happy there. None of us are supposed to be here forever. Some hear about the Mountain of

Regret and think it's made up, so they never try to find it. They's so broken they choose the island over the possibility of peace. That's all right; that gives me more kids to play with. But others want more. They hear about the stars from a mermaid, or a kid, or a nice old man by the docks, and they find the sky before the island takes them for good."

"Stop talkin'," Jay whispered.

"Come on, Number Two. You can't keep this from her. Lou, the reason no one comes back from Soul Rock the same is 'cause the ones who make it that far see what the stars have to show 'em, and they go on."

Lou clawed at her skull, the headache pounding behind her eyes. "None of this is real. I am imagining it."

"The island is more real than anythin' you had back home in a lot of ways." Peter cocked his head, and a smile curled across his face. "The crocs, the pirates, the curses . . . it's everythin' good and evil about the world. You always wondered what life was really like outside your pretty house and pretty dresses, didn't you? Here it is. The island, your world—both are beautiful and ugly. Except your mommy can't come to this place to pull the wool over your eyes."

Lou shook her head against a faint memory; she'd heard those words before. In another place. But none of it mattered. She was tired, and Rosie was curled up in bed, soaking the pillows with tears. Tears *she* was responsible for. "I saw her . . . my sister. I cannot let her think I've abandoned her forever."

"But you did. You came here."

"Not by choice!"

Peter's clan fanned out ahead of her, and Lou spotted Bell a few paces behind him, her snarl a permanent fixture on her twisted face.

"For once, you're right. This place wasn't made for you, Lou," Peter said. "You're a grown. You were never meant to end up here.

But we gotta be flexible with the rules sometimes. I didn't let Jay go back to you when you were a kid, but I let you stay now, as a favour to Jay. You got one memory left before things go back to the way they were always supposed to be. Once you see it, you get to decide what you wanna do."

Jay swung his dagger in a vicious arc. Steel hissed through the air between them, missing Peter by inches. He yelled, lunged again.

But Peter was quicker. He spun away on light feet and circled Jay like a tiger stalking its prey. Peter trapped Jay with his steady gaze, and the pair froze. "This place was paradise to me, always an adventure waitin'," Peter said. "But I stayed too long. I missed my chance. And the stars gave me a choice: I could go on and leave the island for good, or I could stay here and help souls like us decide what to do. I'm gonna help you, Lou. Even if Jay don't want me to."

Jay swiped again, but he cut through open air. "Help? You keep us here like prisoners. You promise us adventure and games without rules, but all you did was steal us and trap us in a pretty brig. All your rules—"

"Were to keep you *sane*!" Peter spat. "You're lost, Number Two! Look at everything you've done! If I had let you go back to the Land of the Grown whenever you wanted, you'd have gone crazy. You woulda seen the mess your daddy left behind—the mess in the closet you were never supposed to see."

"You don't know that."

Peter laughed. "I used to sit outside my momma's window for days, watchin' her read, countin' the sweaters she used to fold on her lap one by one. She never saw me, but I waited anyway, hopin' she would." He stepped closer, those bright eyes infinitely sad. "It's not a fate I wanted for any of you. So I took in the kids who were lost and made sure you all got a fair chance."

"If I'd stayed with Lou longer, she might not have become lost at all!"

Lou's world spun. She was fading. The stars flickered gold, a vast treasure chest in the sky, and their whispers returned. She strained to listen, and with every spoken word, Jay and the others slowly disappeared. The trees shone through their bodies, solid shapes through ghosts long past.

"Jay. My friend," Peter said, his voice cracking, "Lou's here *because* of you."

"Don't say that!"

"Can't you see it? You tried to change the course of her life when you had the chance, and it worked . . . for a while. But her daddy got sick. If that baby hadn't come along, Lou might have come here a long time ago, like she was supposed to. Rosie kept her alive a little longer, not you. She didn't need you anymore. She needed her sister."

"No."

"When I saw that Lou's path hadn't changed, I knew there was a new kid who would need a friend. I coulda sent you back to take care of Rosie, but you were too distracted. Too angry. When Lou finally left, I needed someone focused to take care of Rosie. So I sent her Timber."

"No!" Jay struck out, and, this time, the blade scratched Peter's arm. A fine crimson line snaked down to his wrist. "You sent Timber to make me suffer. All you ever did was make us *suffer*!"

Sadness clouded Peter's features. "If you had just left things alone . . . If you had let Lou live and die without you tryin' to meddle, she woulda left the Land of the Grown and gone where *they* go when it was her time. But you betrayed me to the pirates, and Sammy managed to break through the barrier."

"You leave Sammy alone!" Jay cried. "Sammy's the only one who ever cared what I wanted."

"I'm not gonna hurt Sammy, Number Two. It's not his fault he broke through and pulled her over here. He was able to do it because the island was weak." Peter twisted his palm to the sky, and blood dripped into the snow. "Who knows? Maybe she left the Land of the Grown *because* of Sammy."

Jay froze. His brow pulled low over his eyes. "What are you talking about?"

"All this time, you thought Lou needed you to stay alive. Instead of fightin' pirates, you wasted away tryin' to go back to *save* her. So you got me captured. You messed with the island's magic. Maybe seein' Sammy—seein' what wasn't supposed to be there—is what finally broke her. Maybe it's all your fault. Wouldn't that be somethin'? A real bad joke, huh?"

"Stop lyin'!" Jay's shoulders shook, and spit flew from his mouth. "Stop playin' with my head. I'd never do anythin' to hurt Lou."

"Not on purpose," Peter said. "But we only know the difference between a mistake and a good idea after we see how our choices play out."

"What's that even mean?"

"That no matter how you look at it, Lou's here because you couldn't let her go. But hey—this is what you wanted, right? To see her again, no matter who you hurt?" Peter advanced slowly and blinked back tears. "That's the choice you made, Jay. It's done, mistake or not. You gotta live with the fallout now."

Lou spluttered as water filled her lungs and the eyes of a bespectacled boy blinked at her through the murky waves. "Jay, something is wrong . . ." she said. "What is happening to me?"

The memory came unbidden. Her engagement was announced. Rosie retreated in on herself. She was afraid, not angry; Lou could see that now. But once Rose had pulled away, all Lou had seen was grey and fear and pain and a sister who suddenly despised her.

And so Lou let the darkness take her.

You'll take me with you? If you go off exploring or find a small apartment on a terrible street somewhere, I want to come too. Do not leave me here alone. Promise it.

Oh, how she wanted to keep her promise.

The waves had taken over Silverton Lane before she could make things right. Water from the walls had flooded the house and crashed into the garden. They'd been so real—as real as Sammy had been.

Sammy.

She had seen the boy in her home.

Chased him through the garden.

Into the woods.

The woods.

Her head would surely split open from the pain. She'd suffered headaches for years, but they'd been curiously absent once she'd stepped foot on the island. The colours, the vivid smells, and the very pulse of life beating around her had only returned when she'd found Jay.

When she'd found the *island*.

"I changed my mind. I don't want to remember," she said, her sobs making her ribs ache. So many memories, so much sadness. "Please, make it stop."

Peter and the lost children swarmed her.

"You can't stop it," Peter said. "You need to know why you're here."

"Sammy brought me here."

"Maybe."

Jay swung his dagger, and his blade caught flesh. A bright red line sliced across Peter's chest, but the boy did not flinch. Bell hissed. "She needs to see it, Jay," Peter said. "Let this happen. She's almost there."

Jay glared, fury painting his cheeks red. "See what?"

"That she had a family that loved her, and she left them behind because she couldn't understand their kind of love." Peter turned to Lou, his expression unfathomable. "Your mother couldn't look at you all those years because she felt guilty. She was scared she'd messed you up because she'd made so many mistakes."

"Shut up," Jay growled.

"Your momma had her own problems, but she wanted to give you what she thought would make you feel better," Peter said. "But you two didn't want the same things. Momma and kid, bound by blood but so different. She pushed and pushed and forgot how much damage growns can do with even the best intentions. She showed you she loved you in the wrong ways, Lou. She chose wrong. But she tried."

Lou's life had always been planned in clear detail: learn her manners, be a doting daughter and loving sister, marry well, restore the family name Father had destroyed by dying at the inappropriate time. She'd resented her mother's plans, had seen them as anything but an expression of love. So Lou had let the Briarwood, the sword fights, and nights playing in Mermaid Lagoon slip away.

Melancholy truly was a monster with large teeth.

Lou's cheeks burned. Her collar was soaked, but she didn't care. Children faced one another, primed to attack, but the stars shifted, calling her back to another vision, and she had no fight left in her to resist.

"Show me," she whispered. The sky scooped her up and swallowed her.

Lou was back in the Briarwood. Her life had become too hard to hold on to. She'd taken to the trees because that was the only safe place left. Safe from the lie of her life. Safe from the demands.

The lake waited deep in the woods. Her feet found the familiar path while her mind warred with itself.

"I . . . I remember."

Pain. So much pain endured that day. She'd needed to escape it.

She'd followed Sammy and the water into the Briarwood. But there had been no boy. There had been no flood.

There had only been the lake.

The water had been cool and murky. The soft waves had lapped at her legs as she'd stepped into the abyss. Stars had watched from above as she'd slipped under and exhaled her last breath. There was too much pain.

"Leave her alone!" Jay sobbed. "I can't lose her again!"

The constellation took on an unfamiliar scene, and Lou knew she was no longer in a memory. She was back in her room, *really* back. Rose slept, the tears coming even in the depth of dreams. Her body was a hill under the comforter, her knees tucked into her chest as though bracing for a blow. Anne Webber startled awake, her face bleached white under the moon. She'd forgotten to draw the curtains, and with one look at her younger daughter, she slipped out of bed. Just as Lou had done so many nights before, Anne made her way soundlessly to the fluttering curtains and stared out over the Briarwood, the dark sway of a thousand trees rocking back and forth to a tune all their own.

"Mother," Lou whispered. Anne Webber's eyelashes fluttered, and her left hand, still wearing the thin circlet of a gold wedding band, flew to her mouth. "Can you hear me, Mother?"

Droplets of sorrow coated Anne's lashes, darkening them to ink. Her teeth trapped her bottom lip as though biting her sobs into submission. Lou's mother collapsed to her knees at the window where Lou and Jay had fought so many pirates, saved so many treasure chests from destruction, and learned the names of so many birds.

"Lou," she moaned over and over. *Lou, Lou, Lou.* "I love you. I am so sorry. I failed you." Her tears overcame her, muddling the words—*Lou, Lou, Lou*—until they rolled into one another, incoherent syllables professing love the way she never had when her daughter was alive.

Through it all, Rose slept, her tears finally run dry. A child should never see their parent be anything less than strong, so Anne Webber suffered alone too; Lou knew that now.

"I understand." Lou wouldn't let Jay or Sammy or any of the others see how much it cost her to accept that she had to leave. That she was already gone.

"You did right by her, Jay," Peter said. "But when I heard you'd sold me out to the pirates, there was nothing left for me to do than to let this play out."

For the first time, Jay's blade faltered. "You *knew*?"

"How many times I gotta tell you. Nothin' happens on the island without me knowin' about it. I let them take me prisoner and keep me down in the brig. And when the island's magic started to fall apart, I let Lou come here. I had no idea if she was already gone or if your meddlin' would bring her here, but I knew you hadn't learned your lesson." Peter's face was drawn. Tired. "The only way you were gonna understand what I go through every day was to lose the thing you loved most by your own hands."

Treacherous tears poured down Jay's cheeks. "You let me think we were all gonna die. You scared my kids. *You* killed Benji! *You* did this to Lou, not me!"

"There're consequences to messin' with the balance of things. Sometimes lessons are learned better the hard way. You don't gotta like it to understand, right Jay?"

Their voices dulled to a low hum as Lou let herself fade. It was no one's fault but her own that she now drifted in the ether, but she couldn't tell anyone that. She had no body. No voice. Instead, she hovered in the land between the island and the world she'd grown up in.

Her father was right: duty was, indeed, a pirate. And in trying to be everything for everyone else, the biggest pirate had claimed her. She'd been a child wanting to become a woman, then a woman reminiscing about the freedom of childhood. In that way, she had never allowed herself to be a child or a woman at all. She had loved fiercely in a world too small to allow that sort of complexity.

Lou sighed, no longer feeling the cold. The air whispered across her arms, her legs, her windburned cheeks. "It wasn't my fault. I was enough—I just couldn't see it."

Love wore many faces: the admiration of a sister; the fear of a mother; a father's love, even when his time was short. She hadn't understood the variations of love before. Lou wished she had. It might have made a difference.

But it wasn't her place to question such things. Not anymore.

The birds can touch everythin' you see. They just glide over the trees, so close the branches tickle their bellies. Can you imagine being one of 'em? Free, just flyin' wherever you want to go?

That was all she'd ever wanted—to fly, to be as free as one of the birds she'd studied in her books. Now she only wanted her mother. Her sister. To see them and hold them and brush the tears from their cheeks and the hair from their eyes. To tell them she finally understood. That she was home again. For good.

While Peter and Jay circled each other, each with their own band of lost souls waiting to endure another war that would change nothing, Lou drifted off, away, away, away.

She laid her head to rest in the tender place between the child she'd been and the woman she would never become. A memory and a constant, doomed to remain stuck and unchanged. And in another life, that thought may have saddened her. But in the life where Jay and Rosie, her mother and father and Peter and his children all loved her in their own way, she was content with her fate.

"That's it, Lou," Peter said, tipping his face to the sky. He sighed, breathed in deep, and in that moment, he could have been weightless. "It's about time you learned to fly, little bird."

If not for the stars, the night sky would be nothing more than a stretch of endless black. Even then, one, two, a thousand stars were mere specks of light, useless in a fight against the darkness. They could no sooner approach one another than Lou could have reached out a finger to touch one from her place on the ground. How lonely those stars must have been, doomed to watch one another from a distance. Useless.

But there were more than one, two, a thousand stars before Lou. Together, millions of those lonely spots of light ate away at the darkness, creating balance, creating a light more powerful than the oblivion between them.

Lou counted herself lucky to be one among the many lonely stars. She had a purpose, a way to be part of a whole when she'd only ever been a collection of broken pieces—one lonely speck of light left to stand still as the darkness swallowed her light. She would never be alone again.

While the island raged and her mother and sister sobbed in each other's arms, Louisa Webber finally touched the stars. And they reached back.

CHAPTER 36

LOU

NOW

Since the age of four, I dreaded the day death would claim me. But when I finally faced my end, I understood death was a fear of my own making. Everything looked worse in the dark, and my life had been painted black for so long.

Until then.

But I wasn't finished. Not yet.

Jay.

I wasn't sure when the balance of the stars tipped. It might have been when colours turned to smells or my body became one with the breath of the wind. Either way, I slid back to the coves and lagoons, through Soul Rock's watchful eyes, up the snowy mountain peaks and into the barren trees.

I had no body, no fingers with which to hold Jay's hand like he always held mine. The thought didn't bring me sadness, only the burning desire to make him understand that it was not Peter's fault or his. As ready as I was to let go, Jay had forever clung to the possibility of life, of *me*. If I'd still had a beating heart, it would have burst with love for him. For them all.

The snow wafted through me as I returned to him. I drifted

past Sammy and Henry to rest beside the boy who would forever be my friend. His auburn hair billowed around his head as he moved in precise circles, driving his dagger around in sharp lines.

Who are you? I'd asked him the first time we met.

Just a kid. Like you, only bigger. Nothin' more to it.

That answer had made sense. Then again, I was only five and had no idea who *I* was. Or who I'd become.

Woman.

Daughter.

Sister.

A sad girl.

A little bird.

Free.

Soon, but not yet.

Jay's back was taut, his teeth bared. *Please don't fight,* I begged, but my voice was air, and I couldn't speak. Instead, I drifted beside him, tethered to the small space between worlds.

"You're a stinkin' traitor," Jay said. "Didi, get your bow!"

"Boss, Kiran's not lookin' too great—"

"Do what I say!"

"Jay?" It was Sammy, his voice coming from the folds of Henry's arms. "Lou's gone. Please. I don't wanna lose anyone else."

I'm right here.

Jay turned, and his terror was absolute. He scanned the path we'd taken up the steep slope, looked over the mountain's edge, around the trunks and gnarled branches blistering in the cold. "No. No, she was right here."

"I told you, she didn't belong here. She's got people who love her, and she finally heard what the stars had to say." Peter sighed and took a step closer to Jay, the pity in his eyes surface deep. "Let it go, Number Two. We don't have to be enemies anymore."

"You took her away from me again," Jay said through a throat thick with tears.

No, Jay. I'm right here. I didn't leave you.

Sammy reached out a hand to pull Jay back, but it was no use. He swatted Sammy away as though he were a lowly irritant, not a friend. "Bring her back."

"I can't."

He can't.

Jay howled into the gathering night, not a crocodile or a pirate, but a wolf, a wounded animal hovering on the edge of death. He swung wide. Bell's scream shook the trees, and she charged, wings of spun silver unfurling behind her, a terrible angel.

Peter avoided the blow, but only just. "Let it go! There's been enough death today!"

"You bring her back, or there's gonna be one more." Jay lunged, and Henry made to stop him, but fury was more powerful than strength or size. Jay was a boy possessed, his narrow frame quivering and shifting in his rage.

Who are you really?

A boy. A friend. That's all. That's all I ever wanted to be.

That was all Jay saw himself to be. But I knew better.

I know who you are, Jay. You are better than this.

Peter stood his ground, his eyes as worn as the old trees back in the Briarwood. I remembered those woods now—the light that reflected jade on my skin, the distant chittering of insects and snapping of twigs. Home. The lake. My grave.

Jay's chest heaved. "Fight me!"

Listen. I'm here. Turn around. I focused on my legs, tried to go to him, to rest a hand on his to steady the blade aimed at Peter's heart. But I had no arms or legs, no will of my own in the place between places.

Peter scowled. "I don't wanna fight you. But if you don't put that blade down, you won't give me a choice. I won't have you killin' any more of my boys."

You are a leader, Jay.

You are kind.

You are safety.

You are loved.

You are my brother. Forever.

Warm arms wrapped around me, and the smell of cloves and oranges filled me up where once I'd been empty. *Not yet.* I was fading again, this time for good. There was somewhere else I needed to be. But I could not leave the boy who'd kept me in his heart until I told him he would always be in mine.

A mane of raven hair splayed across my pillow threatened to overcome the sight of Henry pulling Sammy behind him, of Kiran collapsing to his knees while Bell advanced on him like a hungry beast.

"Jay, don't do this!"

"*Get them!*"

Arrows flew, and children charged across the snowy peaks of the Mountain of Regret.

Jay.

I love you.

I'm sorry I left you.

I won't say goodbye, because goodbye means forever.

Jay struck down a boy no older than eight with a cry of satisfaction. Blood spattered the snow, and Peter drew his own weapons as Bell targeted Kiran, the weakest of their party. I did not want to remember Jay that way. In my heart, I saw only the boy with the chipped tooth and eyes like the sea. The boy who'd been a best friend all my own, my private brother, my everything.

Didi pulled the string of her bow and let an arrow fly. With a hiss, the metal head buried itself in Bell's wing. A scream pierced the sky, flying from cracked lips and jagged teeth. The fairy stumbled, forgetting she was magic made flesh. Everyone, it seemed, forgot.

"That's what you get for tryin' to touch my brother!" Didi cried.

So much blood.

Jay only had eyes for Peter. The pair clashed swords, stumbled, and lurched around and around across the tainted snow. The harder they fought, the harder the stars pulled me away from them. War erupted on the mountain, and all I could do was watch and fight to stay. As slow as the sun rising over the horizon, the mountain turned to the orange, yellow, and autumn red.

Please, a little longer.

Bell shrieked again, and Peter's restraint finally broke. He lunged and slashed and moved like a snake, but it was Jay who shed his humanity like a second skin. Eyes like oceans froze to ice, and his arms grew thicker, longer, striped with new muscle.

Jay . . . stop this. Don't forget who you are.

But Jay couldn't hear me. No one could or would ever again. If he had, his arm would have faltered instead of slicing through Peter's shoulder. Jay hovered over the king of the island, smiling as he leaned in for the kill. Kiran stood by his sister, his good arm skewering attackers with a blade dripping in gore. Everywhere, red spilled and spattered, paint thrown against a canvas. It was such a human thing, to crave violence when violence was so pointless.

The faint tang of fresh earth and mouldering leaves was jolting against the backdrop of copper.

Jay! I screamed. But the fighting was too loud, and I was too weak, and maybe I didn't exist at all.

Jay's skin dripped with blood that wasn't his own, and new stubble bubbled across his jaw. "I used to think you were my friend. I looked up to you. But after all these years, I finally see that you're nothin' more than a beast. The king of crocodile swamp! How do you like that title, *boss*?"

"I'm no croc, Jay. Put the blade down before it's too late." Peter's chin quivered. "You're changin'."

"Don't tell me what to do!" Another slash, and Peter's sleeve bloomed red. They moved up and away from the chaos as though they'd danced that dance before, twisting toward the peak of the mountain together.

Peter blocked a fist to the jaw with a quick hand. "Don't make me hurt you, Number Two."

"My name's Jay."

Henry took a kick to the stomach that knocked him flat on his back, and he lay in the snow, blank eyes roving the sky. Empty eyes, sad eyes, eyes made only for the boy buried in the tunnels underground. He did not try to avoid the boot that crunched down on his nose or staunch the fountain of coppery blood spouting from both nostrils. Henry let himself become an easy target, and Peter's boys picked him clean.

Get up!

Henry's pupils fixed on the sun, his tears mingling with the blood.

I was tired. Jay needed me, but I needed rest. He never got to say goodbye, and neither did I. Such was the awful symmetry life offered to the unfortunate like us. My heart broke for Jay, for me, for the lives I'd touched and never appreciated until it was too late. If I could have wept, I would have been soaked in my tears.

Steel gnashed against steel over the grunts and screams. Sammy huddled behind a tree, watching Jay with wide eyes, and I could only imagine the racing of his heart, as quick as a rabbit's in his narrow chest. As Jay's shadow on the snow grew longer, Sammy's fingers grew thicker, his wide eyes beginning to crease with the quick passage of time.

"Look at me," Jay demanded in a new deeper voice. "I was your slave, but I'm free of you now. I'm *better*. I'll find Lou again.

I'll get her back, and then I'll spend every day of my life hating you and the crocodile you are."

"You can hate me all you want, but that hate's gonna change you. And you won't be able to come back. Look at you—it already started." Another step backward, and Peter's feet kissed air. "Or you can get over this and come back to the Tree. Your choice."

Jay stopped. His jaw went slack, and his legs stilled, two sturdy tree trunks planted deep in the ground. "You . . . You'd have me back in the fold?"

"Just like old times. We forget any of it ever happened and move on. We can make sure no other lost soul suffers like you did. Like Lou did." Peter's voice was even. Honest. "Remember how much fun we had? We can have it again. Forever. I don't want you changin' like this."

Forever. A promise I couldn't make him. Jay was fading along with the cold, and when he answered, his voice came from a distance. "You're tryin' to distract me 'cause you still think I'm weak. That's bad form." He ran at Peter, blade ready to impale him, to push him over the edge.

But the boy who would never grow up had the fairies and stars on his side. He was the first of his kind, and that sort of magic was greater than hatred. He leapt into the sky, and his dagger flashed liquid silver under the moons. The blade caught Jay above the wrist, and the ball of flesh that had once been a hand spiralled out over the edge and into the waiting island waters.

Jay screamed and buckled to his knees, and I screamed with him. Bell swooped out of the trees and collected Peter in her arms, whisking him into the sky with one wing crumpled behind her. Children scattered in the snow, leaving behind a trail of blood and cheers of victory.

I tried consoling the boy who was no longer a boy as he nursed his mutilated arm. But I couldn't do anything but leave him. It was time.

I recited their names over and over in a silent prayer: *Jay, Henry, Sammy, Kiran, Didi. Jay, Henry, Sammy, Kiran, Didi. Benji.*

They would be remembered.

Blood everywhere. Heavy breathing. Jay limped away from the edge, taller and bleaker than I remembered him. The chip in his tooth was gone, filled in and whole, but his arm was forever broken. His many years finally stood on full display, with new lines and grooves tracing his face, thick black stubble, and faint scars decorating the rest of him.

My poor Jay.

I was so tired.

He moved to inspect the closest body on the ground and grunted under his breath in a voice too low, too cold. "Time to go."

Didi and Kiran stumbled to his side, mouths open as they took in his new body. The body of a man, straight-backed and sinuous, had taken the place of the leader they'd once known. He knelt beside a fallen boy wearing a long red jacket and peeled it from the still corpse. Blood spattered at his feet, but Jay threw the jacket over his shoulders and tucked his bleeding arm into the sleeve with quick, sure motions.

"Where's Henry?" Jay asked.

Didi sniffed. "He's gone."

I expected pain. Instead, there was only ice. "Fine. Let's go."

"But—"

His eyes flashed, and he bared his teeth. "You questionin' me, twin?"

"No, sir," Didi said, pushing Kiran behind her. "Never."

"Sammy? Sammy!" Jay spit blood, but the swelling in his mouth was too severe, butchering the words and crumbling them to mulch. "Where are you, boy?"

Instead of the barefooted child with the kind face and round glasses, a paunchy man wearing clothes much too small for his size staggered out from behind a tree. "I . . . I'm here, Jay."

The air shifted as Sammy shuffled over to him and retrieved a belt from one of the fallen. Always the most loyal and devoted of Jay's boys, it was no surprise that Sammy had followed in his footsteps. With thick fingers, he wrapped the cracked leather around Jay's bleeding stump and tugged it tight. Fear flickered across Kiran's and Didi's faces, but they followed him as though attracted by a new form of gravity.

Please don't do this. This is not who you are.

"Where are we goin', boss?" Kiran asked, new colour high in his cheeks.

"Back to the den. We gotta clean ourselves up and clear out our things before we go down to the cove."

No.

"We're going to see the pirates?" Kiran asked.

"We are. I have some business to take care of with Blackbeard."

I pulled against the current, but the oranges, grass, rich pull of wet earth, and gurgle of running water were stronger. Jay led my friends down the mountain without a backward look at where I'd last stood. And there, under the light of the moons and stars, I knew I'd lost him forever.

I let the current pull me back.

And then I was gone.

CHAPTER 37

The Briarwood greeted Lou like an old friend.

She whispered through the trees, flicked a leaf to reveal its velvet underbelly, rustled a shrub to scatter flower petals like confetti on the mossy ground. Shadows swayed and moved, but they did not bother her like they once had. Souls wove together like the roots of an ancient sycamore, braiding into the world, birthing sounds and colours and life, and she was part of them.

A shift in the wind swept her back, and Lou slipped into the tide with ease. She snaked through the trees, marvelling at how the grains of bark and roots were so different but could quiet her mind just the same. How the earthworms hummed, and the critters moved together in a living web. In the past, she wouldn't have appreciated a drop of it. But in this new form, she let the energy of the Briarwood tug her along, trusting it to lead her home.

Another sound now. Light steps squelched the earth in even, tentative beats. There was sadness in the way the forest leaned away from that sound, a bleak grey seeping into the greens and plums and vibrant reds of the woods. Instead of recoiling from that dark intruder in the bright woods, what remained of Louisa Webber moved toward it. She floated, leaving strands of herself in the branches, letting the scent of lavender and the memories of boar-bristle brushes and black velvet ribbons fill her up.

The girl slipped like a shadow out from behind an evergreen. Hair hung limp down her back, the blues and reds of soft black strands muted in the sunlight. Satin shoes shone in the dull light, her skirt was starched and rigid, and her collar was buttoned to the chin. But it was her *eyes* the trees feared: deep as onyx, trimmed with lashes curling to the sky and filled with emptiness.

Rosie. My Rosie.

The young girl knew the trees, traced her fingers along the ripples of old bark, avoiding debris in her path. Her bloodshot eyes stared into nothing.

Her. *Rosie.*

Another life.

And Lou's entire reason for holding on.

Lou opened her thoughts to the Briarwood, and the forest reached back, accepting her request. The wind curled around her, and she filled herself with love and light, with pleas for forgiveness, memories of stories told over lace-trimmed bassinets, and days spent scaling the trees to reach the sky. She no longer had a dark heart to slow her down, to cause her pain. She was happy. Letting that golden light warm her, Lou shivered through the branches and visited her sister one last time.

Rose frowned at the sudden gust of wind. It was not cold as it should have been this deep into the fall. It was balmy and bright, love, laughter, ribbons, brushes, and bears in a tousled bed. It was their life together, and it had been a *good* life.

The thump of Rose's footsteps stopped. Her lips parted, drinking in every emotion Lou laced into the world. Her eyes widened in awe, not fear.

I really am a bird, Lou thought, tousling Rose's hair, fluttering her too-straight skirt. *Be free. Remember me at my best. I love you, little one. Always.*

Tears slid down Rosie's cheeks, a pink flush tickling her pale skin. She choked on a laugh and a sob, and Lou reached into her sister's arms to soothe her heart, to take away her pain.

Rosie had needed Timber because Lou was always destined to go on. And now it was Rose's turn to fly on her own.

Lou stayed for as long as she could. Final messages of love and hope flashed through her, and she pressed each into her sister's ear: *Forgive Mother. Love each other. Don't forget me.* Over and over, Lou sent what was left of her soul into the Briarwood and the person she loved most in the world.

When Rosie smiled, brought her fingers to her heart, and uttered, "I love you too, Lou," she knew it was enough. It was everything.

With a sigh that could have been a whisper of leaves against the earth, Lou was gone.

Away, away, away.

CHAPTER 38

JAY

RIGHT WHERE IT STARTED

My first memory of Lou was the day I knew my life could mean something.

I hated moving back and forth between worlds, but here I was. Again. Taking on another kid wasn't something I wanted to do, but it was supposed to be my last one. Peter had promised me so. I stood in the shadows with a toy boat and some table scraps, waiting. On the upside, it was summer, and the day was warm, soaked in sun. On the downside, the fact that I'd landed in another forest was pretty depressing.

Whatever this new kid needed, I wasn't it. There was too much to be done at the Hanging Tree, too many raids needing organized and new faces to be initiated and protected from Peter's special brand of love. The newest victim, Sammy, was too young to be left alone with Peter for any length of time, and this was all beneath me. Pointless.

Years meant precious little, but I still hated wasting my time.

I picked at the callouses on my fingertips with my dagger and let the bark of an old tree bite into my back. She'd be here soon, and if she didn't show, I'd leave. "Take your time, kid. Give me a reason to leave. *Please.*"

Peter had been cruel enough to keep this kid's story to himself. Some were assigned to me because they needed a friend during a plague, through a separation, because of some rough hands, or simple loneliness. Those cases weathered me down the most; I got close, spent years talking and playing, just for them to shake me off when they were through picking my bones clean. But every so often, there were those doomed to die, and I knew I might get the chance to keep them a little longer. On the island.

Watching them grow up was worse than seeing them die. Death was permanent, forced on mortals with a complete disregard for their need to stay alive. They didn't *like* to leave me, and for that I was grateful. But growing up meant they'd seen me, spent time with me, and decided something else was more important.

That hurt. That *always* hurt.

How would this one hurt me?

It didn't matter, because this was what Peter wanted. So, I waited, surrounded by greener, more suffocating trees than the ones I called home, and tried not to hate the kid before I'd even met her.

Then there she was, first in sound with her footsteps on the leaves, then in scent with a hint of lavender on the wind.

She was a small thing—four, maybe five—trapped in shoes too white for the dirt and a dress too long for the heat. Her hair wasn't quite blond, or brown, or red, but a blend of all three. Like the feathers of a northern cardinal, delicate and unique. Light brown eyes spaced a bit too wide on her face, the freckles spattered across her cheeks like a sunburn. Except this girl was pale, a creature of the indoors. Sunflowers—dozens of them—scattered across her full skirt. She wasn't an orphanage kid, or an abandoned kid, or a kid with no money. This one had a collar buttoned tight, shoes shining under the sun. Everything about her was starched and smelled of privilege, and yet she slipped her finger under the lace collar of the dress, pulled at the neck, and wrinkled her nose.

She hates it. Huh.

So, what was it, then? Issues with her parents? Trouble making friends? Her shoulders hunched in, curving her spine protectively over a frayed colourful book. She looked harmless. Pitiful, even. So small, so pale, so lost, just like all the rest of them.

I stayed deep within the trees for my last few minutes of peace. Whether I was ready or not, whatever time she had left in her childhood was going to be spent with me creeping in through open windows and sneaking into her house at night. Hopefully she'd come and go quick and I'd forget her. Hopefully she was as forgettable as she looked.

But then she tipped her face to the sky. She stumbled over roots and twigs, those ridiculous shoes slipping over leaves and catching on half-buried rocks. So many things to make her fall, to hurt and bring her down. But the sunlight brightened her pale face, and she grinned, her smile so wide it could only have come from a place of pure joy. She spun on the spot, her voice humming off-key like she was relieved no one was listening. Whatever her demons, in that moment, with the sky on her face and a book swirling through the air around her, this girl was happy. And I wanted to join her, just to see what all the fuss was about and maybe feel . . . something. Happy was asking a lot, but *something* would be nice.

Whoever Louisa Webber was, she was a kid, and she needed me. And I had a chance to be in her orbit for a little while.

Some lost and forgotten part of me wriggled free. I lifted my face to the sun. Just to share one small thing with the girl who was destined to consume my world for however long she let me into her life.

And suddenly, I was smiling too.

One day, she was going to leave. But there, in the trees behind her home, we were alone. Together. It was enough to share a secret with a new friend for a little while. To be part of something bigger than the small island I'd chosen to spend the rest of my eternity on. To be a kid instead of just . . . lost.

I stepped out of the shadows, ready to have my heart broken for the last time.

ACKNOWLEDGMENTS

exhales
cracks knuckles
laughs deliriously and begins to pound on an overheated keyboard

Yay, I made it! The end! La fin! And getting here would have led to mandatory institutionalization had it not been for an amazing team and support system who are worth infinitely more than the page space used to thank them.

- My first thank-you goes to Chelsea, my content editor. You struck the perfect balance between encouragement and tough love with your comments, suggestions, and reactions. Developmental editing is both exciting and terrifying, and your input was invaluable. I'm also sorry I upset your dog. I truly didn't mean for that to happen.
- A treasure chest full of thanks goes to Natalia, the chief editor at Enchanted Ink Publishing and my copy editor. From your positive attitude and professionalism to your knowledge of the craft, attention to detail, and patience, you are truly the best. You took my book baby and made it shine. I also apologize for the sea creatures featured in this book. They're harmless, I swear.

- Franziska, you have such an eye for gorgeous cover art, and I'm so grateful to you for designing my book cover. Seriously. Look at it. *squeals like a three-year-old* Thank you for giving my book baby such a pretty face!
- To Cathy, my first reader, my no-bullsh*t feedback-giver, my Pazza-in-chief, and my cheerleader: I am forever grateful for your insanity and aggressive text messages demanding more chapters. Also, the fact that you named your kid's bear Benji after having read the first draft of this book is higher praise than you know.
- Sab, you were so proud when I published my first book, and you continue to be so genuinely enthusiastic. I don't tell you this enough, but your enthusiasm helps me feel less crappy about my crappy first drafts. You're probably the most positive person I know, and without that positivity, I would have likely abandoned this project a half dozen times. Thank you.
- Frank, you were one of the first to say that writing a book was *cool*. Then again, you're a fellow Star Wars nerd, so I shouldn't be surprised. You gave me a place in your gym, put my life back on track with positive thinking and a healthy lifestyle, put a copy of my book on your front counter display (despite not knowing if it was any good yet), and have become one of my best friends. Don't let all that get to your head, though—it's big enough as it is.
- Justin, Grace, the New Life team, and all the members—you're amazing. If they ever figure out how to bottle positivity, they definitely should pay you a visit. I owe each of you a giant hug.
- Mom, you read the first draft of this one. Dad, your Facebook posts bragging about me are adorable. Both

of you told me to keep going, so I did. And I'll keep on doing the thing just to see your pride all over again.

- Nonna, you don't read English, but you try to read my books anyway. That says it all.
- My babies. My world. You are the reason this story exists. It's my honour to raise you. It's my greatest accomplishment to see you both smile. I know you'll both grow up one day, but until you do, I'll keep smothering you with kisses and baby talk. To be honest, I might never stop.
- My last and greatest thank-you goes to you, hubby. You're the Jim to my Pam, the Luke to my Lorelai, and the Mr. Darcy to my Bridget Jones (minus the bad Christmas sweater because a thematic tie and pair of socks are more your style). You talk me back down to reality while encouraging my dreams, and you do it all while supplying caffeine. Sometimes a little vodka, too. Plus, you're really pretty to look at.

ABOUT THE AUTHOR

WWW.VANESSARACCIO.COM

Vanessa Raccio, author of the *Rathburn* series, has a bachelor's degree in psychology from Concordia University and a certification in personal training. After years of balancing "the jobs" with "the hobbies," she decided to pursue "the dream." Vanessa lives in Canada with her husband, two beautiful children, and a chihuahua who is both fierce and afraid of spiders in equal measure.

facebook.com/vraccio

instagram.com/authorvanessaraccio

goodreads.com/138301805-vanessa-r

tiktok.com/@authorvanessaraccio

Ingram Content Group UK Ltd.
Milton Keynes UK
UKHW042142070623
423069UK00014B/285/J